WALLFLOWER

WALLFLOWER

samantha leigh

Cover design by Echo Grayce at Wildheart Graphics
Editing by Killing It Write
Proofreading by My Notes in the Margin

A catalogue record for this book is available from the National Library of Australia

ISBN: 9978-0-6459988-2-5 (paperback)
ISBN: 9978-0-6459988-3-2 (e-book)
ISBN: 978-0-6459988-4-9 (hardback)

For introverts and daydreamers and hopeless romantics
who feel safer when they're looking at the ground...
Eyes up, wallflowers, and keep them up.

AUTHOR'S NOTE

Please note that some details of professional hockey have been modified in this story for your reading pleasure.

My books are low on angst and big on feel-good vibes, but they occasionally touch on topics that may be difficult for some readers. *Wallflower* features a side character who has depression and explicit sex scenes.

To see a complete list of content warnings for all my books, including *Wallflower*, please visit my website at samanthaleighbooks.com or scan the QR code below.

And most importantly, take care of yourself.

xSam.

ONE

✿

Chord

I SWING THE CHERRY-RED sports car into a basement parking space marked *reserved*—not for me, but I don't give a shit—then hit the lock button on my way to the elevator. Once inside, I tap the button to close the doors and another for the fourth floor, then turn to face the floor-to-ceiling mirror.

I'm in a tailored navy suit custom made to fit my shoulders and thighs. White shirt. No tie. A new Rolex on my wrist. I pinch my fingertips through my dark hair, taking care not to undo all the good work—and product—I put in this morning, then stand back and appraise the final picture.

Not bad for a thirty-four-year-old NHL legend who was just dumped by his team two years shy of retirement.

I snort and tug on my shirt cuffs. Fuck 'em. I'm going to spend the rest of my career making sure those assholes regret the way things fell out this year.

1

The elevator dings, the doors slide open, and I step out into a gray-carpeted hall flanked by stark white walls adorned with San Francisco Fury memorabilia. Framed jerseys. Signed headshots. Black-and-white photographs of the team's best wins. Directly opposite the elevator is a sign, and I scan it for directions to Boardroom One.

Loaded silence ushers me up the corridor and, like always, the press of eyes makes me want to turn and leave. I never thought I'd get sick of people looking at me. Women begging for my number. Fans shoving markers in my face and telling me I was the best player they'd ever seen. I never thought being so fucking good at something that it gave you the world would one day feel like living in a cage.

I walk fast with my gaze forward and jaw clenched. Maybe I should relax. Fury headquarters is technically my home now, so I shouldn't need to be on my guard. My mouth tips up in a sardonic smile. Home isn't always where a person is safest—or even wanted.

Ah, shit. A pretty blonde with a predatory look in her eyes, a tight canary-yellow skirt wrapped around her hips, and tall black heels on her feet slides into the hallway at just the right moment to catch the curve on my mouth, and I screw up by meeting her interested glance. She takes it as an invitation to approach, and I'm about to scowl hard enough to scare her away when a familiar figure steps out after her.

Around us, people pretend they're not watching, but heads pop up over cubicle partitions like a game of whack-

TWO

Chord

BARELY A THIRD OF THE chairs around the monstrous table are occupied, but I assume someone chose this room because it's the biggest and the best. The Fury knows they got a good deal when they signed me for a fraction of what I'm worth, and they're probably wondering what the hell I'm doing here.

In the hours since we signed the contracts, I've asked myself the same thing.

Campbell is on my right, Courtney from marketing is on my left, and there are reps from what looks like every other department arranged around the table. I don't know that they all need to be here, but it looks like everyone wishes they weren't. So they can stay.

After he makes the obligatory introductions, Coach braids his fingers together and sets his hands on the table.

"Before we get to business, I want to offer Chord a warm welcome to the San Francisco Fury." He turns to me. "I know this is a big change, and it's not done under the best of circumstances, but the team here is taking this as an opportunity to make a fresh start, and we hope you will, too."

He pauses, offering me the floor, and I give him a tight smile that barely touches my lips.

"Hey. You." I tip my chin at the guy with the open laptop. "You're from the media relations team, right?"

He licks his lips and nods like there might be a wrong answer—or like he wishes he could say no.

"Good. Take notes because I'm only going to say this once."

I flex my fingers where I rest my hands on my thighs, stretching them out before curling them into fists again. I don't want to have to say this at all but it's something I have to deal with, and I want our media relations team to have the right lines to feed to the press.

Around me, eyes dart everywhere but in my direction. I can feel the anticipation. It's a bit like skating out onto the ice before a big game. Everyone waiting for the first hit. The first goal. The final horn. The crowd can smell blood, and these idiots are waiting for me to spill mine.

And it's all there. Right on the tip of my tongue...

The team that took twelve of my best playing years recruited a twenty-something douchebag who stole my team and screwed my girl. Then they dumped me when I had a problem with that. They can go fuck themselves.

But saying those words out loud would be stupid, so I grind my teeth and spit out the same bullshit I gave to the press when I was waiting to get the hell out of Calgary.

"I'm grateful to the Calgary Crushers for buying out my contract and giving me the opportunity to sign with the San Francisco Fury. I wish my former team all the best for the coming season, but my focus now is taking the Fury all the way to the Cup."

The words taste bitter, but ice is better than fire. Frost is preferable to flames. If I ever actually said all the things I want to say, I'd lose all control, and nobody deserves to know how much the last year fucking hurt.

I glance around, and the only person who doesn't look disappointed is Coach. What did these people expect from me today—a therapy session?

I run my tongue over my lips and look around for the drinks I asked for. Green juice. Protein shake. Hot black coffee. Iced vanilla latte. Freshly squeezed orange juice—no pulp. Iced water. I don't know why I do diva shit like ask for six drinks when one would have been fine, other than the fact that keeping people on their toes also keeps them from getting too close. Six drinks, and there's nothing on the table.

"Any chance of getting one of those drinks I asked for?" I say to the room.

Courtney's the first one to speak. Of course, she is. "We had a little miscommunication this morning, but they're on their way right now." She snatches her phone from the table and taps out a message. "I'll get an ETA while we continue."

I grunt, and Coach clears his throat, shooting me a look that draws down his brows as well as the corners of his mouth. I'm too old, too rich, and too jaded to care about disappointing anyone, but like a reflex, I sit up straighter.

"Thank you, Chord," he says, though he's talking to everyone. "I think that means we're all moving in the same direction—forward, not back. But let's not sugarcoat this. We've got a lot of work to do. Playing for San Francisco won't be anything like playing for Calgary. We're rebuilding, and we've made a few bad contracts trying to do that, but I'm determined to turn things around, and we need a veteran to help us reach our potential. Our boys need an experienced captain—a leader and a mentor, on and off the ice. We need *depth*." Coach claps me on the shoulder. "That's where Chord comes in. Sixteen years in this game, and nobody's ever been better on the right wing. His determination and that famous wrist shot are going to take us to the playoffs next year. I guarantee it."

Hell, yeah, I'm leading this team to the playoffs. And if karma has my back, I'll be taking home the Cup.

"So." Courtney smiles and leans forward with her elbows on the table. "There are just two items on our agenda for today. Let's take care of those before we get to the points you raised in your email, shall we?"

My eyes dip to the generous swell of cleavage peeking out from the neck of her loose black blouse, and Courtney's mouth tips up at having won a point. It takes all my strength not to roll my eyes, so I settle for a cool stare. If a woman flashes me her tits, I'm going to look. Doesn't mean I'm interested. Doesn't mean a damn thing.

Her lashes flutter—is she trying to *flirt*?—and I decide I don't like this woman. I break her gaze by reaching for a glass of water that isn't there.

Jesus Christ, what does a man have to do to get a drink around here?

"Fine," I reply. "What do you need to—"

The boardroom door crashes open, and a woman falls through, righting herself and blushing brightly when she notices that everyone is staring. She's tall and attractive but swimming inside baggy beige trousers that cinch in at her small waist and an open matching blazer that's at least two sizes too big. Her dark-rimmed glasses are too large for her pretty, heart-shaped face, framed by strands of dark hair that have pulled free of her long ponytail, and she's balancing a cardboard tray in each hand, both loaded with drinks.

My drinks.

Her big, anxious eyes land on me and widen briefly before she drops her chin and hurries down the length of the room. She keeps her gaze low as she sets the trays at my elbow and plucks the cups from their holders. I watch with mild curiosity as she avoids looking at me, fumbling a little as she pulls at the drinks, and once the six paper cups are lined up in front of me, she practically bolts for the doors.

Around the table, the Fury team ignores her, which annoys me. Even an intern deserves a nod of acknowledgment.

I choose the iced water and take a long draw, but before the mysterious brunette can make her escape from the big, bad Chord Davenport, Courtney obnoxiously clears her throat and then stabs her finger at the end of the table. And when I think I couldn't dislike the marketing manager more than I already do, the girl freezes like she's frightened, gives a jerky nod, and sinks into the chair closest to the door. She unloops an ugly battered satchel from across her body, pulls out a notebook and pen, and hunches over the page like she wishes she could fade into the furniture.

Someone needs to tell her that's absolutely impossible.

"Now, where were we?" Courtney waves her hand at the media relations guy, who wipes a bead of sweat from his brow and shifts in his chair. "Steve, would you like to raise your concerns with Chord?"

"Concerns?" I echo, forgetting all about the girl. "What *concerns*?"

"We just... Ah, that is..." Steve looks around for help, which makes me huff out an irritated sigh, and Coach jumps in.

"Your relationship with the media could be better, Chord. They say you're hard to talk to, and I think you'll agree that you don't give them a lot to work with in post-game press. It's something we hope you're willing to work on."

He rubs a wide hand over his jawline, meeting my glare with solid confidence, and for the first time, I notice the lines around his mouth. The thinning hair. The experience in his dark brown eyes that wasn't there more than a decade ago. I breathe deeper as some of the tension leaches from my hands.

Bobby Campbell was an awesome center in his day, and when I was drafted to the Tampa Bay Titans at eighteen years old, I'm not sure who was more excited about me playing for a legend of his caliber—me or my dad. Campbell knew me as a kid, helped shape me into the player I am today, and next to my father, he taught me the most about how to be a man. I played four years with him until I was traded to Calgary, and I never thought we'd be on the same team again.

Until yesterday.

Everyone waits for me to speak, but I don't. Nobody's going to like what I have to say, which is the media can go to hell. For my last two years with Calgary, they were up my ass about the value of my captaincy, and when news broke that our cocky new trade, Spencer Cook, had been sleeping with my girlfriend for months—and that a few of the guys on my team knew about it—the press made my life a living nightmare. So, I give them as little as I can, as infrequently as I can. And that isn't going to change.

The media relations guy shifts in his seat, and Coach shoots him a look that tells him to keep his mouth shut.

"One more thing, Chord, and then we'll move on," Coach says instead. "I need you to make yourself available this summer. We're building a new team, and not only do we need to get to know each other on the ice, but we've got some bonding to do." He spares me a sympathetic glance. "This is a fresh start, all right? For you and the Fury."

"No can do," I reply, and his eyebrows shoot up. I pick a drink at random—it's the green juice—and lift it to my mouth, taking my time until I'm sure the next time I speak, it won't sound so sharp. "I'll be in Sonoma this summer, and I don't intend to leave."

That's a lie. I don't know how long I'll be home.

My hand involuntarily strays toward my pants pocket. I haven't stepped foot on my family's vineyard in three years, and it's not like I needed an invitation to go back, but it was nice to finally get one.

My fingers press against the folded piece of purple paper tucked away where I won't lose it, the words scrawled across it carefully formed and with sparkling pink stickers around its edges. My six-year-old niece wrote and asked me to come for a family game night, and hell will freeze over before I ever tell that little girl *no*.

"Well, then." Coach scratches his forehead with one thick finger. "You've got a nice set-up there, right? I think I read an article five or so years ago in one of those fancy architectural magazines. The property's huge, and you built your own house. It's got a complete gym. A full-size pool. Secluded and private."

I narrow my eyes. "Yeah."

"Then it's no problem." His eyes brighten above his satisfied grin as he taps a palm on the table. "We'll come to you."

My molars grate together before I change the subject. "It might be time to talk about my email and the list of things I need from the team. It's been a long season, and I need support for recovery between now and October."

Courtney straightens so quickly she bounces. "Yes. We can arrange it all. No problem."

I meet her eyes. They gleam in a way I don't like, and it pisses me off. "Game tape? For the team and any new trades?"

"We're on it now and will send you everything you requested."

"Personalized eating and exercise plans?"

She checks something on her laptop and nods to herself. "We've sent your information to the team's sports nutritionist and trainers, and they'll be in touch within forty-eight hours."

"Physio? I need someone who can come to me at least twice a week over the next couple of months."

I don't need to add that I'm not in my early twenties anymore. Years of hockey and the injuries that go with it mean I can't slack off in the off-season. Everyone here can read between the lines.

"Absolutely," Courtney agrees. "And if the team physiotherapists can't make it, we've got a list of wonderful freelancers who—"

"And a personal assistant? I need someone to handle my move from Calgary to San Francisco. I'll be preoccupied with training and my family, so I need someone who's hands-on."

Her eyebrow quirks and I immediately regret my choice of words.

"I couldn't agree more." Courtney tucks her blonde hair behind one ear, and her tongue glides across her glossy bottom lip. "I think it would be beneficial to assign you someone from the marketing team. As discussed, we need to massage some of those relationships you have with the press, and the marketing team is best positioned to facilitate that. In fact, *I* could—"

"No." I don't need binoculars to see where she's going with this. "I need a personal assistant, not a handler, and not a media coach. I need someone to answer my emails and find me a new apartment and deal with the shit I don't have time to deal with."

"I assure you, I'm perfectly—"

"And I need them to come with me to Aster Springs."

I don't. I really don't. There are eighty-seven days between now and next season—I've counted—and I need to spend every one of them focused on my game. The last thing I want is an assistant hovering nearby and buzzing in my ear, but I'll say anything to stop this woman from scheming her way into my personal life.

Unfortunately, my demand has her leaning forward.

Can't she take a fucking hint?

"I can definitely make that work."

I challenge her hot stare with one coated in ice until movement at the other end of the table catches my eye. It's the intern doing her best to disappear into the high-back boardroom chair. I glance at her, but it's obvious she doesn't want to look at me, and it gives me an idea.

I need someone who isn't going to throw herself at me and someone who won't give me any trouble. I want someone who keeps to herself, stays out of my way, and won't drive me crazy. I need someone invisible.

She's perfect.

I fling up my arm and point. "I want her."

"Oh, no!"

The intern's hands fly up to cover the roses in her cheeks, and the way her eyes grow round like she can't believe she said that out loud makes my lips twitch. I almost feel bad for her, but Courtney's scornful sniff makes my dickish behavior worth it.

The marketing manager visibly collects herself, flipping her hair over her shoulder and rolling her mouth against a condescending smirk. "That's Violet James, one of our junior marketing executives, and she will *not* be working with you."

Is that right?

I stand and button my suit jacket. *Well done, lady. You've just gone and guaranteed that this little wallflower is mine for the summer.*

"If you need anything else," I say to the room as I stride toward the exit, "send requests to Violet—my assistant."

I set my hand on the door, but before I walk through it, I pause next to Violet and wait for her to raise her head. It takes a long second, and her gaze drags up my body like she's delaying the moment she has to meet my eyes. When she does, I almost cancel the whole thing.

How much of an asshole do I have to be to demand this woman work for me when I can tell by the crease between her brows and the way her plush pink lips are parted that she wants to tell me something but can't?

I hear Courtney get to her feet, but I can't look away from Violet. There's a question in those deep chestnut-colored eyes, and it's on the tip of my tongue to tell her she's off the hook.

Courtney is suddenly at my shoulder. "You've changed your mind," she says, and the relief—or maybe it's hope—in her voice is palpable. "Good. I offer my—"

"No."

The chill in my stare is for her, not Violet, but Violet's on the receiving end because I can't bring myself to look away. Her eyes widen, and I blow out a frustrated breath.

Fuck it.

"Be at Silver Leaf Ranch & Vineyard at ten a.m. tomorrow," I tell her. "Don't be late."

THREE

❧

Violet

CHORD DAVENPORT SMELLS SO GOOD I can't think straight. Clean like powder. Fresh like mint. Earthy like cedar with mouthwatering base notes of man. Tall, intimidating, devastating *man*. The fragrance goes straight to the pleasure center in my brain, but it's his eyes that freeze every muscle in my body. He's got thick, dark brows—the one on the right sliced with a single scar—over cold cobalt blues that pin me to my chair and suck the air from my lungs. And I can't look away.

We're in a room full of people, yet Chord stares at me like there's nobody here but us. He's waiting for me to say something, but there's no chance I can string a coherent sentence together.

Tell him you can't be his assistant. Tell him you can't spend a whole summer on his ranch. Tell him he terrifies you. That you have responsibilities. That you're the wrong person for this job!

My lips part, and Chord's gaze drops to my mouth. His eyes trace the shape of it, sweeping from one corner to the other and back again and triggering a warm flush across my chest. The small hope I had of stopping his plan before it goes too far is lost in the silence between us.

"You've changed your mind," Courtney says. I didn't even notice her approach, and I should probably acknowledge her, but Chord's eyes remain fixed on mine, and until he lets go, I'm at his mercy.

"Good," Courtney goes on. "I offer my—"

"No."

The change in Chord is swift, and even though I'm almost positive his problem is with Courtney, it's terrifying to be on this end of his icy glare. My fingertips press into the leather of the boardroom chair as I remind myself breathing isn't optional, and I should probably start again if I want to live long enough to tell my dad about this.

Chord clenches his jaw as a frustrated sigh puffs from his flared nostrils. "Be at Silver Leaf Ranch & Vineyard at ten a.m. tomorrow," he orders. "Don't be late."

He walks out, leaving the doors open behind him, and I watch him walk away. Smooth bronzed neck and a tousled mop of dark hair. Broad shoulders that strain against his navy suit jacket. Narrow waist and pants that are just snug enough to hint at what's underneath—thick muscle and a tight ass. And the way he *walks*. Like he owns the world. Like he's never heard the word *no*.

18

It's not until Chord rounds a corner that I remember where I am. The first thing I see is Courtney, and it's clear that I'm in big trouble.

She crosses her arms over her chest, red nails tapping her upper arms. People collect their notebooks and laptops in awkward silence, and as they shuffle around us to get the heck out of here, I stare at my hands. Not even Courtney can blame me for what just happened, right?

I shoot her a darting glance.

Oh, yeah. She can, and she does.

Courtney throws up her hands. "How could you let this happen? Your instructions were perfectly clear. Sit in the corner, take notes, and"—she bites back a mocking smile as she gestures at my outfit, eyes dancing at the picture of my pristine white sneakers peeking out from underneath my wide-leg tapered beige pants and the matching oversized blazer swamping my frame—"*blend in*."

I wish I had the nerve to put this woman in her place. Just once.

I majored in fashion design in college, I know how to dress myself, and I'm quietly proud of my look. All I ever wanted was for *Violet James* to be the name people gave when someone asked about jaw-dropping wedding dresses and stunning haute couture, but my dreams didn't pan out. My personal style and a bedroom covered in sketches are all I've got left.

Fortunately, I'd double-majored in business marketing, which is how I landed this job with the San Francisco Fury.

And though it's not to Courtney's taste, I always wear beige. Or tan. Or gray or white or black. A monochromatic color palette makes it possible to mix and match a smaller wardrobe, plus it's much easier for me to...

I sigh inside my head. *Blend in.*

"You won't last a week," she continues. "You know that, don't you?"

I do know that.

"I... That is, I mean..."

Trepidation bursts in hot prickles across my collarbone, but then Coach Campbell steps between us. He offers me a business card and I take it with confusion.

"Call me later in the week, and we'll talk about setting up those summer training sessions." He plucks the card from my fingers, flips it over, and returns it. There's another number scrawled on the back. His personal line, I realize, and when I glance up at him with a small, questioning smile, he gives me a comforting wink. "If you need anything, I'm happy to help. And no need to look so worried, Violet. Chord's a good guy at heart. His bark is worse than his bite."

I wish I could tell him how grateful I am for his kindness, but instead, I tuck the card away to hide it from Courtney's suspicious glare.

"Have a good day, Courtney," Coach says before he leaves.

She ignores him, and I get to my feet, hoping that this is the day my extra height equals confidence. It isn't.

I hate the way this woman makes me feel: stupid and small—figuratively speaking. I'm five foot nine, and she barely clears my chin. And I hate that, on some level, I envy her. She's smart. Attractive. All confidence and power, self-assurance and sex. Courtney wears her crimson nails and ruby-red lips as if she paid for them in blood. Come to think of it, maybe she had.

Courtney purses her lips. "I expect you to be online during work hours in case anything comes up here that requires your attention."

She's letting me do it?

My heart thunders so fast that blood roars in my ears, and I realize that part of me was holding onto hope that Courtney would find a way to shut this wild plan down. For a few moments there, it was kind of exhilarating to imagine being claimed by Chord Davenport and whisked away from the monotony that is my life, but only because I never dreamed it would happen. I don't want to go. I *can't* go. I have too many responsibilities here.

"Oh, no." The words come out dry and cracked, so I clear my throat and try again. "I can't—"

"You absolutely can." Courtney sweeps through the doors, and I scoop up my notebook and satchel before chasing her down the hallway. "You'll just have to make time for your actual job while you're sunning yourself by the pool and organizing his mail and facilitating the team's *training* sessions."

"That's not what I meant. I can't—"

"Find a way." She pulls up short, and I stumble to avoid crashing into her. Her eyes sweep up and down my body before she shakes her head with a sigh of resignation. "For reasons I cannot fathom, Chord Davenport wants you."

My entire body flushes red-hot, and I wonder if I can reach the nearest bathroom before I throw up. Maybe. If I run.

"And it's our job," Courtney adds bitterly as she walks away, "to give that man what he wants."

FOUR

Violet

I OPEN THE DOOR TO the two-bedroom apartment I share with my dad, and the comforting aroma of ragu makes me smile—for about three seconds. I've spent the entire day thinking about how to break the news I'll be gone all summer, and I still don't know how to do it. The thought of leaving him in his own company for months ties my stomach in knots.

The door clicks shut, my keys hit the ceramic bowl on the hallway table, and Dad's head pokes around the corner. "Dinner is ready when you are, Blossom."

"Thanks, Dad," I call on my way to my room. "Give me a couple minutes to freshen up, and I'll come right out."

He knows me well enough to read between the lines, and this evening is one of those times I need to be alone for a while.

I'm grateful but not surprised when he replies, "Take your time. No rush."

I disappear into my room, drop my satchel on my desk, and collapse face down on my bed. Ugh. What a freaking day.

And starting tomorrow, my dad will be alone for the first time in probably thirty years.

His world is so, so small. He spends ninety minutes every morning walking around our neighborhood, cooks us a homemade dinner every evening, and supports the San Francisco Fury like it's his religion. He also sees his therapist twice a month. That's all he has. Walking. Cooking. Hockey. Therapy. And me.

With a groan, I roll and reach over to turn on the lamp on my nightstand, then glance around my room. When we moved to San Francisco ten years ago, it was so I could start my fashion degree, and this shoe-box apartment was the best we could afford. Dad insisted I take the larger bedroom with the ensuite bath because "young women need privacy, and young fashion ingenues need space to chase their dreams."

When I mentioned I wanted to line the walls with oversized gray felt-covered boards, he installed them all in a day and surprised me with them after class. All this time later, they're covered with layers of my sketches, hundreds of fabric swatches, a bunch of inspirational quotes, and photographs of wedding dresses by my favorite designers. Evidence of a dream I gave up but a calling I can't ignore.

I pick up my vintage—okay, thrifted—beige leather satchel, tug my sketchbook free, and open it to the design I started this morning but didn't have time to finish. I put on my headphones and turn up the gritty rock track, then start to draw. It's not long before I'm lost between the beat in my ears and the smooth paper under my palm. Another minute, and my heart rate slows enough that I can no longer feel it thumping.

Cocking my head to one side, I add shadow to the feminine silhouette on the paper. Lengthen the skirt. Refine the waist. This particular design isn't new. It's a dress I've committed to paper a thousand times over the last ten years, but I'm trying something new in the bodice. A little less lace and a little more skin. A subtle blush instead of the classic ivory I've favored in the past. Sometime later—I know it can't be too long because Dad hasn't come looking for me yet—it's done.

I tear the page free from the binding and look around. I ran out of blank space years ago, so I find a spot where a pin can pierce through the layers to the board and add my latest work to the collection. Versions of the same dress appear on all four walls, each one a little different in ways nobody but me would notice. My latest attempt at a sample of it hangs from the dressmaker's dummy in the corner. I should let this one go, but I can't until I get it right.

After a quick social media check—no new likes, no new followers—I shower, change into comfortable sweats, and then sit at our two-seater dining table. Dad is in the kitchen spooning noodles and sauce into bowls, and when he sets one down in front of me along with a bowl of grated parmesan cheese, he gives me a look he's perfected over the last twenty-eight years. The one that says *spill it*.

"I have some news," I begin, twirling a knot of spaghetti onto my fork. I slide it off when it grows too large and start again.

"Yeah?" Dad picks up his knife and fork, slices into his spaghetti, and chops the strands into rice-size lengths. I've suggested we cook penne or fusilli instead of spaghetti, but slurping noodles was one of my favorite things as a kid, and he refuses to let it go. "Did you get a promotion already? I knew it wouldn't be long before the Fury realized how lucky they got when they hired you."

I spare him an indulgent smile. Lucas James is my biggest cheerleader, and I appreciate his confidence, but he's my dad. He's obligated to believe in me.

"Not exactly."

I stuff a forkful of pasta into my mouth, but I have to swallow eventually, and Dad's waiting with questions written all over his face.

"Chord Davenport came into the office this morning."

Dad's hands stall mid-cut and I can't help but grin at the wonder in his eyes. "You met *Chord Davenport*?"

"I did."

"And?" He circles his fork in the air, prompting for more. "What's he like in person?" Dad shakes his head. "The Fury's going to be unstoppable next season with a player like Davenport on the right wing. Just what we need to turn things around, right?"

"Right."

I set down my fork, take a gulp of water, and then tuck one hand between my knees to stop them from bouncing.

"What's going on?" Dad leans back to glance at my legs, still vibrating under the table. "Are you nervous?"

"A little."

"Why?"

He gives me a confused look, so I suck in a deep breath and let the words tumble out.

"He came in to talk about next season, but he needs an assistant for the summer, and I think my boss wanted to do it, but for whatever reason, Chord didn't want that. So anyway, one thing kind of led to another, and in the end, he said he wants me."

Dad's brows climb high enough to carve creases in his forehead. He's only forty-eight and still has a thick head of hair—dark, like mine, with silver around the edges. "But that's... That's great!" He grins as he lifts a forkful of his dinner halfway to his mouth. "Think you can get me his autograph?"

"Maybe. But Dad..."

He senses there's something I'm not telling him. His expression grows serious as he sets down his cutlery. "What is it, Violet? What are you worried about?"

I huff out a resigned breath. "He's spending the off-season on his ranch in Sonoma County, and I... I have to go with him."

"Go with him?" I watch as Dad tries to puzzle it out. "To where? His ranch?"

I nod, and Dad's eyes cloud with emotion. Understanding. Disappointment. Worry.

It's been two years since he last had a serious depressive episode, but that doesn't mean I don't think about it every day. Suddenly, I'm talking a mile a minute, hoping that dropping a load of uninteresting trivia will distract us both.

"I looked it up online today at work. His family owns a property called Silver Leaf Ranch & Vineyard just outside of Aster Springs. His parents bought it in the early 1980s, and when they passed, Chord and his four siblings took over. They make wine—mostly chardonnay and pinot noir—but they also have a small organic farm with heirloom vegetables and fruit and an olive orchard. A few animals—chickens and horses and sheep. There are accommodations and a restaurant. They host weddings and functions, and the property is something like a hundred acres, so Chord built his own house with a pool and... Oh, Dad." He's staring through the table and probably hasn't registered a word I've said. I reach out and set my hand on his. "Are you okay?"

"What?" He clears his throat and tops my hand with his. I do the same, so our hands are stacked together, and he smiles. That's something else we've done since I was little. "I'm fine. This is a once-in-a-lifetime opportunity, and you should feel good about it. Don't worry about me. I'm going to miss you. That's all."

"I'll miss you too, and I don't know what there is to feel good about. I didn't apply for the job or anything." I lift my shoulders and let them drop. "It's a case of wrong place at the wrong time."

"I'm sure that's not true."

"It is, but it doesn't matter. What matters is that you'll be okay. I'll call every day, and I was thinking maybe you could ask around the building for some handyman work. You haven't done that in a while, and it would keep you busy, plus the extra money might be nice. I'll also speak to Jennifer upstairs about checking in on you—"

"No, you won't." Dad pulls his hands free and scoops up some pasta. "I don't need a babysitter."

"I know that." I drag my hands back and collect my fork, but I only play with my food. "But she's a nice person, and you could both use the company."

He snorts. "I can take care of myself."

He can, I reassure myself, but my voice is small when I reply. "I know."

We eat our meal in silence, and if it weren't for the fact that my paycheck keeps this roof over both our heads—and that the Fury was willing to add Dad to my health insurance—I'd quit my job right now and forget all about Chord Davenport. Instead, I have to find a gentle way to tell my dad I'm leaving in twelve hours.

I'm still searching for words when I stand to clear away the dishes, but Dad stops me with a hand on my arm and guides me back to my seat.

"I'm sorry. I don't mean to be so hard to talk to, but I hate it when you worry about me. It reminds me that I've screwed up this whole parenting thing, and it's too late to fix it."

My heart breaks as I shake my head. "You haven't screwed up anything. It's not your fault you have depression."

"But it *is* my responsibility, and it's not the most important thing right now. You are." His brown eyes, the same deep chestnut shade as mine, soften. "How do you feel about the job?"

"I don't know," I confess. "Nervous. Kind of overwhelmed. He's an intimidating guy. Tall—much taller than he looks on the screen—and big. Arrogant. Demanding. He didn't say much today, but everyone in the room was hanging off every word. There's something about him, you know? Charisma isn't the right word. More like, um... magnetism. It's hard not to look at him."

"I didn't know you were such a fan." Dad's eyes sparkle as he fights to hide a smile.

"Oh, I'm not." I don't want to burden Dad with the truth that I'm more than a little scared of my new boss, but a version of my worries comes tumbling out. "I've never been anyone's personal assistant, though, let alone to someone who's used to getting what he wants when he wants and how he wants it. I'll probably screw up a hundred times within a week, and he'll send me straight back home."

"I don't believe that for a second." Dad takes my hand and squeezes my fingers. "You're too smart and too gentle for anyone to treat so badly. Just be yourself, and you'll do great."

He's got no idea about Courtney and what I put up with at work. The day I told him I got a full-time marketing role with his favorite hockey team, his face lit up brighter than a kid at Christmas. It would shatter him to know how much I loathe it, so I smile and grip his hand before letting it go.

"Thanks, Dad."

"And who knows what opportunities might come from this? Impress him enough, and it'll open doors for you at the Fury. You'll be running that place in no time." I roll my eyes, and he boops me on the nose. "Just do your best, Blossom."

"My best means keeping my head down, staying out of Chord's way, and doing my job well enough to survive the summer." I huff out an anxious chuckle. "I'll be counting down all eighty-seven days until I come home."

"You said he's got a family on this ranch?" Dad asks, and when I nod, he looks thoughtful. "Maybe dealing with Chord Davenport on his home turf will soften him a little. You might even become friends."

I nibble my lip and try to imagine a version of the man I met today without all the ice and edges. I can't see it, and the possibility of being his friend is even more ludicrous. I've never been able to relax in social situations, and aside from the fact the San Francisco Fury signs both our paychecks—his with a lot more zeroes than mine—I have nothing in common with Chord Davenport. There's a higher chance of seeing one of my dresses on a red carpet than there is of a man like him taking an interest in a girl like me, but I can tell Dad likes the idea.

"I really doubt it, Dad, but I suppose you never know."

"When do you go?"

I wince. "I have to be in Aster Springs at ten a.m. tomorrow."

His face falls, and he rubs one finger under his nose the way he does when he's feeling overwhelmed. But then he brightens so quickly that his enthusiasm can only be for my benefit.

He gets to his feet and claps his hands together. "If you have to go, tomorrow is as good a day as any. I'll clear away the dishes so you can pack."

Before he can collect our empty bowls, I jump to my feet and throw my arms around his middle. I'm tall, but Dad's taller, and I press my cheek against his chest.

Dad wraps his arms around me and rests his cheek on my head with a sigh. "This is a great adventure," he murmurs into my hair. "And you'll only be gone a few months. Everything will work out fine. After all, how much can possibly happen in just one summer?"

FIVE

Chord

85 DAYS TILL HOCKEY SEASON

IT TAKES ABOUT AN HOUR to get from San Francisco to Silver Leaf Ranch & Vineyard, and even though it's been years since I last went home, I could never forget the way.

I zip through traffic, cruise past sleepy country towns, and then reach the Redwood groves, rows of vines, patchwork farmland, and rolling green hills of Sonoma. The twilit landscape is blanketed by last night's fog, making the damp air glow. I slow down and take it all in. It's fucking gorgeous.

The sun is creeping over the horizon when I roll past a familiar set of enormous white timber gates bracketed by low stacked stone walls, and a tingle of loss pinches the bridge of my nose. My mom painted those gates herself every spring and every fall, and even though they're much more weathered around the edges now, I can see the paint is fresh. Not that

I'm surprised. My sister, Charlie, runs the ranch now, and she'd never let those gates—or anything else—fall into disrepair.

I snort. Charlie—smart, stubborn, her-way-or-the-highway Charlotte Davenport—would shut the place down before she let it go to shit. And it's almost come to that. It's been eight years since our dad died, and this winter, it'll be ten years since we said goodbye to Mom. Once they were gone, business was never the same. Our family was never the same.

Daisy turned eighteen just before Dad's death, so we were all adults by then and living our own separate lives. Without Mom and Dad to bring us together, it got too easy to stay fractured. And even though Charlie, Finn, Dylan, Daisy, and I inherited everything, and none of us wanted to sell, we never found a way to run this place like they did.

I've tried over and over to invest, but Charlie won't take my money. She doesn't want a single cent of what hockey's given me, and it drives me fucking nuts.

The gates are flung open, revealing a long country lane wide enough for two cars to pass, bordered by old silver-leafed olive trees. I don't need to turn in to know the driveway is covered with dusty gravel that crunches under both boots and tires or that there's a turning circle at the end in front of a white-clad reception house and tasting room.

But I'm not a visitor, and I don't stop until I've driven farther around the perimeter of the hundred acres my family owns. I turn onto a dirt road forking off to the right, stop at a gate marked *private property*, and take a second to appreciate the fact that I'm finally here. I haven't lived at Silver Leaf since I was eighteen, but I've never felt at home anywhere else.

I leave the car running as I get out of the car to swing open the wide metal gate. As I wind my way up the long asphalt drive to the house I built at the rear of my family's land, it feels like nothing has changed. Not the house, a masterpiece of white wood and glass and stone hugged by a wide porch that overlooks our vineyards on one side and the river on the other. I picture the infinity pool on the far side, and my muscles relax at the thought of sinking into the water when the heat hits later in the day. Until then, I open an automated door on my five-car garage, swing the coupe into one of the free spaces, and consider my next move.

Do I go into the house first, maybe unpack and get in a quick workout, or do I let my family know I'm here?

It's tempting to leave the hard stuff for later, but that girl—woman—from the Fury will be here mid-morning, and I need to talk to Charlie about organizing a cabin for Violet to use for the summer.

The grumble in my stomach settles things. I leave my luggage in the car, lock the garage with the press of a remote control, and start the walk around to my little brother's restaurant.

It's a little more than a mile—near enough for me to get there on foot, not so close that visitors might accidentally wander too close.

As I follow a dirt track framed by tumbled boulders, I pass the old dam and cast my eye over the rows of vines stretching in every direction. This deep into the vineyard, I see the strain we're under. More fields lie fallow than they should, and more than half are bordered by broken wire-and-timber fences. I skirt closer to the vines that are green and full, take note of the open canopies, and silently approve the crop load. At least the vines we do have look like they'll give us a good pinot noir this year.

My hike lasts about fifteen minutes before the first building comes into view. Named The Hill because it's perched at the top of a low rise, our family restaurant looks like the rest of the buildings at Silver Leaf Ranch & Vineyard—the cellar door with our wine-making operations and tasting rooms, the main house where Charlie and Dylan live, the lines of cabins that make up the guest accommodations, and the private bungalow by the water. They're all classic white wood, rough stacked stone, and oversized glass windows that take full advantage of the landscape. Even indoors, you can't escape the effects of nature. When it came time to build my own place, I made it my mission to honor the style my parents loved so much.

I take the stone steps cut into the side of the rise two at a time and let myself into the kitchen. My brother stands with his back to me at the stove, and fuck, for a second, I feel like shit. I'm an asshole for not seeing him more often.

"What does a man have to do to get a decent breakfast around here?"

Dylan spins, and I ignore the way the kitchen staff double-take at the sight of me. Dylan stalls for a moment, but time starts again as he launches across the room and throws himself at me. I crush him to my chest before letting him go.

"What are you doing here? Wait. Let's just..." Dylan looks around and calls over a middle-aged woman in matching chef's whites, gives her a few rushed instructions, and then jerks his head in the direction of the private function room. I follow him as we leave behind a silent kitchen that bursts into excited whispers the second my foot is on the other side of the door.

"Food shouldn't take long," he says as he moves through the empty space with its vaulted ceilings and stacks of tables and chairs pushed up against the walls.

One side of the room is made up entirely of tall glass doors that open up onto a balcony looking over the vines. There's a single long table set up on this side of the glass with a few chairs around it. Dylan walks straight to it, takes a seat, and kicks out another chair as an invitation for me to join him.

Dylan's five years younger than me, and he was only thirteen when I was drafted to Tampa, so we didn't always have a conventional brother relationship. But in those days, Mom and Dad were still around to bring him to games, and I came home every summer back then, so we were close enough.

He's not as tall or broad as I am, his brown hair is a little lighter than mine, and his bright blue eyes are much warmer, but nobody would doubt that we're related. Dylan was such a goofball as a kid, and he kind of reminded me of a puppy, but all that changed when he became a father. He was only twenty-three years old and not in a serious relationship with Izzy's mother then or now, but raising his daughter full-time forced him to grow up damn quick.

I drop into the seat, stretch out my legs, and cross my arms over my chest. Dylan cocks an eyebrow and shakes his head.

"You sneaky son of a bitch. Why didn't you tell us you were coming?"

I shoot that eyebrow right back at him. "Why do you think?"

Dylan winces before passing a hand over his jaw. "Charlie."

"Who said you can't be smart and beautiful?"

"Fuck off. I'm smart enough to know that surprising her like this is going to be worse for you than giving her a little warning."

"And I'm smart enough to know that this way, she didn't have time to change the locks."

He laughs, but it's short and shallow. "She wouldn't do that."

"She would."

He's saved from pretending he disagrees when a server comes in bringing us breakfast. I fall on the plate the moment it hits the table.

"Slow down, bro." Dylan watches me with horror that may actually be genuine. "That's fine food you're shoveling in right now. Savor it. *Appreciate* it."

"Huh?" I glance at Dylan and then back at my half-demolished meal. "It's eggs and sausage. Bit of toast. Some other stuff." I poke at the things I don't recognize. Whatever they are, it's all delicious, and I scoop another forkful into my mouth.

Dylan uses his knife to give me a tour of the plate. "Poached eggs and house-made sujuk. Potato and corn fritters. Pumpkin hummus. Capsicum and chili chutney. Garlic labneh. Microherbs. Grilled sourdough baked fresh this morning."

I follow along, wishing he'd shut up and let me eat, and he takes one look at me and rolls his eyes. "Next time I'll get you a bib and a pail."

"Sounds good," I say around another mouthful of sausage. I mean *sujuk*.

"But seriously." Dylan spares me a sidelong look as he cuts into his breakfast. "What are you doing here? How long are you going to stay?"

I stick my hand in my pocket, pull out Izzy's invitation to family game night, and smack it onto the table without a word. Dylan's brows draw down as he picks it up, but after a cursory scan, he shakes his head with a small smile and sets it down again.

"She didn't tell me she was doing that."

"She didn't?" A stab of disappointment takes me by surprise. Part of me thought the invitation might be from Dylan, too—maybe even Charlie—but it seemed that my niece was operating alone. "How'd she find my address?"

SAMANTHA LEIGH

"No fucking clue. That kid runs circles around me, Chord. I'm terrified of what the next ten years are going to do to me."

I smirk. Better him than me.

"How is the little punk? I miss her."

"She's great. Murdered kindergarten, but we knew she would. I'm talking to her mother about the possibility of getting her tested for giftedness, but I don't know. Something about it feels weird."

"In what way?"

"Shouldn't a kid get a shot at a normal childhood? Izzy is bright—like, off-the-charts smart—but she's a lot of other things too. I don't want her to be defined by the one thing she happens to be good at and lose touch with everything else."

I don't notice my fork has stalled halfway to my open mouth until Dylan looks away with a sheepish grimace. I lower my hand and frown at the way my heart starts beating harder.

"Is that what you think happened to me?"

"No. Maybe. I don't know." Dylan rubs the back of his neck and shrugs. "Look, I didn't mean—"

A wide set of doors at the opposite end of the room crashes open, and Dylan grins at what he sees over my shoulder. I spin in my chair and beam at the little dark-haired girl marching into the room like she owns the place. She's got a camouflage-print t-shirt on with a bright pink tutu, and filthy tooled leather cowboy boots on her little feet.

"Daddy, I came to tell you—"

"*Chord?*"

The sharp squeal behind Izzy comes from the throat of my baby sister. I mean, she's twenty-seven, but she'll always be the baby, and she's supposed to be in South America for the summer. With her long blonde waves, pink cheeks, and permanent smile, Daisy is pure sunshine, and something loosens in my chest at the unexpected sight of her.

After Daisy screeches my name, Izzy's eyes widen as she realizes who I am, and when I drop to one knee, arms outstretched to entice her into a hug, she races into a flying leap so fast that I'm twirling her around before I've taken another breath.

"Uncle Chord!" Izzy squeezes my neck tight enough to cut off oxygen for a moment, then releases me and gives me a bright smile. "Did you get my invitation? Is that why you're here? What did you think of the stickers? I saved all my best ones for you."

"I got your invitation and that's exactly why I'm here." I bop her on her upturned nose. "I couldn't say no to my best girl."

"What does a sister have to do to get a little affection around here?" Daisy punches me in the ribs to get my attention, and I scoop her against me with my free arm. I regret it when she pinches me hard in the side. "Why didn't you tell us you were coming?"

"Ow! You're one to talk. Aren't you supposed to be in Argentina or Chile or something?"

"Eh. I wasn't feeling it, so I'm spending the summer here."

Warm breath tickles my neck, and I twist my head to find Izzy gazing up at me, big brown eyes glued to mine before she wraps me in another hug. Her body softens with a happy sigh as she flops her head onto my shoulder, and I rest my cheek on her dark hair.

"Funny thing that," I say to Daisy. "So am I."

SIX

Chord

DYLAN RETURNS TO THE KITCHEN after breakfast, so Daisy and Izzy take me on a tour of the ranch. I don't need it, but it's Izzy's idea, and I can't stand to disappoint her. Plus, an hour or so walking around the property means another hour I can delay dealing with Charlie, and that sounds like a good idea to me.

Izzy skips on ahead, leading us away from the restaurant and down an unsealed road toward the stables. I breathe in clean air laced with the scent of dirt and lavender courtesy of the herb gardens planted around the restaurant. I turn my face toward the sky and silently appreciate the endless blue.

Hockey's never far from my mind, but out here, it feels far away.

Daisy waits until Izzy's out of earshot before she nudges me with her shoulder.

"So, what are you really doing here?"

"Me?" I shrug and kick at the little stones studding the dirt path. "My niece invited me."

Daisy snorts, and when I respond with a flat look, she rolls her eyes and bumps me again. "Fine. Talk to me. Don't talk to me. I don't care."

"Izzy invited me," I repeat, "and in case you haven't heard, I signed with the Fury two days ago, which means—"

I'm three steps ahead when I notice Daisy isn't beside me anymore. I turn, and she's staring at me, brows drawn like she's working out a riddle.

"You're moving home?"

"I'm moving to San Francisco, yeah."

Her face lights up, and she leaps at me. "You're moving home!"

I catch her and hug her hard enough to crack a rib. Her joy takes me off guard, and though it warms me a little, the high fades when I remember Daisy doesn't live here. She's never been interested in where I've made my home before, and I don't know why she cares now.

After I set her down, I give her a suspicious look that has her grinning like an imp.

"What aren't you telling me?"

"Nothing."

Daisy starts strolling again, glancing up the way to check that Izzy's still in sight. Our niece is passing the chicken coops, twirling and kicking up puffs of dust before skipping through them like it's some kind of magic and not airborne dirt that Dylan will have to wash out of her clothes tonight.

I'm growing impatient as I adjust my pace to match Daisy's much shorter stride. "I call bullshit. What's going on?"

"*Well.* You're here. I'm here—"

"And why are you here, exactly?"

"That's for me to know and you to find out, Mr. Grumpy Pants." I roll my eyes, and she sticks out her tongue. "Charlie and Dylan live here, and as for our troubled middle child—"

"Finn? Do you know where he is?"

I shove my hands in my pockets at the thought of our brother serving overseas. I don't like to think about it, and I'm good at avoiding thoughts that don't feel good, but I'm the oldest. I should keep closer tabs on my brothers and sisters, but it's like Daisy said. Charlie and Dylan never leave the ranch. Daisy packed her suitcase the day after Dad's funeral, got on a plane, and we've barely seen her since. And then there's Finn. He enlisted straight out of high school and is a Navy SEAL now, so...

I do the math in my head. He's been gone for thirteen years. Fuck. Somewhere in there, I missed his thirtieth birthday.

"I do." Daisy looks like a cat who caught a mouse. "He's in Mom and Dad's bungalow."

It's my turn to stop dead still. The bungalow is a little house our parents built right on the river, and though they said it was reserved for private rentals like honeymooners, bachelor parties, and celebrities, I don't ever remember them

45

SAMANTHA LEIGH

renting it out. Instead, one or both of them would disappear out there for a day or two at a time. Dad would take his fishing rod. Mom would take a book. They'd both come back a little happier and more relaxed. It made more sense to me now than it did then. Living on a property that welcomed a constant stream of strangers must have been exhausting, not to mention raising five kids. But they loved each other. Fiercely and always. I suspect they never had any intention of using that bungalow for any other reason than as their own escape when they needed a break.

"Finn's here?" I take hold of Daisy's arm and turn her to face me. "Why? For how long?" Panic grabs me by the throat. "Is he all right? He's not injured, is he?"

"No, he's not injured, and I don't know for how long, but... He's been discharged, Chord. He's not a SEAL anymore."

A sound of surprise and relief escapes in a rush of air. Our family isn't what anyone would call close, but the fact I didn't know this information about my brother still stings.

"I had no idea."

Daisy gives me a sad smile, and I wonder what she heard in my voice. "Don't feel bad. He didn't tell anyone until he got here, and that was only three days ago, but he's been discharged for three months."

"Three *months*? Where has he been all this time?"

Daisy shrugs. "You know Finn. He's not exactly an open book, but the best I can make out, he traveled around for a

46

while and caught up with old friends. Picked up a stray dog. Now he's home, and we're all together again." Daisy skips forward a couple of paces so she can walk backward and beam at me. "How great is that?"

"Yeah. It's great." Daisy's optimism is contagious, and for a moment, I can almost believe that this will be the summer our family gets its shit together.

The moment doesn't last long.

"Meanwhile." She waves a hand up and down at my body, her nose scrunching in disapproval. "Are you trying to impress a girl or something? What the hell are you wearing?"

I look down at my black t-shirt and dark blue jeans. Both designer. Both fucking expensive. "What's wrong with this?"

She rolls her eyes. Little sisters were made to annoy big brothers, I know that, but she does it so well and with so little effort that it's extra irritating.

"We've been out here for fifteen minutes, and your shoes are already filthy. I give your shirt another five before it's covered in dust as well."

I glance at my feet and frown at the dirt caking the white leather. "I walked from my house, so it's been longer than fifteen minutes."

She snorts and spins so we're walking side by side again. I note her scuffed-up work boots, worn jeans, loose tee, and wide-brimmed hat and suddenly feel overdressed.

"Step onto this ranch in white sneakers and twenty-five-hundred-dollar jeans again, big brother, and we're going to have words. Wear that fancy watch one more time and you might never see it again. You're a country boy, Davenport, not some rich dick from the city." Just when I'm starting to feel stupid for not changing after the drive, she glances up at me. "And put on a hat. You don't want that pretty face of yours to burn."

I flick the brim of her hat, sending it flying to the ground. "Did anyone ever tell you how annoying you are?"

After a decent pinch to my ribs that makes me grunt, she picks it up with a shake of her head. "You're such a baby."

Up ahead, Izzy stops in front of the abandoned stables.

"Aunt Daisy says there used to be horses in here," she tells me as I tug on the closed door. "Is that true, Uncle Chord? Did you ever ride the horses?"

A quick look inside confirms that aside from some old bales of hay and a punch of stale air, the stable is empty. Daisy pokes her head in with a wistful sigh, then takes Izzy's hand as we keep on walking.

"We used to have horses," I confirm. "But I didn't ride them much."

"You were too busy playing hockey," Izzy declares like it's a well-known fact.

"Uh, yeah." I rub the back of my neck. "I guess I was."

"There used to be twelve horses here," Daisy says.

"Twelve?" Izzy's eyes grow round. "That's a whole dozen!"

"That's right. And when your grandmother was still alive, she used to take people out on guided trail rides. She taught me how to ride a horse, and one day I'll teach you, too."

Izzy drops Daisy's hand and spins in a delighted pirouette. Her little red cowboy hat falls off, catching around her neck by a cord, and I set it right again as she babbles with excitement.

"Are we getting horses, Aunt Daisy? Are they coming this week? I'm going to call mine Mabel."

"Mabel?" Daisy shares an amused look with me. "Why Mabel?"

Izzy throws up her hands like that's the silliest question she ever heard. "I don't know. I just like that name."

"Well, when we have horses again, you can name one Mabel. Until then..." Daisy scoops up Izzy and sets her on her hip. "Uncle Chord, crouch down a second, will you?"

I'm not sure what Daisy is planning until I squat low to the ground, and she deposits Isobel on my back. I look up at her with flat eyes.

Daisy responds with a shit-eating grin. "Giddy up, horsey."

I stretch up to full height and grunt as Izzy kicks her hard little heels into my sides. I take off at an easy walk, then increase my pace as she whoops her hat over her head, yanking on the collar of my very expensive shirt, giggling and shouting, "Yeehaw!"

Behind us, Daisy cackles because, apparently, this is hilarious.

I don't care what anyone says. I'm buying this kid a fucking horse.

SEVEN

Violet

DAY 1 AT SILVER LEAF... ONLY 85 TO GO

I TURN DOWN THE VOLUME in my car until Aerosmith is barely audible and concentrate on the instructions given by my GPS. *Estimated time of arrival at Silver Leaf Ranch & Vineyard is thirty minutes.*

Anticipation flickers in the hollow of my throat, but I tighten my fingers on the steering wheel and force myself to appreciate this moment. It's a big one, and I don't want to miss it.

The morning sky is all blue today, with only a few cottony clouds scudding along the horizon, and the fog has all but lifted, so I'm graced with views of never-ending fields and vineyards that meet green hills and low mountains. The beauty of Sonoma Valley is breathtaking.

I've lived in San Francisco for a decade and never been here. Wine country is the kind of place you go for romantic escapes with a boyfriend or boozy weekends with the girls. I have neither a boyfriend nor the girls, so I've never had a reason to visit.

The truth is, I've never traveled anywhere. Never chased adventure. Never spent any time away from home. I'm twenty-eight years old and about as worldly as a toddler. I owe it to myself to live this experience. I owe it to my dad, too.

When we said goodbye this morning, he was positive in a way that felt real, which made me think that even though neither of us expected this separation, it might be good for him.

Before I know it, I'm outside the tall white wooden gates of Silver Leaf Ranch & Vineyard. I pull over and hesitate, leaning over the steering wheel to get a better look at what's inside.

There's a long, wide driveway bordered by tall trees with silvery foliage, giving it the look of a quiet country lane. It's too long to see what lies at the end, and sitting here doing nothing isn't settling the butterflies, so I take a breath, turn the wheel, and ease my foot onto the gas pedal.

I go easy over the loose gravel because I'm not used to driving on anything except city roads, and I'm captivated by the ranch itself. I lower my window to get the full experience. Summer air that smells like clean, damp earth. Lush green vines in perfect rows and empty fields lying beyond. Woodlands behind that. Glimpses of water—a river, maybe? A lake? Mountains in the distance. A panoramic picture of paradise.

Eventually, a bright white structure with a sign declaring *Silver Leaf Ranch & Vineyard* above it comes into view.

Hedgerows appear on either side of the driveway just as perfectly planted garden beds turn the wild landscape into something tamed but no less beautiful. Next thing I know, I'm pulling around a turning circle in front of a building with a welcome sign and easing into one of a dozen car spaces marked *guest*.

I shut off the engine and take a deep breath. I did it. I'm here.

And... I've got no idea what to do next. I peer out the car windows, front, back, both sides, but there are no signs of life. My only instructions were to be here at ten a.m., but I'm early, and I'm in no rush to see Chord Davenport again, so I sit back in my seat and nibble my lip while I debate my next move.

I'm still sitting here five minutes later, knees bouncing and stomach getting tighter, when a tap on my car door scares me half to death.

A woman about my age, maybe a couple of years older, gives me a polite smile. She's got warm brown hair pulled back in a ponytail and a black shirt with a Silver Leaf Ranch & Vineyard logo embroidered on one side.

"I'm sorry. I didn't mean to scare you, but you've been sitting here a while, and I thought you might be lost."

"Oh. Thanks, but no. I'm not lost." She steps back as I open the car door, and I thrust my hand at her in an awkward attempt at confidence that's fooling nobody. "I'm Violet James. Chord Davenport is expecting me."

The woman shakes my hand, but her professional friendliness fades away at the mention of Chord's name. "I'm

Charlie, Chord's sister. It's nice to meet you, Violet, but you must have your wires crossed. Chord's not here."

My heart, which only a moment ago was flying like a bird in my chest, freefalls to the ground. "He's not?"

"No."

Charlie walks away, and I practically fall the rest of the way out of the car, scrambling to follow her long strides toward the building behind us.

"I'm sorry you've come all this way for nothing but—" She cuts off, turning and regarding me with narrowed eyes. "Are you from the press?"

"Me?" I squeak. "No!"

"A puck bunny?" She shakes her head and huffs out a disgusted chuckle. "You'll have better luck going to his games, and tell your friends, too. Save yourselves the drive and the embarrassment."

"A *puck bunny*?"

She takes off again, gravel crunching under her boots, and I hurry after her.

"No, I'm from the San Francisco Fury and—"

"It doesn't matter where you're from." Charlie stalks toward the set of enormous white timber doors fronting the reception building, then tugs one open and holds it ajar. "Like I said, Chord's not—"

"Aunt Charlie!"

A little girl comes careening around the corner of the building, skipping and skidding over the loose stones. She's a curious sight in a red cowboy hat, khaki camouflage tee, neon pink tutu, and tiny cowboy boots caked in mud and dust.

I smile a little as she slides to a stop in front of Charlie, then grins up at her from under the brim of her hat. "Guess what?"

Charlie lets the door swing shut as she leans down and tweaks the little girl's chin. "What?"

"Uncle Chord's here!"

Charlie's head jerks up, and she looks at me like I've tricked her. My stomach drops as I raise my palms, not sure what to say, and two more people stroll around the side of the building.

I release a sigh when I recognize Chord, looking so sexy in a simple black t-shirt and dusty Wranglers that I'm at risk of choking on my own spit. But my relief is short-lived once I see the hard look on his face. Any hope I might have had that Chord would be softer—or at least less intimidating—around his family evaporates on the spot.

"You're early."

My mouth pops open. Yes, I'm early. In some parts of the world, that would make me responsible. Reliable. An enthusiastic go-getter. In Chord Davenport's world? It makes me a nuisance.

"Chord." Charlie's glance bounces between us, and her suspicion is obvious. Does she think we planned this? The idea would make me laugh if I wasn't at risk of sounding hysterical. "When did you get here?"

"Just this morning."

Charlie crosses her arms and blinks with disbelief. "And you were going to tell me... *when* exactly?"

"Daze?" Chord turns to the woman he arrived with, a pretty blonde with big hazel eyes and a mouth that looks on the verge of smiling. I get the impression it's always like that—she's got a warmth about her—and I wonder if she's Chord's girlfriend. Not going to lie, they make an odd match. "Take Izzy back to the main house for breakfast, will you?"

The girl—Izzy—skips toward him. "But I already had breakfast, Uncle Chord."

"Have it again," he replies. The way his tone softens is subtle, but I hear it, and I'm surprised. He straightens the hat on her head. "Little girls who want to ride big horses need to give their body energy to grow nice and strong."

"Did you hear that, Aunt Charlie? Uncle Chord's going to buy me a horse!"

An odd noise sticks in Charlie's throat, and the blonde woman chuckles as she lifts Izzy's hand. "Careful, Izzy. You're going to give Aunt Charlie a few more gray hairs."

Izzy giggles. "Aunt Daisy! She doesn't have gray hair. She's not a grandma!"

Ah. Another sister, then. For some reason, I'm relieved. Chord on his own will be hard enough. Chord with a girlfriend? The stuff of nightmares.

"Wrinkles, then?" Daisy pushes at the crease between Charlie's brows, trying to smooth out the line.

Charlie swats her away, but the corner of her mouth twitches. "I don't have wrinkles, either."

Daisy chuckles. "Not yet anyway."

Daisy leads Izzy away, and I'm tempted to take a long step back as Chord and Charlie stare at each other, but they're glaring so hard I already feel as good as invisible. It takes my discomfort to all new levels.

"So." Charlie shifts her feet as she crosses her arms. "What are you doing here?"

"Izzy invited me."

She gives him an exasperated look. "Our six-year-old niece *invited* you?"

"That's right. To a family game night."

Charlie rolls her eyes to the sky. "Good Lord."

"And I'm not sure if you heard but I signed with the San Francisco Fury."

"I—" Charlie clears her throat and shakes her head. "No, I didn't know that."

I'm not an expert at these things, but I get the impression Charlie just told a big fat lie.

Chord pins his arms over his chest, mirroring Charlie's defensive stance. "Yeah. I'll have a place in the city soon, but until I get that all worked out, I'm going to hang out here."

Charlie's brows shoot up. "Here? For how long?"

His nostrils flare a little, and tension feathers in his sharp jaw. "Until the season starts."

"October? You're going to be here for the entire *summer*?"

"I've got a house here, Charlotte. I have every right to stay. Silver Leaf is my home too."

She snorts. "Yeah, sure. Home."

A vein throbs in Chord's neck, but instead of losing his cool, he shakes his head and expels a loud breath. That's when I notice I'm holding mine as well.

"This is Violet." He waves in my direction but doesn't look at me. Maybe I should be relieved about that, but it makes me feel like more of a nobody than I already do. "She's my personal assistant. I need you to find a cabin for her to stay in while I'm here."

Charlie's chin dips as her brows shoot up. "*You* need *me* to find her a cabin to stay in for *three months*? What do you think this is, Chord?"

"A hotel?" he snaps.

"It's a *business*," she retorts. "And *I* run it. Not you. There are no cabins."

"There were twelve cabins last time I checked."

"And none of them are available."

Chord's hands, tucked under his hard biceps, flex in and out of fists, but his tone stays even. "Not one cabin is free for the entire summer?"

"No. Not one."

Charlie lifts her chin, daring Chord to argue, and a silent moment passes when I think he might. This is so awkward. I'm the reason they're arguing, which is bad enough, but it also feels like witnessing a family moment that should be private.

I take a small step back, but gravel crunches under my sneakers and I freeze. They whip around to pin me with identical frowns, and Chord's eyes are cold enough to make my heart sputter.

Charlie shakes her head with a nasal grunt of disapproval. "If you're so rich and so important that you need a twenty-four-seven personal assistant, Chord Fergus Davenport, you can find a room for her in that big fancy house of yours."

A laugh that sounds suspiciously like a whimper bubbles up my throat. She wants me to live with Chord for *three months*? His middle name is *Fergus*?

Chord glares at his sister as blood tips his ears red, but he remains silent. It's a standoff until, to my surprise, Charlie breaks it by turning to me.

"It's nothing personal, Violet. I hope you enjoy your stay."

"Sure." My nervous humor fizzles into dread as my eyes bounce between Chord and Charlie. Is he really not going to say anything? My heart has never raced this fast. "Uh, thank you."

She gives me a tight smile before she turns on her heel and disappears behind those huge, heavy white doors. I watch them in case she returns to tell me this was all a big joke, but there's only silence.

"Key."

I whip my head around to Chord, who is standing closer than I realized, all irritation replaced with blank coolness, watching me with his hand out, palm up expectantly.

"I'm sorry?"

He twitches his fingers and raises his brows, distracting me with that sexy scar. "Give me your car key."

"Oh. Sure. Okay."

I don't stop to wonder why he wants my key. I'm too busy processing what's happening while dealing with the fact that Chord is talking directly to me. His smooth, rich baritone slides down my spine as I fumble in my satchel, pull out the car fob, and offer it to him. When he takes it, his fingers brush across mine and sparks fly all the way to my elbow. My eyes widen at the feel of it, and Chord gives me a curious frown before turning away.

My stomach does a tight little flip. My nerves are out of control.

Chord takes a few long strides toward my car, and when I don't follow, he stops and turns with an exasperated look. "Are you coming?"

"Yes. Of course."

I hurry over as he reaches the car and slips behind the wheel. I get in on the passenger side just as he's adjusting the driver's seat to accommodate his long, athletic legs, but it hardly helps at all. He slides the seat forward, then back. Forward again. Back again. The car is small and he's simply too big for it, and his chiseled jaw hardens as he battles to get comfortable. The sight of this big, powerful hockey player folded into my little old car is suddenly irrationally funny, plus... *Fergus*. I let out an unintentional giggle that sounds too much like I'm choking back a snort.

SAMANTHA LEIGH

Chord shoots me an irritated look as he starts the engine. "Everything all right?"

My heart stops and my eyes grow wide. "What? Oh, yes. I was just thinking that uh... I can drive if you want. It's my car, after all, and it's small. You don't look... comfortable."

His eyes drop to his legs at the same time mine do, but whatever I found funny about this situation is gone like it never existed. I'm distracted by the way his dark jeans strain over his thick, muscular thighs, and... Oh, God. I'm ogling him.

I look away as fast as I can, but he's too attractive and he smells so delicious that I can't find anything else to focus on. My glance darts back, and I'm met with the hard curve of his tricep and the broad lines of his shoulder. I skim my gaze down his arms, but his forearms are muscled, too, and there are his hands—huge, strong, tan, gripping the steering wheel like he knows how to handle it. The skin over my chest starts burning as I try to meet his eyes, but they're too cool, and by the time I've traced his perfect jaw, the smooth column of his neck, and the way his dark hair curls around the edges, I panic and glance at his crotch.

His freaking *crotch*.

My cheeks flame as I spin around and stare out the window, my breath coming too fast and prickles springing up on the back of my neck because I can *feel* him watching me.

Holy hell, I'm not fit for society.

It's quiet for an awkward moment, and I don't trust myself to turn around when Chord clears his throat and backs out of the car space. "I know the way, and this car isn't made for rough terrain. It's safer and faster if I drive."

"Okay." I wrap my hands around the leather strap of my satchel, then brave a sideways look at Chord. He's concentrating on the road, expression blank, and I breathe a little easier. Maybe he didn't notice the way I practically undressed him with my eyes.

Oh, crap. Now I'm thinking about him naked. The smooth hard muscles of his chest, his shoulders flexing as I gaze up at him from the pillows. Hovering above me and touching me with those incredible hands. They'd be gentle but rough. Calloused from hockey. Confident, of course. Firm. Demanding. Talented. Relentless.

My cheeks blaze again, and I jerk my head away, staring hard at the scenery sliding past the car.

I'm suddenly thankful that Chord Davenport is the way he is—cold, distant, and difficult to read. Even under the same roof, he'll want as little to do with me as possible, and it's so much better that way. *I'll* feel better that way.

It might be fun to think about a man like Chord looking at me in a way that makes my breath catch, but I'm not ready for that. I'll never be ready for that.

Chord's the sexiest man I've ever met, but I'll never understand him or be comfortable when he's around. If I want to survive the summer and keep my job, I need to focus on the work and make myself all but invisible to the person sitting next to me.

I kind of want to laugh again because who am I kidding? He's the hottest, richest, and most recognized player in the NHL. I'm a plain little marketing assistant with a confidence problem and a sketchbook full of broken dreams. Chord Davenport would never look twice at a girl like me.

EIGHT

❧

Chord

I DON'T SAY ANYTHING AND neither does Violet as we get into her car. It's tiny and old, and no good for driving on country roads. I'm already pissed off and Violet's transportation isn't my problem, but the fact that my assistant drives this sorry excuse for a vehicle makes my mood even worse. She can't rely on this all summer, which means she'll need the key to my truck.

I adjust the driver's seat over and over, trying and failing to make room for my legs. If I was the kind of guy who grumbled, I would.

I knew my reunion with Charlie was going to be difficult, but I wasn't prepared for an audience and Violet's early arrival put me at a disadvantage. The only person in the world as determined as me is Charlie, and if I tried to argue with her about whether or not we have a cabin available, she'd have burned the books—possibly the cabins, too— before admitting she lied.

And dropping my middle name like that? Didn't even bat a fucking eyelash and she knows how much I hate it. Facts are that my sister plays dirty, I was about to lose the fight, and I wasn't about to let anyone witness that. Not even my assistant.

A weird noise from the passenger seat interrupts my thoughts. Violet looks startled, like she accidentally swallowed gum or something.

I frown with irritation. "Everything all right?"

She looks at me with wide eyes and squeezes her fingers around the strap of that ugly leather satchel. "What? Oh, yes. I was just thinking that, uh... I can drive if you want. It's my car, after all, and it's small. You don't look... comfortable."

Her eyes fall from my face to my legs, and I follow her gaze. I'm sure I look ridiculous in this tin can, but I'm not letting her drive. I'm about to tell her as much, but then stop.

I usually know when a woman is checking me out, but I'm not sure about this one. Her eyes dart all over the place, bouncing across my body like drops of water on a hotplate. When she spins around like she's been caught doing something naughty, I decide she *is* checking me out, but that she doesn't mean to. It's not what I'm used to, and it's cute as fuck.

I fight the amused twitch of my lips because cute or not, she's not my type—thank God—but even if she were, I know better than to get distracted by a woman this year.

I throw the car into reverse and back out of the parking space. "I know the way, and this car isn't made for rough terrain. It's safer and faster if I drive."

"Okay," she murmurs, but I can barely hear her with her face turned toward her window.

Silence suits me and we drive the distance to my private road without conversation.

When we get past the gate and finally roll onto asphalt, I drive a little easier. I'm not taking in the scenery the way I was earlier in the morning, though. I'm too busy fuming about how my summer got screwed and now I've been saddled with a housemate I don't want, but then a gasp from Violet pulls me back to the present.

She's leaning forward and craning her neck to get a better look out the windshield, and when I follow her line of sight, I see she's staring at my house.

Okay, yeah. It's awesome.

I swing the car around with one hand, taking the corner as wide as I can to give her the best view, then pause outside the house to fish out my phone, swipe to my home automation app, and open the garage door. When I pull her car into a free space, it looks ridiculous next to the sports coupe to our right and my truck on the left, but I don't want to embarrass her so I keep my head down as I pop the trunk and take out her bags.

She's got two suitcases—one large, one smaller—but when I reach in to pull out an oversized black canvas tote wedged into the back seat, she lurches forward and snatches it up before I can get a hand on it.

"I'll take that one," Violet says. "It's personal."

I give her and the bag a curious look, wonder what's in it for a fleeting moment, then decide I don't care. I don't need to know what she's hiding.

"I can take these too." She reaches for the larger suitcase. "You don't need to—"

"It's fine." They're not so heavy I can't lift them, but she'd struggle trying to wheel them over the rough ground outside the house. I might be an asshole but I'm not about to make a woman carry her own luggage.

I walk around to the front entrance as the garage door slides closed behind us. "There's internal access from the garage, but it's locked. I'll give you a set of keys so you can come and go as you please."

"Okay. Thank you."

She walks beside me with her tote slung over one shoulder and her arms crossed over her body like she's trying to disappear inside her oversized clothes. I wonder how long it'll be until her mousiness gets on my last nerve.

As I punch the access code into the security panel near the front door, I feel unexpectedly vulnerable. I've never invited anybody into this house, and now I've got a summer guest who's going to have keys and the passcode and access to everything. It's not as if I've spent all that much time here over the years but this place has only ever been mine.

My somewhere to go "one day" when hockey isn't my life anymore.

I push open the wide door, set Violet's bags on the light hardwood floors, and look around. It's exactly as I remember it. The white walls and wide dimensions and natural light pouring in from every corner. The foyer opens directly onto a wide staircase straight ahead, then a home office on the right and an enormous living room on the left, both furnished by the interior designer I hired to get everything just right. Some of the pressure in my chest loosens, and the first thing I do is open the nearest window.

"I guess it's a little stale in here," I mutter as I hurry over to the glass doors separating the living room from the front porch and fling those open too. "I haven't been here in a while."

I glance over, prepared to see her face screwed up with distaste, but Violet doesn't seem to notice the stuffy smell of building materials or dust motes floating in the air. Her eyes roam over the vaulted ceilings, the cold stone fireplace, and giant soft white sofa, and a pretty look of wonder shines on her face.

"It's beautiful," she whispers.

I drop my hand from where it was worrying the back of my neck. "Oh. Thanks."

I return to where she stands by the door and slip off my runners. Violet does the same, setting them neatly beside mine, and without the extra half-inch of height, her baggy gray pants pool around her feet so that only the toes of her white socks poke out.

Violet's tall but the way her clothes fit makes her look tiny. It reminds me of the pictures Dylan sent me of Izzy in dress-up clothes, and I wish this woman would stop giving me reasons to smile.

"So, uh. Let me show you around."

She sets her tote down next to her bags and removes her gray blazer. I try not to stare as she hangs it on a hook by the door. She's wearing a plain white tank underneath, which shouldn't be sexy, but it's tight like a second skin, showing off her slender frame, tiny waist, and full, heavy tits.

Well, fuck me. I wasn't expecting that.

I drag my gaze away as she pulls a notebook out of her satchel, and I'm relieved to turn my back as I lead her into the house. When I glance back to make sure she's keeping up, she holds a pen at the ready, and I realize she's taking notes.

Cute. As. Fuck.

"Kitchen," I say as we pass through the open room with a white marble island, six-burner freestanding stove, and white Shaker cabinets. I dart to the far side to slide open the heavy glass doors leading onto the porch, then circle back around to the oversized pantry hiding behind wide double doors.

"I only just got here, so there isn't any food. You can visit the restaurant on the property whenever you like, but the first thing on your list should be to pick up some groceries."

She scribbles on her notepad. "Groceries. Got it."

"Until I hear from the sports nutritionist, just get essentials." I list a few things as I move around the room and open all the windows. "Eggs, bacon, oats, nut butter, fresh vegetables, salmon, chicken, protein powder, almond milk, yogurt, bananas, and Pretzel M&M's."

Violet's pen flies across the paper, then stops. The look she gives me from under her lashes is suspicious. "M&M's?"

"Pretzel." I'm not ashamed, and I give her a look that dares her to laugh.

"Right," she says, and I'm distracted by the way she nibbles her full bottom lip to stop a smile. "Pretzel M&M's."

I pull out my credit card and hand it over, then retrieve a set of spare keys from a drawer and hold them out. "Take the truck."

"The truck?" She glances at the keys in my hand like they might bite then actually takes a step back. "That's okay. My car works just fine."

"As long as you're here, you'll drive the truck." I close the distance and drop the keys onto her notepad. "It's safer."

"Right." Violet nods and makes another note, but I get the feeling she's talking to herself now. "The truck. I can do that."

I walk in silence through the house, stopping to open windows, and give Violet a brief introduction to each room. It's something like a reintroduction for me too, and in every space and on every surface, I'm reminded of how much time I put in with the architect and interior designer to finish this place exactly the way I wanted it. With each new room, I find myself anticipating Violet's small sounds of admiration, and it's weird how her opinion, which shouldn't matter, makes me feel a little better after what just happened with Charlie.

Once we've finished on the ground floor—kitchen and dining, two living rooms, home office, two guest baths—then the basement—complete gym and rec room—we make a circuit of the wrap-around porch and a brief visit to the wet-edge Olympic-length pool before Violet follows me upstairs.

"My bedroom's that way." I gesture down a long hall to the closed double doors at the end. It's more of a suite than a bedroom, but she'll never see it, so the details don't matter. "And you can stay…"

I trail off as I consider the four closed doors at the other end of the hall. Each bedroom has something going for it, but there's one that's a standout, and I go straight to it.

I open the last door on the left and step into the largest of the four bedrooms. They each have an attached bathroom so any would give Violet privacy, but this one has a king-size four poster bed, a deep desk set in front of tall glass windows looking over the vineyard to the west, and a jaw-dropping oversized walk-in closet.

I move aside to let her in and watch for her reaction as anticipation tightens the muscles across my chest.

Violet's only two steps into the room before her hands press against her cheeks. "Oh, my…"

Her steps falter before speeding up again, but instead of going to the gigantic closet like I expected, Violet's only got eyes for the desk. Her fingers dance over the smooth wood finish as she lowers herself into the deep chair, and her palms caress the glossy surface as she devours the incredible view.

A moment ticks by, then another, and she still hasn't said anything. It's almost like she's forgotten I'm here but I don't even care. I'm enjoying this. I get off on being the best and having the best and showing it off, but right now that's not it. Or not all of it. I'm too surprised by the way Violet sat herself behind that desk like it belongs to her and too amused at the way she apparently couldn't care less about me. It's a little like glimpsing the person Violet might be when she's alone, and I like that she feels safe enough to be that person here, even if only for a moment.

And where the hell did that come from?

I scowl at nothing and clear my throat. "I'll get your bags," I say with one foot already through the door.

I jog down the stairs and get to the front door, then loop the handles of Violet's tote around one wrist before picking up a suitcase in each hand. I turn to go back the way I came, but Violet's hurrying to intercept me.

I pause at the urgent worry on her face. "What the—"

Violet's eyes widen as she slides in her socks over the smooth hardwood floor, crashes against my chest with a high-pitched whoop, then saves herself from losing her footing by latching onto my shirt. I drop the bags so I can steady her, wrapping my hands around her bare upper arms and pulling her close.

And I don't let go.

It's the way she smells—floral and so subtle I needed to be this close to notice it. Her skin is soft and warm, and I'm distracted by the way her deep brown irises are dusted with flecks of gold and how her nose is sprayed with barely there freckles. I follow the tip of her tongue as it traces the shape of her mouth, full and pink and glistening.

"Chord?" she murmurs.

"Mm?"

She glances down at my fingers.

Shit.

I drop her arms and step back, flexing my fingers to erase the memory of her warmth, before spinning around and picking up her suitcase again. Violet's hand darts toward her tote and away, like she's not sure she should try her luck getting it away from me, so I pick it up and hand it over, and I don't look back as I climb the stairs. I'm not capable of handling that much connection, so I do what I do best. I reach for the ice.

I step inside Violet's bedroom door and deposit her luggage on the floor. She's right there when I turn to go and we're close—too close—but one look at the frost in my gaze and she takes a quick step back before glancing at her notebook.

"I'll go out for groceries now," she says quietly. "Then I'll start making inquiries about an apartment in the city. Coach Campbell asked me to call and set up those training sessions with the team, and after that I'll see about having your personal items shipped from Calgary."

The reminder about Coach's training plans for the summer sends my mood further south, and I'm sure it shows because Violet licks her lips and lifts her chin, but blinks too much for me to believe she's feeling confident. I feel like a prick for using my old tricks to push her away, but it's better this way, I remind myself. Easier. Safer.

"Fine," I tell her. "If you need me, I'll be in my gym."

I'm gone before she has a chance to respond.

NINE

❧

Violet

DAY 4 AT SILVER LEAF... ONLY 82 TO GO

I PULL THE TRUCK INTO the garage, cut the motor, and sink into the seat with relief. The silence seems loud after the deafening thrum of the engine, and I breathe a little easier knowing I've made yet another trip to the grocery store and returned this monster without a ding. I cast a wistful look toward my silver hatchback, then grimace at the sleek red sports car on the other side of it. I'm still trying to decide if Chord wants me to drive this thing because it's safer, like he said, or because he's embarrassed to have his assistant drive around in a dusty old clunker.

Looping my satchel across my chest, I climb down and go around to the trunk to collect the groceries. There's more of them today than I bought the morning I arrived. In the four days since then, the Fury's nutritionist provided a comprehensive list of the things Chord needs to keep on hand. With the amount of food I bought today, I shouldn't need to go out again for at least a week. I hope. The less I have to drive this thing, the happier I'll be.

I stand at the door of the open garage for a moment to appreciate the views. Even from here, there's so much to see. Never-ending sky and sunlight hitting secret pockets of water and lush green rows of perfectly planted vines heavy with fruit. And on the far side of the nearest field, where he's been every afternoon for the past four days, Chord working on the broken fences.

I pause for a moment to watch him, wondering for the hundredth time why he goes out there all alone every day when he could pay someone to do the work for him.

It's a mystery with no clear answer, just like the question I have about why none of his family has been to see him since he arrived.

I almost feel sad for him until I remember that he's a ridiculously attractive, megarich pro athlete with an overstuffed ego. If he's alone, it's probably because he wants it that way.

I give up with a shrug and return to the groceries. It's none of my business. I'm here to do a job and stay out of Chord's way, which has been easier than I anticipated. Easier and infinitely more awkward because I'm almost certain *he's* avoiding *me*.

After waking up on my first day here, I nervously tiptoed through the house and couldn't find him anywhere, but there was a to-do list on the fridge. I took it, ticked everything off and added some notes of my own, then put it back where I found it with a little prayer that this kind of back and forth was what Chord had in mind. Apparently, it was because there was a new list in the exact same spot the next day. And that's become my routine.

The sun comes up, and Chord's nowhere in the house. I work in his home office. We bump into each other once or twice. Exchange a handful of sentences a day. So far, I feel less like an employee and more like an uninvited house guest. It's uncomfortable, and Chord is living up to his reputation as cold and superior, except...

I think about what happened in the hall the day I arrived. For a split second, something was different with him. His hands on me, his body so close, his eyes infused with something other than ice. But the moment passed like it never happened, and he's been a walking snowman ever since.

It takes four trips to carry the groceries from the car to the kitchen, and I'm lugging in the last bag when Chord walks in through the heavy glass doors to the back porch. I freeze like he's a wild animal because... Why? If I don't move, he might not see me? Ironically, it almost works.

His snug dark jeans are marked with dirt, as are his heavy boots. His black t-shirt has muddy marks where he's wiped his hands down his chest and stomach. He smells like fresh earth and hard work, and I don't know why that's a turn-on, but it is.

He looks more real like this. More vulnerable somehow. Suit-and-tie Hockey Chord is hot, but down-and-dirty Farmer Chord is so breathtaking it makes me ache.

He's halfway to the kitchen when he raises his head and notices I'm standing there. I rush to set the last bag on the counter, pretending like that's what I was doing all along and not getting an eyeful of his hard chest and muscled thighs and rough, capable hands. His gaze flutters down my body, and I resist the urge to hide behind the island.

I've traded my sneakers, blazers, and wide-legged pants for sturdy boots, faded Wranglers, and a loose vintage Guns N' Roses tee. These clothes are practical for the ranch, and outside of the city, my oversized suits make me stick out like a sore thumb.

"Hey." Chord clears the crack in his voice and drops his gaze to the floor as he starts moving again like someone just hit the play button. He heads straight to the fridge for a bottle of water. "Didn't know you were in here."

His face is flushed from the sun or exertion or both, and his dark hair curls at the edges with sweat. Oh God, I'm staring, and was that a question? It looks like he's waiting for an answer.

I hide how flustered he makes me by turning my back and unpacking groceries. "I wasn't until now. I mean, I was out picking up the things your nutritionist recommended. I just got back."

There's a long silence, and when I can't pretend to unload empty bags anymore, I turn around with a tub of yogurt in one hand and a carton of eggs in the other. Chord looks... kind of annoyed? He scans the bags and I worry that I bought the wrong things or I'm not working fast enough. I hold my breath, but the waiting is too much, and just when I open my mouth to say something unnecessary about protein, he finds his voice.

"Right. Thanks."

Then he crosses the kitchen in long, quick strides, and like lightning, he's out the door.

"You're welcome?" I reply to the empty room, and the words come out breathy.

I suppose this reaction is common when a nobody has to deal with a somebody, but Chord is so overwhelming. Just one interaction and my stomach flips like I've stepped off a rollercoaster.

I remember the groceries in my hands and give myself a shake. I'm a professional, and I need to *be* professional. Chord's a person just like everybody else.

Once everything is stowed away, I disappear into the home office and log on to my computer. Maybe I should set myself up in my bedroom and let Chord have the house to himself, but I can't stand the idea of using that gorgeous space for something as mundane as work.

The moment I saw the room and the view, I couldn't wait to sit in there and sketch, and now I live for six o'clock when I can go to my room, check in with my dad, and spend the rest of the night with my designs. That bedroom is what gets me through the day.

The afternoon passes the same as the ones before. I make phone calls and answer emails about Chord's move from Calgary to San Francisco, set his physio appointments, manage his calendar, deal with his inbox, and answer media inquiries. Next, I check my work phone and emails to make sure I'm not giving Courtney any reasons to fire me. Finally, I reach out to Coach Campbell to discuss the Fury's teambuilding and training sessions, which he still wants to do right here at Silver Leaf. Right on time, I smack an updated list on the fridge, nuke a microwave dinner, and pour myself a glass of red before heading upstairs for some alone time in my new room.

"How was your day, Blossom?" Dad asks, his face filling my phone screen.

I'm curled up on the most comfortable bed known to man with the most ordinary mushroom risotto I've ever tasted. I think of Chord's comment that I can eat at his brother's restaurant whenever I want, and my stomach rumbles, but the tension between Chord and his sister makes me too uncomfortable to risk it. Bad food with my dad on the phone is preferable to good food with a side of family drama any day.

"Fine," I tell him. "Same as the last three days. How about you?"

"Oh, you know." He shrugs and scoops up a forkful of mashed potato. "Fine. Same as always."

Dad wants to know all about Chord, and I'm struggling to find new things to tell him, but I talk about the ranch and the fences while listening carefully for signs that Dad isn't coping with my absence. He's eating normally and looks well rested, and though he doesn't know it, I'm in touch with Jennifer, our upstairs neighbor, for daily updates. As far as we both can tell, everything is okay.

Twenty minutes later, I say goodbye to Dad, and though it's a lousy way to look at it and I feel bad for even thinking it, that phone call is the last item on the list of tasks I need to tick off every day. Even at home, early evening has always been my favorite part of the day because finally, I get some time for myself.

I sneak downstairs to wash up my dirty cutlery and refill my glass of wine. The fact that the kitchen light is on should have warned me, but I'm so eager to get back to my room that I'm halfway to the dishwasher before I notice Chord sitting at the island. His chin lifts and his eyes land on me before I can disappear.

"I'm sorry." I hurry to drop my bowl and cutlery in the sink, then ditch the wine glass, too. "I didn't know you were here. I'll just—"

I risk another glance his way, only this time I see he's got a first aid kit open at his elbow, there's a ball of gauze in his fist, and he's cleaning a long, nasty gash in his right forearm. I inhale sharply and cover my mouth, and the look he gives me is barely veiled amusement.

"Don't suppose you know how to sew, do you?"

I give him a puzzled frown and drop my hand. "I do, actually, but what's that got to do with..."

I trail off at the cool mirth in his expression, and when he shakes his head, I suddenly understand. I wouldn't say I have a weak stomach, but the thought of stitching together muscle and skin makes me wish I hadn't forced down that awful mushroom risotto. At my audible swallow, Chord smiles. It's small and fleeting, but it's there, and I take an involuntary step forward.

"I'm joking," he murmurs.

Without thinking, I cross the distance to get a closer look at the cut and only then realize how deep it is. "Oh, my God. What happened?"

Chord grunts. "I got careless with the fence wire."

A fleeting glance out the glass doors confirms that although it's summer and the days are long, the light started fading a while ago. "Have you been out there all afternoon?"

"Yep."

I think again about how he doesn't need to be fixing the fences at all, but even if I were brave enough to ask him about it, it's not the kind of thing a practical stranger should care about. Instead, I say the next thing that comes to mind.

"Can I take you to a hospital or call someone or—"

"No." His glance flickers toward me and away again as he concentrates on dabbing away the blood. "I've had plenty worse on the ice. I just need to clean it and cover it up, and it'll be fine."

"Are you sure?" I risk another look at it, then grimace at the gore. "It looks bad."

Chord keeps his eyes on his arm, but I can see the way the corner of his mouth tips up, and I like the way it makes me feel. Warm and a little triumphant. "I'm sure."

It doesn't feel right to walk away, no matter that it's the sensible option, so I ignore the way it makes my heart race and gesture at the first aid kit. "At least let me help you dress it. It'll be hard for you to manage with only one hand."

He says nothing for long enough that I start to feel foolish, but apparently, it wasn't a totally stupid suggestion because he finally says, "All right."

Chord sets aside the bloody gauze and pulls out the antiseptic and cotton wool, and I watch in helpless silence as he applies it. With most of the blood wiped away, I can see the gash isn't as bad as I first thought. When he retrieves a stack of mismatched bandages, he finds the appropriate size and hands them over without looking at me.

"Would you mind?"

"No." I gently clear my throat and try to talk a little louder, but I'm only now realizing I need to touch him to do this, and my heart skips a beat. I can't believe he's letting me do this. "Of course not."

I peel away the backing and pause to consider the wound, but I'm instantly distracted by the size and strength of Chord's arms. Lean, ropey muscles stretch from elbow to wrist, smooth skin bronzed by the sun and dusted with fine dark hair. His hands are strong, too, and decorated with rich blue veins. Thick, calloused fingers, broad palms and neat, smooth nails marked with evidence of a day spent mucking about in the dirt.

He has a wide, pale scar down the inside of his left wrist, most likely the result of a game injury, and even that's appealing. Everything about this man screams power, and I bet there's not a thing he can't do with these arms. These hands. These fingers.

"You might need a few," he says.

I startle and try to cover it by tearing open another packet. "Yeah. It's, uh... big."

Warmth prickles underneath my collarbone. It's *big*?

Seriously, Violet. Even you can't be this ridiculous.

My fingers tremble as I carefully apply the first of three large bandages over the cut, and even though I wince at the way they rub against the wound, Chord doesn't flinch.

It's hard to swallow as he watches me press the material to his arm, and though I'm going slow to get it right and not cause him pain, I might also be taking my time because I like the way my body buzzes when I'm next to him.

I attach each bandage with gentle motions, smoothing the material over his skin in long, slow strokes that end when my fingertips graze his skin. I feel every touch in my core. Chord's warmth crackles like static, and it only takes the lightest touch to ignite a spark.

When I'm done, I take a shaky breath while I gather up the empty packets and toss them in the trash, then stand in the middle of the kitchen, unsure what to say next. Chord sits there staring at his arm for long enough that I decide he wants me to leave so he can be alone.

I move toward the hallway and hover at the edge of the room. "Goodnight."

Chord doesn't look up. "Goodnight."

I shake my hands by my sides as I climb the stairs to my room, like I can shake away the hum in my blood, but it doesn't work. My pulse lurches every time I replay the feel of Chord's skin under my fingertips and the high lingers long after I've turned out the light.

TEN

Chord

80 DAYS TILL HOCKEY SEASON

I BREATHE PAST THE STRAIN in my lungs as I power around the empty field beside the old barn, running at max pace toward the dam. The sun has only just cleared the horizon, and although its glow is muted by damp clouds of silvery morning fog blanketing Silver Leaf, I'm slicked with enough sweat that I peeled my shirt off ten minutes ago and secured it in the waistband of my shorts.

I like running. I like the sensation of ground passing beneath my feet, the burn in my muscles and the expansion behind my ribs. I like pushing my body to see what it can do, so even if Violet wasn't living in my house, I'd be out here covering the exact same ground day in and day out. But she *is* in my house, and I'm determined to avoid her, so I've made it my mission to be busy every hour of the day. Mornings running alone or with Finn. Breakfast with Dylan, Daisy, and Izzy at the restaurant. Hours in the gym. Laps in the pool. Afternoons fixing the fucking fences.

I absently brush a hand over the bandages on my forearm and think back to the electricity of Violet's hesitant touch as she applied them. What the hell was I thinking sitting in the kitchen just waiting for her to appear? There shouldn't be electricity. There shouldn't be fascination. There shouldn't be *anything*.

This woman is shy. She's withdrawn. She wants nothing to do with me, and that's why she's the ideal assistant. But I find myself watching her sometimes when she doesn't know it. Driving in and out of the garage as she white-knuckles the steering wheel of my truck. Pacing the porch with her phone to her ear. Sneaking up and down the stairs with her dinner at night.

Why was she hiding in baggy clothes when I met her? What's she thinking behind those big glasses? What is she afraid I'll see in her dark-lashed chestnut eyes that she keeps them locked on the floor at her feet?

I pick up speed to stop myself from thinking so much. The faster my mind moves, the slower my muscles fire, which is why I won't let myself be distracted this summer. I'm an elite athlete, for God's sake. I've built a career on strength and self-discipline. I'm a pin-up boy for focus and control. I'm not about to lose it over a banging body, a mysterious set of eyes, and the occasional temptation of a pretty pink blush.

I'm on the last stretch to the house when something moves ahead. A shadow in the fog, the height and shape of a person at a fork in the path like they're not sure where to go next.

I pull up short, breathing heavily and squinting into the distance, ignoring how my racing heart skips at the possibility that it's Violet. Whoever it is, they're too slight to be Finn and too tall to be Daisy. It might be a guest who wandered off the walking trails that crisscross the ranch, but it's unlikely that lost hikers would pass this close to my house before finding their way back to the main property.

It's got to be her.

I creep closer to confirm her identity, moving through an ethereal haze that pulls back from the heat of her body like it wants to hug her curves but can't get close enough.

I empathize with a quiet groan.

She's wearing skintight white leggings that cling to her high, rounded ass, black trainers, and a baggy khaki-colored hoodie. Her phone is in her hand, pods in her ears, and her warm brown waves are piled on the top of her head, wisps pulling free around her face and catching on her glasses.

The casual athletic look has never really done it for me—but then again, I've never seen it on Violet.

I drag a regretful hand down my face and take a few steps back, intending to let her walk back to the house alone because a fantastic ass in yoga pants is definitely a distraction I don't need, but seconds pass without her moving. I could—*should*—turn around and take the long way back to the house, but I can't force my stupid legs to move, so I stand there like a moron, half-hidden in the fog.

Violet looks at her phone, takes a few steps to the right like she's finally decided that way lies her destination, then stops and moves to the left. Her head lifts, whipping around like she's trying to get her bearings, and she steps to the right again. When she checks her phone for a third time, then stomps her foot in frustration and takes off on the left trail with a long, determined stride, I cover up a chuckle and follow. She's fucking lost and it's adorable.

"If you're interested in a job picking grapes," I call, "you'll have to come back in September."

Violet jumps clear in the air, spinning with wide eyes that flash ever so briefly with fear, then murder, before she slumps and smacks her hand onto her heaving chest. "You scared me!"

I mash my lips together because her reaction shouldn't amuse me, but it's cute, and the glimpse of something in her that isn't timidity or nerves makes me want more.

"I didn't mean to, but if you keep going that way, you're going to end up in the pinot noir vines."

Violet's brow furrows as she glances at her phone and then back down the trail. "Oh."

I gesture in the opposite direction. "The house is about ten minutes' walk this way—assuming that's where you wanted to go?"

She glances at my hand, then her rounded eyes bounce from the dirt to my bare chest and away again before returning to my body and lingering a little longer. The corner of my mouth lifts as a flush rises in her face, and I resist a real grin when she spins toward the correct path.

"Um. Yes. Thank you."

"No problem."

I suppose I could put on my shirt, but I'm not going to. And I don't ask if she wants company either because I'm not going to risk her saying no.

When Violet realizes I intend to escort her the rest of the way, she blinks a few times before plucking the pods from her ears and stuffing them in the pocket of her hoodie.

We walk for a short time in silence while I study Violet from the corner of my eye. Her plump pink lips part occasionally, diverting me to interesting, *distracting* thoughts that I refuse to entertain. I get the impression she's searching for the courage to start a conversation, and on her third failed attempt, I save her the trouble of trying again.

"So," I say, "have you spent much time in Sonoma?"

Her throat moves before she answers. "None."

"None?" I ask with surprise. "How long have you lived in San Francisco?"

She goes from looking straight ahead to watching the dusty ground disappear under her feet. "Ten years."

"Ten years," I echo. "And not a single visit?"

She shrugs and folds her arms over her chest. "No. This is my first time."

"You've never wanted to explore the area?"

"I guess... I mean... I suppose I wanted to visit but never really had the time."

I take note of the curve to her shoulders, the stoop in

her back, and mentally kick my own ass for coming off as a judgmental prick.

"Does that mean you like wine?" I ask.

Her brows pull down, and she casts me a wary sidelong look. "Sure. I like wine."

"How about farmers' markets?"

"Yeah." Violet's mouth turns down a little as she thinks about it. "That sounds fun."

"Botanical gardens?"

She drops her arms as a small smile—a hint of potential ease and confidence—flits across her mouth. "Of course. Who doesn't like flowers?"

Why the fuck does it feel so good to see her open up a little?

"And art?" I ask. "What do you think of galleries?"

Her eyes light up, and she forgets herself long enough to turn toward me. The unguarded joy on her face makes her so damn pretty I forget to watch where I'm going and stumble over nothing.

"Shit," I mutter as I right myself. Violet stretches out a hand to help me, but I'm an embarrassed idiot who steadies himself too quickly, and she pulls back before making contact.

Violet clears her throat as we continue walking, the house coming into view up ahead. "I *love* art," she says. "Is there a local gallery nearby?"

"Yeah. Great restaurants and wineries and coffee too.

There are some tourist brochures up at the reception house. Feel free to take off an afternoon while you're here and do some exploring."

I slow as we approach the house, not ready for our conversation to be done, and Violet keeps pace at my side.

"That's nice of you," she says. "Thanks."

"No problem."

We climb the front porch steps together and reach the front door at the same time. I punch in the code and swing it open. "After you?"

Violet drops her eyes with a small smile and walks past me. I breathe in the sweet, floral air she leaves in her wake and, without thinking, brush the base of her back to usher her inside. My hand presses against the fabric of her hoodie, her hip just out of reach of my fingertips and the top of her ass only a short fall away from my palm.

She freezes at my touch, and so do I, but whatever this is lasts only a moment before Violet inhales deeply, drops her chin, and hurries into the house.

I stare at her ass as she moves down the hall, losing a chunk of time in exchange for the memory of white spandex hugging her curves when she walks. But when she turns a corner and is out of my sight, I straighten from my stupor.

Fuck me.

I slam the front door and glare at nothing as I storm through the house, adrenaline buzzing like I haven't just run eight miles. I grab a towel on my way to my gym, then go to the nearest station and launch into a set of pull-ups, impatient for the burn to start.

Sweat rolls down my temples, my neck, and my spine. My grip falters, but the fatigue only makes me work harder. I'm focused. I'm disciplined. I'm in control. I know what I want and a woman isn't it. It's hockey. It's the Cup. It's to be the fucking best.. So, no more distractions. No more temptation. And no more thinking about Violet James.

ELEVEN

Violet

DAY 8 AT SILVER LEAF... ONLY 78 TO GO

I'VE SPENT A WEEK AS Chord's personal assistant, and here's what I've learned: I need to try harder to stay out of his way.

It shouldn't be this hard. It's a big house. It's an enormous property. His busy schedule and the daily instructions stuck to his fridge can only be strategies he's using to limit direct contact with me. And that's smart, I reassure myself. Logical and practical and I can't take it personally. If anything, I should be relieved.

Chord and I don't need to be friendly for me to do my job, and after all, professional distance was always my plan. Keep my head down. Do my job. Survive the summer without making a fool of myself or getting fired.

There's no good reason I should be surprising Chord when he's nursing bloody wounds in darkened kitchens or disturbing him while he's on his half-naked morning runs.

Oh. My. *God*.

I twist in my sheets, away from the soft morning sun streaming into my room, and squeal into my pillow. I will never, ever get over the sight of a shirtless, breathless Chord Davenport, his gray workout shorts slung low enough to show the carved dips of his hips, t-shirt dangling from his waistband, every hard muscle on his body glistening with sweat and tight with strain. Dark hair, damp and matted. Blue eyes, nowhere near cool enough to counteract the extreme heat of his extraordinary physique.

I'll never forget how my pulse raced when he set his hand on my back.

But I'll also always remember how inadequate I felt when he learned I've lived in San Francisco for ten years without ever driving out to Sonoma. How agonizing it was to force small talk with a man who would rather converse via sticky notes.

Resolved to try harder to keep out of sight, I find a pencil and scrap of paper and scribble down what I know about Chord's schedule outside of the appointments I set for him. He leaves the house early to *run practically naked* around the ranch. Passes an hour in the gym before lunch. Swims until two p.m. He spends the late afternoon performing tasks around the property and eats dinner alone long after sunset.

Satisfied I can work around him for the next seventy-eight days and counting, and with a little more confidence than I had last night, I shower and dress, throw my hair in a knot and my glasses on my nose, and head down to the kitchen.

As I expect, there's a new list of tasks on the fridge, Chord's messy scrawl covering the square of yellow paper, but that's not the only thing stuck to the stainless steel this morning. For the first time, there's something else, and even with my glasses on, I can't work out what it is until I've slipped the stack of brochures out from under the chunky black magnet and spread them out over the kitchen counter.

Tourist information for Sonoma County. Wineries and restaurants. Historic gardens and hiking trails. Bicycle rentals and horseback riding. Guided tours and swimming spots. Markets and galleries.

I look up and around, half-expecting Chord to be watching nearby, but I'm alone, so I allow myself a small, honest smile of excitement and gratitude, which is chased by a falling rush of incredulity. I'd dismissed Chord's suggestion to take an afternoon for myself off as empty words to fill a silence, but maybe he meant it. He went out of his way to collect these for me, and that's... Well, it's sweet, and not at all the kind of gesture I expect from my grumpy, self-absorbed boss.

I glance around again, wishing it were one of those times we might run into each other so I could thank him, but the house is quiet, and I'm alone. Before I talk myself out of it, I tear a square of paper from the stack on the counter, dash off a quick "Thank you for the brochures—Violet" and attach it to the fridge, then scurry from the room.

After that, I'm so nervous I eat my breakfast in the office. Lunch, too. A dull, fluttering ache in my chest reminds me how silly it is to want to *accidentally* bump into him, but when I visit the kitchen later in the afternoon, and my thank-you note is no longer on the fridge, the ache drops into my stomach. All this effort to avoid him and I'm disappointed that it worked.

Frustrated with my daydreams and ready to take a breather from sorting through Chord's unhinged fan mail, I run up to my bedroom and scoop up armfuls of dirty laundry.

The eight days of worn clothing is more than the compact bathroom hamper can hold, but I shove in as much as I can and balance the overflow against my chest. I've been waiting for a safe time to do it and now, while Chord's working on the fences and I'm guaranteed a few hours without interruption, is as good a time as any.

The laundry room in Chord's house is plucked straight from an interior design magazine. It's located in the basement adjacent to a full bathroom with an infrared sauna attached to the spectacular gym, and it's at least as big as my kitchen back home. Completely outfitted and finished with the same white Shaker cabinets and dark-veined marble surfaces as the kitchen upstairs, it also has sleek, top-of-the-line, front-loader washer and dryer machines with every bell and whistle—a fact I filed away when Chord gave me the tour.

No more washing my lingerie in the bathroom sink for me.

I drop the clothes hamper with a thud and dump the extra armfuls of laundry on the smooth, clear counter. I sort it into three loads—whites, darks, and delicates—and put the largest in to wash first. I locate laundry detergent and fabric softener in an overhead cupboard, choose a thirty-minute cycle, and hit *start*.

Once I return the empty hamper to my bathroom, I spend the half hour in the home office setting Chord's physiotherapy appointments for the next two weeks. Back in the laundry room, I transfer my wet clothes to the dryer and add the next load to the machine. With another thirty minutes to kill, I sort through Chord's official Fury correspondence, including event invitations and media requests, and hurry back just as the machine beeps to signal the end of the wash cycle.

The last load to go through is my underwear. Half of it is made up of the sensible white sets I prefer during the day. The other half is a rainbow of the soft, silky pieces I've been wearing at night.

I've got dozens of sets like these: bright, pretty, some of them sexy pieces I've never worn because I was saving them for the day I didn't live with my dad. Joke's on me, I suppose. When I started collecting lingerie all those years ago, I never imagined I'd be twenty-eight and still waiting to take them for a spin. But they were the first thing I put in my suitcase when I packed for Silver Leaf.

I navigate my way to the "delicates" program, add the underwear to the drum, and close the door. It's a longer cycle than a standard wash, so after I've folded the first load and stuffed the wet items into the dryer, I take what's clean back to my room and disappear into the home office once again.

When I return to the basement, the washer is still spinning, but there are dry clothes to fold so I busy myself with those. There's something soothing about the act of laundry, I decide, when it's not done in a rush in a communal utility room.

The sound of heavy footsteps outside the door straightens my spine, and with butterflies in my stomach, I twist toward the doorway just as Chord walks in, the knees of his jeans covered in mud, his boots caked with it too, his ridged abs flashing and flexing as he drags his filthy white shirt over his head. Dirt streaks his forearms and neck, and once his t-shirt is over his head, he freezes at the sight of me.

"I didn't know you were in here."

"I'm not." I force myself to stare at the floor instead of the fine trail of dark hair leading from his belly button into the waist of his jeans. "I mean, I'm nearly done."

The washing machine beeps to signal the end of the cycle, and Chord tosses his shirt over one shoulder as he crosses the room and opens a cupboard with a basket inside that looks like the receptacle for a laundry chute. It's full of clothes, and Chord heaves it out before closing the cupboard door.

Oh, no. No, no, no. This cannot be happening.

"Um." I shoot a panicked glance at the multicolored jumble of lingerie visible through the transparent door of the washer. "Do you have laundry? I could do it for you if you like?"

Chord spares me a sideways glance as he reaches into the overhead cupboard and takes out the detergent. "Housekeeping isn't in your job description."

"I don't mind. I like doing laundry. It's relaxing. Satisfying. You know. Uh, fun."

His brow furrows with confusion—or is it concern? I'm not surprised. I sound like a lunatic. A dirty-clothes-huffing lunatic.

"I can do my own laundry," he says. After a pause, he adds, "But thank you."

"You're welcome."

I wring my hands and glance at the washer again, then back at Chord waiting on the other side of the room with his large arms crossed over his glorious chest and an expectant expression on his stony face.

Right. The machine is done. I need to leave. I've got a stack of dry, clean clothes to carry upstairs, plus an armful of sexy, lacy lingerie that nobody's ever seen but me. Piece of cake.

Just do it. Drag those damp panties out of the washer and run!

With a purposeful and probably peculiar-looking nod, I lean over to put my body between Chord and the contents of the machine, yank open the door, and haul out my underwear. My heart races and my hands grow clammy as I drop a pair of white cotton panties and a pale pink sports bra twice before I've balanced my cargo securely in the crook of one elbow. When I'm certain I can stand without losing anything, I straighten and turn around.

Chord's focus darts up to my eyes, and I blink. Was he... was he looking at my ass? By his steely look of disinterest,

I desperately hope not because if he *was* checking me out, he's not particularly pleased with what he sees.

"I'll just take the rest of this stuff and get out of your way," I tell him, crossing to his side of the room where my clean clothes are stacked on the marble counter.

I have to deposit my underwear next to them before I can maneuver my t-shirts and jeans into a tower between my forearm and my chin, and it wobbles when I scoop my lingerie against me with the other arm.

A lacy red bra escapes, and I drop everything to retrieve it with a mortified swipe, then try again to perfect my balancing act.

It's not working, and I'm starting to sweat when behind me, Chord clears his throat and silently offers me an empty laundry basket.

I accept it with a murmured "Thank you," dipping my chin to hide a rush of embarrassment that I didn't think of it first.

I load the stack of clothes first, stuff my underwear into the gaps around it, and heft the basket with two hands.

I'm nearly free and clear in record time when a pointed cough from Chord pulls me up short. I know before I turn around that this isn't good.

Lying there on the floor, equal distance between us is a coral-colored bra and a pair of black silk bikini-cut briefs.

My cheeks flame as we both stare at them, equally stunned into immobility.

I wouldn't mind if a nice, big hole opened in the ground right about now.

Chord takes a step like he's going to pick them up, but I dash forward before he gets the chance. Of course, when I lean over to collect them, half a dozen other pieces tumble out of my basket onto the floor at his feet.

He takes a step back as I keep my head bowed, gathering everything with superhero speed and super-loser clumsiness, blinking back tears and shoving bras and panties into my basket as more fall out.

Finally, I've collected it all, and abandoning any hope of regaining my dignity, I bolt from the room and Chord's cool blue stare.

I maintain speed until I'm safe in my room, door closed against my back, chest heaving with deep, dazed breaths. That was possibly the most humiliating, cringeworthy thing to happen to me ever before and—dear God, please—ever again. I'm not usually that clumsy, even on my worst days.

How on Earth am I supposed to face him after *that*?

You don't, I remind myself. *He wants as little to do with you as you want with him. Just stick to the plan and stay out of his way.*

My earlier daydreams of accidental meetings with my boss now feel more like schoolgirl infatuation. Chord Davenport is way out of my league, but after today it'll be all that much easier to stay out of his way.

If he wasn't already trying his hardest to avoid me before, he's certainly going to up his game now.

TWELVE

Chord

77 DAYS TILL HOCKEY SEASON

IT'S AFTER MIGNIGHT BUT I can't sleep, so I sit at the far end of the long, twelve-seater outdoor dining table on my back porch, staring out over the ranch while it's lit by the pool lights below and the half-moon overhead. I welcome the touch of the cooler night air, breathe in the comforting scent of earth and vines, sip a mug of hot cocoa, and stare up at the midnight sky. And I think about my mom.

A lot about my daily life reminds me of my dad—games, training, travel. He was there for all of it when I was a kid, stayed involved in my career until I was well into my twenties, and in some ways, hockey keeps my memories of him bright and close. Rarely a day goes by when I don't think of him, even if it's fleeting.

I can't say the same about my mom, which kills me to admit. It's just that my life now rarely reflects the moments

I spent with her then on the ranch. Reminders of her—her sandy hair and sapphire eyes, her warm sugar-cookie skin, her full-hearted laugh and her long, hard hugs—are rare and unexpected, and when they come, they hit harder than recollections of my dad.

Here at Silver Leaf, however, I'm surrounded by reminders of both my parents. The way they worshiped each other. The satisfaction they found running this place, building it from nothing, sharing their victories and overcoming their setbacks. How they molded their dreams around their five children. The lifetime of joy they experienced just by loving one another honestly and intensely and selflessly. They were lucky. *We* were lucky.

I set my cup on the table and pull Violet's thank-you note from the pocket of my shorts, and my thumb involuntarily brushes the perfectly formed letters written in black ink. It's just a piece of paper. I should throw it in the trash. Instead, I trace the sweep of her name one more time before tucking it away and returning my attention to the patterns in the sky.

My mom loved handwritten notes in lunch boxes or jacket pockets, under pillows and on bathroom mirrors. She loved late-night conversations and hot cocoa with marshmallows, and she loved the stars.

Light bursts inside the house, spilling out of the open kitchen window at the other end of the porch and interrupting my thoughts. I scramble to feel even a shred of irritation that Violet is once again in my way, but the only feelings within reach are curiosity and expectation as I listen to her move about inside.

The fridge opens and closes. A saucepan is retrieved from a cupboard and, a moment later, lands on the stovetop. A gas burner jumps to life with a *click-click-click* before she rustles in the pantry. A spoon hits the inside of a mug.

I debate the wisdom of going in to... What? Say hello? Tell her I couldn't sleep because I was thinking about her? Ask her if she'll lift her chin for me, just once, because I'd like to get a better look at her pretty pink blush?

But the moment comes and goes before I've made a decision. The light goes out again and I blink to adjust my vision, bristling at the unwelcome disappointment.

Then the tall glass door to the porch slides open, and Violet slips out onto the decking.

Jesus Christ. She should have stayed inside.

Out of my reach at less than a dozen paces away, with bare feet, long legs, and skin glowing silver in the mixed light from the pool and the moon and the stars, Violet's dark hair is in a loose braid over one shoulder, her glasses are on her nose, and she's wrapped in a long-sleeved, short-hemmed silk robe leeched of color in the darkness.

She paces across the porch to the balustrade and sets her elbows on the rail, leaning over to blow the steam from her mug. The action makes the hem of her robe ride higher on the backs of her pale thighs and hints at the soft curve of her ass underneath.

My dick lifts a little, like he's trying to get a look, and I resist the urge to shift in my seat.

I shout silently at myself. *Speak, asshole*, but I don't. Not yet. I just want to watch her a moment longer. Behold this version of Violet, without her self-conscious defenses.

She takes a swallow from her cup, hums with appreciation, then turns her face toward the sky. Her eyes drift closed like she's praying or wishing, and my mouth is suddenly dry.

She's so exquisite with starlight kissing her cheeks, mouth curved in a secret smile, calves tight while she's pushed up on her toes, long fingers wrapped around her cup. Her lips move like she's talking to herself, and I have a desperate longing to know what she's saying. What she's thinking. What she's feeling.

I wait for her to open her eyes, finish her drink, and go back inside, but when she stays in the same place long enough to make me realize I shouldn't be here anymore, I think about slipping away. I consider it. I decide it's the right thing to do. I dismiss the idea. Then I clear my throat.

Violet jumps, turning and spilling her drink over the side of the cup, and I choke back a groan when she lifts her wrist to her mouth and licks away a rivulet of liquid with her delicate pink tongue.

"I'm sorry," she says, turning her hand and collecting up another droplet of moisture with her lips. She squints to better make me out in the shadows, then glances down at her bare legs. "I didn't know you were here. I'll just—"

"I couldn't sleep."

Violet drops her hand and furrows her brow as she tilts her head to one side. "Me neither." She glances into her cup, then toward the kitchen before she raises her drink between us. "I made warm milk. Did you want some?"

I lift my mug in response. "I beat you to it. Hot cocoa with marshmallows."

"Cinnamon and maple syrup here."

"I'll have to try that sometime." I nod at the chair closest to her, the farthest from me at the other end of the table. "Have a seat."

She chews on her bottom lip before pulling out the chair and lowering herself into it. I take a swallow from my cup and she does the same, dark eyes watching me warily over the rim of her cup. I guess I deserve it, but it doesn't feel great, so I sit there in moody silence, growing more frustrated with my own assholery.

"I've seen pictures of skies like this one and wondered if they were real," she murmurs quietly. "You don't see stars like this in the city."

"Nothing like a Sonoma sky," I agree.

"Do you know much about them?"

"The stars?" When Violet nods her head, I reply, "Yeah. I know about the stars."

"Could you..." She pauses and adjusts her glasses. "Could you tell me about them?"

My skin tingles a little at her timid request, but before

I think better of it, I swipe at my phone lying on the table to switch off the pool lights. We plunge into near-darkness, and I move off the porch to stand on the lawn below. Violet shadows me, stopping a long pace away and craning her neck at the magic arching over us into infinity.

I point to my favorite constellation. "Cygnus," I tell her. "Or the Swan. You see those five stars there?" I sweep my finger across the sky to draw her attention to a row of three bright spots followed by one above and another further below. Violet nods with a serious frown of concentration. "That's the Northern Cross. It marks the Swan's chest."

Violet tugs at her lip, upward eyes shining until understanding dawns with a lift of her brows and she finally connects the dots. "I see it!"

I fight a smile and move a step closer to her, pointing to a nearby section of sky. "See those four extra-bright stars over there?"

She hums, alight with curiosity and focusing hard on where I direct her. Her lashes are dark and long, the tip of her nose a fine point, her lips plump and parted, and I swallow with difficulty.

"That's the Keystone," I explain. "Hercules' torso. See those stars around it? Those are his arms and legs, and that constellation beside it is Draco—the dragon Hercules defeated."

Violet catches her lip between her teeth, and I stare as it pops free. "I *think* I see it."

I move behind her, leaning down to measure her line of sight, ignoring the way her floral fragrance fills my nostrils, and point at the stars over her shoulder. "There. Draco."

"Oh." Violet grows very still before she inhales deeply and releases a shallow breath. Her arm rises slowly as she points to the brightest star in the sky. "Do you know anything about that one?"

"That's Arcturus," I tell her, straightening a little but not moving away. "Part of the Herdsman."

"Arcturus," she repeats. "And the Herdsman? I thought it might be something more romantic than that."

"Oh, yeah? Why's that?"

Violet hugs her chest and shrugs. "I don't know. I suppose I've always believed the brightest star in the sky was made for wishing." She shakes her head and takes a few short, quick steps toward the house and away from me. "It's silly. I don't know why I even said that."

"It's not silly at all."

I resist the urge to close the distance between us and glance back at the star in question. "There's a constellation right there called the Great Bear, and Arcturus is its guide. Lighting the way. Keeping it safe. If you were going to trust your dreams to any star, it makes sense to wish on that one."

I realize I've been staring up at the sky for a while by the time the silence between us grows loud, and I turn back to Violet. There's a look of soft contemplation on her face, but her subject is me and not the stars.

"How do you know so much?" she asks.

I screw up my nose as it tickles with nostalgia. "My mom. She loved camping and the seven of us spent our summers sleeping outdoors with nothing between us and the sky. We looked for constellations together every night."

"Oh."

I can't bring myself to look away from my memories or meet Violet's gaze, so we say nothing for a long while, just admire the sky side by side.

"I think I'm tired now," Violet whispers. "Thank you for the company."

"You're welcome."

I'm ready to be alone but if Violet had wanted to stay, I'd be okay with that too.

The way she makes me feel is confusing and unexpected, so I listen as she climbs the steps and disappears inside the house, breathing easier only once I know she's gone.

THIRTEEN

Chord

I'VE GOT A GOOD SWEAT going and my heart rate's up as I leap onto the front porch of the old bungalow. "I win."

Finn's feet land a half-second behind mine, and he shoves me to the side. "Fuck off. You had a head start."

I crack the tiniest smile and bend down to give Finn's old golden Labrador a rub behind the ears. Her name's Dakota, she's got to be at least ten years old, and Finn picked her up at a rescue shelter on his three-month trip across the country.

I knew the minute I saw her why he brought her home. The resemblance between this dog and the Labrador we had as kids is uncanny, and Finn had always been old Bear's favorite.

Dakota turns her head to lick my fingers, and I give her one last scratch before setting a hand on the balustrade and catching my foot in one hand. The stretch through my quad feels good, but beating my younger brother on these morning runs feels even better.

"You're a sore loser."

He snorts and throws an incredulous look my way. I grin for real this time. We both know I'm the one who hates to lose, which is why I never let it happen.

"Do you think Dylan would want to join us tomorrow?" I ask. "The only thing better than kicking your ass every morning would be showing you both how it's done."

"Nah." Finn sets his toes against the low line of timber and stretches out his calf. "Running isn't really his thing."

"And what is?"

Finn shrugs. "Izzy and the restaurant."

I shift into a low lunge, grunting quietly at the pull in my hip flexors, and Finn bites back a shit-eating grin.

"Say it, asshole. I dare you."

"I don't need to, old man. Your body is saying it for me."

I shake my head and switch legs. I know how old I am. I know I can't play hockey forever. But Finn's teasing hits a nerve that wasn't there a year ago.

When I thought I'd see out my career with Calgary, I looked toward retirement with a kind of proud resignation. I was okay with walking away because I was at the top of my game. At the top of *the* game. I was prepared to start something new—maybe here at Silver Leaf, possibly with a woman I loved, in a house that I built for a family. But everything is different now. Now I've got too much to prove.

"How are things going with Charles?" Finn asks.

Charles is Finn's nickname for Charlie.

Born a year apart to the day, they were inseparable growing up. Fair-haired, brown-eyed, barrel-chested, and big-hearted Finn, and the dark-haired, blue-eyed, dirt-on-her knees big sister who always had his back. One never went anywhere without the other right up until the day he enlisted. Dylan and Daisy, born two and four years after Finn respectively, had their own bond as well. Of the five of us, I've always been the odd one out. The oldest, sure, but that was never the problem. Hockey was the problem. It always came first.

"Things are…" I reach an arm over my head and push on the elbow to stretch out my tricep. "Fine."

Finn lifts a disbelieving eyebrow. "Talk to her, bro. Sort it out. We're all too old for this shit."

I change arms and lean into the burn shooting through the muscle. "I would if I knew where to start."

He shakes his head and walks through the unlocked screen door. I follow, holding the door open for Dakota to amble through after us, then move fast to catch the bottle of water that smacks me square in the chest.

"She's our sister," he says. "Start anywhere you like, keep going until she bites, and don't let her push you around."

"I wish it were that easy." I huff out a dry chuckle, but I think about it as I take a long swallow of water. "Has she… said anything about me?"

The look he gives me is wry. "She doesn't have to.

You know the problem. She knows the problem. We all know the problem, and we want you two to fix it."

He punches my arm as he passes me on his way to the sofa, then launches himself over the back of it, points the remote at the television, and starts flicking through his streaming service. Dakota shadows him, and when she heaves herself up next to him, he shifts to make room for her alongside his thigh.

Finn's right. I know the problem. I just don't know how to solve it.

Charlie's stuck on the idea that I haven't done enough to earn my place here. I spent my childhood focused on becoming the next NHL prodigy while she was being groomed to take over the family business. It's a job that would have gone to me had it not been for hockey, and although I know she loves Silver Leaf and probably wouldn't have it any other way, it doesn't change the fact that I got to chase my dreams while she was here doing the grunt work and carrying the burden of Mom and Dad's legacy.

It won't be easy, but I'm going to prove that Silver Leaf means as much to me as it does to her. And if she won't accept a dime of my money, I'll just put my blood, sweat, and tears into this place the same way she has. Why else would I be out there every damn day fixing fences with my bare hands?

"Thanks for the run, bro." I clap Finn on the shoulder. "Same time tomorrow?"

He doesn't look up. "You bet."

I walk out while he's still channel surfing.

I start the run back to my house, easing a little on the pace as I round the last bend, then stopping altogether as I spot movement on the back porch.

It's her. A short, fast flicker of frustration has me narrowing my eyes at her distant silhouette.

I'm not irritated with her. I'm pissed at myself. Hiring Violet as my assistant was supposed to be the easy option. A wallflower who'd never hit on me. Someone I wouldn't look at twice. But ever since she got here, I can't *stop* looking, and I'm losing the will to keep my distance.

What was that I said about my focus, discipline, strength, self-control? I snort quietly to myself. My most prized values might as well line the floor at this woman's feet because instead of doing the smart thing and going around the front, I run straight to her.

I take the porch steps two at a time and stand back while she paces at the other end of the white wooden deck, talking on the phone with her head bent and voice quiet.

Whatever it is looks serious, and maybe now would be a good time to disappear, but I edge closer, seduced by the way her tee lifts on the side with her raised arm, exposing the narrowest strip of smooth pale skin.

Violet's absorbed enough in her conversation that she doesn't feel my eyes on her, doesn't notice me even when I lean into another round of stretches. And I'm so fixated on her that I don't notice the other phone on the long outdoor table until it rings with an incoming call and skitters across the top. Violet shoots it a harried look over her shoulder, but when she sees me, her brows shoot up, and she starts blinking.

"Jen?" she says into the phone. "Thanks for the chat, but I have to go. I'll text you tonight after I talk to him."

Him? Who's *him*? A boyfriend? Violet glances at me once and away again, her throat bobbing in a nervous swallow, and I smooth the irritation from my face.

The phone on the table, which had just fallen silent, screams again. I'm frustrated by how badly I want to talk to her right now, and I don't care that it's none of my business, so I pick it up to see who's bugging Violet—and, by extension, bugging me. It's not a boyfriend, but the name flashing irritates me all the same. *Courtney Reynolds.*

"I'm sorry." Violet accepts the phone from my outstretched hand while tucking the other into the back of her shorts. "I didn't mean to interrupt your morning…"

Her face falls as she sees the name on the screen, and when the call cuts off, I move closer to make out the notification that says she's got two missed calls and two unread texts. All from Courtney.

"Shoot," Violet whispers. "She's going to be so mad."

"Courtney?"

I cross my arms over my chest and keep my tone cool. I'm only too capable and too happy to take care of any issues she has with that woman.

"Yes." Violet licks her lips, tongue sweeping out in a way that makes my dick pay attention, but she waves away her worry like it's nothing. "I'll call her back now. I'm sure it'll be fine."

"And the other thing?"

I'm a demanding bastard, but I've always known that about myself.

"What other thing?"

I nod at her hip to indicate the phone in her back pocket. "The call you were on when I got here. Something serious?"

"Oh." Her hand touches the phone in her jeans, giving me a valid excuse to rake my eyes up her long legs to the curve of her hip. "That was a personal call."

"With your boyfriend?"

A sweet, self-deprecating chuckle dances across her lips, and the sound makes me stand a little straighter.

"Ah, no. I don't have one of those."

"Girlfriend?"

Violet gives me an amused frown, and I cock an eyebrow in return. So fucking cute.

"No. I don't have one of those either."

"So, the serious conversation with the not-your-boyfriend and not-your-girlfriend was with your..."

"Neighbor." Her expression is bemused, but in a good way, if the way she's trying not to smile is anything to go by.

"About your..."

She's still trying to work me out, but the crease that pops up between her brows doesn't sit well with me. "My dad. He's—"

The phone in her hand rings again, and she looks at it with alarm. "I'm sorry. I really have to take this."

"Go ahead."

I mean for her to answer it here where I can keep an eye on her, but Violet interprets my permission as a dismissal and hurries into the house.

My stomach clenches as she walks away, and I'm so damn disappointed to watch her go. It's a small thing in a series of small moments that shouldn't feel so significant, but the disappointment is what tips me over the edge.

I love the sound of her laugh. I could waste an entire day waiting for her smile. I crave our accidental moments together, and I like how I feel when she's near—warmer, somehow. Less guarded. More myself.

The struggle to stay away has become more of a distraction than pursuing her, so why am I trying to fight it? I want this woman, and if chasing her makes me weak? If it flaunts the rules I imposed on myself this year? Then fuck it. I'll deal with the fallout later.

Rules were made to be broken, and I'll break them all to make this girl mine.

FOURTEEN

Violet

DAY 10 AT SILVER LEAF... ONLY 76 TO GO

I END MY NIGHTLY CALL with Dad and immediately tap out a text to Jennifer.

He seemed a little down. He says he ate dinner but I'm not sure I believe him. Do you know if he's been walking in the mornings?

I curl up against the pillows on my bed, hug my legs, and wait anxiously for the ping of a return message.

I saw him go out this morning, so it may be nothing. We all have bad days, after all. I'll invite him around for a meal tomorrow and let you know how it goes.

Jennifer's text loosens the worry in my chest. I've enjoyed being at Silver Leaf more than I thought I would, and I feel guilty that I don't think enough about my dad. There's too much to distract me here. The fresh air and wide, open spaces. The fact that I don't have to see Courtney every day. The ridiculously

118

hot hockey player who has no idea I watch his swim in the mornings but who *does* know how to read a sky full of stars.

It's just so nice to live my own life for the first time ever, but when Jen called me earlier to talk about how Dad has been coping on his own, I started to panic. My first priority has always been my father—he's more than my only family, he's my best friend—and I hate myself for letting it slide even a little.

I send a text. *I appreciate that. Thanks, Jen. I don't know how I'd do this without you.*

She responds with a heart emoji, and I set my phone on the nightstand before inhaling deeply through my nose then sighing out my mouth.

Another day is over, and I can finally indulge in what I've been looking forward to since I woke up. One-on-one time with my sketchbook.

I set my glass of wine on the desk and get everything ready—my headphones, my pencils, and the felt-covered board I picked up from the hardware store on the first day. I pull it out from where I've hidden it under the bed and set it on the floor propped against the wall. It's stuck with a few of my favorite pictures, samples, and sketches. A little piece of home.

Before I settle myself at the desk, I step into the closet and paw through a drawer for something to wear to bed. It's the last step in what has become my nightly ritual, and something I never did at home: a hot shower to wash away a day of ranch dust and country dirt, followed by a clean pair of pretty panties and a matching camisole.

I pull out a lacy combination in a vivid shade of teal that I'd never wear outside the privacy of my own bedroom, and shiver with anticipation. I know exactly how that silk is going to slip over my warm skin and how sensual it will feel under the cool sheets tonight.

For what feels like the hundredth time, I replay today's conversation with Chord, and the moment he asked if I had a boyfriend, only this time I fantasize that his interest wasn't polite or innocent but possessive and jealous.

What might it be like to have a man like that want me? Desire me?

I rub the silk between my fingers. It's mind-blowing how something as simple as fabric, cut the right way and embellished just so, can make someone feel like a different person. That's the magic of fashion and why I love it so much.

I throw the underwear on the bed, strip off my clothes, and spend fifteen minutes under the hot, hard spray of what is fast becoming one of my favorite places in the world. I towel off in the bathroom, pull a brush through my wet hair, and lather my body with lotion before returning to the bedroom and sliding the lacy thong up over my legs. As soon as the cool silk slips into place, a satisfied little moan escapes my throat. I set a hand on the camisole next, then scream when the fastest, fattest brown mouse with the beadiest eyes I've ever seen bolts out of the fabric and scampers across the soft cotton bed covers.

I scream again when it disappears under my pillow.

And I'm still screaming when the door flies open, and Chord bursts into my room.

"What the hell is going on?" he demands before pulling up short with his eyes popping out of his head.

I point at the mountain of pillows. "There's a mouse in the bed!"

"A mouse?" He glances at the pillows and then back at me. He looks stunned, kind of like he's been whacked over the head with something heavy, and realization dawns. He's scared of mice too.

"Yes, a mouse!" I shake my finger at the pillows. Did the little cushion at the front just move? That *creature* was totally big enough and the closer I look... Yes. The cushion in front definitely shuddered. "Get it!"

"Uh, sure." Chord takes a hesitant step forward, then drops his head back and stares up at the ceiling. I catch a mumbled *fuck* before he says, "Jesus, Violet. Could you put on some clothes?"

"What?" I look down at my good-as-naked body and shriek before bolting into the bathroom and slamming the door.

Holy crap. My boss just saw my boobs.

Chord Davenport just saw my boobs.

I snatch up my wet towel and wrap it around my body, then hunch against the door, wishing I could die and listening for sounds in the bedroom.

What do I care now if he finds the mouse? As soon as Chord leaves the room, I'm packing my bags, driving back home, and never leaving my apartment again.

Oh, my God. Chord saw my boobs.

My body shakes from the shock of the rodent, but the heat across my chest is all embarrassment, and tears prick at my throat. I can never face Chord again.

I hear movement in the bedroom, then the rustling of sheets and pillows, a thud followed by a pained grunt. I close my eyes and try to imagine what it means, but even when the room grows quiet, I'm not brave enough to open the door. I have to believe that Chord will say something once he's caught the mouse, and then let me know he's leaving so I can die from mortification alone, the way it's supposed to be done.

I listen, clutching the towel around my chest and trying to calm my shaky breaths. And just when I think he's left without telling me, I hear soft footsteps on the carpet, and what sounds like the linens being torn off the bed.

I lower myself to the cool, damp tiles and sit with my back to the door, toying with the edge of the Egyptian cotton and nibbling my bottom lip as I listen to Chord moving about the room.

Oh, God. I drop my forehead to my knees and let out a pathetic whimper. *He saw my boobs.*

An eternity later, a cough sounds too close on the other side of the door, and I jump. For a moment, I'm terrified he's going to try to come in.

"The mouse is gone," Chord says. His tone is even, like he's trying to pretend he didn't just see me half naked, and

I groan quietly. This is so humiliating. "And I'm going to my room, so you can come out whenever you're ready." A pause, and then, "Goodnight."

I don't move for a full count of sixty seconds, just to be safe.

When I open the door and step out into the room, I'm not quite sure what I'm looking at.

The bed is perfectly made, but the sheets are now olive-toned linen instead of the crisp white cotton they were twenty minutes ago. I creep forward and touch them, just to be sure, then glance at the door and back at the bed.

Chord changed my sheets.

That's when I notice my pretty teal camisole carefully draped over the white desk chair, and the pinboard against the wall, now moved to the other side of the room from where I left it. My sketchbook is right there, too. My favorite dress, almost finished, is drawn large on the open page.

And I realize with a sinking feeling that Chord saw more than my bare skin tonight. He doesn't know it, but he just got a glimpse directly into my soul.

FIFTEEN

Chord

75 DAYS TILL HOCKEY SEASON

I HAVE NO IDEA WHAT time Violet leaves her room in the morning because for as long as she's been here, I've been out the door at sunrise, but I'm skipping breakfast with Dylan, Daisy, and Izzy today to get past the weirdness as fast as possible. I want her to feel safe with me. I want her to stay.

Last night was so freaking *awkward*.

Awkward or not, my cock twitches every time I think about it, and I adjust my pants while scowling at the coffee machine as it doles out my espresso.

The picture of Violet standing there in those flimsy blue panties, luscious tits bare, squealing at a mouse like a goddamn city girl... So damn adorable and so freaking sexy, someone will have to physically carve it from my brain before I ever forget it.

I'm sitting at the informal dining table on the opposite side of the kitchen island, sipping my second cup of coffee and devouring my overnight oats, when Violet appears. I look up just as her eyes widen at the sight of me, and she actually spins on her heel and takes three steps in the opposite direction before she stops herself.

She's wearing denim cut-offs today, exposing her long, smooth legs, and I watch with interest as she straightens her back and tosses her head—obviously giving herself some kind of internal pep talk—before she turns around again and strides into the kitchen, focused entirely on the coffee machine.

"Morning," I say.

There's an imperceptible pause in her movements as she goes to fill a cup. "Hello."

I watch her move about the kitchen with a focus that tells me she plans to look anywhere but at me, but when she checks the fridge for today's to-do list, I clear my throat and hold it up.

Violet glances at it, then me and her brows draw together. "Do you need more time with the list?"

"No. I wanted to go over a few items, if you've got time?"

She adjusts her glasses and casts a furtive look down the hallway. Toward the home office where she works or the front door where she can escape, I'm not sure, and I cover my uncertainty by lifting my coffee cup to my lips. I'm relying on her being too timid to tell me no, but after what happened last night, I'm not entirely certain she won't just bolt.

I give myself a point for guessing right as, with an almost silent sigh, she slips into the chair across from me. "I've got time. What did you want to talk about?"

So many things. The felt board and sketchbook I saw in your room. The flimsy little thong I hope you're wearing under those shorts. How pretty you were with your face bare last night, and how I've wasted too many hours thinking about it.

How I can't stop wondering how well your tits would fill my hands.

I shift in my seat to give my dick a little more room, set down the list between us, and tap the top line. "How are the plans coming along for the move? Any leads on a new apartment?"

Her forehead creases as her shoulders drop. "Oh."

I see the moment Violet gets it that I'm not going to mention the mouse, the sketchbook, or the partial nudity. The tension between her brows fades as she twists the paper on the table to face her and then wraps her hands around her mug.

She still can't meet my eyes, but if reading my notes gives her something to do, I'm okay with that. It means she doesn't notice the way I count the freckles on her nose or watch her lips form each word.

"There's not a lot out there, and I want to get you the best." She touches the paper again before hiding her fidgeting hands under the table. "The realtor sent me a list of options, but only one was anywhere near good enough."

"One is better than none."

"Right." She glances at me from underneath her lashes and offers a tentative smile. "When I've found at least three for you to choose from, I'll set up times to inspect them.

You don't mind returning to the city for half a day in the next few weeks, do you?"

I shake my head. "I'll make it work."

"Great." Violet drags her teeth over her bottom lip as she peruses the other tasks I've asked her to do today, and I lean back in my seat to watch her. "You've got physio twice a week every week from now until the season starts in September, but we can always add more if you need it. I'm sorting through the game tape we have so far and should have another batch for you by the end of the weekend. I've read through all the updated paperwork from the nutritionist..."

She trails off and glances up, and there's a tiny smile on her mouth, which makes the corner of my lips tip up before I even know why.

"I'm sorry, Chord. No Pretzel M&M's in the plan, I'm afraid."

I let my smile stretch a fraction wider. I appreciate her joke, but I like the shape of my name on her lips even more. "But you got them anyway, right?"

She lifts one shoulder, shifting her tee down her arm and exposing a gray bra strap. Now I'm wondering if she saves her colored lingerie for the bedroom, and my cock likes the idea.

"Right," she agrees. "There were just a few other things to sort out today. Invitations to summer events you might want to attend."

"I don't," I reply, rougher than I intended, but gruff is my go-to when I'm uncomfortable, and talking about making a public appearance while I'm also dealing with a hard-on is all sorts of uncomfortable. "You can RSVP no."

Her posture stiffens again, and I try to relax.

"Okay," she says. "Aside from that, there's just one or two other things. You have an email from a warehouse in the city. Whatever you're storing down there needs more room, and they want to upgrade—"

"I'm satisfied with whatever they suggest. Upgrade or move or whatever." I don't want to talk about the warehouse or answer questions about what's in it.

"No problem." She slips her hands under the table again and curls her shoulders forward. "I'll return their email today."

Stop being a fucking asshole.

I take a sip of coffee as a kind of reset. "Thank you."

"You're welcome."

Violet suddenly stands and looks around like she's searching for an excuse to leave, and I curse myself for giving her attitude.

"I'm sure you've got a full day planned," she says. "I don't want to keep you."

She walks away and sets her coffee cup in the sink. My breakfast is only half-finished in front of me, but I follow, keeping a tight enough grasp on common sense to stay on this side of the island where I can still see her face.

"I'm going to go for an early run then I'll get in a few laps." The conversation is starting to time out, and I'm not ready to let her go yet. I scramble for a topic of conversation, and the first thing that comes to mind is the morning I found her on the Silver Leaf hiking trails. "Do you, uh, run?"

"Me?" She smiles to herself as she rinses out her coffee mug. "No, I don't run."

I want to see that smile again. "Swim?"

Violet glances up at the ceiling and considers her answer, and whatever she thinks of teases the corners of her lips again. "I... float."

I can almost see her petals unfolding, and I round the island to get a little closer. "Float?"

"Yeah. You know, like on those inflatable beds?"

"Sure. I get it."

She shakes her head and gives me a shy glance. "I'm sorry to disappoint you, but I'm not much of an athlete."

"You couldn't disappoint me."

The words are out before I can stop them, and we stand there in an odd kind of silence, Violet blinking at me like she's sure she must have misheard me, she's just not sure how.

"Right, well." Violet picks up a towel to dry her hands and gives me a tight smile. "I guess I'd better—"

A buzzing ring sounds from the pocket of her jeans. She whips it out and checks the screen, but I don't miss the way her body tenses, and her throat bobs with a swallow as she swipes to accept the call and holds the phone to her ear.

"Courtney. Hello. How are you?"

A surge of protectiveness swells behind my ribs and

I cross my arms over my chest, not trying to hide the fact I'm watching to see what happens next.

Violet's gaze flickers my way before she drops her eyes to the floor. "No, I haven't checked my email yet this morning."

She licks her lips as she takes in whatever Courtney is saying on the other end of the line. It's Saturday morning. Why the hell is her boss calling her outside of office hours?

"Mm-hm." Violet nods slowly. "Yes, I understand."

Her throat works again, and she wraps an arm around her middle before turning away from me, and something doesn't feel right. I move around to the other side of the island to get a clear view of her face, and she spares me a quick look that gives nothing away.

She probably wants me to leave, and I almost do. Except I can't.

"I know," she says into the phone. "I'll work on it. It won't happen again."

Violet glances at me again, a look that lingers this time, and there's no misreading what's in those big brown eyes now. Powerlessness.

I hold out my hand, palm up, but when she only stares at it, I pluck the phone from her fingers and press it to my ear.

"Courtney? This is Chord Davenport."

"Oh." I hear the way she shifts her attitude. "Hello, Chord. How are you?"

"Fine, but there's a problem here."

"I understand." The restrained triumph in her voice makes me clench my jaw. "Violet will return to her role here first thing Monday morning, and we can arrange a replacement—"

"No, that's not what I mean."

Violet watches with astonishment, her palms pressed together against her mouth, and here I am, wanting to smile again.

"Well..." Courtney falters. "What do you mean?"

"When I asked for an assistant, I expected that person to work for me and only me. Twenty-four-seven. I didn't expect her to perform two full-time roles or split her focus in a way that makes it impossible to do either job well. That stops today. From now until October, Violet is no longer available outside of her duties here as my assistant. If required, I'll pay her salary so you can hire a replacement to cover the gap that leaves in your marketing team."

Silence. And it feels good.

"I'm glad we had this little talk," I add. "Have a good day, Miss Reynolds."

I end the call and offer the phone to Violet. She takes it with an uncertain hand, and the amazement on her face feels fucking fantastic.

"You didn't... I mean, I can't believe you..." A disbelieving chuckle erupts from somewhere deep in her chest, and I'm living for the sound. "Courtney won't like this."

"And I couldn't care less."

I turn away and take my seat at the dining table to finish

my half-eaten breakfast. Violet gives another amazed laugh, then starts to leave the room. I stop her before she goes, unable to resist the chance to make her smile one more time.

"Take the rest of the day off, Wallflower, because starting tomorrow, you're all mine."

Violet's cheeks flame the prettiest shade of pink, and the color does things to me. Things that heat my blood and make my heart race faster than it does on the ice. Things I want to feel over and over. A high I'm going to crave all summer long.

SIXTEEN

Violet

DAY 12 AT SILVER LEAF... ONLY 74 TO GO

I SIT AT THE TABLE on the back porch with my open laptop and an iced tea, for all intents and purposes, enjoying the sunshine while working on something for Chord because, apparently, that's my entire job now. But that's not the whole truth. I'm out here instead of in the home office because Chord is fixing the fences again, and this is the spot with the best view.

I can't prove it, but I get the feeling he knows I'm watching.

Words cannot do this man justice, and the light sheen of perspiration on the back of my neck isn't only thanks to the summer heat. Chord's jeans hug his tight, round ass so well, and they're snug enough to strain across the bulge in front. Between his hours of manual labor, he walks in and out of the house with his tight t-shirt damp enough to look sprayed on, his body hard and carved like granite, his hair dark and curled around the edges.

After a morning spent doing not much more than watching him work, I'm struck by how easy Chord is in his body. Everyone knows he's a powerful hockey player, but his physical ease doesn't end on the ice. He's probably one of those people who's never felt awkward a day in his life, and the way he handles the fences is so confident and forceful. It makes me wonder what he's like in bed.

I startle when the back door crashes open and someone sings out, "Hello! Anyone home?" My impure daydreams disappear beneath a burning rush of guilt.

The little girl I saw the day I got here—Izzy, Chord's niece—dances onto the porch. She wears the same little cowboy boots and hat, but her tutu is blue today, and she's got a yellow long-sleeved one-piece swimsuit underneath.

I'm surprised to see her, given that Chord hasn't had a single visitor since I got here, but also oddly happy that someone has come looking for him. But when Izzy spots me and pulls up with a pouty little frown, I think I should have stuck to working in the office.

"Um, hi." I rest my elbows on my knees and lean over with a smile. "You're Izzy, right?"

"Yes." She crosses her little arms and pops a hip. "Who are you?"

I'm both scared and amused by her attitude. "I'm Violet. It's nice to meet you."

She squints at me and turns her head a little. "Are you Uncle Chord's girlfriend?"

I laugh in surprise and look around for help just as Chord's blonde sister, Daisy, steps onto the porch.

"Violet is Uncle Chord's assistant, Izzy. She helps him with his hockey stuff." Daisy squints out at the field where Chord is working, then hands Izzy the baseball cap and cowboy hat she's carrying. "Go give these to Uncle Chord and tell him you're here to help with those fences. Also, tell him I said the one on the left is crooked."

"Okay."

Izzy skips down the steps, jumps the last one and lands on the lawn with two feet and a *"Yes!"* then bolts in Chord's direction. She must yell out when she's close enough because Chord suddenly straightens and opens his arms to scoop her up and spin her around. When he sets her down again, he takes the cowboy hat she offers and hangs it on a fence post before he slips the baseball cap on his head. Backwards.

I barely muffle an indecent moan.

Daisy snorts. "I knew he would do that." Then she looks at me. "I've been waiting for Chord to be a gentleman and bring you around to introduce us, but this is better." She extends her hand. "I'm Daisy. It's nice to meet you properly."

I accept her hand and shake it. "It's nice to meet you too."

Daisy glances at the jug of iced tea on the table, steps back inside and reappears with another glass, then sits across from me and helps herself to a drink. She takes a sip, watching me over the rim of the glass with inquisitive hazel eyes.

I'm not sure what to make of her or this situation. I glance out at the field and see Chord looking in this direction, but when he notices me looking, he bends back to Izzy and his work.

I guess I'm on my own. I stick my hands between my thighs as a reminder not to bounce my knees.

"Chord's come up to The Hill every morning for breakfast since he got here, but we missed him the last two days," Daisy says. "Izzy and I thought we'd come look for him, and I was hoping to see you too."

It's in my nature to think the worst, but I force myself to ask, "Really? Why?"

She takes off her white wide-brimmed hat and drops it on the chair beside her before reclining a little and setting her booted feet up on the table.

"Because I've been home for weeks, and Charlie won't go with me to The Slippery Tipple. I need to *dance*, Vi. Please tell me you'll give my brother the slip next weekend and keep me company?"

My heart kind of stops before it takes off again as fast as it was, only now its thrumming in my wrists instead of pounding in my ears. Chord's sister wants to go dancing with *me*? I'm as interested as I am anxious—I've never been dancing with a girlfriend, and I'm not even sure I know how—but that's not all. Nobody's ever called me *Vi*. It's a thing only a good friend would do, but Daisy says it like she's known me for years, not minutes, and I love it so much that warmth starts creeping along my chest.

"Yeah, sure. I mean, I'm not officially on the clock after six p.m., so it should be fine. It should be great. You know. Fun."

"My grumpy big brother doesn't work you day and night?" She cocks her head and considers me with lips pursed against a smile. "I think he likes you."

"Me?" I laugh self-consciously and lower my eyes. "I don't think Chord likes anyone." I hear the words too late to take them back and cover my hot cheeks with my hands. "I can't believe I said that. I didn't mean it. I'm so sorry."

Daisy stares at me long enough to make me believe I've messed this up, but then she bursts into laughter and I chuckle along with her without any idea what's going on.

Her eyes are watery with mirth as she reaches across the table and squeezes my hand. "It's okay, Vi. You're not the first one to think that. You might be the first one to say it while sitting on his porch, using his wi-fi, and drinking his iced tea, but that means you've got ovaries of steel, and I like that in a woman."

I take a deep breath and pick up my drink. "I'm so embarrassed."

She waves her hand and leans back in her chair. "Don't be. Chord can be an arrogant, irritable jackass, but he's got a good heart. In fact, I feel like I should apologize to you."

I choke a little on my mouthful of tea and hurry to set down my glass. "To me? Why?"

Daisy glances out to the field where Chord and Izzy are hard at work, then turns back with a rueful smile.

"I'm sorry you got stuck in the middle of Chord and Charlie's discussion the day you arrived. She feels bad about it, and it has nothing to do with you. They've got their own stuff, but it was unfair to air it in front of company."

She purses her lips and cocks her head to one side, examining me like a specimen in a jar. "You work for the Fury, right?"

"Ah... yes?"

She nods thoughtfully. "So, you can't repeat any of what I tell you now, right?"

"Right."

She nods once. "Good. I could use someone to talk to, and it's hard to make real girlfriends when Chord Davenport is your brother. I never know when something I say might end up in an article somewhere, or if someone is being friendly just to get his number."

I sense that whatever Daisy wants to get off her chest is none of my business, but I ignore the little flush of shame for not shutting this down and lean closer.

"Chord was always a hockey prodigy—magic from the moment he was old enough to skate. He knew it. Mom and Dad knew it. And they made sure that me and Dylan and Finn and Charlie knew it. They treated him differently. Never made him do chores, made allowances for him they never gave us, and raised him to put himself and his own goals before everything else, even the ranch. Don't get me wrong—Mom and Dad were amazing parents, and they loved us so big—but

Chord was special. I don't think Chord realizes, even now, how his dreams affected our relationships with him."

I lick my lips and blink a little, trying not to show how her words affect me. Dreams are something I think about all the time—dreams and how they make people do selfish things. My mom chose dreams over her family. I shelved my dreams to take care of my dad. And he never had dreams of his own.

Daisy doesn't notice how I hang on her every word. "It was hardest on Charlie and still is. With or without Chord and hockey, Finn was always going to be a SEAL, Dylan was always going to be a chef, and I was always going to run away the day I turned eighteen. We were never going to stay here and run this place, but Charlie..."

Daisy tips her head from side to side like she's looking for the right words. I'm on the edge of my seat even though I've never felt good about gossip but... Chord saw my boobs. And my sketchbook. I'm going to take my chance to learn something intimate about him.

"Chord's the oldest. You know that, right?" Daisy says, and I nod. "In another world, he'd have been the one to take over here, but in *this* world, that responsibility fell to Charlie. She was prepped from day one to take over Silver Leaf, and she wants to live up to the dreams Mom and Dad had for her the same way Chord lived up to the future they planned for him. Charlie wants to prove herself the way Chord has—show the world she's capable of success. But the problem is she's scared."

"Of what?" I ask before I can help myself. "Chord?"

Daisy shakes her head. "God, no. At least, not like that. I think she's scared that when Chord retires, he'll come back and take what she's spent the last eight years trying to build. That he'll swoop in with his money and his attitude and she'll be pushed aside. Charlie loves this place, and she wants to save it—in her own way and on her own terms."

"Save it? Is Silver Leaf in trouble?"

Daisy raises one perfect eyebrow. "Twenty years ago, this place was something else," she says. "Today, we make just enough from the restaurant, weekend tourists, the occasional wedding, and one catering client's monthly wine order to keep us in the black. Without that, we'd have shut down years ago."

"I'm sorry. I had no idea."

"How could you? Just don't mention it to Charlie. She's working hard to turn things around. We want horses again—that'll be my job—and a spa. Glamping. More private bungalows. All of us have ideas, but we're struggling to make them happen."

"And Chord?" I ask. "He doesn't want to invest?"

Two weeks ago, I might have presumed Chord was cold enough to leave his family to fend for themselves, but now... I glance over at where he's helping Izzy bang on a fence post with a hammer, then smile when he pretends she caught his thumb with a big-swing hit. I've seen too much to believe that about him anymore.

Daisy snorts. "Chord has tried to invest in this place more times than I can count, and Charlie won't take it. If Chord can make his fortune on his own, then so can she—or so says Charlie."

Poor Charlie. Poor Chord. It sounds like a big old mess.

Voices float to us on the summer air, and Daisy and I turn to see Chord leading Izzy back to the house. He's still got that cap on backwards and he's spinning the cowboy hat on one finger. He flicks it at Daisy when he steps onto the porch, and she catches it with two hands.

"Never in a million years, Daze," he mutters.

She rolls her eyes and jumps to her feet. "And the backward baseball cap is *just so cool*." Daisy turns to me. "Don't forget, Vi. Saturday night. Eight o'clock. Oh, no. What's wrong? What's that look?"

I didn't know I had a look, but I was mentally going through the items in my wardrobe and *dancing* hadn't been on my summer bingo card when I packed.

"Just wondering what I'm going to wear," I admit.

She flaps one hand at me. "You can borrow something from me."

Daisy is at least five inches shorter than I am, and I give her a skeptical look that only makes her laugh. "We'll figure it out, but you're coming. Hear that, big brother? Me and Vi are going dancing on Saturday night."

"Dancing? Where?"

"The Slippery Tipple. Where else?"

Chord grunts before his blue eyes slide to me. "*Vi?*"

I shrug self-consciously. "It's short for Violet."

His lips twitch. "I know. I just didn't realize you were collecting nicknames now, Wallflower."

Daisy snorts. "Wallflower? Hell, no. This queen is going to be the brightest, prettiest thing on the dance floor next Saturday night. Isn't that right, Vi?"

I don't answer her. I can't because there's that name again. Chord stares at me with burning blue eyes like he knows what he does to me, and my face grows hot as a million spots of light take flight in my body. The same way they did last night.

SEVENTEEN

Violet

DAY 16 AT SILVER LEAF... ONLY 70 TO GO

"YOU GOT A MINUTE?"

I lift my head from my laptop and Chord's never-ending fan mail and almost choke on my own saliva. Chord's leaning in the doorway to the home office, forearm on the frame, wearing nothing but low-slung sky-blue swim shorts. My gaze drags over his biceps, down his hard chest, across his rippling abs, and past the jut of his hips. It bounces back to his face when I reach the bulge in his pants, and a rush of heat between my legs makes my cheeks burn. Judging by his subtle little smirk, Chord knows exactly where my mind just went.

Someone, *please* send help. I'm not built to handle this much gorgeous.

"Sure," I reply in barely more than a breathy whisper.

"You got a bathing suit?"

That brings me back to Earth, and I narrow my eyes. "Why?"

"It's warm out, and I thought you might like to take a break." He shrugs and straightens as one side of his mouth hooks up. "I'll swim, and you can... float."

I glance out the tall glass windows, past the porch and at the blue sky. It's easy to forget about the heat with the central air in this house, but I know it's perfect weather for swimming because I work on the porch at least twice a day for, ah... fresh air.

But the idea of sharing a pool with Chord makes me nervous, and that's even before I think too hard about being in a swimsuit in front of him. *He's already seen you in less than that*, I remind myself, but the flashback to that night in my room isn't helping things.

"I don't know," I hedge. "I'm pretty busy."

"Come on." He shifts to lean his shoulder on the trim, crossing his large arms over his chest and swinging one ankle over the other. "Just an hour. I won't tell the boss if you don't."

He's the boss, and when I blink too fast at the comment, his right eyebrow—the one with the scar—ticks up. So now, apparently, Chord is charming.

My blush now is more pleasure than embarrassment. "All right. Just an hour."

"Good." He pushes upright. "I'll meet you at the pool in ten."

I wait for the sound of his footsteps to fade before running upstairs to my room, digging through my drawers, and slipping on my white bikini. I grab my hat, a towel, and the sunscreen, and race down the stairs before I change my mind.

When I set eyes on the pool, I burst out laughing.

"What is this?" I ask as I approach the water's edge.

Chord is waist-deep in the water, surrounded by at least ten blow-up novelty pool floats. He spins to look at me, and his eyes slide up my body in a way that makes me very aware of how much skin I'm showing. His dark hair is damp, slicked back and sexy, his hard upper body drips with water, and his throat bobs with a deep swallow. I pull on my hat, drop to the edge of the pool so I can dangle my legs over the side, and try to hide.

Chord wades his way over to a giant inflatable pizza slice and pushes it in my direction. "I swim. You float. Isn't that right?"

I chuckle as I push the pizza away with one pointed toe. It looks precarious, and the last thing I need is to look foolish trying to stay dry on a flimsy piece of plastic in the middle of Chord's perfect pool. "Yes, that's right, but maybe not that one."

He guides a swan to me. "What about this guy?"

The swan has a long neck with handles and a small platform for my bottom. I give him a wry look from underneath my hat. "Do I look like a straddle-and-ride kind of girl to you?" I hear the words after I say them, and heat explodes to my hairline. "Oh, no. Don't answer that."

He doesn't try to hide his amusement, shaking his head with a small smile. "I won't," he promises.

I could get used to this version of Chord. Relaxed. Friendly. Warm.

He makes his way around the menagerie of pool toys, offering them to me one by one. Unicorn. Dolphin. Strawberry. Pineapple. Seahorse. Doughnut. By the time I've slathered sunscreen on every inch of skin I can reach, I've decided on the giant peacock. It's got a wide base made of netting, so I can feel the water on my legs and a tall spray of inflated feathers to recline against. But while I'm wondering how I'm supposed to get on it without looking goofy, Chord nods at the tube of sunscreen in my hand.

"You missed your back," he observes.

"Oh." I look at the tube and wonder if there's a way to have Chord's hands on me without having to come right out and ask for it. "It's hard to reach."

My heart skips as he splays his palms on the smooth travertine coping, flexes every muscle in his sexy athletic arms, and launches himself out of the pool. He sits beside me, dries his hands on one of the towels stacked nearby, and takes the sunscreen.

"Turn around," he orders quietly.

With butterflies fluttering their way up my throat, I remove my hat, sweep my hair off my neck, and twist to offer him my back.

The moment his cool hands touch me, every inch of my body erupts in goosebumps.

I coach myself through each breath as his large, confident

hands massage the lotion into my skin. His palms do most of the work, slipping over my shoulder blades and along my spine. His hands swipe low, to the waist of my bikini briefs, and wide, to brush the sides of my ribcage.

When he tucks his fingers under the strap of my bikini and sweeps them underneath, I freeze. A warm, wet pulse beats at the apex of my thighs, and when he finally pulls away, I embarrass myself with a loud, shaky breath.

I shift to face the pool but can't bring myself to look at him. "Thank you."

His voice is strained when he replies, "You're welcome."

Chord drops back into the water, submerging himself completely and swimming away under the pool floats. The pool is enormous—Olympic size with plenty of room for the toys—and while he's under the water, I return my hat to my head and take the opportunity to arrange myself on the peacock.

Soon I'm safely ensconced on my pretty floating bird, and I sweep my hands in the water to rotate my position and look for Chord. He's tucked into a big brown inflatable teddy bear, its arms curled around like it's trying to hug him. He looks ridiculous and adorable at the same time, and it makes me laugh.

"You *swim*," I say. "And *I* float. Remember?"

He raises his scarred brow as his mouth tips up. "I feel like relaxing right now. There'll be plenty of time for laps later, and I'm not in any rush."

I drop my eyes with a small smile. "Okay."

I adjust my hat a little so I can watch Chord from under the wide brim. He takes a deep breath and lets it out with a satisfied sigh, then closes his eyes and turns his face to the sky. His arms dangle in the water, and he's still for so long that I wonder if he's fallen asleep. It makes ogling him easier, but when he suddenly speaks, I jump.

"So. Sports marketing, huh?"

"What? Oh. Yes. Sports marketing."

"You like hockey?"

"Um."

I wiggle my fingers in the cool water as I search for the right words, but when I take too long, he opens one eye and lifts his head.

"You *don't* like hockey?"

I bite my lip at how offended he sounds. "I like it fine," I assure him, "but I'm not what you'd call a diehard fan. My dad, however, follows the Fury like it's his religion. He was ecstatic when I told him I got a job for the team."

"I'll have to meet him someday."

"Really?" I don't try to hide my surprise.

"Sure."

"He'd love that."

"Is he the reason why you took the job?"

"Um, well..."

It doesn't feel great when people don't care enough to ask about my life, but I'm always uncomfortable when they do. It's a paradox easily managed by avoiding conversation altogether. But this moment with Chord doesn't feel that way. We've been edging closer to something that might be friendship, so it's surprisingly easy to push through the discomfort of talking about myself and lean into the impulse to be more open. "He's part of it, but it's a respectable, well-paying position with excellent health benefits. Anyone would kill for the same opportunity. I'd have been silly not to take it."

"So that means—what? You studied business marketing in college?"

"No, actually." The sun is toasting the tops of my thighs, so I run my cool, wet hands over them for relief. "Well, yes and no. I double majored in marketing and fashion design."

"Fashion. That's cool."

Apprehension flutters in my chest. I get the sense Chord's taking this conversation somewhere specific. Somewhere like the sketchbook and felt board he saw in my bedroom. The walls around my heart slam into place, but then I remember the secrets Daisy shared with me—all the intimate details I know about Chord's life without his permission—and I want to offer something in return. The truth.

"Yeah, it is—or was."

"What do you mean *was*?"

I take a moment to think about my answer. It's hard to put into words the regrets I've kept to myself. It hurts to think of them, let alone say them out loud, but it's almost like they've been waiting for the right time to surface because once I start talking, I can't stop.

"My dream was to design wedding gowns and haute couture. Violet James—the next Vera Wang." I chuckle at how absurd it sounds now. "But it's just me and my dad at home, and we need my income, so while other design students were doing low-paid internships and traveling the world, I was working whatever part-time marketing gigs I could find during the week, slugging it out in fashion retail on weekends, and failing to make an impact on social media." I shrug like it doesn't bother me, but the burn of failure and embarrassment sticks in my throat. "I gave it ten years before I admitted it was time to let go of my dreams. Then this job with the Fury came up, I applied, and I got it. Do *not* ask me how, but I suppose things worked out all right in the end."

Chord is quiet for a moment, and I start to feel insecure about how much I've shared. Perhaps he wasn't angling for my life story. Maybe he was just trying to be polite. I misread the situation, and now I look stupid.

But then he says, "It's just you and your dad?"

"Yep. Just the two of us."

"And your mom?"

A sad sort of smile tugs at my lips. "She was only eighteen when she had me. I mean, Dad was only twenty, so he wasn't that much older, but by the time I turned three, my mom decided she didn't want to be a mom anymore. There was too much adventure waiting for her. Too many dreams she wanted to chase. So, she left, and we never heard from her again."

"I'm sorry," Chord says quietly.

"There's no need to be," I say honestly. "I got over it a long time ago. She was young and beautiful, and she wrote me a long letter explaining how she dreamed of being on the stage. She told me she was sorry, and I was hurt and mad for a long time, but as I grew older and learned more about the world, I began to understand why she did what she did. I'm not sure I would have wanted a mother who didn't want to raise me. I don't want to be the reason for someone else's regrets."

Chord blinks like he's turning my words over in his head. "And your dad?"

A single tear takes me off guard, and I dash it away before Chord can notice it. I'm more reluctant to talk about my dad than anything else, but I miss him so much that the words spill out. "He was always a good father—he's a good man, and I never went without—but he struggles with depression. I've always believed my mother leaving us was sort of the catalyst for that."

"What does he do with himself? Does he work?"

"He did a carpentry apprenticeship when he was young and worked in construction for a while. Then he did odd jobs and handyman-type things."

"So, you take care of him?"

Something about the way he says it makes me frown. "We take care of each other."

"And the designing?" He casts me a look that says he's referring to the sketchbook he wasn't supposed to see—he knows that; I know that; and he knows I know he knows—

but neither of us is going to mention it because it'll bring up *other things*. "You still draw in your own time? You don't share it with anyone?"

I sigh and drop my head back against the fat plastic peacock feathers, pressing my lids closed to ease the way they sting. "I do still draw, and no, I don't share it with anyone."

"Why?"

It's a good question—one I've asked myself many times—without a real answer. I give him the only one I have. "Because I don't know how to stop."

His brows pull together, and his mouth turns down. "Maybe that means—"

"I'm a little warm." I pull my float against the side of the pool and inelegantly drag myself out of it, then offer him an awkward wave without making eye contact. "Thanks for the swim—or the float. I'll see you later."

I fling my towel around my shoulders and hurry back to the house, hoping that if I move fast enough, I can outrun the regret of sharing too much. This anxiety is why I can't make friends. Vulnerability is uncomfortable, and people don't always know when to back off. I know Chord was about to tell me I shouldn't give up my dreams, and I don't want to hear it. It took me a long time to accept that I wasn't meant to be a designer. Hoping for the impossible hurt too much. Hope broke my heart every day.

EIGHTEEN

Chord

68 DAYS TILL HOCKEY SEASON

I SIT ON THE EDGE of my bed, elbows on my knees, and glare down the hallway at Violet's almost-closed bedroom door. She's been in there for an hour getting ready for her night out with Daisy, and I've been searching for an excuse to go with them. The Slippery Tipple is a dive bar with great beer, good music, sticky floors, and a questionable crowd, but it's the only place close enough to Silver Leaf to dance and get drunk and still find a way home at two in the morning. It's owned and run by a woman named Mona Golightly—my mom's best friend when she was still alive and as good as an aunt to me and my siblings—but that doesn't help me right now. I'm too pissed at the idea of Violet moving her body on a hot, dark dance floor, lit by the glow of the kitsch signs, tipsy and flushed and gorgeous, another man pressed against her.

I crack my knuckles on my left hand, then my right, and scowl at her door.

It's been two days since our conversation in the pool, and I can't get it out of my head. I asked a question without much hope of getting an answer, but Violet shared some big things—and part of me wishes she hadn't.

She gave up on her dreams. No. She gave up on *herself*, and it makes me so fucking mad.

I'm halfway up the hall with no idea what I'm supposed to do when a blast of music sounds from behind her door. There's a squeal before the sound cuts out, and I knock before I can stop myself.

"Come in?"

My lips tip up at the way she phrases it like a question.

My eyes land on her immediately, and I blink away the memory of her standing in that exact spot, wearing nothing but her pretty blue panties. It's a small leap from there to the way her skin felt under my palms by the pool—slick with lotion, warm from the sun, so unbelievably soft.

This woman's got no idea how she fucking tortures me.

"I'm sorry about the noise." She picks up her phone and taps to silence the music before setting it on the desk face down. "I was listening with my headphones and didn't realize the volume would be so loud on speaker mode."

Her glasses are on the desk and her bare feet sink into the fluffy white carpet, but she's still in the cut-off denims and old Van Halen tee she's had on all day. I find the vintage rock

154

shirts one more intriguing thing about her. Does she wear them ironically? Is she a genuine fan of their music? It seems like a good opportunity to find out.

"What are you listening to?"

She waves her hand toward her phone and feigns a casualness she obviously doesn't feel. "It's a random mix. I don't know what they play at The Slippery Tipple, and I want to be prepared."

"They play all different things. Country, easy rock, stuff you hear on the radio." Then I narrow my eyes at her last comment. "Prepared for what?"

Violet drops her eyes. "Dancing," she mumbles.

"Dancing?"

I hate the way she nods but doesn't look up, so I close the distance between us and make it impossible to ignore me. When she still won't look at me, I take her chin and lift her eyes to mine.

"Why are you embarrassed?"

Her chestnut eyes shift between mine as she searches for something. "Because I'm not sure what to do."

My pretty little wallflower doesn't know how to dance.

I reach around to pick up her phone, then hand it to her. She spares me a quizzical look before she unlocks it, and I take it back long enough to select a song and adjust the volume. When the first slow country notes sound from the speaker, I set the phone down and extend my hand.

"May I?"

I follow the tip of her tongue as it darts out to swipe her bottom lip, but after only a brief hesitation, Violet sets her hand on mine.

I'm acutely aware of my own heartbeat as I place my other hand on the small of her back. With a little pressure, Violet shifts closer the way I hoped she would. My breath grows short and shallow as I take note of the featherlight touches between us at my thighs, her hips, my chest, her breasts.

Violet presses her eyelids closed as her fingers tighten, then release in my hand, before she risks a shy look up at me and drops her eyes again.

"This is what you do," I whisper.

I move in small rocking steps from side to side. Violet's palm is warm, and her actions are stiff and self-conscious, but she follows my lead and stays on the beat. By the time we get to the chorus, the tension has melted from her arms, and she sinks effortlessly into our easy sway.

I dip my head to set my mouth at her ear. "You're good at this."

She looks up at me with a blush and a smile. "You make it easy."

I turn us a little, angling our bodies so I can sweep my eyes over the room. Her sketchbook is open on the desk again, and her oversized felt board is covered in copies of the same dress.

After our conversation in the pool, I don't think twice about raising the subject again. "You draw the same dress a lot."

"Hm?" She glances over her shoulder at the board as she

rocks against me, and I force myself to concentrate on her words instead of the heat of her body. "Oh, yes."

She pauses, and I get the sense she's contemplating how much she wants to share. I know if I keep silent long enough, she'll rush to fill the void. I'm desperate to understand why she's fixated on this particular design, so I'm a dick and say nothing.

"It's my mother's wedding dress," she says finally. "Well, a version of it. I've played with the design a thousand times over the years, trying to change it just enough to make it feel like mine, but I can't seem to get it right."

"So, it's *your* wedding dress?"

"Yes. No. Maybe?" She groans and forgets herself long enough to drop her forehead on my chest. My pulse jumps, but just when I'm about to turn my head and inhale the fragrance of her hair, she straightens with a sigh. "It's the dress I imagine wearing if I had a different life. One where my mom stayed with me and my dad, and she gave me her gown because it meant something to our family. Hope and happiness. Contentment. Love." Violet gives me a sideways smile, and her voice turns quiet. "But who knows if I'll have that for myself?"

I cast an eye over the drawings as we sway together, noting that at least half of them have a groom's tux sketched in black and white alongside the gown, but it's the way she talks about her desires as if they're ridiculous that fires the muscles in my jaw.

"It's okay to want things for yourself. It's okay to put yourself first sometimes."

She shakes her head. "That's a nice idea for some, but it's

not realistic for most people. That's why they're called dreams. They're just pretty pictures in our heads. Things to distract us when real life becomes too hard—or too sad."

I frown over her head, thinking about my hockey career. "Dreams come true all the time."

"But at what cost?" she murmurs. "What would I need to give up to have the things I want?"

My frown deepens as I absently lead Violet in a small circle. What have *I* given up for the things *I* want? I've got no close friends. Never had a relationship last more than a year. I've got an incredible house that's been empty since the day I built it, and even though I lived there for more than a decade, I'm not leaving behind anyone special in Calgary. My family might love me, but Charlie barely tolerates me, and everyone who matters in hockey thinks I'm a cold, arrogant asshole.

Is there any price I haven't paid to be the best?

These aren't things I let myself think about, let alone catalog like a shopping list, and I remind myself that this conversation is about Violet, not me. I hate the way she dismisses her desires like they're not valid or worthy. Like *she's* not worthy. And I'm going to change it.

I shift my hand higher up her back just so I can brush my fingertips over the indent of her spine. "How do you feel about the dancing now?"

She inhales sharply at my touch. "A little better," she says breathily. "Thank you."

"Good."

Pressing her palm against my chest so she knows to keep it there, I let go of her hand and run my fingers up her arm. There are those goosebumps again, the same that erupted all over her body by the side of the pool. A pretty flush creeps above the neckline of her crew-neck tee, and I give her a tiny smile.

"I think making you blush might be my favorite thing to do, Wallflower."

A little noise, almost a whimper, sounds in her throat, and I gaze down at her, willing her to raise her head. She does, her focus sliding up my chest to my collarbone to my eyes, her pupils dilating before her focus falls to rest on my mouth.

"Chord?"

"Mm?"

I lean in at the same time she does and swallow as her eyes drift shut. Our mouths move closer so slowly, but I don't want to rush it. Closer... closer still... until her breath caresses my lips, and I let them part, ready to—

"Hello! Where is everyone?"

At the sound of Daisy shouting downstairs, Violet springs back and then spins away. I run a hand through my hair, confused and unbalanced. And unsatisfied.

My heart races, and I clear my throat to get Violet's attention, but she doesn't turn to look at me. With a tight, heavy stomach, I realize the moment has passed, and with my sister stomping around the house, there's no way to save it now.

"I'll tell Daisy you're here," I mutter before leaving the room.

I replay the almost-kiss as I pass my sister on the stairs, who's lugging up an armful of clothes still attached to hangers, as well as a small suitcase. I scan them, consider carrying them up for her, and then decide not to. This tiny blonde party girl is the reason my mouth isn't on Violet's this very minute, so I'm not feeling particularly helpful.

"Violet's in the last bedroom on the left," I tell Daisy before slipping past her.

"Thanks, bro."

I don't know where I'm headed until I reach the gym, but all I do is step into the room, look around, and walk straight back out again. I head to the living room at the front of the house instead and sit on the sofa, where I have the best view of the front door. I don't even know why I'm here other than I want to see Violet before she leaves. Get one last fix of her before I'm in this house all alone.

Something is sparking between us. Something alive and exciting and almost innocent. And after all of Violet's talk about dreams and desires and the price she'd have to pay to chase them, I'm determined to show her that when it comes to me, there's no cost attached to taking what she wants.

NINETEEN

Violet

DAY 18 AT SILVER LEAF... ONLY 68 TO GO

DAISY APPEARS AT MY BEDROOM door, drops a stack of dresses on the bed with a satisfied grunt, then drags a compact suitcase up onto the mattress next to them. She unzips it and flings the lid open, then considers her delivery with her hands on her hips.

"This is nearly everything I own. There's got to be something in here that'll make every man at The Tipple take one look at us then proceed to cry into his beer for the rest of the night."

I watch her. I hear her. But I don't *see* her. My heart beats too fast to be healthy, and my thoughts are two minutes in the past, frozen at the exact moment Chord was close enough that we breathed the same air. Warm, delicious air from warm, delicious lips that would have brushed mine if... if...

My eyes focus on Daisy, and with her halo of golden waves and impish grin, she's impossible to hate. Even if she did interrupt the most romantic moment of my life.

Her expression folds into concern as she comes over and clasps my hand. Tight. "Are you okay? Please don't tell me you've changed your mind. I've been looking forward to this all week."

I laugh a little. "No. I haven't changed my mind. I was just... thinking about other things."

Her mouth purses to one side as she arches one eyebrow. "Like my brother?"

Warmth tingles across my cheekbones. "Is it that obvious?"

"A little, but it's not your fault. He came flying down those stairs like I'd caught him doing something he shouldn't be doing." Her eyes twinkle as she drops her head to one side. "Something like his assistant?"

I stare at her blankly until her words make sense. "What? No! I mean, we were dancing, and he leaned in a little, and then..."

Daisy drops her chin expectantly. "And then... you kissed him?"

"No." The blush burns hotter as I admit, "Not yet."

I've grown to know Daisy a little better over the last week. She's brought Izzy around twice more since that afternoon on the back porch, and Chord's baby sister is so vibrant and sweet that I could listen to her talk for hours. She's shown me her tattoos, shared pictures of her hair in a hundred different shades of pink, purple, and blue, and told me about the locations she's been all over the world.

Daisy is my polar opposite and genuinely scandalized that I have no body art, have never dyed my hair, and have never traveled further than the west coast. And while I haven't been nearly as forthcoming with her about my own life—compared to Daisy's adventures, mine is a sad lot of *not much* and *not quite*—I *have* told her a little about Courtney and the boyfriend I had for five minutes in college. She declared me too good for both of them.

I like her, and I love the way she just assumes I know how to do... *this.* Talk. Listen. Relax. Enjoy her company. Share my secrets.

Daisy shakes her head and turns to the bed, tossing clothes left and right. "While I'd *love* to talk about my brother for hours"—the eye roll she throws my way underscores her sarcasm, just in case I missed it—"there are more important things to worry about right now, like what are we going to wear tonight?" She throws a shimmery silver skirt to one side with a sigh. "I've worn everything at least a dozen times, and none of it makes me feel good anymore. I need to go shopping."

I scan the mountain of fabrics without much hope, wondering if there's something—anything—I can salvage in my own wardrobe, but then a hint of deep purple catches my attention.

It's a tight-knit top, and it's got potential. I dig around and discover a pair of high-waisted shorts that match, then remember the belt I've got in my closet that'll bring the two pieces together.

Daisy has a pouch full of costume jewelry in her suitcase, and there are a couple of pieces in there that aren't too flashy, plus she's brought over three pairs of heels.

Within five minutes, I've laid a top-to-toe outfit on the bed. I take a step back and study it with satisfaction.

Daisy materializes at my side, fists on hips again, staring up at me like I've been hiding a secret. "Um... wow?" She runs a critical eye over the clothes and nods approvingly. "I never thought of matching these pieces before, but they look fantastic together. How did you know?"

I shrug to hide the fact that I'm pleased. For just a second, I'm tempted to confess the truth about my degree, but telling a second person in as many days about my failed fashion career is too much. "I just like clothes."

"Well, you're going to look hot in this."

"Oh, no." I consider the outfit again, this time imagining myself in it instead of Daisy as I planned, and an anxious chuckle bubbles out of me. "This is for you."

"No chance. This purple top has your name all over it, Violet. Literally. I'm sure you've got shoes you can wear."

I do have a pair of heeled ankle boots that might work, but that's beside the point. "The shorts are too short for me."

"Bullshit. You've got incredible legs, and you should show them off. Now that's settled, what can you do for me?"

Daisy has the bearing of a tiny drill sergeant, and I don't

like my chances of arguing with her, so I grimace and poke at the clothes again. Another five minutes later, and with a few carefully selected additions from my own wardrobe, I've put together a second outfit that Daisy approves with an enthusiastic round of applause.

"You're a natural at this," she marvels as she strips off her clothes, and the compliment puts little roses on my cheeks. "Now, the quicker we get dressed, the sooner we can do hair and makeup, and the faster I can get a drink in my hand and my booty on the dance floor."

As optimistic as Daisy is, it still takes an hour to get ready because she insists on curling my hair and giving me smokey eye makeup. When she lines my lips with a bright red pencil, I barely recognize myself, and when she asks if I have contact lenses, I begrudgingly put them in. A spritz of perfume later, and she's shooing me out the bedroom door.

Daisy leads the way down the stairs. "I hope you're ready for a big night, Vi. I plan to dance till Mona kicks us out."

"Mona?"

"The owner. You're going to love her. When I was growing up, Mona's daughter was my best friend. Plus, she makes the best white wine sangria you'll ever taste."

I tug at my shorts and think about meeting new people tonight, dancing with strangers, and having my first real cocktail. A wave of worry flips my stomach, and I glance back at the way we came. In another world, I'd be in bed with a microwave dinner, my headphones, and my sketchbook right now. Part of me yearns for what's safe and familiar. Another part—a more powerful part—is too exhilarated to turn back now.

We stop to collect our purses and do a final check of our faces in the hall mirror by the front door. Daisy suddenly jumps, letting out a little squeak and splaying her fingers over her chest.

"Jesus, Chord. Creepy much?"

She turns from her reflection and steps into the dark living room behind us. Only then do I notice the tall, broad shadow leaning on the back of the sofa. Daisy finds a switch and snaps on the light.

Chord's eyes are already on me, his gaze burning across my body. He starts at my white boots and sears a path up my bare legs, over my hips and chest, then reaches my mouth. When he meets my eyes, his fingers tighten where his hands rest on the back of the sofa, and his jaw hardens.

Things flutter inside me. At my throat. In my stomach. Between my thighs.

"Why the hell are you creeping around in the dark, weirdo?" Daisy turns back to the mirror and fluffs her shiny blonde waves. "I know you can afford the electricity bill."

Chord grunts and pushes upright, crossing those magnificent arms over his chest. "I wanted to make sure you know to call me if you need a ride." He pauses while his eyes trail over my outfit again. "Or maybe I'll go with you and keep you out of trouble."

Daisy snorts as she leans closer to the mirror and examines her makeup, running a finger under her bottom lip to catch a smudge. "This is a *girls'* night, Chord, and if there's any trouble, I'll take care of it."

"How are you getting to the bar?" Chord moves closer, and though he's talking to Daisy, his eyes don't leave me. "How will you get home?"

Daisy finds her phone, opens her ride share app in three efficient swipes, and flashes the screen—along with a triumphant grin—at Chord. "Our car will be here in ninety seconds. And like magic, we'll do the same thing at two a.m. when our feet are sore, and our heads are spinning, and we're begging for bacon sandwiches."

He's listening to Daisy, I'm sure of it, but Chord hasn't looked away from me. His focus is intense enough that my heart is a hummingbird in my chest.

I tear my eyes from him and pretend to check myself in the mirror, but all I can see is Chord in the reflection, his stormy blue eyes leaping at these tiny shorts that barely conceal my ass.

My fingers shake as I apply another coat of lip gloss. Chord watches the wand glide across my mouth, and my pulse jumps. I've never been this aware of my body. I'm nervous. I'm aroused.

"Fine." Chord finally graces Daisy with a scowl. "But you'll call if you need me."

"I will, big brother. Thank you."

He clears his throat and softens his tone. "And you, Violet? You've got my number."

I meet his stare in the mirror. "I do, and I will. Thank you."

He nods. "Good."

There's the sound of a car pulling up outside, and Daisy escapes through the door. But as I move to follow her, Chord stops me with a firm but gentle grip on my upper arm. His hand is large enough to wrap all the way around my slender bicep—a reminder of just how powerful this man is—but I love it, especially when his thumb brushes my skin in a reassuring sweep, sending goosebumps rippling in all directions.

"You look beautiful," he murmurs.

I lower my eyes. "Thank you."

Using his free hand, he tilts my chin upward, the way he did in my bedroom, and his mouth lifts to one side as he notes the heat seeping into my cheeks. "Eyes up, Wallflower. And keep them up."

I blink and meet his cobalt gaze, and he holds me there for the longest second before he nods once in approval.

"Have a good time tonight."

I laugh lightly. "I'll try. Your sister is much wilder than me. I'm not sure I'll keep up."

"I meant what I said." Chord lets me go and steps aside to let me pass, but he's still close enough to touch. To breathe in and consume. "Call me anytime."

"Thank you, but I'm sure I'll be fine. Who knows? I might be such a lousy dancer that we'll be home before midnight."

He doesn't laugh, and if anything, his expression grows more serious. "Promise me. I won't sleep otherwise."

The incessant fluttering grows intense, most noticeably between my legs. "Okay. I promise."

I slip through the door and into the porch-lit twilight, aware of his eyes on me as I walk to the neat white sedan waiting on the drive. Glancing back, I see that he watches from the doorway as I slip into the backseat next to Daisy, and he's still there when we turn onto the road and drive out of sight.

TWENTY

Chord

THIS HAS GOT TO BE the longest night of my life. I was an idiot to let Violet walk out of here looking like that, smelling like that, *feeling* like that. So freaking stupid to let her walk out of my house and not beg her to let me follow.

Now I can't shake the jealousy thinking about her dancing with another man. Touching another man. Letting another man touch her. *Fuck*.

Four hours after she left with Daisy—after a dinner I didn't taste, a workout I don't remember, and a movie I didn't understand—I'm in the living room again. Watching the clock. Remembering Violet's long, smooth legs in those shorts and boots. Ignoring the way my dick has been hard since I saw her mouth painted red. Reliving the feel of her warmth on my lips when she was close enough to share the same air. Kicking myself that I didn't kiss her when I had the chance.

I check the time. It's twenty minutes past midnight—only three minutes later than when I last looked. I turn on the television and surf mindlessly through the channels. At twenty-three minutes past twelve, I hit the remote to switch it off, drag a hand down my face, and drop my head back on the sofa. I don't remember ever being this way about a woman—agitated and needy. I should hate the way this feels. I should have the self-control to ignore it. But that would mean either ignoring Violet or categorizing her as one of those distractions I didn't want to deal with this year, and I can't do either of those things.

Another hour passes, and I'm half-asleep on the sofa, my arms crossed and bare feet propped up on the coffee table when a shrill ping from my phone startles me awake. I grope for it and rub my eyes at the notification lighting up the screen. It's a text from Violet.

Wallflower: I can't believe you saw me naked.

I jerk upright, heart thumping in my ears, and read the text again. It takes only a second for me to understand.

She's drunk.

And she's talking about the night I walked in on her wearing nothing but her panties.

I'd be a liar if I said I didn't think about that moment every night with my cock in my hand. Now I know Violet's been thinking about it too, and my dick pulses against my sweats.

Me: You weren't naked, Wallflower.
Me: You okay? Having a good time?

I stare at the screen long after the backlight dims and pray there's more to this conversation than one random text. She's out with Daisy, who certainly knows how to have a good time, and Violet's got the whole bar to entertain her, but she texted me. She wants to talk to *me*. It feels like winning the fucking lottery.

Wallflower: I'm having a fantastic time, but my feet hurt soooooo much... *sad face*
Wallflower: And I *was* naked! You saw my boobs! CHORD DAVENPORT SAW MY BOOBS!

I laugh in the darkness. Inebriated Violet is even more adorable than sober Violet.

Me: Too much dancing, eh? I guess there was nothing to worry about after all. You're a natural.

Wallflower: Don't change the subject, mister. Admit you saw me naked.

I hesitate, wondering how to play this. *Fuck it.*

Me: I'll admit I saw you in a sexy blue thong.

The three dots of her reply fade in and out, and I tap out another message while I wait.

Me: And I'll admit I haven't stopped thinking about it since.

The dots disappear, and so does my hard-on as I worry that I've gone too far, but then the phone vibrates with an incoming text, and her reply pops up on the screen.

Wallflower: I think about it too.
Wallflower: Can you come get me? Daisy is having fun, but I've had enough for one night.

I nearly break my stupid neck tripping out of my sweats, but in ninety seconds flat, I'm in jeans and a shirt and climbing behind the wheel of my truck.

I make it to The Slippery Tipple in less time than it should take me and throw the truck into one of the last available parking spaces. I rush through the overpacked lot, push open the bar's wide timber door, and scour the crowd for Violet like I didn't set eyes on her just six hours earlier.

She's perched on a stool at the bar, alone and stunning, her long legs crossed at the knees, her dark curls wilder than when she left the house and a hundred times sexier. So damn sexy I stop where I am just to drink in the sight of her.

There's an appealing flush in her cheeks, but it's a warm,

damp kind of glow—the kind that comes from too much booze, too much dancing, and too many bodies in one room. It's the kind that comes from exertion and depletion and gratification, and a vision of Violet swims through my head—she's naked, sprawled in my sheets, hair mussed and wild, and looking exactly like this. It's enough to keep my feet rooted to the floor in some kind of stupor, and I'm mesmerized when she brings a tumbler to her mouth, her lips softly greeting the rim of the cup, until...

Oh, Jesus. She's got a glass of Mona's notorious white wine sangria, and that stuff is strong enough to strip paint. Violet's texts suddenly make a lot more sense.

I'm already making my way over when a guy drops onto the stool next to her. He's in dirty jeans and a dusty t-shirt, boots caked with mud and looking like he drove here directly from the farm.

He tilts sloppily in Violet's direction. She leans away with a tight shake of her head, and it's clear to anyone watching that she's trying to rebuff the advances of some drunk asshole who can't take a fucking hint. But when he takes it as an invitation to move closer, I see red.

I shove my way through the crowd, my anger rising, and insert myself between Violet and the dickhead. Her face lights up when she sees the broad chest in her way belongs to me.

"You came," she says with a happy sigh and heavy eyelids that float closed before opening again.

I resist the urge to grin like a goofball—just. It's getting harder and harder not to smile for this woman. "I did."

The guy behind me pokes my shoulder—hard. "Hey! We was talking here."

I ignore the jab and the comment because that's infinitely smarter than turning and decking him, which is what I want to do.

"You said you've had enough?" I ask her. "Did you want me to take you home now, or can I tempt you into one more dance?"

"I—"

"I said, fuck off!"

The drunk falls against my back in what I assume is supposed to be a shove. I barely stumble, but I'm jostled enough to knock Violet's cocktail out of her hand. She squeals as the sticky drink pours down her chest, soaking the purple fabric of her top and coaxing her nipples to stiff peaks. I spare a moment to imagine licking the sweet liquid from her skin before I spin around and kick the legs of the farmer's stool out from under him. He drops to the floor with a string of curses, and I lean down to grab him by the shirt, accidentally tearing the fabric when I do.

"If you know what's good for you, you'll stay the fuck down there until I tell you it's okay to get up. Understood?"

"Hey, man." He's suddenly looking a lot more sober. "It's cool. I didn't know she was with you."

"Shouldn't matter that she's with me, asshole. When a woman tells you no, it means no. Now shut the fuck up and stay down on the floor where you belong."

I release his shirt with a warning shove that drives him to the peanut shell-strewn boards, then straighten. My gaze goes straight to Violet, my eyes running over her body to make sure every inch of her is safe. "You okay?"

She dabs at her wet skin with a soggy napkin, and her chestnut eyes are wide as she stares at me. "That was... That was..."

I pull a lock of her hair from where it's stuck to the moisture on her collarbone and tuck it behind her ear. "That was... what?"

Stupid? Overkill? A disgusting display of male ego that belongs on the ice?

"Hot," she answers with another breathy sigh.

My eyebrows shoot up, and fuck, there's a half-smile on my mouth and nothing I can do about it.

A loud, short cackle sounds from behind the bar, startling us both. It's Mona, and she spares me a wry smile before handing Violet a damp towel—and a fresh cup of sangria.

"You're not supposed to say that sort of thing out loud, honey. Sets us women back decades and gives idiot men ideas that only get 'em into trouble."

"Oh. Sorry." Violet shrugs a little but doesn't seem all that contrite, especially when she downs another long swallow of her drink.

I've known Mona all my life, and in those thirty-four years, she's always had hair so red it could only come from a bottle. Her heart-shaped face grows more attractive with every line, and her no-bullshit attitude makes her the perfect proprietor of The Slippery Tipple.

She rounds the counter to take a look at who I just dropped, then gives me an approving nod before she opens her arms and waves me in.

"Didn't know you were back in town, sweetheart. Come give me a little affection."

I scoop her into a hug. "Hey, Mona. You're looking good."

"You're a hot liar, is what you are." She chuckles. "But I'll take it."

She returns to the other side of the bar and picks up a dish towel to mop up the splashes of Violet's spilled cocktail. "Now, what brings you down here?" she asks before her eyes slide knowingly to Violet. "Let me guess. This sweet girl here, am I right?"

The jerk on the floor tries to crawl away slowly so I don't notice, so I do him a favor and pretend I don't. Violet watches my exchange with Mona with glassy eyes, and she probably won't remember a minute of this conversation.

Still, I clear my throat, tuck my chin, and lower my voice. "Yes, ma'am."

"Glad to hear it. I get the impression this one isn't used to the breakneck pace your sister likes to run at." Mona nods toward the dance floor, then shakes her head. "And she's not alone tonight, so it's even worse. No woman with half a brain would try and keep up with those two."

I follow her line of sight to where Daisy dances in the center of a pulsing crowd, not understanding what Mona means until I spy the woman next to her, similarly small and similarly gyrating, with a shock of red hair I'd recognize anywhere. Penelope. Mona's only daughter and Daisy's childhood best friend.

"Poppy's back?" I ask.

"Mm-hm." Mona shakes her head. "She strolled in here tonight like it hasn't been six years since she's been home, and I'm not convinced the girls didn't plan it this way, but they swear black and blue it was all a coincidence or fate or what-have-you. They've been drinking and dancing and flirting up a storm. Just like the old days." Mona sighs. "There'll be a fight or two before I close tonight. Mark my words."

My mouth twitches. "I'll give Dylan a call. Give him the heads up."

Mona flicks the towel at me. "You leave that poor boy alone. He did enough running around after those two when they were teenagers. Those girls are big enough now to figure it out for themselves."

I huff out a dry laugh as Mona rolls her eyes, an affectionate been-there-done-that twist to her lips. She moves along the bar to tend to her customers just as Violet moans and reaches down to tug at her boot.

My eyes travel the never-ending distance of smooth skin that is Violet's legs, from the hem on her shorts riding high on her thighs to the dainty ankle bones peeking out the top of her low-cut boots, and my cock twitches.

"Too much dancing, huh?"

She nods slowly and groans again. "Uh-huh."

I slip my hands under Violet's arms and hoist her onto the bar. She squeaks and steadies herself by flattening her hands to either side of her bare thighs as I lift one leg and slide off her boot, then do the same on the other. With the shoes clutched in one fist, I slide an arm around Violet's waist, the other under her knees, and swing her up against my chest.

She throws her arms around my neck, and when people start to look, she hides her face against my shoulder. Her hair smells so sweet, like peaches, and her warm breath against my skin, the soft hint of her tits against my chest, the way her fingers dig into the muscles... It's like freaking electricity zipping through my veins.

I pause to check the dance floor and spare a frown for my sister. She spots me and yanks Poppy's arm to get her attention, and they wave at me like drunk teenagers. Daisy goes so far as to give me two goofy thumbs up before Poppy points my way and yells something in her ear, making Daisy nod like a bobblehead.

Daisy and Poppy were hellcats as kids, and it doesn't look like much has changed. With the two of them back in town at the same time? God help Aster Springs.

Mona slides up beside me, one hand on her hip as she shakes her head at the girls.

"Can you take care of Daisy tonight, Mona?" I ask. "I need to know she's safe, and I don't want her disappearing with some loser."

Mona flaps her hands, her dish towel still gripped in one of them. "I was already planning on taking the three of them home after I closed the place. Don't worry about Daisy. She's safe with me, honey."

Satisfied that my sister will be all right with Mona, I stride through the bar with Violet cradled in my arms, her boots hanging from my fingers, and my eyes forward so I can't count how many cameras are pointed in our direction.

When I get to my truck, I juggle a little to open the passenger door. After tossing in Violet's boots, I ease her into the seat, then reach around to get her seatbelt.

My breath and hands are a little unsteady as I slip the strap across her body and snap the buckle into place, but then she stuns me by dancing her fingers into the edges of my hair. I freeze, still leaning over her, our faces so close.

"You look so cute in the backward baseball cap," she mumbles.

I choke out a laugh. "What?"

She gives me a silly smile and rubs the ends of my hair between her fingers. "Yeah. When you're all hot and sweaty, these little bits curl against your neck and around your ears, and it's so ridiculous how good-looking you are. And the hat just..." She closes her eyes and hums happily like she's thinking about it.

She likes the hat, huh? I tuck that piece of information away for another day, close the door and walk around to the driver's side, then get in, and start the engine.

Violet's eyes are closed, and I've decided she's fallen asleep when she asks, "Do you like me, Chord?"

My eyes slide from the dark road to her and back again. "I do."

"Like, *really* like me?"

There's nobody here except the two of us, and Violet's eyes are closed, so I let myself smile for real. "Yeah. Like, *really* like you."

"Oh."

Another long silence, and then, "But why?"

"Why... what?"

"*Why* do you like me? I don't understand." Her eyes ping open, and she pins me with a wild but glassy stare. "Is it because you saw my boobs?"

I laugh. "No, that's not it. You're smart. And strong. And thoughtful. You don't ask for anything, and you give so much. You put your family first. And you don't know how beautiful you are."

Her face screws up like she's trying to understand and failing, so I go a step further with a confession that's been teasing the edges of my mind, something I haven't had the guts to look at head-on yet.

"And I don't think you care that I'm a hockey player, or that I've got money. You don't care that I'm Chord Davenport, the star athlete." I risk another glance at her, and she appears to be deep in thought. "In fact, I think maybe this thing between you and me would be easier if I wasn't any of those things.

Maybe you'd like me, too, if I was just an ordinary guy."

"Yeah. You're right."

She nods the sluggish nod of a drunk person, and the fact that she agrees with me sends pain lancing through my chest. But then she goes on.

"I don't like Chord Davenport the hockey player," she mumbles with her eyes closed, head lolling against the headrest. "Or the rich man. Or the guy with the big house and the big attitude, and the cars and the pool and the gym and blah blah blah..."

She drags her eyes open, reaches over and pokes my cheek, pushing until my lips curl into a smile. "I like the Chord Davenport who wears jeans and boots covered in dirt. The one who makes his niece giggle and gives her great hugs. The Chord Davenport who scarfs down Pretzel M&M's when he thinks I'm not looking, fixes broken fences with his hands, saves me from scary mice, and is such a gentleman he's spent the last week pretending *he didn't see me naked*."

She whispers the last words, and I laugh again.

"And I like the way you make me *feel*," she adds with a cute little shiver.

"Oh, yeah?" I watch her from the corner of my eye. "And how's that?"

She closes her eyes again, slumps in her seat with a happy sigh, and replies like she's halfway to sleep. "Warm. Excited. Like my body is filled with butterflies and light."

I blink at the road and try not to let the whir of my heart

distract me from the task of driving us safely home.

"I like the way you see me," I say, not quite loud enough for her to hear. "I think I like that Chord Davenport too."

I pull the truck into the garage, get out, and walk around to open the door for Violet. She sits with her head rolled back, belt still on, and toes wiggling inside the sheer ankle socks she had on under her boots.

I wait for her to step out, but she stretches her arms toward me and twitches her fingers.

I give her an amused frown. "What?"

She thrusts her bottom lip into a pout as her perfect dark brows crinkle over brown puppy-dog eyes, and she makes grabby motions with her hands.

I dip my chin. "You want me to carry you?"

She nods pathetically. "My feet still hurt."

I shake my head with a smile and reach around to unbuckle her seatbelt. She throws her arms around my neck immediately and sticks like a barnacle as I straighten out of the car. It's so fucking cute that I hold her close and never want to let her go.

"I wonder what you're going to think about all this tomorrow," I mumble, breathing in the scent of her hair again as she nuzzles her cheek against my chest.

She sighs and relaxes in my arms. "I'm going to think this was the best night of my life."

TWENTY-ONE

Violet

DAY 19 AT SILVER LEAF... ONLY 67 TO GO

I WAKE UP WITH MY contact lenses in, a pounding in my skull, a mouth that feels stuffed with cotton, and a sinking sense of regret. About what, I'm not sure until I replay what I can remember about last night and, with sudden panic, realize I forgot to call my dad.

I *forgot*.

Nausea rolls high enough to tickle my throat, and I grope on the nightstand for my phone. It's dead, so I attach it to my charger, then fling back the bed covers with a groan. I want to stay in this bed forever. I also want water and painkillers and a shower and... something salty?

Once I've taken out my lenses, brushed my teeth, and scrubbed the makeup from my face, I step under the hot spray of the shower, sink down onto the tiled bench built into the wall, press my cheek against the cool side, and let the water loosen my muscles. When I feel half-human again and can open my eyes without squinting, I dry off and dress, pick up my phone, and dial Dad's number while heading downstairs.

The call goes through to his voicemail, and I stall on the second-last stair, refusing to give in to guilt and worry as I leave a message. I follow with two texts—one to Dad and another to Jennifer—then tuck the phone into my pocket.

The house is quiet. I slide across the floors on quiet feet to the gym, then the home office, around to both living rooms then out to the back porch, but Chord isn't here.

That odd hollow in my stomach gets deeper in his absence, but I don't know why. It's kind of like the feeling I get when I've forgotten to tick an item off a list or left a conversation unfinished. *Something* feels undone, and now that I know I'm in the house alone, the nagging sensation only gets stronger.

When my stomach growls—very specifically for something salty... and hot... and greasy—I head to the kitchen, phoning Dad again on the way. Again, he doesn't answer, and I coach my way out of panic.

I check the clock on the wall. It's mid-afternoon, and I can't believe I slept a solid twelve hours, but more concerning is that it's been nearly two days since I spoke to my dad.

I chew on my lip and try to think, but it's hard with the pounding in my head. Dad not answering his phone doesn't have to mean anything. He may be out getting groceries or watching television. Reading. Cooking. Walking. I'm not a bad daughter because I forgot to call him one time.

That's what I tell myself, but the gnawing in my gut makes it impossible to believe.

I maximize the ringer volume on my phone and set it face up on the kitchen counter, then go searching for food. Water. Aspirin.

Before I've taken three steps, I stall at the bright pink note stuck to the front of the refrigerator, covered with Chord's messy hand noting today's date and a list of things for me to do.

Oh, no. *Work*. I forgot about work. I need salt and painkillers and fluid in an IV before I can face my computer screen.

I pluck the paper from the fridge and scan the first item.

1. First things first. There's aspirin in the cabinet above the fridge.

Oh, thank God. I drop the note, find the bottle, and down two tablets with relief before scooping up the list from where it fell to the floor. My eyes snap straight to item two.

2. Read last night's text messages.

"Oh, no." The hollow, nagging something explodes into panic as I snatch up my phone and close my eyes, too afraid to look and see what I did last night. "No, no, no, no, *no*."

I open my text messages and my exchanges with Chord jump from the screen. I read them through twice, and then sink to my ass right there on the hardwood floor.

My first impulse is to be mortified—and I am; this is humiliating—but my heart races for another reason. I scroll back and stare at his texts until the words are burned into my brain. Chord thinks about me. Naked. No, sorry. He thinks about me only half-naked and wearing a flimsy blue thong.

I bite my lip as I rewrite every look he's given me, and now that I know he's been thinking bad thoughts, I squeeze my thighs together to ease the needy ache between my legs.

Recalling that there were more things written on his list, I latch onto the counter and haul myself up, find the note, and read the next line.

3. Check your voice messages.

My hand shakes from one-part nerves, ninety-nine-part anticipation as I swipe through to the correct screen. There's a voicemail from Chord waiting for me, with a time stamp at three-oh-seven a.m. I tap to listen, and a heavy breath bursts from my chest at the first spine-tingling note of his deep, smooth voice.

"Hey, Wallflower. I just carried you and your boots to bed. Laid you down. Tucked you in. Swept your hair from your face and turned out the light. We had an interesting conversation on the way home, and I don't want you to forget it, so here's what I told you. I like you—*really* like you—and you asked me why. It's because you're smart and sweet and selfless—all the things I'm not. You're sexy as hell, and I can't stop looking at you. Thinking about you. Remembering you—just like I said in those texts. You told me you like me, too. Not my career. Not my name. Not my car or my house or the parties I could take you to. Just me. And I know you were drunk when you said it, but I believed you, and I'm hoping you don't take it all back when you wake. Sleep tight, and I'll see you tomorrow."

I might be hyperventilating, but I still replay Chord's message three times more from start to finish. *You're smart and sweet and selfless. You're sexy as hell. You like me too. I believed you. Don't take it all back.*

Those words in that voice make me warm all over, and there's no way this moment can get any better, but I still want more when I check the list for the final item.

4. When you're ready, call the restaurant and tell them you're awake. I ordered one of everything on the menu, but if you're craving something special, they'll make it for you. I'm at the main house for Izzy's family game night, and if I'm not back before you go to bed tonight, I'll be counting the minutes until our drive tomorrow.

Tomorrow. I've arranged for Chord to inspect three potential apartments in San Francisco, and he wants me there with him—ostensibly to take notes. Once we're done, Chord needs to meet the manager at the facility where he leases storage to discuss whatever mysterious stuff he keeps in there, and then he has an appointment with his accountant.

He won't want me tagging along for either of those appointments, so I plan to sneak away and see my dad. I haven't mentioned this to either Dad or Chord in case I can't get away, but now that I've missed a nightly check-in and my father isn't answering my messages, I'll have to make it work.

I send Dad another text—a quick *Are you okay?* I try to keep it casual so he doesn't think I'm parenting him, but when he reacts to my text with a thumbs up, I sigh with relief. He's there. He's okay. And this time tomorrow, I can hug him and make sure with my own eyes that he's doing fine.

As the last tendril of worry unravels itself and the aspirin works its magic on the throbbing behind my eyes, I clutch Chord's list against my chest and call the restaurant. Within half an hour, the most divine-smelling delivery arrives on the doorstep, followed by black-clad waitstaff who set the table, arrange everything just right, and leave me with more food than I could possibly eat.

I load up a plate and consider taking it to my room where I can curl up and sketch while I eat, but the empty living room with its deep, soft sofa and wide-screen television is calling my name. So, I find an episode of *Gilmore Girls* and snuggle up with a blanket that I really don't need but can't resist.

Maybe I'm still under the influence of last night's alcohol, but I wonder if this is what it feels like to be a twenty-eight-year-old without worries. There's space in my chest that wasn't there before and a looseness in my muscles that I've never known.

As the *Gilmore Girls* intro sequence plays and I take the first bite of a meal good enough to make me moan, something like contentment settles over me like a second skin.

I know the real world is out there—my dad, my job, my boss, my loneliness, my lost potential—but I don't feel the weight of it right now. And it's all because of Chord.

He thinks about me. He thinks I'm sexy. He erased Courtney from my life, bought me pool floats and slow danced with me in my room, teased out my secrets when no one else could, answered my drunk call for help in the middle of the night, then left me adorable notes and voice messages and ordered me food.

These last few weeks have felt more real to me than my real life. This life has felt more like *mine*.

I pick up my phone and send him a short text, hoping that he senses how big these two little words are to me right now.

Me: Thank you.

My phone vibrates straightaway with his brief reply.

Chord: You're welcome.

Safe. That's the word. I feel *safe*. And I can't believe that of all the people in the world, Chord is the one to make me feel that way.

TWENTY-TWO

Chord

67 DAYS TILL HOCKEY SEASON

IZZY'S GAME NIGHT IS MORE like a game marathon. It kicks off at two p.m. and doesn't finish until well after dark and the little hostess has been asleep for a full twenty minutes.

We tried to wrap it up twice already—once as soon as her eyes started to drift closed, and again when she'd been out for thirty seconds. Both times, she shot upright like she'd been poked with a blunt stick and demanded another round of cards or charades or Monopoly. And we complied every time. Even Daisy, who looks like she'd rather have her head in a toilet.

I'm not the only one this little girl has wrapped around her finger.

We're in the living room in the main house—the house we all grew up in, and the house that Charlie, Dylan, and Izzy live in now. And Daisy, I suppose, though I'm not sure how long she plans to stay.

Not much about this place has changed in the last twenty years. The polished oak furniture has been wearing divots in the carpet since before I was born, and the gray wool is clean but old. Mom's first-edition books, vintage teacups, and family photographs are still on the shelves. Dad's armchair still sits empty.

When I walked in here today for the first time in years, Charlie, Finn, Dylan, and Daisy were already sprawled out in the spots they'd claimed twenty-plus years ago, and it was like I'd stepped out of a time machine. Forgotten memories and old grief sapped the oxygen from the room before a wistful warmth burst inside my chest, carrying with it a simple one-word thought. *Home.*

That was hours ago, and it's been dark outside for an hour by the time Dylan scoops Izzy off the sofa. Her tiny frame is lost in a cloud of lime green tulle, her feet are stuffed into a pair of fluffy white bunny slippers, and her long, dark plait dangles over the curve of Dylan's forearm.

"Do you need a hand?" I ask as I leave my seat on the rug and get to my feet.

"Nah. We're fine. I'll take her to bed and come back to help you guys clean up."

"I've got it." Charlie leaps from her place at the end of the sofa, then collects a half-empty bowl of popcorn in one hand and a couple of empty tumblers in the other. "You have an early start at the restaurant tomorrow. Take care of Izzy, then head to bed yourself."

Dylan looks around the room. "Are you sure?"

He's got to be thinking the same thing I am. It looks like a glitter bomb has gone off in here. Izzy—with Finn as her accomplice—decorated the place with balloons, streamers, and confetti in six shades of pink. Tidying up will take forever.

"I'm sure." Charlie waves him off and rounds the sofa, nudging a dozing Daisy as she passes. "Daze will help me."

Dylan snorts as he disappears up the stairs, and Daisy rolls over, turns her back to the room, and makes a whining sound. She's so freaking hungover. It's hilarious.

"*Daze* is in too much pain to do anything," she moans, wriggling around like she can't get comfortable, then reaching behind her to switch off the lamp on the side table. "There." She curls in on herself with a satisfied smile. "That's better."

Charlie rolls her eyes. "Finn?"

Finn's slouched in an armchair and scrolling through something on his phone, which he immediately tucks away before bounding to his feet. He gives Charlie a kiss on the cheek and is halfway to the door when he replies, "Can't. Leave it, and I'll do it tomorrow."

Charlie stares at the front door as it swings closed behind our brother.

"Fine," she mutters. "I'll do it myself."

Charlie disappears into the hallway, and I snatch up a stack of plates and a handful of dirty napkins before following. She's at the sink when I enter the old but tidy kitchen, so I set the dirty dishes in the soapy suds and step back.

"Thanks," she mutters under her breath.

"No problem."

"You don't need to hang around, you know." Charlie yanks open the dishwasher and starts loading it. "I can clean up. I'm sure you've got things you need to do tonight."

I check my watch. It's nearly ten o'clock. If I leave now, I might get a moment with Violet before she goes to bed.

I imagine her face when she found my note on the fridge. When she read our texts, and then when she listened to my voice message.

I realized last night that when it comes to Violet, I've given up any hope of stone-cold self-control, and I don't even care. I like who I am with her. She reminds me of the guy I used to be. A younger Chord who trusted people and had fun and loved without regret. Before money and fame and betrayal changed things.

But as much as I miss her tonight, Violet is the reason I *don't* rush back to my house. These past few weeks on the ranch have made me more certain than ever that this is where I want to be when I retire. And while I don't need Charlie's permission to do it, I don't want to move back while there's this tension between us. I need to fix whatever's broken between my sister and me. I want to do better. I want to *be* better.

"I don't mind hanging around a bit longer," I tell her.

She shrugs but doesn't look my way. "Whatever you want."

I go back and forth between the living room and the kitchen, quietly clearing away all evidence of game night.

There's not much I can do about the confetti without pulling out the vacuum cleaner, but I sneak upstairs with the balloons and quietly load them into Izzy's room, hoping it'll be a fun surprise for her when she wakes.

I return to the kitchen one last time, lifting the last bowl to my mouth and tipping the final crumbs of the Pretzel M&M's onto my tongue. I offer the empty dish to Charlie, who accepts it with a tiny smile and a shake of her head before stowing it in the dishwasher. "I can't believe those are still your favorite."

I lean back on the counter and cross my arms over my chest, my legs at the ankles. "I can't believe you still only eat plain."

She shrugs and programs the machine, still finding excuses not to look at me. "Original. Classic. Dependable."

I nod. "Respectable."

"Exactly."

There's an awkward silence, and I'm looking for the right words to start a meaningful conversation when Charlie speaks first.

"I guess I'll call it a night, then." She dries her hands on a dish towel and tosses it on the counter.

"Wait."

She pauses with her body half turned from me, then shifts around and lifts her chin, finally meeting my eyes.

I take a long breath. I'm not an anxious person. I'm an arrogant asshole with too much money and a reputation

that encourages people to make my life easy, but Charlie...
Charlie makes me nervous.

"I'm looking at apartments in the city tomorrow. Three of
them to start. I'm pretty sure one of them will be good enough
for the season, so I'll be out of your hair come September."

"Oh." Charlie shifts her feet and stares at her bare toes as
they brush along the smooth, pale, hardwood floor. "Good.
I mean, you know. Good for you."

"Yeah." I rub the back of my neck. "But Charlie..."

Her arms snake across her chest, and she lifts her chin like
she's anticipating a fight.

"I can't play forever, and I reckon I've got two good years
left in me—tops. I built my house here for a reason, and that
reason was my retirement. You have to know I plan to come
home once I'm done with hockey."

Her eyes flash, and her spine straightens. "You can't take
this place from me. I won't let you."

I frown and wait for my brain to catch up, but a few
moments later, I'm still not sure what this is about.

"I don't want to take Silver Leaf from you," I reply.
"I want to be part of it with you. I want to make a life here.
I want to help you."

She chokes back a bitter laugh. "Because I need your help?
I'm doing such a lousy job as CEO that we need you to swoop
in and save it?"

"No." I push off the counter, taking a step closer as she
takes a step back. "Because this is my home. This is where

I want to be. And maybe if you weren't carrying so much of the burden, the ranch could grow a little."

She shakes her head and narrows her eyes. "I knew it."

"Knew what? This ranch is too much for one person to manage alone. Mom and Dad couldn't have done it without each other, and Dad couldn't have done it without you after Mom died. It's not a failure to admit that running a business this complex requires more than one person doing all the management stuff."

"I've got Dylan—"

"Who runs the restaurant and the event catering. Not to mention, he's raising a little girl all by himself. He does enough."

Charlie blinks. She knows I'm right. She's also not going to admit it. "Daisy just got back."

"And I'm sure she'll be a big help, but once we've got horses again, it'll be a full-time job caring for them and running the trail rides. Assuming she sticks around, that is."

"Finn's not going anywhere."

That's news to me—good news—but not good enough to win Charlie the argument. Finn's an asset to the ranch, but he's not about to pitch in with inventory or account management or employee relations or business development. Finn isn't a leader, and Charlie knows that as well as I do.

"And what's he going to do?" I ask.

"I don't know. I'll find him something."

"So why can't you find something for me, too?"

Charlie throws up her hands. "Oh, my God, Chord. Are you serious? Fine. I need someone to pull weeds in the—"

"Charlotte."

"What?"

I inhale deeply and release a loud, measured exhale. Charlie might be our CEO, and our siblings might make their own contributions to operations, but the ranch has a solid team behind it, and most of our employees have been with us long enough to remember Mom and Dad. Oscar—our lead winemaker. Lillian—who manages hospitality and accommodations. Bryan—head of the farm team and seasonal hires. Sonya—the tasting room manager.

On top of that, we run an organic operation. Weeds are taken care of by a flock of freaking sheep.

"I'm coming home, Charlie, whether you like it or not, but I'd rather do it with your blessing. Let me be someone you can rely on. Someone who can share the load."

Charlie's eyes flash with rage. "Where were you when Mom died, and Dad needed someone to *share the load*?"

I can't believe she's asking me this. I thought she understood.

"That was ten years ago. I was at the top of my game in Tampa. I couldn't just walk away."

"And where were you two years later when Dad passed?"

"The trade with Calgary was too fresh. You know that."

"And when Isobel was born, and I was here without you, without Finn, without Daisy, and almost without Dylan because he was struggling to figure out how to be a single father—where were you then?"

I grit my teeth. "I can't just walk away from my life, Charlotte. I've worked as hard for my career as you have for yours. Sacrificed just as much. And I've tried to give you money over and over and *over* again, but you refuse to take it."

She scoffs. "You want me to take your money to soothe your guilty conscience."

I blink back the hurt. "That's not fair."

Charlie rolls her lips and pales a little. "Maybe not, but life hasn't been fair to me either. It's been hard, and I've worked through it all. Alone—and fine, without much to show for it—but it's all I've got. And at least you go to sleep at night knowing you made Mom and Dad proud."

Tears spring up in her bright blue eyes, and my throat grows tight. I raise a hand in her direction. "Charlie—"

"Forget it." She raises her palms to fend me off. "I can't stop you from coming home. I can't stop you from loading your money into this place and *saving* it from me, but I won't tell you it's okay. It won't erase all the years you weren't here. I'm not Mom or Dad. You don't get a free pass. Not this time."

I only notice she's still in her Silver Leaf uniform—black shirt, dark jeans, boots—as I watch her stride from the room and rush up the stairs.

I stare into nothing and think about what she said. Did I try to give Charlie money because I felt guilty about not being here? Maybe... but it just never felt that nuanced to me.

My family had a problem, it caused pain for the people I loved, and money could fix it. *I* could fix it. I didn't give any thought to what offers of cash would look like to Charlie or what she thought they meant. I didn't think I had to. My motivations weren't that complicated.

I run a frustrated hand through my hair. I've screwed up a lot of things in my life—my career, my captaincy, my romantic relationships, my family—but for the first time in as long as I can remember, the weight of each of those things doesn't tip the scales the way they used to.

I think about Violet and the things she's given up for her father. I don't agree with it, I don't approve of it, but right now, I'm closer to understanding it.

TWENTY-THREE

Violet

DAY 20 AT SILVER LEAF... ONLY 66 TO GO

CHORD IS UNUSUALLY QUIET ON our trip to San Francisco. It's not the cold, intimidating silence that made him famous. It's an introspective kind of quiet like he's lost in his own thoughts. And it makes me anxious.

I've told myself his behavior is not about me at least a dozen times over the last five hours. In the car on the drive to San Francisco. When we inspected the first apartment on my list of potential new homes. And the second. And the third. But now, as we stand in silence on the street outside the building of Potential New Home Number Three, I've swung back to believing that he's having second thoughts about me. About us.

He's staring at his phone like he's forgotten I'm here, and all I want is to run away from the awkward humiliation and hug my dad.

After a long moment passes without Chord looking up, I rock forward on my toes and try a tight, uncertain smile. "So, what did you think of this one?"

"Hm?" He frowns at his phone before locking the screen and stowing it in his pocket. He glances up at the residential building behind us, squinting toward the wall of glass on the penthouse floor. "It's nice. Definitely the largest of the three we've seen today. What do you think?"

"Me?" This is the first time he's asked for my opinion, and I'm not sure what to say. Compared to my cramped, aging apartment, all three properties are palatial. "Oh. Um, I like them all."

Chord crosses his arms, and for the first time today, a little life warms his blue eyes. The flutter of anxiety in my middle swirls into butterflies.

"But if you had to choose...?" he leads.

I frown. "If I had to choose... what?"

His mouth ticks up. "Which would it be?"

I take a moment to consider it. He's asking for professional advice from his personal assistant, so I forget about my own preferences and think about it from his point of view.

"Well, apartment number three *is* the largest," I reason out loud. "It's the most modern, and it's the closest to the arena. It has great security, and it's the most expensive, which means it's probably the best... right?"

Chord shrugs. "Probably, but that's not what I asked. Out of the three we saw today, where would *you* choose to live?"

"Me?"

At his amused nod, I bite my lip and recall the first place we saw. It was the smallest by far, but it had the most warmth with its cream-colored walls and living room with built-in bookcases and wood-burning fireplace, vintage fittings everywhere, exquisite natural light, and a beautiful view over a park.

Chord rolls his lips against a smile. "It's apartment number one, isn't it?"

I press a palm to the heat on my face. "Am I that obvious?"

"No. I'm just getting better at reading you."

Out of nowhere, Chord takes my hand, threading his thick, callused fingers through mine and latching on tight. Tiny, teeming, white-hot sparks burst through my body, not only at his touch but at being touched like this in public. Because people are *looking*.

Wherever he goes, people look at Chord. They may or may not know he's the best hockey player of his generation, but they do know a beautiful face when they see one. And it's his energy. His magnetism. He demands attention. It's easy to forget that when it's just the two of us alone in his house, or when we're with Daisy and Izzy. His family doesn't look at Chord the way strangers do.

He tugs me in the direction of the sports car he chose for the drive from Silver Leaf and opens the passenger side door to usher me in.

I glance at the vacant seat. I so badly want to do as he says and get in, but I also want to see my dad. This was the moment in today's itinerary I was supposed to slip away.

"Aren't you going to that appointment at the warehouse?" I ask. "I thought I might—"

"Yes, and I'd like you to come with me." He sets a soft hand on the small of my back and guides me closer to the car. The next thing I know, I'm buckling my seatbelt and watching Chord round the hood.

I'm not prepared for this. Chord has been cagey about his storage facility on the three occasions I was forced to mention it. My empty stomach is now a little queasy with a mix of anticipation and reluctance. I haven't eaten since breakfast, and it's already mid-afternoon, but I didn't worry about lunch as I had plans to pick up a box of Dad's favorite pastries on my way over to our apartment.

Chord slides behind the wheel and starts the engine.

"Are you sure you want me to go with you?" I ask. "I don't want to intrude."

My stomach growls, and I blush as Chord's mouth quirks to one side.

"I'm sure," he says. "And you're not intruding. In fact, I need your help with something. But first, let's get you something to eat."

He checks his blind spot, pulls out into the street, and then reaches across the center console to find my hand again. He collects my fingers and settles them on his knee, and all I can do is stare at the way we fit so perfectly together.

"I've been distracted today," Chord says as his thumb caresses the back of my hand. "I apologize for that, but if you can tolerate me for the rest of the afternoon, I want to explain."

He pulls to a stop at the next set of lights, where he throws me a sideways look that makes me melt. Literally. I squeeze my thighs together, and his eyes fall to my lap like he knows why. Heat rises from my core to paint my chest and collarbone.

"Okay." My breath sounds loud in my ears. "I can go with you."

Chord stops at a local sandwich shop on the way, where he buys us both salads and green juices to go. While we stand at the counter and wait for our food, I watch a couple of young kids jostle each other in the corner, whispering and pointing at Chord.

He notices it, too, because as soon as he has our lunches in his hand, he walks toward them, sets the food on a table, and says hello. He's surprisingly warm and friendly. A couple of selfies and signed t-shirts later, we're back in the car and speeding toward our appointment.

"That was nice of you," I say as I spoon the delicious cold chicken and couscous salad into my mouth.

"I like kids," Chord says. "Nine times out of ten, they're not assholes."

I lift one brow. "Only nine times?"

Chord huffs out a dry chuckle. "There's always one."

He digs his fork into the open takeout box he's wedged between his thick thighs. I wonder what it would feel like to be in that position—pinned between his hard, muscled legs, and mere inches away from the bulge behind his fly.

Hello, new low. I'm jealous of a cold chicken salad.

We reach the storage center, pull into a parking space, and Chord collects the takeout containers to deposit in the nearest trash can. I watch with admiring amusement as he uses a paper napkin to trap the crumbs we drop. He's a perfectionist, this man. In all areas of his life. And I like that.

He holds my hand again as we approach the entrance, pulling me against his body like we're a couple. I shift my old satchel so it's not hanging between us and shamelessly press myself against his warmth.

The heat from his arm seeps through the fabric of the oversized blazer I wore today—this trip to the city gave me an excuse to revisit my old wardrobe—and a quick glance up at the smug half-twist on his mouth tells me he knows what I'm doing.

It's so unlike me to be this bold, and maybe I should put a little distance between us, but it's like whatever fog he was under this morning has lifted and taken my reservations with it. Chord's cocky but silent acknowledgment of my interest makes me feel safe in brand new ways.

It also turns me on.

Chord approaches the reception desk and introduces himself, and within minutes the facilities manager leads us through a maze of buildings to the warehouse leased under Chord's name. He holds my hand the entire time, and when we arrive, the manager opens the door for us and steps back.

Chord leads me through, flicks on the light switch, and as the fluorescent bars buzz to life overhead, I look up and around and gasp.

"Chord." I reach up and squeeze his bicep, so distracted by what I see that I don't even know I've done it until I register the hard, glorious muscle under my fingers. I jerk my hand away. "There must be thousands of bottles of wine here. More. What is this? What are they for?"

Chord rubs the back of his neck with his free hand and turns to the warehouse manager. "Could you leave us, please? I'll come by your office when we're done to finalize the paperwork."

The manager hands Chord the keys. "Of course. Take your time."

When we're alone, Chord moves further into the cavernous space, towing me along with him. The room is fitted out with tall, wide shelves that span its full length, and there are six aisles of them. As I draw close enough to a shelf to make out the labels on the individual wine bottles, I frown at the image printed on a yellowing white square. It's a Silver Leaf Ranch & Vineyard bottle of pinot noir and the vintage is seven years old. There's an identical bottle next to it, and another next to that. There are even more above and behind. There's a whole section of the same bottle set on sleek, sturdy wine racks that look purpose-built for this space.

I walk a little further as Chord follows, silently watching me, and stop in front of a batch of Silver Leaf chardonnay. It's a year younger than the pinot next to it.

Chord runs his thumb over a label and then drops his hand. "I haven't told you much about the ranch, have I? What we do now? What we used to do? How much trouble it's in?"

I grimace with guilt. "Daisy filled me in on some of it. I hope that's okay."

Chord's brows lift before he rolls his eyes, but there's an affectionate tilt on his perfect lips. "Of course she did. And yes, it's okay. She has as much right to talk about it as anyone, and at least she had the good sense to talk to you instead of someone else. So, you know that the ranch isn't doing as well as it should."

"Daisy said as much. She told me your mom used to run trail rides, and there were plans for a spa."

We stroll up and down the aisles of wine, Chord checking random bottles as we pass. "Yep. And it's the end of July. The height of wedding season in this part of California. Do you know how many weddings we've got booked this summer?"

I've noticed none since I arrived, and I've been on the ranch for three weeks. It seems cruel to point that out, but my silence speaks volumes.

"Exactly," Chord says. "There was one earlier in the month, and there's another in August, but it's not enough. Once upon a time, we were turning couples away three years in advance. But we haven't had the funds to improve our facilities in years, and people are choosing more modern venues."

"But what about the restaurant? Daisy said it does well."

"It does all right. Dylan's a talented chef."

"And the weekend tourists?"

"They help," Chord agrees.

"And then there's that big catering client. The one that orders all that wine every month."

Chord stops and turns to face me, his eyes burning into mine as he tries to tell me something without words. It takes a moment, but when understanding dawns, my mouth drops open, and I look around the warehouse again, more in awe than before.

"*You're* the big catering client?" I whisper. "You bought all this wine from your own business?"

Chord lets out a resigned sigh and looks up at the shelves of wine over our heads. "Yep. Every month for ten years. And I think I fucked up."

"What?" I frown and take hold of his hand, tugging until he looks at me. "What do you mean?"

"Nobody knows about this. Not my brothers. Not Daisy. And not—"

"*Charlie.*"

A loaded breath hisses from my puffed-up cheeks as I scan the room, trying without success to calculate how many bottles there are and the value of each one. How much money has Chord spent over the last ten years keeping his family's business afloat? It's got to be tens of thousands of dollars. Hundreds of thousands. Quite possibly a million. And his family knows nothing about it.

"Oh, my," I mutter.

Chord's rich chuckle startles me, but not nearly so much as the broad grin on his gorgeous face. I look up at him, stunned at how beautiful this man is when he's happy. I get the distinct impression that he's laughing at me, and maybe I should be offended, but I'm not. I can't be. Not if I've done something to make him smile like this.

The electric heat of his touch dulls against the nuclear warmth exploding inside my chest.

"*Oh, my*?" Chord laughs again. "That's a pretty mild curse for the fact that I've been lying to my family for a decade and given them three million dollars against their will. No, against their express wishes. Charlie's going to cut off my appendages one by one when I tell her."

Three million dollars? Chord spent a fortune to stop his family's business from going under because they were too proud to accept his help. My dad is the most important thing in my world—if three million dollars could solve his problems, I'd beg, borrow, and steal to give it to him—so Chord's gesture quite literally takes my breath away.

But I can't see how a secret this big can be kept forever, and it sounds like he wants to confess the truth to his siblings, but why now? And why am I the first person he's told?

"Chord, I'm confused." I roll my lips and search for a polite way to ask what I want to know. "Why did you bring me here? What does any of this have to do with me?"

"I had a… conversation with Charlie last night. I said some things. She said some things. Not many of them felt good.

I've spent every minute since trying to see this situation from her perspective."

He grimaces and rubs the back of his neck. "Hockey has been my life since I was a kid, and it was always going to be that way until I had to retire. So, I left Silver Leaf to Charlie and Dylan, knowing I'd come back when the time was right—for me. I never thought about how that might hurt my family. She accused me of trying to give her money to soothe a guilty conscience. Like I've been trying to buy my way back into the family, and the truth is, I never gave it that much thought."

My brow creases with puzzlement, and Chord shakes his head with a self-mocking smirk. "You were thinking for a minute there that all this wine made me some sort of selfless hero, right? I'm not. I've been too self-absorbed to lose sleep about not being on the ranch when my family needed me. It's just the way things had to be. I knew the business was struggling, and my money was the fastest way to solve the problem. It was the only way I ever thought to help."

"Oh, Chord."

I drop my eyes to hide my dismay, but Chord lifts my face with his fingers on my chin. "I know it was wrong, and Charlie said something last night that turned everything on its head. *'At least you know you made Mom and Dad proud,'* she told me, and it cut like a skate to the wrist. That's all she's been trying to do—make our parents proud on her own terms, in her own way, off of her own power. And I get that. I get that so much."

He glances around at the wine. "I've undermined her by lying about the money all this time, and I'm an idiot for not taking the time to ask questions sooner. To make the effort to understand."

His throat bobs in a swallow, and I bite the inside of my cheek as I watch the subtle changes in his expression. There's doubt and regret, and I sense that he's not used to either.

"You did this because you love her," I tell him. "You love your family, and you love the ranch. This was the way you knew to show it."

Chord stares at me for a moment before pulling me against his chest and wrapping his arms around me. I loop my arms around his waist as he sets his chin on my head and sighs. With my cheek against his chest, I breathe him in and close my eyes. This moment—our first real embrace—will stay with me forever.

"Why are you showing me this, Chord?" I ask. "What can I do?"

Chord hesitates before he replies. "The way you talk about your dad and the sacrifices you've made to care for him in real, honest ways... It's made me think about things differently. Made me hope that things could be different with Charlie and me."

Real, honest ways. Something about those words makes my throat tighten. I love my dad, and I'd do anything for him—including hiding my truth to protect him.

I've never told him I hate my career. I've never confessed how desperately I want to quit every job I've ever had so

I could intern with design houses the way my peers did. He doesn't know that I dream about moving to Paris or London and living on my own. Dad doesn't know that every time I sketch Mom's dress, I imagine myself wearing it and living a life that feels impossible. One where I don't have to choose between duty and dreams. One where love lasts forever.

I breathe slowly through a pang of sadness. Dad has always supported my dreams to design. I could have told him all my hopes and fears years ago. My salary and health insurance and his unemployment and depression... None of that should have held me back. My sense of responsibility got in my way because I let it.

The truth hits me square in the chest, but I can't examine it too closely right now. Chord is obviously on the cusp of a profound personal discovery, and I want to be present for him.

"So, what do you want to do?" I ask.

"I need to tell Charlie the truth, and I need to let her stand on her own two feet. And then, I have to hope that by putting it all on the table and removing any tension between us, she'll trust me enough to ask for help. When it happens, I need to show up. No questions, no excuses. I'll be there."

He sounds so confident, with the tone of a man who makes a plan, executes it well, and always achieves his goal. I have no doubt that he'll make it happen because when has the world ever told Chord Davenport *no*?

My thoughts trail away as I become hyper-aware of the way Chord grows still. His fingers ghost over my body until he finds his favored place on my chin, but when he tips up my face, it's different than all the other times before. His blue eyes are warm with desire, his throat bobs in a deep swallow, and as his gaze falls to my mouth, he moves a little closer. This time, I *know* he's going to kiss me.

My hands find their way into his hair. "Chord?" I whisper. Like a promise. Like a prayer.

The moment between—the hover, the hesitation—is divine and endless until the instant his lips meet mine. And then... *fireworks*.

It's been a long time since I've kissed anyone, but Chord takes the lead. He cradles my head, angling me so he can explore my mouth the way he wants to before he pulls back and brushes his lips, so warm and gentle, back and forth against mine. He teases my mouth open again with a hint of his tongue that I desperately chase with my own. I feel the grin on his mouth, and it snaps the last thread of reserve I have in me.

I press myself against his chest and grip his t-shirt with two fists as our kiss turns frantic. His lips tug at mine, and his tongue sweeps a little deeper, inviting me to reciprocate. And I do. I kiss him until I'm breathless and can barely stand, gripping his shirt like it's the only thing holding me up.

Oh, God. I could kiss him like this forever.

Chord's the first one to pull away, though he continues to cradle my face. "Violet James," he says, thumbs caressing my cheekbones as he stares into my eyes. "Wallflower. What the hell have you done to me?"

"I haven't done any—"

"Yes. You have." He drops his forehead to mine and closes his eyes. "I don't know how you do it, Wallflower, but you make me want to be a better man."

TWENTY-FOUR

Chord

66 DAYS TILL HOCKEY SEASON

WE FINISH AT THE WAREHOUSE later than expected, so I reschedule the appointment with my accountant, and we head back to the ranch earlier than planned. I hold Violet's hand every single second of the drive home, and we spend most of it talking about how I'm going to tell Charlie—and everyone else—about the wine.

Violet makes smart, sensitive suggestions, and we volley a few ideas back and forth, but the further we drive from the city, the more I get the sense something is off. Violet grows quiet and reflective. Withdrawn. She carries her phone in the hand not holding mine and checks it constantly, and her knees bounce in a way I've come to recognize as nerves.

She was into the kiss. I know it. We were both into it and fuck if it wasn't the best kiss of my life. She keeps glancing at our intertwined fingers with a small, disbelieving smile, tracing her thumb over the blue veins of my hand in a way that makes it difficult to swallow. But when she isn't doing that or staring at her phone, she's gazing out her window. And when our conversation fades away to nothing, I know something isn't right.

I pull the sports car into the garage, shut off the engine, and get out, but before I can round the hood to open Violet's door, she's already out and inside the house.

"Are you hungry?" I ask as I follow her down the hall from the garage. "We could go to The Hill for dinner or find somewhere in town?"

Our first official date. I like the sound of that.

"Um." She stops in the kitchen and looks around like she's searching for an exit. "I'm sorry. What?"

I'm trying to understand and not worry, but the change in her is odd.

"Are you hungry?" I ask again. "Do you want to change and—"

"Oh, no. Thank you." She nibbles her lip, checks her phone, and glances toward the hallway, then the stairs. "I'm a little tired, so I'm just going to go to my room. I'll, uh... I'll see you later?"

I don't get a chance to reply before she's gone.

She's tired?

I stand there, staring at the now-empty staircase. I didn't get a *tired* vibe from her. I got nervous and uncertain, maybe a little uneasy...

Oh, shit. Does Violet think I expect to sleep with her tonight? I pray that's not the case, and I rack my brain for another explanation, but this is the only thing that makes sense. The closer we came to the ranch—to this house and to nightfall and the possibility of taking our kiss to the next level—the more introspective she grew.

I would gladly drop to my knees right now and show that woman what she does to me. I would bury my head between those smooth thighs, palm her heavy breasts, and make her scream my name so loud everyone within a five-mile radius would hear the echo for days. But I was pretty fucking happy with her hand in mine today. Pretty fucking pleased with the way she kissed me.

It took me three weeks to get over myself enough to get this far, and when a little voice reminds me that my world needs to be all about hockey and women are distractions I can't afford, I shut it down. Hard.

Violet isn't a fucking *distraction*. She's so much more than that. And if she wants to go slow, that's what we'll do.

I deliberate in the kitchen for too long, pacing and scowling at the clock, before I head to the gym and lift weights to pass the time. I shower. I call Dylan to arrange for food to be delivered when dinner service starts.

When enough hours pass that the sun is almost set and Violet still hasn't emerged, I'm agitated enough that I climb the stairs and ease my way down the hallway, then hover outside her bedroom door. It's closed, and because this is as far as my genius plan went, I'm trying to decide what to do next when I hear a muffled sound through the timber.

I freeze, waiting for another, going so far as to lean close enough that the shell of my ear brushes the door, and I hear it again. There's no mistaking it now.

Violet's crying.

And then I'm knocking. And opening the door. And pushing my way in without an invitation because Violet is crying, and every cell in my body needs to know why so I can make it better.

"Wallflower?"

The light in Violet's room is a mix of pinkish gold and shadow. She sits on the bed, wet hair falling around her face and down her back and leaving damp circles on her silky dark pink camisole. The bed linens cover her bottom half in a way that gives me a glimpse of bare thighs underneath, her headphones lay discarded next to her glasses, and her sketchbook with pencils and shavings has been pushed to the foot of the bed.

Violet dashes at her cheeks, then tugs at the sheets to make sure she's covered. "Oh, hey."

"Hey." I take another step into the room. "You're crying."

Okay, so I'm not the most tactful person on Earth, but the sooner she tells me what's wrong, the sooner I can fix it.

"No." She offers me a watery smile as tears spill down her cheeks. "I'm fine."

"You're not fine. Talk to me."

I take another step closer just as the front doorbell rings. It'll be our dinner, and I glance over my shoulder.

"Are you hungry?" I ask.

Violet chuckles under her breath. "Actually... yes. A little."

My relief at being able to do this one small thing for her is disproportionately enormous. I hold up a single finger and back up a couple of steps. "Don't move, okay? I'll be right back."

I race downstairs to collect the food from the server and decline his offer to set the table and plate up. Instead, I grab a bottle of wine and two glasses from the kitchen, stuff a handful of cutlery and napkins in with the takeout containers, and hurry back to Violet's room.

"Dinner is here," I announce, holding up the bag in one hand and wine in the other. "Do you object to a bedroom picnic tonight?"

She blinks and fights a surprised smile. "No. That sounds good."

I set the bag on the bed and unpack the boxes as I watch Violet from the corner of my eye. Her eyes are red, and her skin is blotchy, but, to my relief, she's not crying anymore.

She inhales deeply as she reaches into the second bag and sets a couple more boxes on the bed. "This smells amazing."

"It does." I pour us both glasses of red, set the half-empty bottle on the table beside the bed, and hesitate at the edge of the mattress. "Do you mind if I join you?"

Her cheeks flush a pretty shade of pink. "Not at all."

I settle myself on the mountain of pillows piled up against the headboard, then straighten again immediately. "Dammit. I forgot plates. Let me go—"

Violet sets a hand on my shoulder, and my heart skips at the small smile on her mouth. "I'm good to share like this if you are."

"Yeah." I ease back onto the pillows, taking a box of Dylan's signature roast duck with me. "I'm good like this."

I stab my fork into a crispy slice, pop it in my mouth, and then pass the container to Violet. She accepts and takes her own piece, and I watch as her pink lips wrap around the fork.

Violet drops her eyes like she knows what I'm thinking, and I don't even care. I want her, and I want her to know it.

"So, do you want to talk about it?" I ask.

Violet's fork freezes before she returns to poking at a container of roasted vegetables. With a sigh, she sets the food aside and picks up her wine. I wait while she takes a sip, sensing that this is another one of those moments where if I'm silent for long enough, she'll start talking. And I want her to talk so badly.

"I called my dad a little while ago," she finally admits, staring into her glass of pinot noir.

"Okay." When she doesn't elaborate, I offer her another dish, which she absently accepts while setting down her drink.

"I called my dad," she repeats, "and he sounded a little down. And when he's down, I'm down. Or, at the very least, I start to worry."

"Because he has depression."

Violet gives me a look that says she's surprised and a little bit pleased. "Yeah. I can't believe you remember that."

"I listen. But he's had this condition for a long time, right? What's different about today?"

She sets down her food, taking care not to spill anything as she bends her legs under the covers so she can wrap her arms around them and set her chin on her knees. "I've never lived away from home. Dad hasn't been on his own since before I was born. The two of us—we're the only family we have. This separation is hard on him, and I feel guilty."

I frown as I finish what's left of the crispy duck and choose another box. I'm at risk of saying something stupid here. Something along the lines of Violet being a grown woman who probably should have moved out of her father's house years ago. Something about hating the idea of her taking responsibility for someone else's happiness—even if that person is her father. Something about the injustice of a child worrying about a parent the way he should worry about her. But I'm smart enough to know that none of this is what she needs to hear.

As I analyze and discard every piece of advice I can think of, another possibility occurs to me. Is this Violet's way of telling me she wants to leave?

My spine is suddenly lined with sweat. I can't keep her here. She's an employee, not a prisoner, but I *am* her boss. And she needs this job—ironically, to pay her father's therapy bills and for the insurance. It would be a simple adjustment to finish our contract and release her back into the clutches of Courtney and the Fury marketing team, and I consider it. I do.

For about six seconds.

I can't let her go before the end of the summer. It's not long enough as it is, and I don't know what will happen when it's over. Violet is mine every minute of every day until the end of September, and I'm not letting her go, so I'll have to find another way.

We eat in silence for a while. When most of the boxes are empty, I toss everything back into the delivery bag and set it on the floor, then clear my throat.

"I don't have any experience with depression, so I don't want to sound insensitive, but you've done nothing wrong by being here. And I'd like to think your father loves you enough to not make you responsible for his mental health."

"Of course he does. That's not the problem." Violet dashes a single tear from her cheek. "I feel bad because I should have found a way to see him when we were in the city today."

A stab of regret shoots through my middle. "I'm sorry. If I'd known you wanted to see him, we could have made it a priority."

"It's okay. It's not your fault, and it's not the real problem." Violet breathes in deep and sighs with her exhale. "These last few weeks have made me so happy, and I'm sad that he wasn't around to share it."

"Yeah? You're really happy here?"

God, I'm an arrogant motherfucker, because all I heard in that sentence is how the last few weeks have made her happy. The last few weeks with *me*.

Violet turns her head where it rests on her knees and smiles. "Yeah. I'm really happy here."

I nod once, like I've been awarded a prize, and after that awkward gesture, I'm pretty sure it's for "Dork of the Year." On the plus side, it makes Violet's watery smile stretch wider.

"I'm glad to hear that. But there's just one problem now."

Her face falls as she straightens from her slouch. "Oh. What?"

I resist the upward pull on my lips and reach over to twist a lock of her damp hair around my finger. "You saying things like that makes me want to kiss you, and—"

"You can kiss me," she says in a rush.

The heat in her voice is all the invitation I need. I lean across the short space between us, slide my hand behind her neck, and pull her mouth against mine.

There's none of the hesitancy of our first kiss, and Violet laps against my tongue with needy whimpers that draw me closer to her and deeper onto the bed. When the taste of her lips feels nowhere near enough, I twist my fingers into her hair, gently pull her head back, and kiss my way across her jaw, her neck, her collarbone. The flavor of her skin is sugar on my tongue, and I respond to the sweet little moans in her throat with husky growls of my own.

Violet slides her open palms up my arms, around my shoulders and down my back, then slips her cool fingertips underneath the hem of my shirt and brushes them along my lower back. Goosebumps jump up at her gentle strokes, and I groan as my cock fights the confines of my jeans. Her fingernails dig into my sides as she latches onto the muscles above my hips, and I respond without thinking, pushing myself up and over her body, straddling her hips, pinning her slender frame between my thighs.

I cradle her head and kiss her, my body arching over hers as she sinks deeper into the pillows.

When Violet's hands disappear further under my shirt, her palms tracking a smooth course over my back, I mirror the move by skimming my fingers down her neck and shoulders. The flimsy straps of her camisole fall off her shoulders, the remaining fabric clinging to the soft swell of her tits and nothing else.

I moan at the promise of them—of her—then kiss the dip behind her earlobe just so I can breathe in the scent of her hair.

"Is this okay?" I ask. "Do you want me to stop?"

Violet moves her mouth to the shell of my ear. "Don't stop," she whispers. "I want to feel good. I *need* to feel good. Please."

Her words ignite a chemical reaction in my blood—a mixture of desire and desperation and challenge.

I run the tip of my nose across her collarbone, swirling my tongue across the hollow at her throat, and keep my voice low. "Wallflower?"

She arches back, pressing her tits against my chest, and I resist the urge to tear her clothes off with my teeth. "Yes?"

"Can I make you come?"

"Oh, God."

Violet closes her eyes, her chest rising and falling with her quickened breaths. I hover over her, watching the flush creep up her chest and tease her cheeks, wishing I could free the painful hard-on trapped inside my jeans.

She's so beautiful like this—wet hair sprawled across the pillows, skin pink and damp, her body on the edge of wanting and needing and *having*—so when she bites her bottom lip and nods, I groan and stretch my body over hers, the sheets still between our hips, and fall on her neck as I tug her silky top down and free her incredible breasts.

"Damn, Wallflower." I wrap my palm around one breast, tweaking a pink peak that's already pebbled and perfect, and capturing the opposite nipple in my mouth.

She gasps when my hot mouth closes over the sensitive zone, then hardens further under my tongue, her fingers tangling in my hair as she gasps and groans, her pelvis twisting beneath the covers as she hunts for friction.

I set my lips to her ear and whisper, "I've thought about you like this so many times, but touching you now is better than even my wildest dreams."

I glance up at her, wanting proof that I'm doing what she asked and making her feel good, but her eyes are closed. Yes, her body writhes beneath my touch. There's a salty, sensual sheen of perspiration across her neck. Her hair is tousled, she's making lusty little noises in her throat, and I know if I touched her between her legs, I'd find her wet and wanting, but it's not enough. Not for tonight and not for me.

Watching her face to see how she reacts, I skate a deliberate palm over Violet's breast, skim her ribcage, and then lightly brush my fingertips over her smooth, flat stomach. I tease the edge of the lacy thong she's wearing underneath the sheets, hooking a finger beneath the elastic and running it around to her inner thigh, and her leg falls open in invitation. Violet's expression reacts to my every movement, her breath grows shallow, her hips lift, and she talks in hot little whimpers, but her eyes remain shut.

I kiss her mouth and snake my hand down her body, circling a peaked nipple with my palm, squeezing her hip on my way to her inner thigh. She blindly and desperately shoves the linens away to remove the barrier between us, and I use my hips to spread her legs.

I slip my fingers between her thighs, and I'm right. She's soaked.

I start slow with a single finger, dipping the tip in to start, then push her panties aside to swirl the moisture over her clit.

Violet's whimpers turn needy, and I spread her lower lips, running my palm and fingers over her soaked warmth until she coats my hand. I want to lick it—I want to lick *her*—but if I've learned anything about this woman, it's to go slow. So, I fill her with my fingers. I sink in the first, then the second, and the way her back arches, the way she opens her thighs so I can go deeper, is enough to make me come a little in my pants.

I fuck her like this for ages, dragging my fingers in and out, teasing her clit with my thumb, stroking the soft, sensitive spot deep in her core that sets her pussy fluttering. But she's not getting there. I coax her all the way to the edge, but she keeps falling off the wrong side. She's thinking too much. I can tell by the way she keeps her eyes closed, squeezing them tight like she's trying to block out the world.

And I'm not having it.

I remove my fingers from her pussy, ignoring her pouty whimpers as I cradle her head with my free hand. Violet sucks fast breaths in through her nose and waits.

"Eyes on me," I order.

Her lashes flutter and she meets my gaze, her brown eyes hot and hazy and almost golden in the last light of the sun. "Good girl. Now keep them open—and keep them on me."

I hold Violet's stare and refuse to let it go, and when I'm satisfied that she's going to do as I say, I resume the tight, wet circles over her clit. She responds with quivering thighs and a thwarted whimper.

"You're going to get there, baby," I say, slipping my fingers deep into her. "I won't stop until you do. I swear to fucking God you're going to come for me."

Her breath catches on a needy moan, and she lifts her knees with a pleading nod, begging silently for more.

I pump in and out of her in long, slow drags, and loop my

arm under her shoulders to anchor her to my palm so she can ride my hand the way she needs to. Soon, the telltale flutter of her orgasm moves against my fingers, and I know it's different this time by the way her eyes widen on mine and her hips buck against my hand.

"That's it, Wallflower. You're nearly there." Our eyes remain on each other, her attention never wavering, and it's the most erotic thing I've ever done. "Can you feel it? Can you feel me inside you? Do you know how badly I want you to come on my hand?"

I curl my fingers inside her, playing her like an instrument, and grit my teeth as the precum of my own orgasm beads at the tip of my cock. Our eyes are locked, hers bright with the promise of her climax, and as her core clamps down around my fingers and her pussy soaks my hand, she finally tears her eyes away from mine, arching and crying out and cutting her nails into the deep muscles of my shoulders.

"There it is," I murmur against her ear, breathing in the smell of her as she shudders through her climax. "You did so well. You feel good now, don't you, Wallflower?"

She responds with a self-conscious little laugh, dragging her hands through her hair. "Oh, God. So good. Thank you."

She lifts her head and plants the sweetest, softest kiss on my mouth, then runs her thumb across my bottom lip. "I can't believe we just did that."

I capture her thumb between my teeth so I can kiss it before she takes it away. "Why?"

"Because nights like this only happen in my dreams," she murmurs, watching my lips trail up her wrist, her forearm, the crease of her elbow.

"That's music to my ears." I sweep the hair back from her face and kiss her as reverently as she did me. "I'm all about making dreams come true."

TWENTY-FIVE

Violet

DAY 21 AT SILVER LEAF... ONLY 65 TO GO

MY EXPERIENCE IN THE BEDROOM begins and ends with the short, underwhelming sexual relationship I had with my college boyfriend. I've never climaxed from a man's touch, and I've lived with my father my entire life, so I haven't done a lot of self-exploration either. My orgasms, when I have them, are fast and no-fuss. Get in, get off, get out.

But this... This was the hardest, most bone-shattering climax I've ever had. So overwhelming that the orgasms I've given myself don't even warrant the name.

I lay staring at the ceiling as my beautiful boss traces the shape of my collarbone with his tongue.

Oh, *God*. Chord Davenport made me come.

And I've got no clue what to do next. I can feel the hard ridge in his pants pressing against my thigh. His hairline is dark and curled with sweat, and his hands roam my body like

231

they're only just getting started, but now I'm on the other side of my climax, and I'm a little lost.

Do I peel off his shirt? Shove my hand down his pants? I mean, it's got to be bad form to accept an orgasm and not return the favor, but this already feels like a lot. And after all the crying and eating and coming, I kind of want to... snuggle?

Chord pushes up on his elbows, hard biceps flexing, and looks down at me with a crooked, cocky smirk. "You look spent."

I wet my lips, liking the way his eyes drop to my mouth to watch my tongue sweep out. "It's been a big day."

"Do you want to go to sleep?"

"Uh." I glance around the room. It's dark and probably not unreasonable to turn in, but it seems like the wrong thing to say after what just happened. "I don't know?"

His blue eyes sparkle with understanding, and he kisses the tip of my nose. "Do you want me to go?"

"No!" I blush at my vehemence and try again. "I mean, you don't have to go if you don't want to."

"I don't want to, so I guess we'll have a sleepover." He gives me one last kiss before pushing up and away. "Just give me a minute to change. I'll be right back."

Chord slips away, and I take the opportunity to use the bathroom. I clean up a little, brush my teeth, and run a comb through my hair, but no amount of cold water splashed over my cheeks can erase the pink glow of satisfaction. I ball up my damp lingerie and toss it into the hamper, then wrap myself in a towel and dash to the walk-in closet to pick out another set. But after sorting through my extensive collection, nothing feels right. My body is loose and sluggish, and I kind of want to sleep like that too. All curled up under the covers, Chord's arms around my body, snuggled up in something oversized and comfortable.

I screw up my nose at the old, stained sweats I packed for these kinds of nights. I can't bring myself to wear them in front of Chord.

I'm still in the closet, wearing nothing but a pair of white cotton briefs, when I hear Chord enter the room.

"You didn't run away, did you?" he calls.

I laugh and poke my head around the closet door. "No. I'm here. I'm just looking for something to wear to bed. After... that... I feel like sleeping in something a little more comfortable than my, uh, underwear."

"And you don't have pajamas?"

"Not in the traditional sense, no."

Chord frowns in thought, then grins. "Be right back."

He darts away again, and I wonder what he's up to as I hold my old tracksuit pants up to triple-check the tear in the bottom and the stain on the knee.

Nope. I can't do it.

"I've got something for you," Chord calls from just outside the door.

I startle and cover my bare breasts with one arm, though he doesn't try to come in, and thrust my other hand through the half-open door while wiggling my fingers.

Chord chuckles as he puts something soft in my grip. "Here you go, Wallflower. See how you feel in that."

It's clear at first sight what he's given me. It's a hockey jersey—and an old one, by the feel of it. I stretch it out, running my fingers over the colors of the Tampa Bay Titans, turning to see Chord's name and number on the back.

With a little shiver, I slip the shirt over my head and let it fall over my skin. I'm tall, but Chord is much taller, and his shirt is large enough that I feel small inside it. I lift the collar to my nose and inhale. And then, feeling a little self-conscious, I step out of the closet.

Chord sits on the end of the bed, dressed now in cotton shorts and nothing else, and his muscled frame, hard jaw, and dark mop of hair make it impossible to maintain a steady breath. His elbows are on his knees as he stares into the distance, but he straightens as soon as I appear, and the expression on his face is a million kinds of validating.

"It suits you," he croaks, then clears his throat and gets to his feet, closing the distance and turning me around with two gentle hands on my shoulders. He sweeps the hair off my neck and carefully arranges it to one side before he's silent for a moment.

"It suits you *very* well." His breath on my skin makes me shiver before his mouth meets the curve of my neck. "My name on your back..." His tongue sweeps out between his lips like he's tasting me. "It almost has me rethinking my promise to let you rest."

Warmth pools in my cheeks and the cleft of my thighs as I glance over my shoulder. Chord looks hungry. Like he really does want to make me come all over again. I'd probably let him, but before I can say something bold and out of character, he picks up my hand, leads me to the bed, and pulls back the covers.

I slip inside and he pulls the linens up over my body before he walks around and gets in beside me. Chord sprawls out on his back, scoops me against his side, and I settle against the firm warm plane of his chest, wrapped in his warmth, his scent, and his strength.

Safe.

I open my eyes to a bedroom flooded with warm, sweet sunlight and indulge in a long full-body stretch. It's much later than I'd normally sleep on a Tuesday morning—I can tell by the way the light angles through the tall glass windows—but there's a reason for it. I've never slept that well in my life. So deeply and so soundly with so little worries. Never.

I reach across the bed to touch the reason for my wonderful night, but my arm sweeps over the empty space where Chord should be. I sit up, and my stomach flips at the sticky note on the sheets.

You were too beautiful to wake. Back soon.

With a moan of blissful relief, I roll over to his side of the bed, bury my head in his pillow and breathe him in, but it's no better than the smell of his jersey on my body. Tampa, he told me, because he has better memories of his time there than he does with Calgary, and he doesn't have his Fury gear yet. I prefer his Tampa jersey, anyway. It's so worn and comfy, and I adore the idea that a twenty-something Chord wore this once upon a time, and it was significant enough for him to keep.

I check the time on my phone, and when I see that it's already ten a.m., I shove aside the conscientious voice that says I should have started work an hour ago. Instead, I throw back the covers and go looking for Chord.

A quick check of the house, the porch, and the pool tells me he's not only not in my bed but also not anywhere on the property. My assumption that he'd be *back soon* from his morning workout was obviously wrong.

I check the garage and his sports car is gone, so I return to my bedroom and pick up my phone but stop short of actually calling him. He's probably gone out to get us breakfast or something, and I don't want to be *that girl*, so instead, I swipe to check my messages—I have none—then, out of habit, open my social media account.

I've all but given up on making anything of it now that I'm only designing for myself, but when I open the app, I'm stunned to see notifications for nearly five hundred new followers. I flip through my feed to see if I've been hacked. No.

Everything is the same as it was, but then I notice I've been tagged in a dozen or so posts.

I'm too confused to be alarmed, but panic flickers in my pulse as soon as I navigate to one of the images. It's Chord at The Slippery Tipple, carrying me out of there in his big strong arms. His face is hard and cold, mine is buried against his neck, and there are my boots dangling from his hand. In the background, other customers have their phones raised and pointed at us.

I scroll through to more tags and more pictures. A few more are from that same night—I don't remember sitting *on* the bar, but there I am with Chord slipping off my shoes like I'm some sort of drunk Cinderella—but the rest are from our trip to San Francisco. Chord holding my hand on the street. Chord guiding me into his car with a hand on my lower back. Chord looking at me with a small smile on his mouth. Me gazing at him like he hung the moon.

I'm almost afraid to read the comments, but I swipe my thumb against the screen anyway. About halfway down the thread, someone identifies and tags me as the woman in the pictures, and that explains the boost to my follower count.

Maybe I should be happy about this, but I'm not. Something about it feels icky and exposed.

I tap to open my profile info and debate the idea of replacing my bio picture with something anonymous. I've almost uploaded a blank white circle when I hear the crunch of tires on the gravel driveway. I drop my phone on the bed and dash to the window to see Chord's sports car pull up to the front of the house.

One of the knots in my chest unravels and I smile to myself as Chord gets out of the car. But weirdly, the passenger-side door swings open at the same time, and someone else steps out.

I gasp and spin around, rushing down the hallway and almost tripping on the stairs in my hurry to get to the front door. I fling it open and throw myself through it, skipping down the porch steps and straight into the open arms of my dad.

"Well, that's a warm welcome, Blossom." He chuckles before dropping a kiss on my head and tightening his embrace. "I've missed you too," he murmurs against my hair.

I pull back and look at him with a kind of wonder, then concern. When things are good, my father is young and fit and, if not vibrant, he's at least got energy. But in the three weeks since I last saw him, he's lost a little weight, and there are shadows under his eyes. It's not drastic enough that anyone else would notice it, but my relief at seeing him gives way to a pang of sadness—and a little fear.

I offer Chord a grateful smile, but he hangs back with an expression that's part satisfied and part... entertained. His blue eyes dance as they sweep down my body and back up again, which is when I realize I'm standing in the driveway, ignoring the sharp stabs of stones underneath my bare feet because I'm so happy to see my dad—and I'm wearing nothing but Chord's jersey.

If it were possible to self-combust from embarrassment, this would be the moment for it to happen. Every inch of my body bursts with shame, and I tug at the hem of the shirt to try and give it more length. When that doesn't work, I shift from foot to foot and attempt to smooth my bed hair.

Dad rubs his jaw to hide a frown just as Chord shakes his head and closes the door to the car.

"Perhaps we should have called first," Dad says. "Given you a chance to, ah... freshen up."

"No, it's okay. I, um..."

I throw a pleading glance toward Chord, and he moves just close enough to keep a respectable distance. I don't know where to look—at Chord, at my dad—so I settle on somewhere awkward between the two.

"I thought you and your dad could catch up over a cup of coffee before I take him around to his accommodation," Chord explains.

That gets my attention. "His accommodation?"

"Yeah." Chord gives Dad a friendly nod, which he returns with an appreciation and humility that breaks my heart. "I asked Mr. James—I mean, Luke—if he might have some time to help me on the ranch this summer. Those fences are taking a lot longer than I expected, and with team training kicking off this week, I'll feel better knowing that the work is getting done even when I can't be out there doing it myself. Charlie was able to find an empty cabin for a few weeks at least, and Luke mentioned he was available to stay a while."

Dad scratches an eyebrow and tilts his head so he's not looking straight at the daughter wearing the rich and famous hockey player's jersey and not much else. "Chord mentioned there might be other things that need doing. Handyman-type things here and there, and I didn't have anything urgent keeping me at home. You don't mind your old man hanging around for a few weeks, do you, Blossom? I promise not to get in your way. You'll hardly know I'm here."

"No! I love the idea. You'll be a huge help. Let's go inside and talk about it, and then you can get settled in."

I grab Dad's hand and blink away the sting in my eyes as I throw Chord a look of gratitude. *Thank you*, I mouth. He responds with a straight-faced wink that makes me giddy.

"Luke," Chord says. "You go on in and make yourself comfortable. The kitchen is easy to find—follow the hallway, and you can't miss it—and Violet will be in soon. I just need to have a word with her first."

I squeeze Dad's hand. "I won't be long."

Dad disappears inside the house, and I pull the door almost closed to give me and Chord a little privacy. He stands with his arms crossed and a cocky twist to his lips, and unashamedly drags his gaze down my body, lingering on the spot where his jersey meets my thighs.

"You're fucking stunning, Wallflower."

I blush and look around even as my heart flies with pleasure. "*Chord.*"

He grins and moves closer, then snakes his arms around

my waist to pull me against him for a soft, lingering kiss.

I should pinch myself to make sure this is real, but if it isn't, then I don't want to wake up. "I can't believe you did this."

"I don't want to see you cry," he says as if he thinks he has the power to protect me from heartbreak. The stupid thing is, I believe he might. "Whatever you need, whatever you want, it's yours."

"Thank you."

I offer my lips, and he takes them again in a kiss a little less gentle, a little more needy.

Chord skates his palms over my arms. "Before you go inside, there's something I need to talk to you about."

"That doesn't sound good."

"Not good. Not bad." He smiles tightly, but his lips have a sardonic twist to them. "Just a fact of life when you're spending time with the hottest player in the NHL."

He's not usually so self-deprecating, and I don't like it. "Is this about the pictures?"

His eyebrows shoot upward. "You know about them?"

"Yes. I woke up to a dozen social media tags attached to pictures of us at The Slippery Tipple and in the city—plus five hundred new followers."

"Okay. Interesting." Chord nods slowly as he slides his hands around my waist, but there's a crease between his brows that wasn't there before. "I know it's too early to put any labels on us... right?"

I force myself to meet his earnest gaze. Like the way we danced, like our first kiss, like the way he touched me last night, Chord knows how to lead, so I agree with him even though I'm not sure I want to. "Right."

His throat works as his grip tightens on my hips. "So, we have to work this out with the world watching. Does that bother you?"

"I mean, it's uncomfortable and weird..." The line on his forehead grows deeper and I stop myself before I can admit that I am, in fact, a little troubled. "Why? Does it bother you?"

He hesitates. "No, but I'm used to it. It's part of the job."

"Are you sure?" I rub my thumb over the line on his forehead. "I bet there are lots of lousy things that are part of the job, but they can still upset you."

Chord presses his lips together as focus turns inward. "At the risk of sounding like a poor, rich professional athlete, the truth is that dating in the public eye hasn't worked out well for me. I seem to attract either women who see hockey and money and throw themselves at me or women who see hockey and money and run in the opposite direction." His hands move in slow circles over my lower back, as if by soothing me, he can soothe himself. "I know you're not the first kind, and I'm hoping like hell you're not the latter."

I look at Chord—really look, so he knows I mean this— but still, his eyes are a little guarded.

"Well, here's the thing." I skate my hands up over his arms, following the carved lines of his muscles from wrist to shoulders, then cup his face. "When I look at you, I don't see hockey, and I don't see money. I don't see the fame or any of those things that might have burned you in the past. I see a good man with a big heart. I see you and like you, despite—not because of—all those other things."

Chord's shoulders relax, and he pulls me close so he can rest his chin on the top of my head. "So, you think you'll be okay standing with me in the spotlight?"

"Next to you?" I twine my arms around his neck and press myself against him. "I'll be okay anywhere."

TWENTY-SIX

Chord

63 DAYS TILL HOCKEY SEASON

MY SAN FRANCISCO FURY TEAMMATES are due to arrive at Silver Leaf at ten a.m., but Coach Campbell pulls up to the house half an hour early. I greet him on the porch with an outstretched hand.

"Wasn't sure we were going to make this happen," he says with a wry look.

I might have to go along with this whole training-and-bonding-at-my-place plan, but I don't have to like it. And this close to retirement, I've earned the right to not have to pretend. It's taken three weeks to set this up, and the delays have all been mine, but I don't rise to Coach's bait.

Instead, I shake his hand and hold the front door open. "You're the coach, right?"

He huffs out a dry laugh. "Good to know you don't need another reminder."

I lead him through the house to the kitchen and gesture toward the stools tucked under the island. "Coffee?"

"Please." Coach pulls out a chair and takes a seat, then braids his fingers and sets them on the marble top. It's his serious pose, and I remember it from our early Tampa days. "Look, Chord. I know we got off to a rocky start at the meeting earlier this month, but I meant what I said about bonding with the team before the season starts. You're a good captain, and you've got the potential to be great, if..."

He punctuates the sentence with a meaningful look. We both know what went wrong last season and if it were anyone else, I'd change the subject right about now. But this is Bobby Campbell. I wouldn't say he raised me—my mom and dad did that—but I was only a teenager when I was drafted to Tampa, and eighteen was too young for me to be out in the world without a solid, dependable presence in my life. Campbell was that person and the fact he's sitting in my kitchen now conjures a forgotten, dormant drive to make him proud.

I blink away the picture of my father on the empty chair beside Coach—two giants of my early career who believed I could do anything. I'm not sure if sixteen years of experience and screw-ups make me remember those early days with more fondness than they deserve, but whatever this feeling is in my chest, it makes it easier to talk.

I slide a mug of coffee in his direction. "Do you know what it feels like to find out the woman you've been dating for a year has been cheating on you with the guy traded to your team to replace you?"

Coach shakes his head and wraps his hands around the steaming cup. "You don't know he was there to replace you."

I raise one brow. "I'm pretty but I'm not stupid, Coach. Spencer Cook's stats mirror my own at his age. He's an asshole but he's a strong player, and he's got a solid seven years left in him—at least. He's going to spend that winning games."

Coach grimaces but nods.

"Emma was screwing him for months before I got word of it, and at least three of my boys knew about it. I was their captain, and they didn't say a fucking word."

He raises his eyes before lifting his chin, blinking at the heat in my voice before dropping his shoulders with a sigh.

"I'm sorry Calgary let you go. I'm sorry things ended the way they did. But you had four good years at Tampa before you were traded, and the first half of your contract with Calgary was stellar. Then you got hard and, yeah, you got hurt, but I'd hate to see pain and rage be the only things you bring with you to the Fury."

I set down my coffee and release a heavy breath. "If you're asking me to forget it ever happened, you're asking too much."

"I'm not asking you to forget. I know that fire is going to be the fuel we need to carry us to the championship. I know anger will serve us on the ice. I'm just asking you to apply it the right way and at the right times. I'm proud of the team we've put together this year, but it won't work if you're not putting your captaincy above your personal problems."

"Meaning?"

"These aren't the boys who screwed you over, Chord, and they deserve your trust until proved otherwise. It may seem like I'm asking a lot for you to give them a chance, but the truth is we're not going to win shit if you're not leading them the way you should."

"And what way is that?"

Coach shrugs one shoulder and lifts his cup. "From the heart."

"Chord, I— Oh! I'm sorry. I didn't know you weren't alone."

Coach and I turn toward the sound of Violet's voice. She hovers between the kitchen and the hallway, clutching her tablet to her chest and obviously unsure if she should interrupt. Her neck is a little flushed, and it reminds me of how she looked last night in her bed.

She let me touch her again, and she came a lot quicker this time, then we snuggled after, and I slept like a freaking baby.

That makes it three nights in a row. A fucking hat trick.

"Violet!" Coach gets to his feet and offers her his hand. "Nice to see you again."

Violet spares me a quick glance as she hurries in to shake Coach's hand. Pretty color tints her cheeks, and I'd bet half of this season's salary that she's thinking about last night, too.

"It's good to see you too, Coach," she says, "but I can come back later if you two need more time to talk?"

"No need for that." Coach nods at the tablet in her hands. "Is that the schedule for today?"

"It is. Yes."

She offers him the device, and he takes it, casting an eye over the screen. "Pool. Track. Gym. Rehab." He hands it back with an approving nod. "The assistant coach and I have divided the team into first, second, third, and fourth lines, and you'll rotate through stations. Chord, you'll spend most of the day with Hayden Shore, Theo Reed, Jake Wilde, Max Breaker, and Weston Payne."

I know them all by name, I've looked at their stats, and I've studied their form. All good players, but I've got no idea if they're good guys.

I grunt, which earns me a sharp look, so I smooth my features. "Fine."

"I was just coming in to let Chord know that the physiotherapists are all set up in the pool house," Violet adds, "and the restaurant is on track to deliver the special menu for lunch, so we're good to start as soon as everyone arrives."

Coach claps his hands, then rubs his palms together. "Fantastic. Thanks, Violet." He looks at me but tips his head Violet's way. "This woman is worth her weight in gold, you know. She's done all the work to get everything set up for today. Made my life a hell of a lot easier."

Violet drops her eyes, uncomfortable with the attention

and the praise, and I fight the urge to lift her chin and remind her to keep her eyes up. But she must feel the press of my gaze because she raises her head and subtly rolls back her shoulders.

"You're welcome, Coach," she says.

He replies with a firm nod. "Now, I wouldn't mind a quick look around the place before the team arrives. Chord?"

It takes effort to tear my eyes away from Violet, but I manage it—just. "Let's do it."

I transfer our empty coffee cups to the sink, round the counter, and slide open the back door. At my gesture, Coach walks through, but I pause before following him so I can get a moment alone with Violet.

Thanks to the pictures all over social media, our involvement is hardly a secret. It's not defined either, I remind myself with a hint of regret as I recall our conversation on the front porch, but it's not something we need to hide. That said, today is a workday for both of us, and I don't want to do anything that might put Violet's professional reputation at risk.

"I won't see you much today," I tell her, skimming my fingertips down her arm and then loosely twining my fingers in hers.

She bites her lip to stop a smile. "But I'll see plenty of you."

"Oh, yeah?"

"Mm-hm. Coach has asked me to hang around in case anyone needs anything."

I frown. "That's not your job, and you don't have to do that. I'll talk to him."

She chuckles lightly. "It's hardly work to spend the day watching a team of professional ice hockey players get all hot and sweaty. I'll just... hover. Nobody will even know I'm there."

"Hm."

I like the sparkle of mischief in her chestnut eyes. There's a lightness in her expression that wasn't there before, and I assume it's because her dad is on the property, eliminating the worry she's kept to herself all these weeks. Of course, there's an equal chance that Violet's relaxed mood is the direct result of my magic fingers. I cast a quick look outside to check on Coach—he's already halfway to the pool house—then give Violet a quick pinch on the ass.

"You better be looking at one of those hockey players and one only," I warn, and her grin grows wider.

It's a joke—mostly—but after the conversation I just had with Coach, it makes me think about my ex, Emma, and how it felt to have my girlfriend cheat on me.

We'd been dating for a year when I found out about her and Cook. It was a blow to my ego, but I wasn't surprised. We might have had feelings for each other early on, but over time, our relationship became one of convenience, not depth. Emma was a social climber: in it for the money, the cars, the travel, the notoriety of dating the NHL's most controversial player. I was done with sleeping around and too focused on hockey to care that Emma was like most other women I'd dated in the past.

Sticking with one woman was supposed to be less of a distraction than hooking up with many, and it was probably true, but it didn't equal love. When Emma finally admitted to having an affair, she was already halfway out the door.

Anyone would think I have trust issues after everything I've been through but with Violet in my arms, looking at me the way she is, I'm stunned by one revelation: I've never trusted anyone the way I trust her.

Emma might have caused me a shitload of trouble but thank God she didn't have the power to break my heart. I must have known even then to never let her close enough to try.

My last session for the day is cool down in the gym, and when I'm finished with the stretches prescribed by the physiotherapist, I find a foam roller and set myself up on a mat near the door. Beside me, left winger Hayden is on his back, wincing and sweating on his own roller as he pushes through a series of lat releases.

The energy between me and the guys today has been dry—not hostile, but not what anyone would call friendly— and Coach has given me enough side eye to start a fucking fire. But I've spent almost a year actively shutting people out, and I wasn't exactly approachable for a long time before that. One day of team building and training isn't going to make these boys family. But I *am* thinking about what Campbell said.

I need to put the anger and the resentment where it'll do the most good, and that's on the ice. It doesn't belong inside the team I'm supposed to lead to the Cup.

There's just one big fucking problem. I've earned my reputation as a cold, distant asshole, and it's not the kind of status I can erase in one afternoon.

I lower myself to the floor, arrange the foam roller under my pelvis, brace myself on my elbows, and rock in a thrusting motion that loosens my hip flexors. It hurts in a good way, and I lose myself in the steady rhythm of rolling back and forth.

"Oh, my."

I suppress a smirk at Violet's version of a curse, lifting my head just enough to take in her boots before running my eyes up her bare legs, over her denim cut-offs, and across her vintage Metallica tee. I know I'm supposed to be on my best behavior today, but I can't fight my shit-eating grin when I see her wide eyes pasted to my rocking ass. I slow the movement down a little, pressing harder into the foam and clenching my glutes, and watch with amusement as her eyes follow the thrust of my hips, her pink tongue darting out to swipe her bottom lip.

"Hey, Wallflower." I cock an eyebrow as her eyes dart from my ass to my face. "Do you need me?"

"Oh, I, uh…" Violet clears her throat as her cheeks brighten and she looks around the room, eyes bouncing from man to man before she finds a spot on the floor to stare at. "I'm here to let Coach know that the post-training food and drinks have arrived, and according to the schedule, it's almost time to wrap up."

I roll off the foam tube and jump up. "Great. Thanks."

Beside me, Hayden groans as he climbs to his feet, rolling his shoulders as he tests the muscles in his back. "Jesus Christ, Davenport. When did you learn how to smile? Give a guy a little warning before you grin like that. It's fucking unnatural."

I scowl at him—hard—but Violet rolls her lips like she knows she's the reason for my good mood, and it's hard to keep the frown on my face.

"You're a riot, Shore," I mutter.

He gives me a wide smile. "Fuck, yeah, I am. Wait until you hear my knock-knock jokes."

I roll my eyes but gesture toward Violet. "Hayden—this is Violet James. She's with the Fury marketing team and my summer assistant. Violet—this is Hayden Shore. Left winger and funny man, apparently."

Violet offers him a shy smile. "Nice to meet you."

"You, too, Violet. I'd shake your hand, but I'm a sweaty mess."

"Oh, of course. No problem."

Coach makes his way over from the side of the room. "Are we cooling down over here or having a tea party?"

"I'm sorry to interrupt your session, Coach, but the post-training menu is on the dining table," Violet replies. "I've let the other groups know it's time to call it a day, and this is my last stop."

Coach raises his palms and gives her a *mea culpa* face.

"I take back the tea party comment, Violet. Thanks for letting us know and for all your assistance today. You've been a lifesaver."

"It's my pleasure."

Violet shoots me a short, warm look from underneath her thick lashes before she slips out the door, and I stare at the spot where she disappeared, wishing the house were empty so I could chase her down the hallway, pin her against the wall, and kiss her senseless.

"You heard her," Coach bellows as Theo, Jake, Breaker, and West drop to their mats in varied states of pain and exhaustion. "Wrap it up and hit the showers. I'll see you all in the kitchen in fifteen minutes."

Hayden waggles his brows at me as he makes his way to the bathroom attached to the gym, and I shake my head with reluctant amusement. Hayden's another new trade for this season. He's in his late twenties, so he's old enough to know a thing or two, but still young enough to be having fun. A fantastic player waiting for the chance to prove himself.

Coach hangs back as the other boys follow Hayden. West approaches first, and he surprises me with a handshake as he passes. I return his firm grip and respectful nod, and I appreciate the acknowledgment that passes between us. West has been in the game for ten years as a solid and dependable defenseman, but he's flown under the radar for most of his career. Recently divorced, if I remember right, but I'm probably wrong. I don't listen to rumors.

Theo, Jake, and Breaker line up like fucking puppies once West clears the door, jostling each other and shaking my hand with about half the level of West's maturity. Their young, objectively pretty faces should piss me off—guys at the start of their careers, their best years still to come—and a year ago, they probably would have. But their energy is less irritating and more inspiring right now, and fuck if I know why.

When it's just Coach and I left in the gym, he stops me from walking out with a hand on my shoulder. His brows are drawn and his mouth is turned down, and my stomach tightens at the dissatisfaction painted on his face.

"I know, you need me to be better. Friendlier." I shake my head with an uncomfortable grunt. "I'll work on it for next time."

His brows pull tighter. "If I'm honest, Chord, today went better than I thought it would. Not perfect, and we can talk about how to improve before the next session, but that's not what I want to discuss."

I rub my neck, working at a kink that probably needs a professional touch. "It's not?"

"No." Coach crosses his arms over his barrel chest. "I got a call from Courtney Reynolds this afternoon."

I want to ask him why I should care, but I'm supposed to behave less like a prick, not more, so I settle for something more neutral. "Okay."

"She says you declined to attend the San Francisco Fury Foundation gala later this month."

I blink in surprise. "This is the first I've heard about a gala."

"So, you didn't RSVP *no* to the event?"

"No. I mean..." With sudden insight, I realize Violet must have declined on my behalf, just following my instructions to keep me out of the way of the press for the summer. I pinch a bead of sweat from my nose to hide my chagrin. "Actually, yeah. I probably did. I told Violet to decline all my invitations over the off-season. I don't want to deal with cameras and questions before October."

He gives me a flat look. "Not going to fly, Davenport, and you know it. Not for the biggest fundraiser on the Foundation's calendar."

"I know," I grumble, already irritated at the thought of putting on a tux and smiling for the goddamn media packs.

"Good. It's a red carpet affair. Black tie. Classy. We've asked the entire roster to do their best to be there. The coaching staff too. Everyone from HQ. There's an impressive legacy guest list. It's a big deal, made even bigger because you're our new captain, and with our line-up, we've got a real shot of making it all the way."

Coach tilts his head to one side like he's sizing me up, and I stand a little straighter. "I know you don't want to smile for cameras," he says. "I know you don't want to answer questions about Calgary. I know you just want to play but we need you front and center everywhere, not only in the arena, and take it from me: next year will be a lot easier if you make peace with this part of the job. Consider the gala just another way to start fresh, okay?"

I give him a short nod. I know he's right, but I wish he wasn't.

He claps me on the shoulder. "Good. And here's a wild idea: why don't you bring a date? The invitation includes a plus one and it's got the potential to be a great night. Maybe walking into that room with someone by your side will make the whole concept a little more appealing, eh?"

My thoughts dart straight to Violet, and the idea of that beautiful woman on my arm for an entire night—showing her off, dancing with her, telling everyone she's mine—really does change the way I think about things. It also gives me an idea, and suddenly dressing up and smiling for the cameras doesn't sound like a bad idea after all.

TWENTY-SEVEN

Chord

62 DAYS TILL HOCKEY SEASON

I KNOCK ON VIOLET'S NOT-quite-closed bedroom door right at seven p.m. When she doesn't answer, I knock louder and hard enough for the door to swing open a little. She's exactly where I knew she'd be: pretty in her purple silk lingerie and propped up against the pillows on her bed, chunky headphones over her ears, sketchbook on her knees, and all her attention on the lines of her pencil skating over the white page.

I watch her for several minutes. She's so damn beautiful like this. The graceful slope of her neck. The braid of dark hair over one shoulder. The concentration creasing her brow, and the way she rolls her lips whenever her pencil isn't moving. The unconscious sexiness of her wearing those vibrant, lacey panties and camis to bed.

I lean against the doorway and take a long breath in, then out. I'd stand here forever just to memorize the way she looks right now, but I've got dinner in my hand—and why should I only look when I can touch?

I clear my throat and step into the room, the sound and movement finally catching her attention. Violet's eyes land on me and brighten instantly, and my body lights up in response. The way she looks at me... It's different from how fans watch me when I play, or the way people stare when they recognize me in the street. It's not the same as women ogling me in bars. It's more real, and I want to be looked at like this.

Violet drags off her headphones and tosses them aside, removes her glasses, then sets her open sketchbook and pencil on the end of the bed. "Whatever that is, it smells amazing. And I'm starving."

"Me too." I pull the boxes out of the delivery bag and arrange them on the bed covers. "Dylan sent over two kinds of pasta. Three kinds of salad. Freshly baked bread and a bottle of Silver Leaf olive oil to go with it."

Violet moans with hungry appreciation as she curls her legs underneath her and presses her hands together under her chin. "Your brother is a culinary genius. Everything that comes out of his kitchen is a masterpiece."

"You'll get no argument from me," I reply, setting down the last container and then taking my usual spot next to Violet on the bed. I lift my shirt and smack my hard stomach. "Not sure my nutritionist would approve of all this indulgence. I'm pretty sure Dylan's secret ingredient is butter."

Violet's gaze drops to my abs, and she doesn't look away

until I pull my shirt down to cover them. I smirk at the spots on her cheeks as she drags her eyes up to my face.

"I don't think you have anything to worry about."

I wink. "Noted."

Violet selects a dish and starts to eat, and like we've done every night this week, we trade boxes back and forth while we talk.

"How is your dad settling in?" I ask.

Violet smiles, and she's so freaking pretty I have to blink to clear my head.

"He's happy here. He doesn't want to get in my way, and I appreciate that, but he's been coming by the house for an hour every morning and again every afternoon so we can spend some time together." She shakes her head in disbelief as she trades a salad for a bottle of water. "He was fifteen minutes late today, and it didn't even bother him. I get the impression that Charlie is keeping him busy—in a good way—and he's thriving with this new independence. I need to thank her."

I need to thank her, too. She really stepped up when I asked her for this favor. Didn't even make me beg. I explained the situation and alluded to Violet's distress and Luke's need for support, and she was immediately on board with finding him accommodation for as long as he needed it. I didn't acknowledge Charlie's miraculous discovery of an empty cabin, and neither did she, though she offered to find one for Violet, too, if she wanted one.

I shut that down real quick.

"I'm glad it's working out," I reply.

"It is." Violet shifts to her hands and knees, leans over, and kisses me softly. "Thank you again."

I lick my lips to capture the salt she left behind and sink into her grateful gaze. "You're welcome again."

Her eyes drop like she's embarrassed about initiating a kiss, and she settles back into her seat. I love that I make her nervous.

I smile to myself as I peek into the nearest boxes, find them empty, and start tidying up. Everything goes into a bag on the floor, except the open bottle of olive oil. I can't find the cap, so I set it carefully on the side table just as anticipation settles over us.

Dinner is just the first step in what has become a nightly ritual. We eat together. We fool around. I make her come. She puts on my jersey, and then I hold her in my arms until morning.

And I know she feels how hard she makes me. The wait for her to touch me is torture, but the pain is worth it. Violet is worth waiting for.

I scoop up the last of the takeout boxes and set them aside, eyeing her closed sketchbook the whole time. She's never offered to show me what's inside, but she hasn't gone out of her way to hide it either. So, I pick it up.

She doesn't protest, so I turn it over in my hands and run my fingers over the worn leather binding. "Have you ever shared your work with anyone?"

Violet smooths her palms over the tops of her bare thighs. "Only the designs I did in college, and a handful of sketches on my social media pages, but in real life..." She shrugs and shakes her head. "No. Nobody's ever seen my designs."

"Is there a reason?"

She captures her bottom lip with her teeth, and I'm distracted by the way she nibbles it while she thinks. "I've never felt close enough to anyone to share them. It's always been private. My sketchbook is my safe place."

Something hitches in my chest when I realize the only thing to bring her joy in this world is a piece of paper and a pencil, and I can't stop the irrational determination I feel to change that.

"I know I'm asking for a lot here, but I'd really love to see your designs. Would it be okay if I had a look?"

I wait, wanting so desperately to be welcomed into this part of her world. She hesitates, and I decide it's not going to happen, but then she nods.

"Yes, that would be okay."

My heart lurches because the significance of her permission is not lost on me. I settle back against the headboard, stretch out my legs, set the oversized book on my lap, and open it.

The first page shows the wedding dress I've already seen—the one that belonged to her mother—but I'm searching for something else. I leaf through the pages until I find something original, pause for a moment, then decide it's not the one I'm looking for.

"These are beautiful, Wallflower. You're talented. I hope you know that."

She flushes as I turn the page to another incarnation of her mother's wedding dress. This one has numbers scratched in the corner, and I brush my finger across them. "Do these mean anything?"

Violet fidgets a little. "They're my measurements. I don't know why I wrote them down."

I do. She wants to wear this dress someday. And maybe the idea of getting involved with a woman who dreams about her wedding dress should freak me out, but it doesn't.

I might have never thought about it in exactly these terms, or even consciously over the years, but I want a happily ever after too. That's the reason I built this house in the first place. I want what my parents had. I want to build a life and provide for my family. I want to love another person more than I ever dreamed possible. One day when hockey isn't my everything, I'll make my wife my world.

"Do you have any favorites?" I ask.

"Um." Violet relaxes against me, and I put my arm around her and kiss her temple. She snuggles in closer and thumbs through the book, considering one dress after another and rejecting them all. But then she hesitates and returns to a silhouette she initially dismissed. It's a strapless gown with a bodice of intricate lace and floral detail in teal, silver and gold, threaded with beads and shimmering flowers. The long skirt is a flowing, ethereal mass of layered blue fabric that somehow has just enough transparency to show the shape of the legs underneath. It's feminine and striking and sexy.

It's perfect.

Violet runs her fingers over the lines of her design. "If I had to choose a favorite, it would be this one."

"It's beautiful," I agree. "And you'd look beautiful in it."

Her laugh is scandalized. "I design the dresses. I don't wear them."

I close the book and carefully set it aside before I turn to Violet and lift her chin. "Who says you can't do both?"

Her plump pink lips are upturned and waiting, her lids heavy, so I kiss her before she can respond.

My hands are greedy for the soft texture of Violet's hair as I push my fingers through her tresses. My tongue recalls the taste of her and anticipates the way she opens her mouth to welcome me. She tilts her head further, inviting more, and presses her body against mine, seeking contact and heat at her breasts, her stomach, her hips, her thighs. A week of this, and it's hard to remember a time when I wasn't kissing her. I never want it to stop.

I trail my fingers down her arms, lift the hem of her camisole, and brush her hip bone lightly enough to leave goosebumps. She whimpers and kisses me harder, latching onto my shoulders like she can't get close enough. My cock thickens.

I swipe a finger into the waist of her panties and a subtle rush of arousal colors her cheeks. She's so fucking pretty like this that I want more.

I lean closer and whisper against her ear. "I love the way you blush for me, Wallflower."

A flush of pink bursts underneath her collarbone, and I drag the tip of my nose across the swell of her breasts to inhale the gentle floral fragrance of her, then press my lips to her warmth.

"And you bloom prettiest when you come."

I can feel the rush of blood pooling under her skin. It makes me think of heat rushing to other parts of her body, the way it's rushing to my cock right now. I think of her swollen, wet and throbbing, and slide a hand up her inner thigh.

"Wait."

Violet sets a hand over mine, and I immediately freeze. Her eyes are hot and wide, her lips pink and swollen, and her breath comes in fast little pants that drive me wild.

"What's wrong?" I ask. "Are you uncomfortable?"

She shakes her head and closes her eyes like she's gathering strength.

"I want..." Violet's tongue darts out of her mouth, her eyes dropping to where our hands are locked together between us, and she expels a breath in a rush. "I want to touch you."

My dick swells so hard and fast it's painful. I growl and push a hand into her hair, gripping a handful of the strands and yanking her closer to me for a hard kiss. Fuck. I want her to touch me too.

She returns the kiss with enthusiasm, nails digging into my shoulders, before pushing on my chest and pulling back. There's a small but pleased curl to her mouth, and I bite my own lip to stop from leaning in and nipping hers.

"I want to touch you," she repeats, "but I want to do it right. You know exactly how to touch me, and I want to do the same for you."

"Wallflower." I run a thumb over the pink tinge on her cheekbones. "I'm ready to come just thinking about your hands on me. You couldn't do it wrong. It's impossible."

The color in her cheeks brightens, and her eyes drop to my crotch before bouncing upward again. "Could you show me what you like? Please?"

I swallow, arousal and expectation whipping through my blood. "You don't have to beg me for anything. Whatever you want is yours."

She rolls her lips, and I can see nervousness behind her eyes, but then she lifts the hem of my shirt like she wants to remove it. I oblige, reaching around to the back of my neck and slipping it off over my head. Violet blinks rapidly, eyes tracing the lines of my pecs, arms, and abs, and when her focus reaches the waist of my jeans, she swallows and fumbles at the fly.

"Relax," I tell her, taking her hands as I lie back on the pillows, stretch out, and unbutton my pants. "We can go as slow as you want to go."

Violet nods and kneels on the mattress beside me, her bottom lip trapped between her teeth, and I watch her reaction as I slowly push my jeans over my hips, taking my underwear with them and letting my cock spring free. The slight widening of her eyes and the tiny gasp she tries to hide makes my blood pulse and my dick jump.

With a fiery blush, she lowers her gaze, and I lift her chin. "You okay?"

Her tongue darts out again, and I picture it circling the crown of my cock. It twitches again, and Violet nods as she stares and whispers, "I'm good."

"Give me your hand," I order, my voice cracking with anticipation.

Violet extends her arm, and I turn her hand over. I pick up the olive oil on the nightstand, drizzle a little of the golden liquid into her open palm, and set the bottle aside. I massage the oil into her skin, both of us unable to look away as our fingers slip and slide against each other. I don't stop until her skin is slick and the oil is warm.

I guide her hand toward my cock, moving slowly so she can pull back if she wants to, but Violet just bites her lip and stares at her small hand cupped inside my much larger one.

With my fingers framing hers, I start with a light brush of her fingertips. I almost jump out of my skin at the first touch, squeezing my eyes closed and breathing through the torturous sensation of her touch sweeping along my length from root to tip. I swirl her thumb over the crown of my cock, dragging it through the bead of precum balancing in the slit, then curl her hot hand around me and guide her grip up and down. It sounds like sex and feels so wet, so tight, but I move slowly, slipping my dick through her oily fingers as I settle into the feel of her.

I open my eyes when she moans quietly in the back of her throat, and it's near impossible not to blow at the mere sight of her—bright-eyed, pink-cheeked, aroused by my cock in her hand.

Violet shifts forward, her gaze moving from my dick to my face and back again, like she's not sure where to focus, and I know exactly what she's feeling. I don't know where to look either. The wonder and lust on her face are breathtaking. Her hand around my dick is fucking everything.

I breathe harder as I watch her slender hand move beneath mine. I pump her grip up and down and circle her palm over the crown. I squeeze her hand to indicate more pressure, my abs get hard, and my ass clenches as I thrust into her grip, and I reach over to guide her other hand to my balls. I curl her fingers around and underneath so she's cupping me, then groan with need as I give a little tug.

Violet breathes almost as hard as me, and I grunt as I fight the urge to explode. I work her hand firm and fast, playing with the tip, concentrating on the base, until I just want to see her fingers wrapped around me and nothing else, so I let her go.

She doesn't falter as she takes over the rhythm I've set. My cock slips in and out of her tight fist, and I claw at the sheets as she brings me to the edge.

"That feels incredible," I pant through fast, heavy breaths. "You're doing it just right. Keep doing it like that. Just—like— that. Ah... *fuuuuuck*!"

My orgasm hits me hard, my cock pulsing in her hand as cum shoots across my stomach and over her fingers in thick, sticky ropes. Every muscle in my body contracts with the intensity of my climax, but then I wrap my hand around Violet's again, slowing the pace of her pumps into something smoother and slower to ease me out of it, coating her fingers and mine in my cum.

Finally, my orgasm ebbs away, and I release Violet's hand. She holds me for a second longer before freeing my dick, and I slide my clean hand up her spine so I can wrap my fingers around the back of her neck.

"You did so good, Wallflower." I pull her mouth to mine. "That was really fucking hot."

"Yeah." She glances at my stomach and then her fingers, both covered in my orgasm and a sweet, disbelieving chuckle tumbles from her lips. "It really was."

"Did it make you wet?" I know it's a question that'll make her blush, which is why I ask it.

She rewards me with a downcast glance and red-hot heat burning all the way to her hairline. "Yes."

"Good." I swipe up a couple of discarded napkins and clean Violet's hands before wiping up what I can from my stomach. "Give me a minute to tidy up while you get ready for bed. When I get back, I'm going to make you come, but tonight you'll be wearing my jersey when I do it." I lift her chin so she's looking at me. "I want you wearing my name while you moan it like a prayer. How does that sound?"

Fresh color floods her cheeks. "Really fucking hot."

"Goddamn, Wallflower." I kiss her again, my dick already rallying at the sound of the curse word on her tongue, then climb to my feet. I hike my pants up around my hips and hurry to the door before stopping and looking back. She's a vision.

"Skip the panties and be ready in sixty seconds," I command. "I can't stay away longer than that."

TWENTY-EIGHT

Violet

DAY 26 AT SILVER LEAF... ONLY 60 TO GO

TWO DAYS LATER, I WAKE up with Chord curled around my body and the morning sun streaming in through the floor-to-ceiling glass that makes up the entire east-facing wall of his bedroom.

I say *bedroom*, but it's not like any bedroom I've ever seen. It's more of a suite. His oak-framed king-size bed is dwarfed by the size of the room. Layered rugs top the clean white carpet that stretches into an adjoining sitting area with a television and fireplace. A personal study hides behind tall double doors to the right. A complete ensuite with a double shower and oversized bath is to the left. And the generous timber-decked balcony that stretches the length of the east side and overlooks the ranch has comfy outdoor sofas arranged around a fire pit. It's stunning and indulgent but also warm and comfortable. It's Chord.

Chord's chest moves against my back, rising and falling with the deep, even breaths of sleep. His hard, heavy arm traps me against him in the best way possible, his hand cups my breast even in sleep, and I smile as I think about where I am and who I'm with. I'm in Chord Davenport's house. In his bed. In his arms. How is this my life?

I try to lay still because I never want this moment to end, but Chord must sense the change in my muscles because he nuzzles the back of my neck with the quiet moan of someone surfacing from sleep.

His pelvis shifts, and the hard length of his erection presses against my ass. My breath catches as I remember the feel of him in my hand, slipping through my fist while watching him unravel at my touch. I've never felt so powerful or in control—or so turned on.

"Good morning," he mumbles against my hair, not bothering to hide the way he breathes in the scent of my shampoo. His arm tightens around my middle as he pulls me harder against him. "Sleep well?"

"So good. And you?"

"The best." He drags the collar of the jersey I'm wearing to one side so he can line my shoulder with kisses. "And that means I'm ready for our date today."

My heart leaps, and I spin to look at his face. "Our what?"

Chord grins. "Our date. Are you free?"

I smile wide enough to sprain a cheek. "I'm free."

"Good." He lightly spanks my butt, then throws back the

272

covers. "We've got a lot of ground to cover, so let's get started."

"Where are we going?" I sit up and watch as he walks from the bed to the bathroom in nothing but his underwear. Not only do I get a good look at his million-dollar ass, but his hard-on is obvious through the dark cotton, so it's hard not to stare.

"Eyes up, Wallflower," he murmurs, smirking when my face floods with heat. He pauses on this side of the ensuite door. "I thought I'd take you on a tour of Aster Springs. We've spent nearly every minute this summer here on the ranch, but there's a lot more to this place than the Silver Leaf grapevines. What do you think?"

"I think that sounds fantastic."

"Good." He flicks on the bathroom light. "Think you can be ready in half an hour?"

"Absolutely."

I jump from the bed and hurry to my room with Chord's light, amused chuckle following me down the hallway.

Forty-five minutes later, we're driving toward the main street of Aster Springs with Chord behind the wheel of his truck. I've got butterflies in my stomach, and I stick my hands between my knees to stop my legs bouncing, but there's not much I can do about the smiling.

I haven't felt this way in years—maybe ever. My body buzzes with excitement and anticipation. This is Chord's hometown, and spending a day together like this feels a lot like getting a glimpse into his past—and his heart.

It only takes ten minutes driving through wine country to reach the town proper, marked by a sign that says *Aster Springs: Population 1209.* We pass The Slippery Tipple, closed and quiet, on the right before Chord pulls into an empty space outside a bustling little cafe on the left. It's got cute red and white striped awnings out front, the menu painted on a sidewalk signboard, and a line out the door, so we join the queue for takeout French pastries and sweet, milky coffees.

It doesn't take long for the people around us to notice that Chord Davenport is here, but when they do, the whispering takes off like wildfire. Chord ignores the murmuring and long, obvious looks, but he holds my hand like he knows I need reassurance. I hang on tight, practically glued to his side, as we approach the counter.

Chord pulls out his wallet and nods to the woman at the register. "Morning, Sophie."

Sophie's hair is more gray than dark, and the deep lines around her eyes and mouth hint at a life spent laughing. "*Bonjour*, Chord," she says with a warm smile and a gorgeous French accent. "It has been too long since I saw you last."

"My fault," he agrees easily. "But I missed you."

Sophie laughs. "You missed my *kouign-amann*." She retrieves a paper bag from under the counter and uses a pair of tongs to transfer a pastry before she glances at me. "Would you like one also, or perhaps you want to try something else?"

I scan the glass case with shelf upon shelf of mouthwatering pastries, and though I linger a little longer on a plate of sugar-coated *beignets*, everything looks so good that I can't decide. "I'll have the same," I say. "Thank you."

"Plus two *cafe au laits,* please, Sophie," Chord adds. "And half a dozen *beignets*."

I narrow my eyes at him, but he just bites back a smile and gives me a wink.

We return to the car with our simple breakfast, the hushed commentary of other patrons chasing us out the door.

"That wasn't too bad, was it?" Chord asks. His tone is light, but his dark brows are pinched.

I don't mean to hesitate. Chord warned me that he came with a spotlight, and I meant it when I said I could stand in it too if he was by my side, but I've never liked the attention. I think about my new social media followers and how the boost to my numbers makes me equal parts hopeful and terrified. It's my instinct to hide, but I don't want that to always be the case. I drink in the smooth, straight lines of Chord's gorgeous face and remind myself how lucky I am to be here right now.

I don't want to be scared all my life.

I take his hand and kiss the back of it. "I'm having French doughnuts for breakfast, so I'd say this date is off to the perfect start."

The relief on his face warms my heart, and the day only gets better. We leave the main thoroughfare of Aster Springs and drive a little way out to a small local art gallery. We walk out with an abstract canvas I adored at first sight, then stop at the village market for lunch supplies.

Chord drives us to a nearby park with stunning historic ruins and enchanting tumbled-down stone walls overrun with flowering vines. He retrieves a soft plaid blanket from his truck, and we find a shady spot looking out over the valley to share our generous haul of local produce—olives and bread, heirloom tomatoes, sweet and juicy stone fruits—expertly matched with a dry white wine that Chord picked himself. We've got no glasses, so we trade sips straight from the bottle, and that somehow makes the whole thing more romantic.

When we're done, I recline on the blanket and stare up at the sunlight filtering through the leaves above. Chord stretches out beside me, propped up on his elbow and watching me with soft blue eyes and a gentle tilt to his mouth.

"What?" I ask, swiping at my face to remove any crumbs that might be stuck to my skin. "What are you looking at?"

"Just how flawless you are," he murmurs.

My cheeks warm, and Chord grins as he slips his hand behind my neck and leans down to kiss me.

"I've had the best day," I murmur. "Thank you."

"You're welcome," he replies, "but it's not over yet."

My heart skips. "It's not?"

"Nope." Chord sweeps a strand of hair from my face, dragging it from my neck where my hairline has grown damp from the heat of the day. "I've done my duty as a good Aster Springs boy and shown you all the tourist traps, but there's one more place I'd like you to see—somewhere only the locals know, so you have to promise to keep it a secret."

I sit up and cross my fluttering heart. "I promise."

Chord gives me a megawatt grin that makes my pulse race faster. "Let's go."

The route to Chord's secret location takes us back down Aster Springs' main street, past acres of vineyards and farmland, then down a rough dirt road that barely warrants the name. He drives confidently through terrain that only a truck could handle, down a narrow path that gets rougher and more remote as the trees around us grow thicker and bright yellow and purple wildflowers begin bursting through the underbrush. Though it feels like forever, it only takes another few minutes for Chord to pull to the side of an unmarked road and cut the engine.

I look around, searching for a sign or something—anything—to indicate we aren't in the middle of nowhere, but there's no such thing.

"We're here," he announces.

"Um." I squint out at the wall of nature outside my window. "Okay?"

Chord grins harder, reminding me of a kid with a secret, and climbs out of the car. I'm still worrying about how I'm supposed to hike in my bare legs and sneakers when he opens my door.

"It's not far," he reassures me when I hesitate.

I don't think I could deny this man anything, so when he slips his hands under my arms to lift me out and set me on the ground, I go with it.

Chord takes my hand and leads me around the car, stopping to take out the blanket, and now I can see there's a beaten track through the forest that's only visible on foot. We follow it down a gradual decline until the trees give way and a wide blue-green lake comes into view. It's still and stunning, with the light of the sun skipping along its surface and the blue sky stretching on forever overhead.

"Oh, my," I whisper as Chord draws me closer to the water's edge. "This is incredible."

"I think so too." Chord drops the blanket on the soft grass at our feet and squints out over the water. The shore on the opposite side is far enough away that I couldn't swim the distance, and he points to what looks like the end of a long wharf jutting out into the water. "You can't see it from here, but there's a little beach around that corner. That's where most people go to swim, and where local kids go to get drunk and make out. You can drive right up to the water on that side, so it's easier to get to, and it's a good spot for parties and bonfires."

I can picture it now, and although it makes me want to smile, I'm sad that my childhood was nothing like that. I spent all my free time at home. "Sounds like fun."

Chord shrugs with a reflective, almost wistful, twist to his mouth. "I was too busy and too serious about playing hockey to spend much time out here, but I sneaked out a few times before I was drafted to Tampa."

"Were you bad?" I tease.

He loops his arms around my waist and holds me close. "The baddest."

I bite my lip to stop a giggle. "I find that hard to believe... Chord Fergus Davenport."

Chord's eyebrows lift before his ears burn red, and he chuckles lightly. "You've been waiting for the perfect moment to throw that out, haven't you?"

"About a month, give or take a few days." I laugh and trace the shell of his ear with a fingertip. "It's only fair I see you blush for once. Don't you think?"

He growls and kisses me hard, and I laugh against his mouth.

"So, why are we here instead of over there?" I ghost my palms over the carved lines of his upper arms and ignore the adorable flush creeping up his neck. "It sounds like the beach over there is a lot more convenient."

Chord narrows his eyes as a mischievous smile passes his lips. "Because this side is a lot more private."

He lifts the hem of my tee high enough to expose my belly, then stops with a question on his scarred eyebrow. My heart races as I raise my arms so he can slip the tee off my body. He lets it fall to the ground, and his throat bobs in a deep swallow as I do the same for him, dragging his shirt up over his torso and as high as I can up his arms before he has to finish the job.

We stand there, me in a lacy white bra and shorts, Chord bare-chested, his fingers twisted loosely in mine, and our bodies brushing with every breath.

"Do you want to go swimming?" he asks in a low rumble.

I'm so lost in his blue eyes that I nod without even worrying about what's going to happen next.

Chord drops to his knees and unlaces my shoes before lifting one foot, then the other, to slip them off. He looks up at me as he unbuttons my shorts, and I shiver in the full heat of the sun as he drags them down my legs. I step out of them, and he skims his hands up my legs, and when he traces the line of the little white thong I'm wearing, I close my eyes with a whimper.

Chord stands and pulls off his own shorts, and when we're both in nothing but our underwear, my nipples hard underneath the lace of my bra and Chord's erection obvious behind the fabric of his underwear, I bite my lip and fight the temptation to remove my bra and panties. I want to be naked with him. Still, I'm too scared to be that bold. Chord hesitates like he's thinking about it too, but then he removes my glasses and sets them carefully atop my clothes, takes my hand, and leads me into the water.

Although the water is cooler than the air around us, it's surprisingly warm, and we wade far enough in for the depth to reach my shoulders.

Chord sinks beneath the surface first, rising like an Adonis with trails of water dripping from his dark hair and over his temples, down his smooth cheeks, his collarbone, his muscular chest. I follow, dipping quickly into the water, then rising back up, pushing my hair off my face.

When I open my eyes, Chord's watching me with the kind of expression that triggers a wet, achy pulse between my thighs.

"Come here," Chord says, his voice husky, reaching out and dragging me to him.

I glide through the water and latch onto his hard, wide shoulders as he kisses me. Our wet lips slip against each other in a way that's new and sensual, but his tongue is familiar, and I wrap my legs around him with the need to be closer. His fingers briefly dig into my ass before finding their way up to my waist, and although I can feel his arousal between my legs, his kisses are slow and reverent. And perfect.

"Can I ask you something?" I murmur against Chord's ear as I cling to him in the water.

His palms sweep over my back, my ass, my thighs, as he nuzzles my shoulder. "Anything."

"I know we agreed it was too early to put a label on... on... *this*... but..." My voice grows smaller as I grasp my hopes and fears tight against my chest. "What are we doing?"

Chord presses his lips to my shoulder, pausing there like he's thinking about the answer, and my stomach tightens. Each day I spend with Chord leaves me feeling safer than the day before. I've let down my guard, and finally, for the first time in my life, I feel like it's okay to be the real me. But maybe... maybe it's too much to want to ask how he feels. The wrong answer would wreck me.

But then Chord draws back and looks at me with so much heart shining in his cobalt eyes that I can barely breathe.

"I don't know about you, Wallflower," he whispers, "but I'm falling for you. Hard."

Light. Butterflies. Everywhere. I tighten around him—arms, legs, soul—and burrow into the crook of his neck. Chord's arms grow snug, his lips go to my hair, and his heart beats fast against mine as I murmur my reply against his wet skin.

"I'm falling hard for you too."

TWENTY-NINE

Chord

53 DAYS TILL HOCKEY SEASON

"YOU OKAY THERE, WALLFLOWER?"

Violet hangs off my arm as we approach the front door to the main house. This is her first time visiting my family home, and she's about to meet my brothers in the potentially overwhelming scenario of our second family game night. So, although the way she squeezes my bicep gives away the fact she's nervous as hell, I pretend to believe her when she says, "I'm okay."

I still tighten my grip on her hand.

It's been a week since our Aster Springs date and the declaration I made in the lake. I meant it all. Every single word of it. And it was so damn romantic—the kind of stories oldies tell their grandchildren—until photos surfaced online and social media shit all over it.

Violet insists there's nothing for me to feel guilty about, but I do. I'm pissed at myself for putting her in that position. I should have been more careful. I should have known *practically private* wasn't private enough for the most precious person in my life. Violet trusted me, and I fucked up.

But I'm resolved to make it up to her tonight.

Izzy declared her first game night such a success that she had to host another one, and this time, she graciously agreed to extend the invitation to Violet and her dad.

I say graciously with heavy doses of sarcasm and begrudging admiration. I asked her if it would be okay if I invited two extra people, and she lit up like a firefly before inexplicably narrowing her baby blues. Then she negotiated. Hard. I got to add Violet and Luke to the guest list. Izzy walked away with a sneaky stash of candy plus a contract—drafted in purple marker and signed by me with Daisy as a witness—that sooner rather than later, I *will* buy her that horse.

She'll make a killer sports agent someday.

We enter the house without knocking, and the sound of my brothers and sisters talking in the living room floats out to us in the hallway. I lead Violet in that direction, wading through a sea of blue and green balloons on the carpet and streamers overhead.

This is the first time Violet will be in a room with everyone in my family at the same time. I know she wants to make a good impression, and even though I wish she wouldn't worry, the fact that this is so important to her means a lot to me.

"Uncle Chord!" Izzy jumps up from where she's playing cards with Finn at the coffee table and launches herself and her enormous purple tutu into my arms. "Did you bring my hor—"

"I'm working on it," I interrupt, casting a furtive glance around the room for Charlie, but she's nowhere to be seen. "Do you remember my friend, Violet?"

She gives Violet a look that reads something like *can you believe this guy?*

"Of *course* I remember, Uncle Chord. We've met *seven times* already."

"Sorry." I roll my lips to stop a smile and notice Violet is fighting one too. "Of *course*, you two know each other." I point to the pair of extra-large whiteboards set up in front of the cold fireplace. "What are these for, Iz?"

"We're playing Pictionary tonight! Boys versus girls, and we're going to win! Aren't we, Vi?"

Violet chuckles at Izzy's use of Daisy's nickname. "You know what?" she says in a conspiratorial whisper. "I think we will."

I feign an offended snort. "You want to bet?"

Violet covers her smile with one hand as Izzy scowls and sticks out her little hand. "A million bucks says the girls win."

I pretend to frown back as I shake on it. "Done."

Izzy wriggles out of my arms and runs over to Dylan. "Dad! Guess what? We're going to be rich!"

Violet laughs, and I draw her to me, wrapping her up and clasping her wrists at the small of her back. "You think I'm joking? I'll bet you a million bucks too. You know I'm good for it."

"But I'm not. If the boys' team wins, what will I give you?"

I dip my head to her ear. "Oh, Wallflower. I'll think of something."

We're interrupted by the sound of someone clearing his throat, and when I realize it's Violet's father, I stand straighter.

I've spent a little time with Luke over the twelve days he's been on the ranch—passing him in my kitchen when he's there for coffee with Violet, discussing the state of the fences when I'm available to help with repairs—and so far, our interactions have been friendly.

He's aware that I'm dating his daughter and, according to Violet, he supports the idea because it makes her so happy. But his brown eyes, so much like Violet's, are a little guarded tonight. It might be my guilty conscience talking, but I wonder if he saw the pictures of Violet and me almost naked in the lake.

"Luke," I say, extending my hand. "It's good to see you again."

He nods and gives Violet a quick kiss on the cheek before accepting my handshake. "It's nice to see you too, Chord. Thank you for inviting me tonight."

"Of course. We're happy to have you."

He gives me a small smile, then tips his head toward Izzy and Daisy, who are fussing with the last preparations for the game night—testing the whiteboard markers, shifting the angles of the boards, setting up the game on the coffee table, Izzy studiously examining the dice.

"I didn't realize this was so serious," says Luke. "Little Isobel has read me the rules twice already." He chuckles dryly and shakes his head. "I'm starting to get nervous."

"I'd say it'll be fun, but Izzy's a tiny tyrant," I reply, only half-joking. "I live for competition, but even I'm starting to sweat."

"That might be because you've got a million dollars riding on your drawing skills," Violet teases.

Luke's eyes widen. "A million dollars!"

I scowl at Violet and pretend to be irritated when in fact, I love this side of her. She gives me an impish grin, then her dad a sheepish shrug, which makes him laugh, and I conclude that Violet's growing confidence is because she feels more comfortable with her father around. Maybe it's even her growing familiarity with Isobel. I let myself hope it's also a little bit about me.

Izzy appears at my hip, takes my hand, and yanks hard, but not hard enough to move me.

"What are you doing, Iz?"

She grunts with effort as she tugs. "You're a boy. You have to—come—over—here."

Violet play-shoves my shoulder. "You heard her, and don't worry. I'm sure my drawing skills are *nothing* compared to yours, Mr. Hotshot Hockey Player. Your million dollars is safe."

Violet flutters her lashes, then blushes prettily when I laugh out loud in surprise at the way she's teasing. "Oh, it's on, Wallflower."

Her blush deepens as Izzy tows me away.

My niece starts barking orders, corralling Finn, Dylan, Luke, and me onto the long sofa on the far side of the room. As soon as her head is turned, Finn gives her the slip and reappears with a couple of cold beers just as Daisy throws a balled-up napkin at my head and waves hello. She's already ensconced on the opposite, smaller sofa with Violet snug against her side, and something clicks open in my chest at the picture of them together.

Charlie walks in from the kitchen and shoves a bowl of Pretzel M&M's in my hands before crossing to the other side of the room and squishing onto the girls' couch. I consider breaking rank to say thanks or hello or *something*, but before I get the chance, Izzy blows a silver whistle that's going to get really old real soon.

"Where the fuck did she find that?" Finn mutters.

Dylan elbows him hard enough to make him grunt, but then he sighs. "No freaking clue. There's a free dinner in it for you if you can make it disappear."

Finn snorts—Dylan's dinners are a given any night at The Hill—but he says, "On it."

"Okay!" Izzy shouts. "The second Davenport Family Game Night is now in session! On your marks!"

On the other side of the room, Violet starts nibbling on

her lip, and her hands are wedged between her thighs the way she does when she's nervous.

You okay? I mouth.

Her legs stop bouncing, and Violet gives me a subtle nod. An even tinier smile. *Yep.*

As Izzy thrusts the rule book in Violet's hands and she bends her head to read, I dig one elbow into Finn on my left, the other into Dylan on my right. They respond with affronted grunts before they both assault my ribs at the same time. I don't give them the satisfaction of acknowledging it.

"What the hell, bro?" Dylan asks.

"That's Violet," I say with a nod in her direction.

"Ah." Finn nods and takes a slug of his beer. "*That's* Violet. I thought she was a figment of your imagination. She's pretty."

"She's fucking perfect," I correct him.

Violet must sense that we're looking at her, talking about her. She raises her eyes without lifting her chin, checking us out from beneath her long dark lashes.

"Say hi," I order under my breath.

"Hey, Violet." Finn waves with a polite smile. "Nice to meet you. I'm Finn—Chord's younger, fitter brother."

"Fuck off," I mutter, and he snickers.

"Hi, Finn," she replies with pink cheeks, a shy smile, and a voice that just carries the eight feet between us. "Nice to meet you too."

I nudge Dylan and practically hear him roll his eyes. "Glad you could be here, Violet. I'm Dylan—Chord's younger, cuter brother."

"Jesus Christ," I mumble.

"Hi, Dylan," Violet replies. "Um, your food is excellent."

Dylan gives me a smug look. "You hear that, bro? Apparently, I'm younger, cuter, and more talented too."

"Go find a mirror, would you?" I say with a good-natured shove.

Violet chuckles, and I give her a wink that heightens the color in her cheeks. I hope she's thinking the same things I am. This feels good. Natural. Easy. Right.

The sound of the front door crashing open and slamming shut reverberates down the hallway moments before tiny, redheaded Poppy bursts into the living room.

"I'm here! I'm here!" Poppy squeezes onto the sofa between Daisy and Violet, then circles her hand at Izzy, who has her fist raised and ready to toss the dice. "Go ahead. Don't mind me."

Beside me, Dylan chokes on his beer. I smack him on the back as he forces it down with watering eyes.

"Jesus." He wipes his mouth with the back of his hand and keeps his voice low. "Where the hell did she come from?"

I watch Izzy roll the dice and move the marker four places on the board as I answer Dylan's question. "She's been back in town for a couple of weeks. Didn't Daisy tell you?"

Dylan makes a sound in his throat. "Ah, no."

Finn hides a chuckle behind his hand. "This should be good."

I'm a dick for laughing, but I can't help it. Daisy and Poppy made Dylan's life hell growing up. He's only two years older and was always picking them up when they got drunk at parties, covering for them when they cut school, saving their asses when they got into fights, and swooping in when they wanted to get rid of ex-boyfriends or guys they weren't interested in. In return, they acted like typical teenage girls. They basically tormented him.

"It's been a long time," I tell him. "I don't think you'll be called up for big brother duty any time soon."

On the other side of the room, Poppy notices us looking her way, and she wiggles her fingers at Dylan with a pretty, devilish grin.

Dylan rolls his eyes with a groan and pushes to his feet. "I need another beer."

Three throws of the dice into the game, and it's Violet's turn to stand at the board. She keeps her eyes on the carpet as she makes her way over, picks up the marker, and accepts the word card from Izzy. I should be watching Finn as he scribbles on our board, but I'm too distracted by Violet. She doesn't look anywhere but the board while she's sketching, shoulders hunched against everyone's shouts. They're all wildly incorrect guesses until Violet's expertly drawn lines coalesce into a tall, fancy-looking dog with puffs of fur at its ankles, ears, and tail.

"Poodle!" Daisy shouts.

SAMANTHA LEIGH

Violet spins and points at her. "Yes!"

Izzy jumps to her feet with a fist pump and high-pitched whoop while Violet returns to the sofa with pink cheeks, a pleased smile, and an awkward high-five from Poppy.

Finn takes one look at his board and the squiggles that look more like a puddle than a poodle, compares it to Violet's masterpiece, then tosses his marker at me and drops onto the sofa.

"Let's call it now. Violet's got us over a barrel."

He's right. By the time the girls have won the best of five games, I'm down a million bucks—and it's the best money I've ever spent. Violet's shy hand and anxious posture morphed into confident strokes and genuine laughter less than an hour into the evening, and it's so satisfying to see her bloom.

She draws. She calls out answers. She exchanges secret jokes with the girls and laughs hard enough that she collapses into the cushions. She's so stunning I sit back and watch her instead the game, not even caring that our team keeps losing.

She fits.

When it's time to call it a night, it feels like forever and not hours since I touched her, and I cross the room like a man chasing rain after not drinking for days.

Violet gives me a slightly scandalized look before slipping into the hallway, and I follow her, dragging her further away from the living room until we're deep inside the house and hidden in shadows.

I pin her against a wall and kiss her neck. "You were amazing in there. My family adores you."

She moans quietly and curls her fingers into my shoulders, dropping her head back against the wall to give me access to her throat. "It was fun."

I smile against her skin. "You just won a million dollars. I'll bet it was fun."

She chuckles and rocks her hips against my thigh. I bat her knees apart and hitch my leg high enough to give her something to ride, and heat pulses against the denim.

"I don't remember shaking on that," she says breathily, "but I'm sure Izzy will collect as soon as she can."

I lap my tongue against the hollow behind her ear. "Probably."

The voices in the living room get louder as everyone prepares to leave, and Violet reluctantly pushes against my shoulders. "I need to say goodbye to my dad, and we should help tidy up."

I grunt because she's right and because I'm so fucking hard. "Just give me a minute. I'm just going to go to the bathroom."

Her lips twitch prettily as I try to covertly adjust my jeans. "Okay."

When I return to the hallway a few minutes later, the house is quieter. I head straight for the living room, then turn toward Violet's voice in the kitchen. Before I get to her, I hear Charlie's voice too, and I hesitate. Do I go in and make sure everything's fine between them? Do I walk away and give them a chance to get to know each other?

Or do I stay hidden in the shadows of the hallway and listen for my cue to get involved?

It's C. I choose option C.

"Thank you for helping clean up," Charlie says, "but it's not necessary. I can take care of it."

"I don't mind," Violet replies. "Actually, I was hoping I might get a chance to talk to you tonight. I want to thank you."

The sound of water running starts, and then stops before Charlie replies. "Thank me? Why?"

I'm taken aback at how gentle her voice sounds, and I can almost feel Violet's deep breath in the brief pause before she speaks. "Thank you for agreeing to let my dad stay on the ranch for a few weeks, and for keeping him busy with odd jobs. I'm not sure what Chord told you about our situation, but my dad is the only family I have, and he doesn't do well on his own. You've saved me a lot of worry, but it's not only that. He's having a really good time out here."

"You're welcome," Charlie replies, "but it wasn't a hard ask. Chord explained that your dad needed support, and we're in a position to offer it." There's a beat of silence before she goes on. "Plus, I figured it might make up for my behavior the day you arrived at Silver Leaf. I'm not what anyone would describe as warm and fuzzy—that's Daisy's thing—but I like to think I'm polite and professional. I embarrassed myself and put you in an uncomfortable position. I apologize."

"You don't need to," Violet reassures her. "It wasn't that bad."

There's an odd silence that lasts long enough that I consider rushing in to fix whatever's gone wrong, but then they start laughing.

"Okay, it wasn't the best start," Violet admits. "But it didn't cause any permanent damage."

"Good. I'm glad to hear it." Another pause before Charlie adds, "So... If that's all, I guess we should probably get back out there."

"Um. Wait. There is one more thing."

"Okay?"

"The San Francisco Fury are coming to Aster Springs a week from tomorrow to train at the rink just outside of town," Violet says in a tumbled rush. "We've hired it out for the day and everything."

There's another pause, and I frown as Charlie asks the exact thing I'm thinking.

"Why are you telling me this?"

"It's a closed session, but I'm going to take my dad along to watch—he's a huge Fury fan—and I thought... I mean I wondered if perhaps you'd like to come too? All of you— Finn, Dylan and Izzy, and Daisy. I know it's been difficult in the past to get away from the ranch and travel to Chord's games, but I bet he'd love to see you at training. You don't have to be there for the whole day, of course, but it might be fun to stop by and take a look?"

More silence, and I swallow thickly.

"I don't think so," she says. "Maybe some other time."

I love Violet for trying, but I knew there was no way Charlie would want to watch me train. And even though I was expecting it, her answer kicks me in the gut.

"Oh." Violet's voice is small, and I hate that she's disappointed on my behalf. "Okay. But if you change your mind, we'll be there all day for drills and practice and team-building games. You can drop by anytime."

"I—" Charlie stops, and I hold my breath. "I'll think about it."

Violet's exhalation echoes my own. "Great," she says. "That's... That's great."

At the sounds of movement in the kitchen, I move further into the hallway and wait for Violet to appear before I follow her into the empty living room. I clasp her hand before she knows I'm there, and she gasps as I spin her into my arms.

"I don't know what I did to deserve you, but I'm so fucking lucky you were in the Fury boardroom that day."

She slides her hands around my neck and, with a puzzled little smile, twists her fingers into my hair. "Where did this come from?"

I rock our bodies from side to side as if there were music, slow dancing with my girl in the silence. "Tonight was just that good."

"I had a nice time too." She hums and snuggles against my chest, then chokes back a giggle.

"What?" I look down, but she's burrowed against my body. "What's so funny?"

"Nothing. It's just..." She finally meets my eyes. "What you said about being in the boardroom that day. I was so scared of you that I wanted to fall through the floor. I went home that night and told my dad I was in the wrong place at the wrong time, and Chord Davenport had hired me to be his assistant. My only plan for this summer was to reach the end of it without getting fired."

I swallow a lump of shame and hold her tighter. "And now?"

"Now I can't believe how lucky I was that you saw me at all."

I'd give almost anything to rewrite the way we met, but I'm determined to make it up to her for as long as she'll let me. "I saw you, Wallflower. I saw you, and I haven't been able to look away ever since."

She rests her head on my chest and sinks against me with a sigh.

"A million dollars for your thoughts?" I ask.

"I was just thinking how much has changed. I didn't want this summer to happen at all, and now..." It should be impossible for her voice to grow quieter, but it does. "Now, I never want it to end."

I stroke her hair, set my cheek on her head, and share my dream in a whisper. "Maybe it doesn't have to."

THIRTY

Violet

DAY 41 AT SILVER LEAF... ONLY 45 TO GO

I STAND AT THE ENTRANCE to the ice arena located twenty minutes outside Aster Springs and welcome the San Francisco Fury as they arrive one by one. As a junior marketing executive, I don't have much contact with the players, but that changed when I became Chord's assistant. This is session number four in the summer training schedule, and the process is familiar enough that I'm not a bundle of nerves anymore. Today I'm directing players to the locker rooms inside so they can get ready for today's sessions, but there's a lot of standing around to do, and I spend the lulls anxiously scanning the parking lot for Chord's family. So far, none of them are here.

Coach Campbell and Chord are already inside, and we've rented the entire place out to give the team time together on the ice. It probably would have been easier to do this at the home arena in San Francisco but with eight weeks until the official start of the season, Coach liked the idea of keeping things low-key and informal by using a small-town venue.

I send another player inside just as a sleek black SUV pulls into an empty space, followed by a similar model in white. Hayden steps out of the first car, then Weston out of the second, just as a convertible jeep with the top down screeches into the lot. The driver swings into an available space, barely coming to a stop before Breaker, Theo, and Jake jump out—literally. They don't bother to open their doors before launching themselves out of the vehicle, landing on the asphalt with the ease of wild cats.

I tilt my head and admire how good-looking they are. Athletic, obviously. Tall, hard, strong. Different ages and different features—tattoos and scruffy, clean cut and boyish—and without exception hot.

As they draw closer, I stand straight, clear my throat and smile, but there's nothing I can do to stop the heat creeping up my neck. "It's nice to see you all again. I hope you didn't have any trouble finding the place?"

Hayden flashes a cocky grin. "Set my GPS to *nearest beautiful woman* and it led me straight to you."

I cover my snort as West smacks him over the head, and the other boys groan, but then an unimpressed grunt sounds behind me, loud enough to make me jump. I spin to find Chord scowling over my head, and I take a small but subtle step away from Hayden.

"These guys just got here," I explain. "They're about to head inside and find the locker room."

Hayden's grin gets wider as he mock-salutes his captain. West shakes his head, and I roll my lips as Chord crosses his arms over his chest and glares while his teammates file inside.

Once they're gone, Chord takes my hand and pulls me away, rounding the corner of the building, and then pinning me against the wall the moment we're out of sight. His hips press against me, and his big arms cage me in as he dips in to kiss me. I kiss him back, my tablet clutched to my chest until we're both breathing fast.

"A little reminder of who you belong to," he says, dropping a gentle sweep of his lips against mine before brushing the tip of my nose with his.

Goosebumps ripple where his warm breath hits the side of my neck. *Who I belong to.*

I close my eyes and give over to the warmth that pools in my core whenever Chord's mouth is on my body, even as a whisper of anxiety swirls in my chest. My life is perfect, and perfection is so foreign to me that it's becoming uncomfortable.

For years I wanted to design couture and travel the world. I never once dreamed about being a personal assistant for the NHL's hottest player, and I never imagined falling in love with him. I never pictured being happy out of the city on a California ranch. Never dreamed I'd find a place where I could live a life all my own, my dad close enough and happy enough that I wouldn't worry about him every minute of the day. I never knew I wanted this, but now that I have it, I don't want to let it go.

And I know Chord said our summer together doesn't have to end, and it's a sweet promise, but no amount of money or sentimental words can stop time. October will be here before we know it and what will happen then? I don't want to ask and break our magical summer bubble, but I think about it every day.

Chord will leave the ranch, and I assume Dad and I will move back to our apartment in the city. I'll return to Fury headquarters under Courtney's rule. Chord will be at away games half the time, driven and focused on getting to the playoffs, and I'll spend my nights without him, sketching and listening to music. Nothing to keep me warm at night except a blanket and my dreams.

I close my eyes and rest my head on Chord's broad chest, soothed by the warmth of his body, the smell of his skin, and the beat of his heart, before he rubs his palms up and down my arms and presses a kiss to the top of my head.

"Okay, Wallflower. I know you're busy. I'm going to check in with Coach and get things started. I'll see you in there?"

I offer him my upturned lips, and the corner of his mouth tips up before he takes my face in both hands and kisses me gently. We walk back around to the front of the building side by side, Chord brushing the back of my hand with his and giving me a quick wink as he disappears inside.

I stand at the front of the arena and check my list for the hundredth time to confirm that everyone who is supposed to be here is already accounted for. Everyone who needs to be here is already inside, but still, I wait and stare out across the parking lot, hoping that hope alone will conjure a Davenport. It doesn't, and my stomach drops as I go inside.

I speak to a couple of staff members on my way through the complex to make sure everything is under control, then enter the arena and make my way over to my dad, who sits in the stands with youthful exuberance brightening his face.

Dad is thriving at Silver Leaf—he's a little stronger, fitter, and happier every time I see him—and I love the change in him, but a flutter of anxiety catches in my throat. How will he manage when it's time to leave?

"I needed this," he says as I hand over one of the coffees I picked up in the foyer. "Thank you, Blossom."

"No problem." I settle into the seat next to him, take a sip from my own cup, and check the time. "Shouldn't be long now."

"That's okay. I don't mind waiting. It gives us time to catch up."

I frown mid-sip and swallow my mouthful of coffee. "Catch up?"

Dad gives me a reluctant smile. "I wasn't going to say anything because you didn't bring it up, and I know you're happy with Chord, but..."

I lower my coffee to my lap, ignoring the way the air

suddenly feels uncomfortably warm and my stomach hollows out. "But... what?"

"This relationship... It's complicated, isn't it? Dating a famous NHL player isn't the same as dating a regular guy. There are added pressures and expectations. People watching and talking about you."

My cheeks burn hot. "You saw the photos, didn't you?"

Dad shakes his head with a defeated sigh. "No, but I read about them."

"We were just unlucky."

I stare at a gum wrapper on the floor instead of Dad's concerned gaze. The photos of Chord and I swimming in the lake *were* unlucky, and of course, they bothered me, but they upset Chord too. Every time a website publishes a new image, Chord's lawyers and PR firm work double time to get it taken down. And for better or worse, we're in this together now. I won't be one of those women who run from Chord when his spotlight shines too bright.

"I'm worried about you, Violet." Dad raises his palms as if anticipating an argument. "I understand you're a grown woman—a smart, sensible, talented woman who can make her own choices—and I haven't always been strong enough for you to lean on, but I have to ask if this relationship is really what you want."

"Oh, Dad." I take his hand with a grateful but watery smile. "I appreciate it—I really do—but I... I think I might love him. This is *really* what I want."

"Love, eh?" Dad rubs a finger under his nose, but it doesn't hide his small smile. "Well, then. I guess you know best, and I—I'm happy for you, Blossom."

I blink back tears as I drag him into a seated hug, kissing his cheek and holding him tight. "Thank you."

Ten minutes later, the Fury glides out onto the ice, and we watch the team warm up, run through drills, and speed along the ice. Dad is captivated, but I get just as much pleasure from his reactions as I do from the players. I wasn't lying when I told Chord that Dad worships the Fury. And even though I mentioned it weeks ago and only once, it was Chord's idea to invite him along today. The gesture was so considerate and sincere that I welled up, and Chord chuckled as he brushed the moisture from my eyes.

The morning wears on, the team is divided into lines and shifts into practice games, and I find myself increasingly invested because even though this isn't the real thing, it's still something to watch. The men are something to watch. They're powerful, fast, and competent, passing pucks and flying past the boards with strength and determination. They're sweaty. They're aggressive. They're loud.

Every one of them knows what he's doing, but there's one who has my full attention. He's bigger and stronger and brighter than anyone else, that magnetism burning like fire even now, and sitting in the stands watching him feels a little like crushing on the popular boy at school. *He'd never like me. He'd never notice me. I'm nobody and nothing compared to him.*

But he glances up, again and again, his gaze laser-focused on me. Things unspoken pass between us, and I feel like I'm floating. Chord might be *that guy*, but he's looking at *me*.

I wish his family was here to see this. I stick my hands between my knees and check the doors for the thousandth time. When an hour passes, then another, I decide it's time to admit defeat. Thank God I kept this little scheme to myself. Chord might pretend not to care when his family fails to show, but he'd feel discouraged about the progress he's made with Charlie, and it'd be all my fault.

Play picks up, Chord sends a puck flying across the ice into the back of the net, and Dad jumps to his feet. I shake my head and chuckle.

"What?" he asks as I grin and shake my head again. "We scored!"

"Nothing. I'm glad you're having a good time. I'm a little distracted, is all."

"I noticed." Dad returns to his seat, then raises an arm over his head and gives a wide wave. "Well, would you look at that? I didn't know they were coming today."

My heart jumps into my throat as Daisy, Dylan, Izzy, Finn, and Charlie walk into the complex. Daisy spies us first and returns Dad's wave, and they make their way over.

I stand as they approach with Daisy in the lead. "You made it!"

Daisy rolls her eyes. "Finally rallied the troops, and here we are. Better late than never?"

"There's not much left of the morning session," I agree, "but if you stick around, you can chat with Chord during the break. I might even be able to round up some skates if Izzy wants a twirl around the ice?"

The little girl jumps up and down, navy-blue tutu floating around her little boots. "Yes!"

Dad gets to his feet and greets everyone as they file into the row of seats behind us, but no sooner does Charlie's butt hit her chair than she shoots back up again.

"I need something to drink," she announces, stepping back into the aisle. "I'll be back in a minute."

Daisy rolls her eyes and starts to stand but I stop her.

"I'm a little thirsty, too," I say. "Does anyone want anything?"

Izzy's eyes grow wide. "Yes! Candy!"

Dylan tweaks her little nose. "You ate before we came."

Izzy rolls her eyes like her dad is the silliest man in the world. "I didn't eat candy."

Dylan sighs. "Something small?"

I smile and wink at Izzy. "No problem."

I find Charlie loitering near a vending machine in the foyer. She has her back to me as I approach, and I gently tap her on her shoulder to get her attention. She turns and glances behind me as if expecting someone else, then offers me a polite smile.

"Violet. Hi. Thanks for inviting us today. I, uh... It was a nice idea."

"I'm so happy you came. Chord will be too."

Charlie laughs under her breath. "Yeah. Maybe."

"Definitely."

Aside from our conversation in the kitchen the week before, I haven't spent any time with Charlie. From what I can tell and based on the few things Chord and Daisy have told me, she spends all her time maintaining the ranch and working on the books. Alone and striving to build a future she's always dreamed about. I can relate.

"I'm glad I've got you alone," I say. "Something crossed my desk a couple of days ago, and I wanted to talk to you about it." I gesture at the sofa in the corner. "Can we sit for a minute?"

Charlie responds with a puzzled frown. "Uh. Sure."

I pull a name and phone number from the pocket of my shorts and offer it to Charlie as we settle on the sofa.

"Fredrick Myers?" she reads.

"Yes. He's the guy in charge of catering and beverage operations at the Fury's home arena."

Charlie's brows draw together, and she gives her head an apologetic shake. "I'm sorry, but I'm not following you."

I heave in a fortifying breath. I don't know if my idea is a good one, but ever since Chord told me about buying wine from the ranch without anyone knowing, I've been racking my brain for ways to limit the fallout. I want to do for Chord what he—and Charlie—have already done for me. Take care of family.

"I'm a little nervous, so I'm not explaining this well," I say. "Let me try again. You know I'm on the marketing team for the Fury, right?"

"Daisy mentioned it."

"Great. This means I know a lot of what goes on with the team and its operations, at least at a high level. I've just found out that the arena is seeking new local wines for their VIP suites, and I thought of you."

Charlie's eyes narrow and she leans back. "Did Chord put you up to this?"

"Actually, no. Chord knows nothing about it."

Her brows shoot up, and she scans the card again. "So why are you telling me?"

"Because I think you're the best person to pitch Silver Leaf Ranch."

Charlie gives me a skeptical look. "That doesn't make any sense."

I clasp my hands together to stop myself from wedging them between my knees. "I'm going to be honest with you, Charlie. I don't know if this will work. The team has solid conflict of interest policies. Chord is new to the roster, he doesn't have the best reputation, and the spotlight's all on him coming into this season. He's signed a contract valued at less than he's worth, and the optics of adding Silver Leaf wines to their VIP beverage list right now are probably too murky to overcome."

Charlie purses her lips and frowns at the paper again. "But you must think it's worth a shot, or you wouldn't suggest it."

"Exactly. I think with the right pitch, full transparency, and a comprehensive public relations plan, you can do this. You just need to think outside the box a little. Make Chord's connection to the team and the ranch work for you—not against you."

She rubs the paper between her fingers, and I can see the gears turning in Charlie's brain. "We could donate a percentage of every sale to the San Francisco Fury Foundation," she suggests. "Nobody else will offer that. Or we can do a limited-edition bottle just for the arena. It'll make the wine more expensive but much less competitive, which will neutralize any perceived unfair advantages."

I smile with a relieved sigh. Charlie is smart and tenacious, just like I suspected, and she's going to nail this.

"You've got this," I tell her.

Her smile is more genuine than I've seen, her blue eyes more open, and I get the impression we just demolished an invisible wall between us. "Thanks, Vi."

The doors leading to the ice fly open, and Chord stalks through. My stomach flips at the sight of him—tall and broad, face flushed, dark hair damp, kitted out in his Fury colors.

His eyes land on us, and his step falters before he clenches his jaw and strides over. Charlie stands a second before I do, and I check the time to see where we are on the schedule.

"Break time?" I ask.

"Yeah." His eyes shift to Charlie and away again. "Kind of. Izzy wants to go for a spin, Daisy's going to join her, and some of the boys agreed to play pick-up with Dylan, Finn, and your dad. Everyone else is going to do off-ice team-building exercises with the assistant coach."

"Sounds like fun. Are you looking for skates?"

Chord rubs the back of his neck, and my heart breaks at how hard he's trying to not look at Charlie. "Yeah. Do you know where I can find them?"

"I'll ask someone about the rentals desk, but everyone will need to meet me there to try them on."

"Great. Thanks."

There's an awkward pause before Charlie says, "I'll take a pair too."

Warmth bursts from my chest as Chord's brows leap, and his hand drops away from his neck. "Yeah?"

Charlie shrugs. "Sure. Once upon a time, I was pretty good on the ice."

"No. You were *fantastic* on the ice." Chord moves a step closer. "Thanks for coming. It's cool that you're all here."

She fights a smile and rolls her eyes like she's embarrassed. "All right. Are we going to do this or what?"

"Yes!" I take a few quick steps backward. "You two go back in while I locate the rentals, then I'll meet everyone back here in five."

Chord reaches over and grasps my hand to pull me in for a quick kiss. I blush and look around to make sure nobody from the team saw it, and his mouth lifts up at the corner.

"Thanks, Wallflower," he whispers.

I'm well out of earshot before I look back down the corridor, warmth radiating to every cell in my body at Chord and Charlie side by side as they head back to the rink.

THIRTY-ONE

Chord

33 DAYS TILL HOCKEY SEASON

I PACE THE LENGTH OF the front porch and discreetly check my watch. As I pass Violet again, curled up with her sketchbook in the white Adirondack chair, she raises her head and spares me a curious but slightly exasperated look from behind her big glasses. She's so fucking cute.

"What's the matter with you today?" she asks. "You're all... twitchy."

I force myself to stop moving and drop into the chair opposite her. Her brows draw together, and when I'm quiet for too long, she closes her sketchbook, sets it and her pencil on the table between us, and clasps her hands in her lap. The look she gives me is affectionate patience.

I check my watch again, then glance anxiously at the driveway. Fuck it.

"Don't get mad," I begin.

Violet chuckles, but her expression is confused. "When have you ever seen me get mad?"

"Then don't freak out."

She presses her lips together before dragging the bottom one between her teeth. "Chord—"

"And don't say no."

"Okay, you're scaring me. What's going on?"

I frown and cup my fist with the opposite palm. This is a pep talk, and I can do that. I'm good at that. I'm five championship Cups good at that. I'm sixteen million dollars a year good at that.

Jesus. I'm pep-talking *myself* now. Get a grip, Davenport.

"Tonight's the San Francisco Fury Foundation Gala," I say.

Violet's body relaxes with a relieved sigh. "You had me worried for a moment. I RSVP'd *no* to that ages ago. You want to stay out of the spotlight this summer, and I'd have told you if the team had any issue with you not going, but nobody said a word."

"That's not entirely true."

From the corner of my vision, I see a car approaching the driveway, and I wish I'd started this conversation half an hour ago.

Violet frowns. "What do you mean?"

"Coach talked to me. They want everyone on the roster to make an effort to be there. No exceptions."

"Okay?"

"He also said I could bring a date."

Understanding passes across her features, and Violet shakes her head. "Oh, no. Not me."

The sound of tires rolling over gravel announces the arrival of the car, and she gives it a quick, puzzled glance. "Who is that?"

"That's your dress."

"My *dress*?"

"Yes. Your dress."

Another car pulls up behind the first, and Violet audibly swallows. "And that is...?"

"Your hair and makeup artist."

She groans and drops her face into her hands. "Oh, no."

I knew this would be a challenge, but I'm so certain that tonight will be a success that I push aside any guilt I feel about dragging her so firmly out of her comfort zone, pull her hands from her face, and draw her to her feet.

"I have to go tonight. I have to wear a tux and smile for the cameras and pretend like I'm having a good time, but I can't have a good time if I'm not with you. I need you next to me."

Violet drops her forehead on my chest and latches onto the sides of my t-shirt. I rest my chin on the top of her head and brush my fingers over her bare arms until she shivers and presses herself against me.

"Please?"

Behind me, the car doors open and close, and I sense people waiting for the right time to introduce themselves, but

I won't rush this moment. If Violet needs time to think, she'll have it. If she really can't do this, I won't make her. I'll cancel the whole thing. Tell Coach I'm sick. But I know in my gut that if Violet puts on this dress and steps onto that red carpet tonight, it'll change everything.

Violet mumbles something against my shirt, and my heart stops.

"What was that?" I ask.

She turns her head so I can hear her. "I said, okay."

"Yes!" I grin and bend my knees, wrapping my arms around her thighs and hoisting her up so I can kiss her. She squeals and leans down until her mouth meets mine, and I spend a good few long moments enjoying the taste of her, not caring what it looks like or how long it takes.

I'm so proud of her.

Finally, I set her on her bare feet and lead her to the top of the porch steps. Below, a sophisticated woman in head-to-toe black and streaks of gray through her dark hair stands with two black garment bags held aloft in one hand and the handle of a wheeling suitcase in the other. She shares a friendly look with the hair and makeup artist, a younger blonde woman in jeans and sneakers who has a larger suitcase propped up next to her.

"Thanks for coming," I greet them. "Violet, this is—"

Violet gasps, her free hand flying to her cheek. "Victoria Hall!"

I fight a satisfied grin, though, by the look on Victoria's face, I'm not hiding shit. Victoria has dressed me for the last ten years, and she's one of the few people I'd consider a friend.

The world-renowned designer of haute couture rolls her cherry-red lips and takes Violet's stunned expression as her cue to approach. I jog down the few steps to relieve her of the garment bags and suitcase, and she gives me a nod of thanks before climbing the steps and offering Violet her hand.

"It's nice to meet you," she says.

Violet's mouth remains open in a little "O" as she accepts Victoria's greeting, and when it's clear that words are beyond Violet right now, Victoria puts a gentle arm around her shoulders and guides her toward the front door.

"I think we'll get started," she says.

"Good idea." I nod toward Simone, the hair and makeup artist Victoria recommended. "I'll bring that up. You go ahead."

I follow the women up the stairs to Violet's room, detouring to my bedroom to hang the second garment bag in my closet, then return with the additional suitcase. Victoria and Simone murmur quietly together as they move into the bathroom to set up, so I pull a stunned Violet to the side of the room with the plan to revive her with a little mouth-to-mouth.

"Are you all right?" I ask.

Violet casts a sideways look toward the bathroom. "That's Victoria Hall!" she whispers. "I cannot believe I'm wearing a Victoria Hall design tonight. Chord, this is... This is too much. I don't know if I can do it."

"You're going to be spectacular tonight. I just want you to enjoy this experience, okay? Let me be the one to worry—if there's anything to worry about, which there isn't. Your only job is to enjoy the moment. Deal?"

She shakes her head with an overwhelmed little laugh. "Okay. Deal."

After one more kiss, I release Violet into the care of Simone for... whatever it is that women do in these situations. Victoria hovers nearby, and I beckon her over.

"So, you'll let me know when it's time to give Violet the dress?" I whisper.

Victoria rests a hand on my arm. "I won't forget. I'm looking forward to it almost as much as you are."

I seriously doubt that, but I thank her with a grateful smile and leave the room.

After a workout and a sandwich, I hit the shower. For the first time since I got to the ranch, I take extra care shaving, put product through my hair, splash on cologne, and then unzip the black designer tux Victoria made for the event. Everything fits perfectly. Pants that give just enough to be comfortable. A tailored jacket with satin lapels and a simple white pocket square that buttons in at my waist. White shirt with black buttons. Platinum cuff links. Black leather shoes. A bow tie I've got no clue what to do with, so I loop it under my collar and leave it loose for Victoria to take care of later.

I unbox the new Rolex I ordered for the occasion and attach it to my wrist, then dip into the jeweler's bag again to retrieve two more black velvet boxes. I head downstairs and set them on the hall table just as a black stretch limousine pulls up outside and Victoria appears at the top of the staircase. My stomach tightens, and I climb to meet her.

"Are we ready?" I ask.

She takes one look at my bow tie and shakes her head before expertly fixing it. "We're ready."

My heart doesn't race this hard in even the toughest games as I follow Victoria to Violet's bedroom. She's standing in front of the oversized full-length mirror in a long, flowing robe, her hair a perfectly styled crown of glossy chocolate curls. Her professionally applied makeup is subtle and accentuates her big eyes, thick lashes, and full mouth, yet simple enough to complement her natural blush.

"You look wonderful," she says breathily before considering me with a puzzled smile. "But what are you doing in here?"

"Turn around," I tell her, my voice gravelly with overwhelm, and with that same curious expression, she slowly spins to face the mirror.

I accept a scrap of silk from Simone as I cross the room, and Violet watches my reflection as I stand behind her and carefully cover her eyes with the soft teal fabric.

"Chord?" she whispers as I tie the silk around her hair with reverent movements. "What's going on?"

I ghost my hands over her arms and she shivers even with the fabric between my fingers and her skin, and I set my lips to her ear. "Do you trust me?"

Her pink lips part with a shaky breath, and she nods. "I do."

"Then relax, Wallflower. It'll all make sense very soon."

With reluctant steps, I back away from Violet and nod to Victoria. She unzips the garment bag holding Violet's dress and carefully removes it from the hanger. It's stunning—so much more vibrant and alive than I imagined from the sketches—and my breath catches with anticipation. As beautiful as it is now, it'll be a thousand times more magnificent when Violet is wearing it. I can't wait to see her face light up when she recognizes the design.

With competent, professional care, Victoria and Simone ease Violet out of her robe and help her step into the gown. She trusts their quiet instructions implicitly, moving her body as they direct, and my mouth is dry as they finally fasten the zipper and arrange the layers of the skirt just so.

Victoria holds Violet's hand as she blindly steps into the silver heels Simone slips onto her feet, and when the picture is complete, air rushes into my lungs and becomes trapped there as Victoria and Simone step away.

I return to my place behind Violet, my gaze sweeping over her reflection. The dress. The color. The blindfold. The lips.

"Chord?" Violet asks with tentative fingers on the scarf around her face. "Is that you?"

"Yes." My voice cracks, so I try again. "It's me."

Her full, painted lips tremble with a nervous smile. "Can I see the dress now? Please?"

I kiss her bare shoulder, and she whimpers quietly. "I've told you before. You never have to beg me for anything."

I tug on the scrap of silk, and it falls to the floor. I watch Violet's reflection for the exact moment she realizes what I've done. Her gasp is followed by a breathless *oh!* Her wide chestnut eyes grow glassy with emotion as her manicured hands hover over her mouth before hesitantly brushing over the dress as if to make sure it's real.

It's real. And it's hers.

Violet is stunning. Elegant. Exquisite. Her neck and shoulders are bare, her breasts accentuated by the strapless corset that wraps around her ribs in a fine, intricate net of lace and flowers. The dress drops from above the waist, falling to the floor in layers of sheer teal fabric that hints at the shape of her long legs underneath.

Blinking back tears, taking shaky breaths, hands exploring the intricate lines of a dress she's only ever seen as a drawing in her sketchbook, Violet blushes so damn prettily. No, not blushes. *Glows.*

I try to swallow, but it hurts, so I run my tongue over my lips and try again. Before I get a word out, Violet reaches behind her to thread a hand in mine and meets my eyes in the mirror.

"How?" she asks.

I reply with a proud grin and cut my eyes to Victoria. "I shared your sketches and measurements with Victoria, and she brought your vision to life."

Violet returns my smile with one of stunned gratitude and turns to search out Victoria. "Thank you so much," she says.

"You're very welcome," Victoria replies from where she stands at the far end of the room with Simone by her side. "It was a pleasure to work on such a gorgeous gown. You have a wonderful eye for texture and movement."

The color in Violet's cheeks deepens with the drop of her eyes until she raises her thick lashes and meets my eyes in the mirror's reflection.

Time stands still. My heart beats painfully and erratically. I've forgotten how to speak. I've forgotten how to breathe.

Then she whispers, "Thank you."

Time starts up again.

Fuck. I'm not falling for Violet anymore. I've fallen. I'm down. I'm done.

"You look—" The words catch in my throat as I take her hand. "You're beautiful."

The color rises in her face, and she gives me the tiniest shake of her head. "I can't believe this is real."

"I'm having a little trouble myself."

"Do you—" She licks her lips, and her throat bobs. "What do you think of the dress?"

"It's the most gorgeous dress I've ever seen, and you look radiant in it." Violet smiles shyly, and I offer her my elbow. "Shall we?"

With her arm in mine, I escort Violet to the stairs, trying not to get distracted by her silver-heeled foot peeking out from under her skirt and hitting the steps in a way that makes her hips sway. Her fragrance consumes me, and I can't feel my own feet meet the floor, but then we're miraculously in the foyer, where her gaze slides past me to the windows.

Her eyes widen. "Is that a limousine?"

It's impossible to look at anything but her when I reply, "Yeah. It's almost time to go."

She blinks, the first real hint of nerves showing on her face, but she nods as if to herself. "Okay."

"Just breathe, Wallflower." I inhale and wait for her to breathe in with me, and we exhale together. "Tonight is going to be great."

"Mm-hm. I know."

I angle her toward the hall mirror and brush a finger along her collarbone, smiling crookedly at the goosebumps. "There's just one thing missing."

Violet glances down at her dress, presses an open palm to her chest, and carefully touches her hair. "I don't think I could handle anymore, Chord. This is already too much. I—"

I set a soft finger to her lips. "Just one more small thing. I promise."

I pick up the first velvet box on the hall table. It's a little larger than my hand, and I set in on my palm and hold it up, but I don't open it yet.

Violet shakes her head and stares at the box like there's a tiny wild animal inside what is clearly a jewelry box. "I can't," she says. "I don't deserve it."

"You deserve the world, and I'm going to do my best to give it to you, but this..." I tap the box. "I got this on loan for tonight, so don't worry about anything other than enjoying it, okay?"

I press the latch, and the lid hinges open, revealing a sparkling diamond pendant inside. Violet gasps.

"Chord. It's beautiful, but it must be worth a fortune. I can't wear this."

"It's not half as stunning as you or worth a fraction of what you bring to my life. And yes. You can."

With hesitant fingers, Violet reaches in and touches the necklace. The temptation is too much, and I snap the lid down like that iconic scene in *Pretty Woman*. The box bites her fingertips, and Violet jerks back before bursting into laughter.

"You did not just do that!"

I warm at the joy in her expression. "I couldn't help it. Here." I set the box on the hall table and turn her to face the mirror above it. She watches in the reflection as I put the necklace around her throat, my fingers brushing her skin as I fasten it at the back of her neck. It's a simple piece—elegant and understated, just like Violet—and she runs a light touch over the diamond as I reach past her for the second box. I slide out a matching ring, press myself against Violet's back, and loop my arms around her to find her right hand. I slide the ring onto her finger as she watches it settle into place.

"This feels like a dream," she murmurs, gazing at the ring before letting her eyes drift shut. "And I don't want to wake up."

I kiss the side of her neck as I slide a hand over her hip. "It's not a dream, which means it never has to end."

"Are you sure?" she whispers.

"I'm sure." I stand by her side like those tuxes in her sketchbook and slip her hand into the crook of my elbow. "And we've only just begun."

THIRTY-TWO

Violet

DAY 53 AT SILVER LEAF... ONLY 33 TO GO

AS THE LIMOUSINE SLOWS AND joins the queue of cars lined up outside the gala venue, Chord squeezes my hand and peers out his tinted window. "We're almost there. Are you ready?"

Butterflies the size of birds beat in my stomach and chest, and my dress is suddenly too tight. *My* dress. I'm about to walk onto a red carpet wearing a gown that *I* designed. People are going to look at me. They're going to ask who I'm wearing. I'll tell them it's my own, and they're going to judge it. They'll judge *me*, and in my experience, people aren't always kind.

Chord ducks his head to meet my eyes, and I realize I've been staring blankly into the distance. "Are you okay?"

"I..."

The limousine pulls to a final stop and Chord picks up

a handset to tell the driver to wait before he gets out to open our door. Then he turns back to me, sincerity large in his cobalt eyes.

"I know you can do this." He brushes my hand in soothing sweeps. "But the decision to walk into this gala tonight is yours. We don't have to get out of the car if you don't want to."

I press my lips together, the smooth texture of my nude lipstick anchoring me to the present, and I admire Chord for the hundredth time tonight. He is the most effortlessly sexy man I've ever seen. The form-fitted suit that hints at the hard, athletic body underneath. The smooth, chiseled jaw and full mouth. The hands—the large, confident hands. That certain smile he only shares with me. The eyes that I once thought were so cold and now set my soul on fire.

I don't want to be scared for the rest of my life.

Am I ready?

No.

Am I going to do it anyway?

Yes.

"Let's go."

Chord alerts the driver, and I take a deep breath. The door opens, letting in the din and flashes of the waiting media pack, and Chord steps out first. Cameras flash with more urgency, the hum of the crowd gets louder, and I slide across the seat while Chord buttons his jacket and adjusts his cuffs. Then he turns and stretches out his hand.

I take it and step out of the car, and Chord sets his mouth to my ear. "You're beautiful. I'm the luckiest man in the world to have you by my side tonight."

I drop my eyes, and he lifts my chin. "Eyes up, Wallflower."

Breathing steadily so I don't lose control, I take Chord's arm and let him lead me down the red carpet. Other guests are ahead of us, and it's clear Chord's done this many times before when he pauses every few steps to let the photographers take pictures from different angles.

"Chord! Chord! Who is your date tonight?" someone shouts.

"Violet James," Chord says in a voice pitched loud enough to carry.

"Violet! Violet!" another person calls. "Who are you wearing tonight?"

"I—" I clear my throat and try to raise my voice, but my mouth is dry, and my heart is racing, and I'm not sure anyone hears me when I say, "I'm wearing a Violet James original."

The cameras flash again, and Chord squeezes my hand as he turns his face away from the cameras and whispers in my ear, "I've been dreaming about the way you taste, Wallflower. I can't wait for the day I make you come on my tongue."

Heat blooms in my cheeks and between my legs, and Chord sweeps a careful knuckle along my jaw. I gaze up at him, and the cameras go wild when his face breaks into a grin. "You looked a little pale there for a minute, and you're so pretty when you blush."

"Chord! Chord!" A photographer leans over the media rope and waves his arm to move Chord down the carpet. "Can we get a few shots of Violet alone?"

"Will you be okay?" he murmurs.

Warmth that feels a little like adrenaline shoots through my veins. "Yes. Thank you."

He kisses my hand and backs away, then watches with crossed arms and satisfaction as I pose for the cameras.

The lights and the noise aren't what I'm used to, but Chord's strong, solid presence makes it possible for me to smile and turn my body as directed. Nerves aside, I've lived a fairytale today. The makeover. The car. The jewelry. Victoria Hall. This dress. *My dress.*

Chord.

For so many reasons, I finally feel enough.

He returns to my side for one last round of pictures, then loops my arm into the crook of his elbow. We make it to the end of the red carpet just outside the venue doors, and Chord pauses, turns his broad back to the cameras, and kisses me.

"You were magnificent," he says.

Tonight, I can believe him. "Thank you."

"And now that the hard part is over, we can enjoy the night." He yanks me against him with a hand on my lower back, and his eyes grow hot. "Or a couple of hours, at least. I don't think I can be a gentleman much longer than that."

I bite my lip and curl my fingers into the muscled arms trapped beneath his suit, trying to tell him without words how I want this night to end. *I need your mouth*, I think. *Your hands. Your tongue. More. All of you. Everything.* And I'm feeling confident and beautiful and brave enough to say it, but then a limo pulls up at the other end of the red carpet, and my heart jumps into my throat.

Chord frowns. "What is it? What's wrong?"

"Oh, nothing. It's—"

With a curious smile, he glances back over his shoulder. Every muscle in Chord's body tenses in an instant, and he miraculously gains two inches of height.

It's the man who ruined everything for Chord in Calgary. His rival, Spencer Cook.

Chord takes my hand and grips it hard enough that I cover it with my other, cradling his fingers in mine.

"What the fuck is he doing here?" Chord grinds out.

"I don't know."

A woman steps out of the limo behind Spencer, and my heart stutters. She's stunning—blonde and curvy in a sexy red dress, a full pout, and loads of confidence. I don't recognize her, but if she's here with Spencer Cook, I know who she must be.

"Is that your ex-girlfriend, Emma?" I ask.

Chord snorts and shakes his head. "Yes."

I don't think Spencer or Emma see us as they take their first few steps on the carpet, then pause and pose, but Spencer doesn't hold my interest for long. I can't look away from *her*. She's bold and gorgeous, and I shrink a little inside. It's easy to see why any man would be attracted to her.

Even more devastating is realizing that compared to this woman's poise and charisma, my performance on the red carpet was amateurish and embarrassing. I didn't give this dress—or my name—the debut I've dreamed about.

I bite the inside of my cheek and blink against the burn of tears as Chord turns abruptly and drags me through the doors.

The gala is being held in a gorgeous ballroom complete with crystal chandeliers, velvet-draped high-top tables, stern-faced servers with champagne flutes and canapes on trays, and a complete jazz ensemble playing on the low stage.

Insecurity twists in my stomach as we fly toward the bar, me hanging onto Chord's hand and lengthening my stride to keep up with the way he weaves between people and tables. He barks an order for a whiskey neat and a glass of white wine for me, then scowls as we wait for the server to pour the drinks.

"Is this about Spencer Cook?" I ask quietly as Chord picks up his tumbler. "Or..." My voice drops along with my self-esteem. "Or is this about Emma?"

He looks at me with surprise, then sets his drink untouched on the bar. "What?"

I look down at my dress with a hint of regret and a meek laugh that I hope will protect me from humiliation, if not pain. "You're acting a little jealous, and... I mean... Do you still have feelings for her?"

Chord slides his warm hand around my neck and leans in, eyes burning into mine. "This is *not* about her. It'll never be about her. Ever. I'm sorry I made you think that for a single second. You are the only woman in my head—tonight and tomorrow and always—and being here with you tonight is the biggest thrill of my life. You're talented. You're beautiful. You're a thousand—a million—times the woman she'll ever be. And I don't love her. I—" Chord clears his throat and blinks a few times. "Please tell me you believe me."

I nod, not because his voice is so fierce and the words sound so true. I nod because I think he was about to tell me he loved me.

Chord exhales with a shake of his head and presses his thumb and forefinger against his eyes for a moment. When he's calmer, he moves his hand to my shoulder, skims down my arm, and stops when his fingers twist in mine. "But I *am* pissed off that Cook is here. What idiot thought it was a good idea to send him an invitation?" He looks around like the culprit might be loitering nearby. "How many players from other teams are here tonight?"

I glance around. "I don't know. There might be a few. Could it be a coincidence?"

"No. I've got good instincts about stuff like this." He looks over my head and scans the people mingling around the ballroom. "Cook's presence here tonight is intentional."

"Do you want to leave?" I ask.

"What? No." Chord closes his eyes, drops his head back, and takes a big breath. "I keep fucking this up. I'm sorry. I don't want to leave. I want to stay and show you off. There'll be time to figure out why Cook's here later, but right now is all about you."

A little of that lost magic sparks its way up my spine, and Chord's lips twitch at the spots of color I'm sure he sees in my cheeks. He collects his drink, sets the other hand to the small of my back, and just when we step out into the crowd, Chord drops his hand below my waist, brushing the curve of my ass and gliding his fingers along the crease of one cheek before he gives me a little love tap. I shouldn't love it as much as I do, but my pulse leaps at his casually intimate touch.

"Okay, Wallflower," he says. "Let's go get 'em."

Forty-five minutes and two champagnes later, I can almost believe that Chord has forgotten Spencer Cook exists. We avoid him completely as we circle the impressive ballroom, stopping every few feet so Chord can make hockey small talk with the Fury's corporate sponsors, high-paying guests, and various representatives of the Foundation's youth charity beneficiaries.

Chord holds my hand the entire time, introduces me by name to every person we meet, and agrees with the kind of pride that makes me want to take off my underwear that, yes, the dress is stunning, and yes, the spectacular woman on his arm designed it herself.

It's the first time in my life I don't feel the impulse to run from the spotlight.

As we extract ourselves from yet another uncomfortable analysis of the Fury's chances at the Cup this season,

Coach Campbell approaches and shakes Chord's hand.

"I was just coming over to save you," he says with a glance behind us. "Martin giving you a hard time?"

"I can handle it," Chord says with a grunt. "And he'll be eating his words come the playoffs."

"I'll look forward to that." Coach grins, and then turns to me. "You're the belle of the ball tonight, Violet. Everyone's talking about the beautiful woman in *that dress*."

Chord watches me with obvious satisfaction as heat paints my cheekbones. "Thank you, Coach. I'm having a wonderful time. And you're looking dapper in your tux tonight."

He chuckles and shakes his head. "You're kind for saying so, but it's been a long time since I looked good in a penguin suit."

"Not true," I insist. "You wear it very well."

An awkward silence falls. The muscles in Chord's jaw start firing and his thumb rubs anxious circles over the back of my hand, but it takes me a moment to work out what's going on. Chord wants to ask Coach why Spencer Cook is here, but he won't do it after promising that tonight is all about me.

I hate to see him upset, and I'm curious about the answer, too, so I gently extract my hand from Chord's and take a small step sideways. "I think it's time for me to freshen up, so if you'll excuse me?"

"I'll walk with you," Chord offers, but I set a hand on his arm.

"You stay and chat. I won't be long."

My relative comfort in tonight's spotlight aside, I still skirt the edge of the room to get to the bathroom on the other side, then linger longer than necessary to give Chord plenty of time to discuss his concerns with his coach. I use the facilities, then reapply my lipstick, smooth my hair, and check over my dress.

I step out of the bathroom and into the adjoining lounge, styled as a little alcove with floor-to-ceiling mirrors and deep armchairs where guests can make a call or catch their breath.

I'm all alone for the first time since I stepped into my dress, so I risk a little spin to make the skirt fan out. This dress was designed to twirl, and I grin when I see the pretty way the teal fabric flares and falls in a mirror, then clutch the back of the nearest armchair when my head spins. After three glasses of wine in barely an hour, it might be a good idea to sit.

Before I get the chance, a pointed cough grabs my attention, and I jerk my head toward the door. My heart flies when I see Emma, wrapped up in her red dress with a thigh-high split showing off her long legs.

I stand as straight as I can and clutch my purse to my chest like it's some kind of shield. "Hello."

"Mm." Her eyes sweep down my dress and up again. "You're here with Chord?"

A bitter feeling of not-good-enough aches in my throat. "I am."

"Good for you. He's not one for big events, you know."

I curl my fingertips against my little clutch and concentrate on the texture of the fabric to calm me. "I know."

"He'll want to leave soon if he isn't gone already."

I know she's trying to upset me, and I know Chord would never leave me here alone, but the mean girl behavior makes it hard to think, and all I can do is blink at her.

She sashays over, stops a foot away, and raises an eyebrow. "Excuse me. I'd like to use the mirror and you're blocking it."

I tighten my grip on my purse. *Don't apologize. Don't apologize. Don't give this woman the satisfaction.*

But my legs won't move. We're locked in an uncomfortable stare. It's too quiet for too long, and I've had enough wine that the words slip out. "I'm sorry."

She gives me a tight smile as I step aside, then passes me and leans in to check her makeup in the mirror.

Her eyes flicker my way, and I realize I'm staring at her. I need to leave, so I turn toward the door, but she speaks again.

"Nice dress." I glance down at it as if I don't know what she's talking about, and she adds, "Off the rack?"

My cheeks burn. "No. It's—"

"I only wear runway to these things." She smooths a hand over one hip, still absorbed in her reflection. "Chord likes it that way. He has good taste, you know? Never settles for anything less than the best—or never settles for long anyway."

Her mouth twitches to make her inference that I'm not the best clear, and my face flames hotter. Is it possible I've already forgotten how awful people can be outside of Silver Leaf and Aster Springs? I want to be away from here, curled up in Chord's arms and Chord's bed, pretending that the world outside the two of us doesn't exist.

I take another step away from Emma.

"I'm *so* glad Spencer and I were able to be here tonight. It's for his father, of course. You know he was a San Francisco Fury legend, don't you? Your marketing team practically *begged* us to be here." Her green eyes glint in the overhead lighting as she looks at me in the mirror. "Spencer is the best and most sought-after player in the NHL right now. Much stronger and more competitive than Chord, who's barely able to earn his keep. From what I've been told, the Fury bosses think Spence would make an *excellent* addition to the team."

My chin jerks up, and when my eyes widen with indignation, her mouth grows smug.

Outrage pulses through me. "That's a lie."

"Excuse me?" She turns and moves closer, and her voice walks the edge of civility. "I know all about you, *Violet James*. Junior marketing executive, temporary personal assistant, failed fashion designer. You might think you've got the upper hand now that you're sleeping with Chord Davenport, but men like him don't stay with women like you for long. The summer will end, and so will this little fling. You'll be nobody again. And Chord? Well, it won't be long until he's washed up right alongside you. Replaced with someone better and hotter than he ever was."

I've never been brave enough to stand up for myself, no matter how I've been belittled and tormented and ignored over the years, but Emma just crossed a line I don't remember drawing. She's saying cruel things about the man I love with the sole purpose of causing hurt and pain, and I won't stand for it.

I blame the alcohol for what I say next.

THIRTY-THREE

Chord

AS SOON AS VIOLET IS well out of earshot, I round on Coach. "What the fuck is Spencer Cook doing here?"

The people closest to us startle at my language, and as they cast sidelong glances my way, Campbell grumbles under his breath and drags me into a quiet corner.

"His father—"

I jerk my arm from Coach's grasp. "You know that's not what I mean."

He pins me with a disapproving stare, and my nostrils flare as I take in a calming breath, but my blood's running too hot, and the oxygen only fuels the burn.

"I haven't even played my first game with this team, and somebody somewhere thought it'd be fine to put me in the same room with him? *And* my cheating ex-girlfriend? With media and cameras everywhere?"

I forget myself and run a hand through my styled hair, then swear under my breath and stuff my hand in my pocket. What I wouldn't give to get out of here right now, take Violet with me, and never look back.

The thought stuns me amid the rage. Even on my worst days, I've never seriously considered giving up hockey, but it's hard to give a shit about any of it right now, and it's too damn easy to be with Violet.

"Are you signing him?" I demand.

"What? No!" Coach shakes his head, but his hesitant expression doesn't fill me with confidence, and then he adds, "Not if I can help it."

I grind my teeth and toss my head, too pissed to be having this conversation in public. And Violet's been gone too long, making me itch like something is missing.

"I'm leaving."

Coach opens his mouth to protest, then closes it and nods. The Foundation does important work for causes that mean a lot to me, but I'm not going to do the Fury any favors by acting like an asshole to our donors. And I've reached my cap on civility.

"That might be for the best," he agrees.

I grunt and stalk away without saying goodbye, glaring across the room and only partially relieved I can't see Cook. I'm picturing how good it'd feel to stumble over him with a fist in his face.

I ignore the familiar weight of everyone's eyes on me as I sweep through the room like a thundercloud and slip out a set of doors into an empty reception area. I scan the space to figure out where to go next, but there are no bathrooms, which means I've taken the wrong exit. I spin to retrace my steps just as Hayden follows me through the doors. He's dressed in a similar tux, his dark blond hair styled and his scruff neatly trimmed, but his wide smile fades when he sees the scowl on mine. It's mostly my beef with Spencer Cook written on my face, but there's a little irritation with Hayden, too. Shore is a fuckboy who flirts with everyone, but I don't like the way he flashes that stupid grin at Violet.

"Listen," he starts.

I try to step around him. "Can we do this later?"

He stops me with a palm to my chest. "I didn't mean to overstep with Violet."

I grit my teeth and meet his eyes, and his throat bobs with a nervous swallow.

"I don't hook up with women I know are unavailable, and I never mess with girls dating the guys on my team. I want you to know that. I'd never do that to you."

I scowl harder. In his own way, Hayden's trying to tell me he's not like Spencer Cook. And another time, maybe I'd appreciate it—even believe it—but with Emma and Cook only a few feet away, I'm not in the mood to make someone else feel better about himself.

Hayden grimaces and drops his hand. "Okay. Well. As long as you know that I'm sorry about Violet. I didn't mean anything by it, and I'll keep my distance if that's what you want."

Someone scoffs loudly behind me, and I spin slowly toward the sound.

Fucking Cook.

"Hayden Shore's not interested in the exquisite woman Davenport brought with him tonight?" Cook's smirk pulls at one cheek, and though he's talking to Shore, his eyes keep sliding my way. "When did you become a monk?"

I ball my fists at my sides while Cook tugs at his cuff like he doesn't have a worry in the world. Like he's got all the answers. Like he knows I'm not going to risk laying a hand on him, and he snickers to himself as he shakes his head.

"You're more stupid than you look, Shore. That girl would be the easiest lay you've ever had." Cook's focus returns to me. "Every player in the league knows the best way to land a woman like that is to make sure she screwed this asshole first. They leave his bed and go hunting for better just to erase the disappointment."

He's goading me, and I'm too old to be goaded, but fuck it. I want to take the bait. I lurch forward, but Hayden's too fast, and he blocks my shot. Cook chortles, then lifts his chin and smirks at something behind me. I glance back as West, Jake, Theo, and Breaker file through the doors. With their expensive tuxes, flashy watches, and perfect hair, they're a well-dressed wall of *don't fuck with us*.

Cook raises his eyebrows, cocks his head. "Aw. How sweet. The whole gang's here." He puts up his fists and throws a few punches in the air. "You here to fight me? Teach me a lesson?"

Theo runs a palm down the front of his tux. "I'd love to, man, but not tonight. I look too fucking good to get your blood on this suit."

Breaker moves up beside Hayden, blocking Cook with a wide-legged stance like he's guarding the net. "And I just don't want to waste the twelve seconds it would take to beat the shit out of you."

Spencer scoffs with an infuriating lift to his mouth. "Davenport's got himself a bodyguard. Cute."

"Don't worry, asshole," Jake threatens in a low voice. "It'll happen eventually, but we'll do it on the ice. Like gentlemen."

Spencer narrows his eyes at Jake as West sets a hand on my shoulder. "Let's go."

"Sure," I agree, pretending to turn around, but as soon as I've got a clear shot, I spin and land a fist in Spencer Cook's stomach. He doubles over with a grunt, and I shake my hand with a sense of pained satisfaction.

"*Dude*," Breaker moans as his head falls back.

"He had it coming," Theo argues.

Spencer tries to straighten, hands planted on his knees, but he's pale and winded, so I give him a hand and drag him up by his collar. "Say one more thing about the woman I love," I demand in his face. "Go on. I dare you."

He groans and tries to glare at me. "You're going to pay for this, Davenport."

"Good," West says behind me. "Send the bill to the fucking San Francisco Fury."

I flex my fingers and recall Cook's peaked, pained face with satisfaction as I follow the guys back into the ballroom. They make a line straight for the bar, where Theo signals to the server and orders a round of beers.

"You guys didn't have to do that," I say as I accept the glass Theo thrusts at me.

"Uh, yeah, we did," Theo replies, one elbow resting on the bar as he looks out over the room. "That douche has been asking to get his ass kicked for years."

"Can't wait for the season to start," Jake adds, cracking his knuckles to make it obvious what he means.

I take a shallow swallow of my beer while looking around the room for Violet. For the first time in a long time, I wouldn't mind sharing a drink with my team, but I'm desperate to find my girl, so I stop at the first sip and set the glass on the counter.

"I have to bail," I announce, offering my hand to Breaker. He takes it and pulls me in for a hug.

"We'll see you at your place next week for training," West says, giving me a couple of thumps on my back.

"Sure." I glance at my barely touched beer. "And why don't you guys stick around afterward? We can try this again at the bar in Aster Springs."

"Don't have to ask me twice," Theo says as the other boys mutter their agreement.

Hayden's the last to say goodbye, taking me aside and muttering under his breath without the other guys hearing him.

"So... are we cool?"

He looks nervous, and I kind of hate myself for being the reason he feels that way.

"We're cool." I shake his hand, then roll my eyes when he grins like a fucking kid. "I'll see you at the ranch on Friday."

I ask a server for the location of the bathrooms, then make my way around the outside of the room and successfully avoid conversation. I loiter outside the women's bathroom door for a few minutes, but I can't be certain Violet is inside, so I move up the corridor a little, pulling out my phone and preparing a text.

A familiar voice stops me dead in my tracks.

"And Chord? Well, it won't be long until he's washed up right alongside you. Replaced with someone better and hotter than he ever was."

Fuck. That's *Emma*.

But it's the reply that makes my heart jump into my throat.

"Why are you behaving like this?" Violet demands on the other side of the wall. "*You* left Chord. *You* cheated on *him*. Why are you going out of your way to say these horrible things about him? Are you not over him? Are you jealous?"

The impulse to storm in and shut this down is overpowering, but I make myself wait. I've never heard Violet speak with such confidence, and something like pride makes me take a deep, long breath.

"You don't know what you're talking about," Emma snaps, "and you've got no idea who that man really is. He's cold and closed off and incapable of real connection. And he certainly doesn't *love* you." She cuts off with a cruel laugh. "Oh, my God. You think he loves you? That's pathetic. Chord Davenport doesn't love anyone but himself. He doesn't know how."

"You don't know him at all," Violet replies, emotion making her voice high. "And if you believe that Chord doesn't know how to love, it means you never even bothered to try. That man is the most loving person I know. He's kind and thoughtful. He's affectionate and sweet. He's a provider and a protector, and if people took the time to look past the fact that he's beautiful and rich and the best damn player the NHL has *ever* seen, they'd know that his independence is because of his strength of character and that he's withdrawn because he's misunderstood. He deserves more than you ever gave him, and *that's* why he's not with you now. It's got nothing to do with Spencer Cook and everything to do with your cruel, selfish heart!"

I blink and swallow the lump in my throat, then enter the little room in three long strides. Violet and Emma see me at the same time, their heads whipping around, but I ignore my ex and rush to Violet, cupping her face in my hands and kissing her hard.

I press my forehead to hers. "I love you," I whisper. "I love you so fucking much."

Her cheeks bloom, her chestnut eyes shine with tears, and I grin. "Let's get out of here."

THIRTY-FOUR

Violet

CHORD PRACTICALLY DRAGS ME FROM the room, his long legs speeding down the corridor and out to the foyer. I work hard to keep up, hiking my skirt up so I don't trip on the hem, and all but running in my pumps. He pulls his phone from his pocket without losing speed, calls our driver, and when he arranges to meet him at a side entrance, Chord changes direction without pausing, leading me down another corridor and around a corner.

My heart flies, not from the pace he's setting but from the thrill of this moment and the words he just said.

I love you.

When we reach the exit at the side of the building and Chord throws open the door, the limo is waiting for us. Chord helps me into the car first, then slides in after me.

His mouth is on mine before the driver closes the door.

Our tongues collide as I tear at his jacket, dragging it off his shoulders while he dips a hand into the corset of my dress and squeezes my breast. Our mouths work furiously, slipping and tugging, lips sliding against each other as Chord cradles my head, fingertips pushing into my curls and pulling them wilder about my face. I yank at his bow tie and then fumble at the buttons on his shirt as he blindly reaches for the control to raise the privacy screen, but as it slides into place, Chord pulls away, eyes feverish and panting heavily.

"I want you to know that I plan on making you come at least six different ways tonight, but the first time I make love to you isn't going to be in the back of a limo."

He slides a hand under my skirts and up my inner thigh, then presses a firm thumb to my clit, rubbing me in tiny circles that make me moan and spread my knees. "But the ranch feels far away right now." He swirls his tongue around the hollow in my throat because he knows how much I love it. "I'd take us to a hotel, but you're too good for that. I can't do it, so we're just going to have to wait."

"No hotel," I agree between whimpers. I drop my head back and bite back a groan as the pressure on my clit brings me closer to orgasm. "But I can't wait. Let's— Let's— Let's— Oh, my God! Chord!"

I release a wordless cry as my pussy pulses around nothing and euphoria flares in every nerve of my body. I moan with release and fall across the long seat, shuddering as my climax ebbs from my system.

"Let's... what, baby?" Chord strokes my hair as he stretches over me and covers one shoulder with open-mouthed kisses. "What do you want to do?"

"Let's go to my place," I mumble, unable to force my eyes open. "It's not far."

"Do you have a key?"

I nod slowly and only once. "I keep an emergency spare tucked into my phone case."

Chord snatches up the intercom handset and asks, "Remind me again—what's the address?"

Once the driver has our destination, Chord pulls me upright before dropping to his knees on the floor of the limo. I whimper at the image of him undoing his cuffs, then again at the panty-melting picture of him rolling his sleeves up over his tanned, muscled forearms.

I bite my lip and dig my fingers into the leather seat as he gathers the fine, soft layers of my dress in his hands and shoves them up over my hips in a pool of silk that takes up most of the long limousine seat. Chord looks up at me with his wild hair and wilder eyes, his gaze sweeping over me like he can't quite believe we're here, like this.

I can't believe it either. I feel so beautiful, so sexy, so powerful, even though my hair is destroyed, my makeup must be all over my face, and my breasts are heaving over the top of my bodice. It's all so heady. The dress and the diamonds and the champagne and the *I love you*...

Chord Davenport on his knees between my thighs.

I gasp as he roughly tugs at my panties, dragging them down my legs and stuffing them into his pocket. A rumble sounds deep in his chest at the first glimpse of my bare pussy and he sets one leg over his shoulder before wrapping his hand all the way around my other ankle.

"I've been dying to taste you," he says as he sets my foot up on the limo's long back seat and spreads me as wide as I can go. "I've been dreaming about your pussy on my lips, and I knew you'd be the sweetest thing I ever tasted, but I never could have imagined a moment like this. I'm about to tongue fuck a fairy princess, and I'm so fucking into it."

My whimpering laugh turns into a strangled cry as Chord dives between my thighs, burying his face in my swollen and sensitive center so fast and so hungrily that I cry out as the pleasure edges into pain. His tongue laps at me with excruciating languor. When I twist my fingers into his hair and tug with frustration, he stares up at me, not letting me look away as he applies his mouth to my clit and sucks hard.

Oh God, it feels so freaking good.

"Damn, Wallflower," Chord says between licks and flick and pulls. "If I knew you tasted this freaking sweet, I never would have waited so long to eat your perfect pussy."

I come again before we get to my apartment.

We're at least respectable when the limo pulls to a stop, and though I should be embarrassed when the driver calls to ask if we're ready for him to open our door, I'm not. I'm too aroused and too satisfied to care, which is an intoxicating mix. My muscles are soft and limp enough that Chord wraps a hard arm around my waist to help me walk, but my thighs are sticky with my own wetness, and I'm throbbing with the need to be filled.

The limo pulls away as we enter my apartment building, and I move toward the staircase, then squeal as he sweeps me up into his arms without warning.

I loop my arms around his neck. "What are you doing?"

"This is a walk-up," Chord says like I don't know it.

"Yes, but we're only on the second floor."

His arms tighten, and his smile turns smug. "I made you come so hard you can barely stand. What makes you think you'll make it?"

He carries me up the two flights and straight down the narrow hallway, stopping at the door with a silver "1" and "B" still attached, the "4" in the middle just a faded imprint where the chrome number used to be.

A flush of embarrassment creeps up my neck as it only just occurs to me that Chord already saw where I lived when he drove out to get my father, and my small, plain home is nothing like what he's used to at his house on the ranch.

Chord scans my face, tracing the crease in my forehead and my down-turned mouth, my eyes stinging with insecurity. But before I can apologize for where I live, he stops me with a hard, hot kiss like he knows what I was about to say.

"This moment is already perfect," he says, his stare burning into mine, "but the only way it's going to get better is if you open this door."

He sets me down so I can retrieve my phone—and the key—from my purse, and I open the door. Like I haven't been gone for nearly two months, I drop the key in the ceramic bowl on the hall table, put my phone down next to it, and move inside.

The apartment feels so small and dark compared to Chord's open, light-filled house, and standing here now, in this dress I designed and with a man I love, it feels like I don't belong here anymore. These walls are a time capsule for a life I haven't thought about in weeks, and I'm a different person than the Violet James who walked out of here with a suitcase and a sketchbook and a stomach full of butterflies.

Chord moves closer behind me, kissing the side of my neck as he tickles my arms with light, warm touches. I shiver as he brushes his fingertips across my shoulders and down my spine, finds the zipper on the corset of the dress, and pulls it down with painful slowness.

I bite my lip as his cock digs into my hip, then inhale sharply as my dress comes loose and drops in a pool of teal silk organza at my feet.

"Where's your room?" he asks in a low, husky voice.

I step out of my dress and walk toward my bedroom in nothing but my heels and a quarter of a million dollars-worth of diamonds. "It's over here."

I glance over my shoulder, and Chord chokes back a strangled moan as he watches me walk away. I stop at the door to my bedroom, turning to stare and whimper at the sudden appearance of his hard, muscled body as he stalks toward me, peeling off his shirt and dropping it on the floor.

Chord scoops me up again and crosses to the bed in three long strides, depositing me in the middle of the mattress and pushing my knees apart with firm, gentle hands.

He switches on the bedside light, and my room bursts with light. My felt boards and sketches are now clearly visible on the walls—Mom's dress and my faceless groom repeated on every surface. The fabric samples and photographs of other people's dresses on red carpets and runways. The dressmaker's dummy in the corner, next to my sewing machine and measuring tape, scissors, needles and pins, spools of thread and scraps of discarded lace. The shelves of sketchbooks filled with failed designs. This is the boneyard of my dreams.

Chord doesn't seem to notice any of it, but I see it all, and I instinctively try to close my legs and hide the most vulnerable part of me.

"Oh, no, Wallflower." Chord kneels on the edge of the mattress and covers each of my knees with a large hand, spreading me open and then pushing my heeled feet back to my ass so I'm on full display. His eyes drop to my pussy, wet and pulsing, and they widen with hunger. "This pussy is too pretty to hide."

I inhale sharply as Chord unbuckles his belt and jerks it free of the loops with one hard, firm tug that cracks through the air like a whip. He shoves off his pants and underwear with a frantic speed that has me hoping he'll give me his

SAMANTHA LEIGH

cock in one hard, feral thrust, but he puts his mouth on me instead, pushing hard on my knees to open me wide, licking me greedily and sucking so rabidly on my clit that I come again in just a few seconds.

My muscles ripple around nothing again, and I thrash on the bed as tonight's third orgasm pushes me closer to the edge of insanity. I need to come with Chord inside me. I can't take it anymore.

I open my eyes, and Chord's kneeling over me with his towering cock slipping in and out of his fist. His heavy thighs are tight, his muscled forearms hard, his blue eyes hazy and hooded, his jaw feathered with restraint.

I nibble my lip as I watch him play, the crown of him tight and dark, and veins throbbing between his fingers. Then he retrieves a condom from the pocket of his pants. I hold my breath and follow the path of his nimble fingers as he rolls it on, fighting the tight rubber to the base like it might not fit.

"You want this, Wallflower?" he asks in a throaty voice.

I nod as a single tear leaks down my face. "Please."

"Don't you remember?" he asks as he moves over me, his powerful shoulder muscles flexing as he balances on one elbow and lines himself up with my soft, swollen center. "You never have to beg me for anything."

He drives home so hard and fast that I cry out and arch toward him. His fingers thread into my hair as he holds still, sweat beading on his forehead, and I dig my fingers into his arms as I adjust to his size.

My hips begin to rock without me realizing it, slowly at first, then with a frenzy I've never known. Chord grunts and curls into me, sweating and still as I take what I need.

"That's it," Chord grunts. "Use me. Use my cock. Use what I have to get what you need."

It doesn't take long. He's so deep and so hard, and my clit is hitting the base of his cock just right, that in no time at all, I've brought myself to the most glorious orgasm I've ever had. Moisture soaks us both, and I moan as my body turns limp.

Chord starts to move his hips in long, slow, excruciatingly delicious thrusts. I'm already breathless, but as the rhythm of his hips gets faster and more forceful, my oversensitive clit aches with every contact. I claw at his firm, round ass and wrap my legs around his waist, doing my best to keep him close.

"Good fucking girl," he whispers, voice strained and cock slamming inside me, hitting something I've never felt before. "Let me give you what you want. Let me make you happy."

"Yes!" I pant as another orgasm builds deep inside my core. "Yes! Oh God! Chord! Yes!"

"And if that's the only thing I do right for the rest of my life," he grunts, sweat slicking his entire body so his hot skin slides against mine so beautifully, "I'll be the happiest man in the whole— damn— world. Ah, *fuuuuuck*!"

Our climaxes crash over us at the same time, mine a full-body wave that saps the last of my strength. Above me, Chord groans and rocks, and I find the energy to kiss the line of his shoulder, the salty moisture of his skin dancing on my tongue.

Chord carefully pulls out and rolls away, then drags me against him so we don't lose contact longer than we need to. With his arm under my head, I snuggle against his side, both of us glistening with sweat, his chest heaving with deep, shallow breaths.

"Holy hell, Wallflower." He curls his arm to bring my head to his lips, and he kisses my forehead. "I—"

"Shh." I set my fingers on his lips to stop him from talking, and he raises his scarred eyebrow with a question.

I blink back more tears because even though I never knew to dream of a night like this, all my hopes for a happy life were about this *feeling*. Maybe it doesn't matter what it looks like. Maybe it only matters that it makes you happy. Hopeful. Content.

Chord's brows draw together, and behind my fingers, his lips turn down with worry, but I press on them harder to stop him from speaking, then draw them away and move in for a soft, romantic kiss.

I rest my head on his chest and smile around a deep, joyful breath. This is it. Chord is it. A life filled with moments like this is all I'll ever want.

And finally, I say it.

"I love you, too."

THIRTY-FIVE

Chord

13 DAYS TILL HOCKEY SEASON

I STEP OUT OF THE house and onto the front porch, too wired to stop for more than a moment to watch Violet all happy and content in her new favorite place—curled up on the Adirondack chair, sketching with her chunky headphones on, oblivious to the world.

I move closer and tap her headphones, and she pulls them off with an adorable smile.

"Can I help you?" she teases.

"You can. I need you to get dressed for a trip to San Francisco. I've got a surprise for you."

Cute spots of color spring up in her cheeks. "What kind of surprise?"

I grin and shake my head. "Not a very good one if I give you any sort of hint."

I move her sketchbook to the table, pluck the pencil from her fingers and set it on top, then hold her headphones up to my ear. A bass-heavy but mellow rock song blasts my eardrum, and I spare Violet a confused smile as I set them on top of her sketchbook.

"Tell me again why you listen to this while you're designing?"

She shrugs and taps her phone to pause the playlist. "One of my teachers at college encouraged us to try classical music, but that never worked for me. I tried techno and boy bands and country, all different styles, but none of them worked like rock." She cocks her head to one side. "It's kind of like the music lures the thinking part of my brain into a loud, thumping mosh, which leaves the creative brain free to do its work."

I gently pull Violet to her feet and loop her arms around my waist. I can't resist her upturned mouth, and she smiles against my lips before I can coax her into a kiss.

"That makes no sense," I tell her, and she laughs, which makes me feel fantastic.

"Is that what you came out here for? To tease me for my taste in music?"

"Nope." I slip a finger under the hem of her tiny denim cutoffs and trace the crease of her ass cheek. "I've got a surprise for you, remember?"

"Oh, yes."

"Good. You've got twenty minutes to get ready, and you can expect to be in the city for the rest of the day."

She bites back a grin and dashes into the house. "I only need five."

Less than an hour later, we cross the Golden Gate Bridge, and my heart starts pounding.

"Are you really not going to tell me where we're going?" she asks for the hundredth time.

I feign an exasperated look when really, I love how excited he is. There's no evidence of her usual anxiety or nerves, and there's been less of that in general in the three weeks since the gala. I'm so happy my plan to coax her out of her comfort zone did exactly what I hoped it would. It got Violet to believe in herself as much as I do.

It made my pretty little wallflower bloom.

"No," I reply. "But we're nearly there."

"Nearly *where*?"

She huffs at my smirk and stares out the window as we cruise through San Francisco. I've memorized the route so I wouldn't have to plug the address into the GPS, and we eventually reach a busy tree-lined street teeming with people moving in and out of antique shops, upscale cafes, indie boutiques, and high-end designer stores. I slow down a couple hundred or so paces from our final destination and pull to the curb.

Violet gasps. "Oh, my."

I fight a grin, surprised but pleased that she's worked it out already. But Violet's not looking at the street, and I don't even think she notices that I stopped the car. Her wide eyes are glued to her phone screen, and one hand covers her open mouth. My grin fades, and my stomach drops.

Ever since the gala, that phone of hers has been a blessing and a curse. Her social media exploded, and her follower count keeps climbing, but for every person who sends messages and makes comments about how talented and beautiful and worthy she is, there are others trying to drag her down. I know what that's like. I know how thick-skinned a person has to be to deal with all the hate and maintain any type of confidence and self-esteem.

My Violet isn't used to the attention, and I've already commissioned my PR firm to filter her messages and comments so she doesn't have to deal with any of that shit.

I just want her to be happy, the way she deserves, but maybe something slipped through the cracks.

"What is it?" I ask. "What's wrong?"

She turns those big, chestnut irises on me, then raises the screen so I can see it. It's an article titled "Rising Designers You Need to Watch," and directly underneath is a picture of Violet at the gala, standing on the red carpet in the dress she created, looking beautiful and radiant and a million other types of perfect I don't have words for.

And it makes the gift I have to give her today even better.

"They've pulled my sketches from my social media accounts, and they're calling my designs original, inspired, and exquisite." She scrolls through the article, flicking up and down and back again with a shaky finger, then finds the line she's looking for. *"Violet James's unusual use of bold lace, modern embroidery, textured fabrics and flowing lines is destined to take the world of bridal couture by storm."*

She lifts her gaze again, wonder and disbelief obvious in the way her eyelids flutter behind her glasses.

I slide my hand behind her neck and rub my thumb across her cheekbone. "You're amazing, Wallflower. And now the whole world knows it."

She shakes her head a little, and I can feel the flight of her pulse under my palm.

"Chord, I don't know. It's all happening so fast."

And I can't wait any longer.

"Can I give you your present now?"

That brings her back, and a look of guarded curiosity moves across her face. "A present? You said it was a surprise, not a present."

"Can't it be both?"

She bites her lip, the first hint of reticence today, and tucks her phone away. "You've done something over the top, haven't you?"

The urge to grin is almost too much, but years of practice help me keep a straight face. "No. I don't think so."

I step out and open her door, then lead her up the street. Violet snuggles against my arm as she surveys the businesses.

"Can you imagine having a store here?" she asks dreamily. "Or a studio? Oh, look!" She points at a fashion boutique, drops my hand to hurry closer, then pauses out front to look at the designs on display in the tall glass window. "That dress is gorgeous."

"Do you want to go in?"

She narrows her eyes. "Is that what this is? A shopping spree? That's very sweet of you, but I really don't—" She cuts off at my chuckle and crosses her arms over her chest. "What? What's so funny?"

"We're not here to buy you pretty things, though I like the sound of that so much we'll come back to it soon." I take her hand again, guide her another dozen steps up the street, and then gently spin her around to face her gift.

Before us is a narrow, white Victorian-style storefront with a simple, sophisticated sign above the black French doors that proclaims it the flagship venue for *Violet James—Bridal Couture*. And in the window, two dresses are displayed on modern, minimalist mannequins. The first is Violet's blue dress from the gala. The other is just one version of the wedding dress she's been re-designing for a decade.

Violet covers her sharp inhalation with two hands, and her eyes flood with tears.

"Chord! What did you do?"

"I bought you a studio."

I don't think she knows she's shaking her head, but her reaction is cute as fuck. "But... but... *how*?"

I paid a freaking fortune, pissed off a lot of contractors, and begged Victoria Hall for help to get it done so quickly, but I'm not going to tell Violet that.

"A designer who's about to take the fashion world by storm needs a studio space, right?"

"Chord, I..." An overwhelmed sob escapes her throat, and she throws her arms around my neck and burrows her face into my shoulder. "I can't believe you did this. Thank you."

I wrap her up and hold her tight, closing my eyes and breathing her in.

I've never felt this kind of triumph before, not even holding the championship Cup. This pleasure and satisfaction that comes from taking care of someone I love. Using the money I've made to hand deliver a dream—and having her accept what I can give her because she knows I just want her to be happy. I'm flying so fucking high.

I blink away the sting in my eyes, kiss her hard and fast, and then let her go so we can both look up at the building. It's the first time I'm seeing it outside of the photographs and emails sent to me by my interior designer.

"Do you like it?" I ask.

She squeezes my hand and glances at me, but it lasts only a moment because she's only got eyes for her studio right now.

"Chord, I *love* it."

I fish the key from my pocket and dangle it in front of her.

"You want to go inside?"

"Oh, my God." She shakes as she accepts the keys. "This is really real."

I step aside as Violet slides the key into the silver lock, and a rush of contentment swamps me at the sound of the mechanism clicking open. Violet gives me a questioning look, and at my nod, she pushes the door open and steps inside.

It smells like paint and building materials, but my designer has created an incredible space. The size is modest but sufficient, with high ceilings and pale wooden floors making it appear larger than it is. The vibe is rich, sophisticated, and understated, with white walls and dark-veined marble surfaces. Aside from the dresses in the window, the shop is empty, and Violet circles the room with reverent silence, passing a fitting area with two private changing spaces and a simple round dais before arriving at a set of closed double doors painted black to match the front.

She gives me a puzzled look, lips twitching with a smile. "What's behind here?"

I shrug. "Open it."

She does, and the head shaking and gasping starts all over again as I follow her into her new design studio.

There's an oversized designer's desk in the middle of the space, illuminated by the task lighting above and stocked with papers and pencils and everything a designer might need. There's a small sofa and coffee table in one corner, a sewing station and dressmaker's dummy in the other, and a surround sound system is installed for her music when she doesn't want to listen with her headphones.

And every inch of the walls is covered with the gray felt covered boards that used to be in her bedroom.

"I had my interior designer take care of this personally," I assure Violet in a rush. "She took pictures of everything and confirmed they're all exactly as they were in your room. And I spoke to your dad about it—to make sure I wasn't overstepping. He helped with the move and insisted on installing everything here himself. Wouldn't let anyone touch it and spent days working with the team to get everything just right. He wanted to be a part of this, too."

Violet isn't trying to hide her tears anymore. She moves to the closest board and runs her hands over a swatch of fabrics, then the lines of the sketch next to it. "Chord, this is too much."

"It's not," I disagree with a lump in my throat. "It's not too much. It's nowhere near enough." I move closer, take her shoulders, and turn her to face me. Her red-rimmed eyes shine with joy and disbelief, and my heart takes off like a bolting horse.

"Violet, I love you. I want to build a life with you and make all your dreams come true. This is it. This is—"

Violet's phone rings suddenly and loudly, making us both jump. She gives me a watery chuckle and slides it out of her pocket, checking the screen and rejecting the call when she doesn't recognize the number.

I coast my palms over her arms and lick my lips, the interruption to my speech making me suddenly nervous. The studio is only the first surprise I have for her today, and even though the studio reveal has gone well, the next gift is bigger. For her. For me. For us.

"There's no reason why we need to rush out of here, but there *is* one more thing I—"

Violet's phone rings again, and she drags it out and checks the screen.

"It's the same number." She grimaces apologetically. "Maybe I should answer in case it's important?"

"Sure." I take a step back and don't let my impatience show. "No problem."

She flashes me a quick smile, then holds the phone to her ear. "Hello? Yes, this is Violet James."

I watch to see if I can work out who's on the other end of the line, but any hope that this will be quick fades as Violet bows her head and frowns with concentration.

"Yes, I'm—" Something catches in her voice, and she clears her throat. "Yes, I'm familiar with his work."

She sounds anxious, and it makes me stand taller.

"Okay," she says. "All right. No, that's... That's wonderful. I'm... Well, I'm a little lost for words."

Another pause.

"My email address? Of course."

Violet recites her contact information, then offers her thanks to whoever is on the phone. She ends the call, her face a little pale and her expression stunned as she stares at the blank screen.

Foreboding sits like a pit in my gut. "Is something wrong?"

She rubs her mouth and shakes her head. "Um, no. Not exactly. That was an assistant for Leonardo Bellucci."

My brows shoot up. "The fashion designer?"

She laughs lightly like she can't believe it either. "Yes, the fashion designer. He— They—" Violet regards me with bright, almost frightened eyes. "Someone on their design team saw the article this morning. They love the dress I designed for the gala, and they want to snap me up before anyone else gets a chance. I can't believe it. They've offered me a *job*."

Blood roars in my ears. This studio suddenly feels too small, and my voice sounds distant when I say, "A job? That's... I mean, that's fantastic. You have to take it."

Violet blinks up at me before she gives her whole body a shake and tucks her phone into her back pocket. "No, I don't."

"You do." I grip her upper arms, and when she refuses to look at me, I tip up her chin until she meets my gaze. "This studio is yours, no matter if you're here all week or just the weekend or once a month or twice a year. And hey, why do you have to choose? Maybe you can do both. Maybe you can—"

"The job is in Milan."

Every inch of me runs cold, freezing my breath and stopping my heart. I've been skating so fast and so blindly toward a completely different goal that for one of the very few times in my life, I don't know what to say. I don't know what to do.

"It's a three-year contract," she adds with her fingers twisting in and out of each other between us. "I'd be on the design team. It would be—"

"Your dream," I finish.

"Yeah." Her face falls, and she glances around the studio I made for her like she can't remember how she got here. "No, I mean, maybe once upon a time, but things are different now. I've got you, and I've got... *this*."

She catches her bottom lip between her teeth, and I swallow my hurt. This is my fault. I put her out in the spotlight because I wanted so badly for the world to see her the way I do. Talented. Beautiful. Humble. Worthy. It shouldn't hurt this bad that everyone did what I wanted them to do. I can't get selfish about sharing her now.

"Violet." I squeeze her arms to get her full attention. "You've worked so hard for this. If Milan and Leonardo Bellucci are what you want, then you have to go."

I think of the second set of keys burning a hole in my back pocket—the ones that will unlock the apartment I bought for us. It's the property Violet liked the day we came to view it—the one with the cream-colored walls and wood-burning fireplace, the vintage finishes and natural light and the view over the park.

My throat feels tight, and I blink to erase the pictures of us I'd been dreaming about these last few weeks. We'd live together in the city while I took the Fury to the championships, and she established herself as a designer. We'd spend the next two years getting to know each other. Live big. Laugh. Have fun. Fall harder and deeper in love every day. Then we'd pack it all up and move to the ranch. I'd build her a studio, or she could commute to this one if she wanted to. We'd get married

We'd have a bunch of kids who would play hockey and make art and collect eggs from our chicken coop. Daisy would teach them how to ride. We'd have the kind of quiet, forever love that Mom and Dad had, and I wouldn't have to fight the world anymore.

We could just... be happy.

It's still possible, I tell myself. Violet isn't gone yet, and she wouldn't be gone forever. This doesn't have to change things—it would only delay them—but three years is a long time to be apart. To live separate lives. To chase different dreams. Three years could change everything. I'd miss her too much.

Violet's focus turns inward, and I hold my breath as she shares the thoughts that pass across her face.

"No." Her voice is firm, and her mouth flat as she shakes her head. "This is what I want. You are what I want. Plus, I have to think practically. I can't leave my father. He'd be all alone, and after what happened this summer with me only an hour away?" She shakes her head again. "I can't risk moving halfway across the world. It would be too much."

Violet throws out her obligation to her dad like it's an insurmountable obstacle when it's not. Still, I reach for it like a drowning man clamoring at a lifeline. Relief burns the back of my throat as I realize I can keep her here without having to be the selfish prick who begs her to choose me over her dreams.

I don't want to be the reason she turns her back on this opportunity, but I don't want her to go. She is my happily ever after, and I'm not wired to let that go without a fight.

"If you're worried about your dad, you shouldn't go," I agree, drawing her to me. She slips her arms around my waist and I hold her tight even as I swallow a thick lump of shame. "Stay right here in California, Wallflower." *Stay right here with me.*

THIRTY-SIX

Violet

DAY 74 AT SILVER LEAF... ONLY 12 TO GO

THE NEXT MORNING, I TELL Chord I'm meeting Dad at his cabin instead of the house for our morning coffee, but it's a little white lie. Instead, I leave early enough to get to Dad just before he walks out, knocking on his door as he's tugging on his boots.

He opens the door and greets me with surprise. "What are you doing here, Blossom?"

I shrug. "I woke early and felt like taking a walk. You don't mind, do you?"

"Of course not. Come on in, and I'll make you breakfast."

I follow him down the short, narrow hallway of his cabin and give the place a quick scan. The accommodations at Silver Leaf are clean, neat, and well-maintained—white-clad cabins with timber floors, white-washed walls, functional kitchenettes, and compact European laundry closets. Half of them have a single bedroom, like this one. The others have two. All have modest but full-size bathrooms and small patios that overlook the green vineyards here and the purple mountains beyond.

I take a seat at the small dining table while Dad fusses at the coffee machine. I've been here twice before, but there's something different about the cabin today. I can't point out any one thing that changes the vibe—maybe it's the way Dad moves around the place, his shoes near the front door and a jacket hanging from the back of the armchair, the groceries stacked in the open kitchen cupboard—but it feels warmer somehow. Lived in.

Dad joins me with two steaming mugs, and I take a careful sip. He mirrors me, his eyes watching me over the rim of his cup, then following my hands as I set my coffee down and trap them between my bouncing knees.

He lowers his coffee to the table, and... there it is. The *spill it* look.

"I have some news," I say, even as I'm silently screaming at myself to leave my father out of this. If I'm going to accept Chord's studio here and not go to Milan, then Dad doesn't need to know about the job offer. But the thing is, I desperately need to tell him. I need someone to tell me that by turning it down I'm doing the right thing. And I need Dad to know the truth.

His brow furrows. "I take it by the look on your face that it isn't good?"

"What?" I try to smile. "No, it's good. It's great. It's... It's wonderful." I can't keep up the act, weak as it is, and I slump with a sigh. "It's complicated."

The lines on his forehead get deeper. "Violet. What's going on?"

"Chord showed me the studio in San Francisco yesterday."

Dad brightens. "He did? That's fantastic. I've been sitting on that secret for weeks, and I hate keeping things from you." He taps a fist on the tabletop. "Tell me: do you love it? Chord worked hard to pull it together so quickly. Approved every design choice to make sure it was what he envisioned for you. He's a perfectionist, and I was impressed."

"He is, and it is perfect. I love it." I tear up at the memory of my new studio, a decade of my dreams pinned to the walls, each and every inch of those pinboards painstakingly transferred and installed by my dad. "Thank you for all the work you did."

I slide my flat hand across the table, and he sets his on mine. I add my other, and he does the same until they're stacked together.

Dad's fingers curl in around mine. "What's wrong, Violet?"

I sniff and huff out a humorless laugh. "I got a job offer yesterday."

"You did?"

"Yes. With a very famous and well-respected designer. Leonardo Bellucci."

Dad scratches his forehead before covering my hands again. "So... you don't want the studio after all?"

I shake my head with an uncertain shrug. "The job is in Milan. If I take it, I'll be gone for three years."

Dad leans back in his chair, hands sliding from mine as he puffs out his cheeks, then releases a stunned breath. "Milan? As in Italy?"

"Yes."

He rubs one finger under his nose, and his voice is uncertain. "Right. Okay. Well... I'm happy for you. This sounds like the chance of a lifetime, and you've earned this. You deserve it." He grimaces and leans forward again, stacking his hands on mine. "I'm proud of you, Blossom. Incredibly proud."

A single tear rolls down my cheek. "I'm not going to take it."

Dad frowns. "Because you don't want to?"

"Because I have a life here," I reply. "Chord gave me this amazing new studio, and if I stay in San Francisco, I can negotiate a part-time contract with the Fury. I'll move back to San Francisco with you, focus on design one or two days a week, and stay with the team so we can keep our health insurance. Hardly anything has to change."

"Violet." He yanks his hands back with a shake of his head. "No."

"Yes."

"Chord is one thing," he says. "I've kept a close eye on him these last few weeks, and he loves you. I'm sure of it. If he hasn't told you yet, he will soon. And if you want to stay because you love him too, I'll support you one hundred percent. But I won't let you walk away from this opportunity for me. It's not going to happen."

"Dad. Please. Just listen to me."

"No." His voice is firmer than I've ever heard it. "You listen to me. I'm not moving back to San Francisco."

I swallow with difficulty. "You're not?"

"No. I like it here, so I've decided to find myself a real job. A new place to live. Make a fresh start in Aster Springs."

I don't believe him. "You're just saying that."

"So what if I am?" he asks. "Dammit, *I'm* the parent. You're my daughter. It's my job to worry about you. You're not supposed to worry about me."

My chest aches, and there's a tickle in my throat. I've used my dad's depression to justify my fear of success over the years, but it's not fair. Nor is it the whole truth.

I stare at my hands and mumble, "I don't want to be like Mom."

Dad's brows snap together. "What?"

"I don't want to do to you what she did to us." My voice breaks as I swallow my tears. "I can't leave you behind to chase a dream that's only mine. How selfish would I be to sacrifice your happiness for my own?"

"Ah, Blossom." Dad gets up and rounds the table, pulling me to my feet and holding me in his arms. I sniffle against his warm, familiar chest, clutching him tighter when he releases a sad sigh. "I never realized how much your mother's choices affected you. I should have seen it, and I didn't." He kisses my hair. "I'm so sorry."

"It's okay." I draw back and try to smile for him. "You had your own pain to deal with."

He holds me by the shoulders, studying me until he's satisfied I'm not about to break down in tears, then gently pushes me back into my chair before returning to his.

"I want you to listen to me, Violet," he says. "You are the kindest, most caring, and most selfless person I've ever met. You're smart and talented. You're beautiful inside and out. I've always known it, and now the world knows it, too. If you want to go to Milan, then you need to go to Milan. I want you to go. You aren't abandoning me. You aren't letting me down. In fact, I'd be disappointed if you let your sense of obligation stand in the way of this priceless opportunity. I don't want to be the reason for anyone's regrets. Especially not yours."

I blink away my tears as his words hit some sort of bullseye in my heart. That was the reason I was able to forgive my mom for leaving me. I never wanted to be the reason she stayed trapped in a life she didn't want.

"Okay," I whisper.

Dad smiles even though his eyes fill with sorrow. "Good. So, what does that mean? Are you going to Milan?"

I stare into my mug of coffee, distractedly noting that it's turned cold.

"I don't know," I admit in a whisper, thinking of Milan and Chord and the San Francisco studio. "I have no idea what I'm going to do."

THIRTY-SEVEN

Violet

DAY 77 AT SILVER LEAF... ONLY 9 TO GO

THREE DAYS LATER, I STILL don't know what I should do. I sit at the desk in Chord's home office, open my email from the headquarters of Leonardo Bellucci, and read it for what feels like the thousandth time. The words are so familiar, and the ones that make the most impact leap off the screen.

Junior designer. Three-year opportunity. Immediate start.
Bridal couture.
Milan, Italy.

A couple more phrases float before my eyes, even though they exist only in my head.

Everything you've worked for.
The life you've always wanted.
A dream come true.

But no health insurance, I remind myself firmly. No way to take care of my dad and no possibility of him coming with me. No family. No friends. No studio in San Francisco. And no Chord.

My fingers hover over the keyboard, and for the hundredth time, I tap out my reply. A polite and long-winded way of saying, *Thanks but no thanks.*

And for the hundredth time I delete it all and start the process all over again.

Junior designer. Three-year opportunity. Immediate start. Bridal couture. Milan, Italy. Everything you've worked for. The life you've always wanted. A dream come true.

I can't say yes. And I can't bring myself to say no. My head tells me to do one thing, my heart aches for something so very different, and I desperately wish one would grow loud enough to drown out the other.

I move the cursor to another tab and my screen lights up with the *Violet James—Bridal Couture* website that Chord had built for me. The colors and branding match my new studio perfectly, and the web designer did a fantastic job repurposing my social media content to make it look like I have much more experience than I do. My "about" page features a bio that makes me wonder who this talented, sought-after Violet James person is and a contact page that includes a photo of my new storefront. A street location. An email address. A way for me to conjure up new dreams and chase them on my own.

No. Not on my own. With Chord.

I bounce my knees and navigate back to my email account. Open the job offer, then click on "reply."

"Hey, Wallflower," Chord says, popping his head into the room. "I was wondering where you got to."

I startle, slam my laptop closed, and jump to my feet, then try to pretend I didn't.

"Oh, hi." I tuck a loose strand of hair behind my ear. "I was just, um, you know. In here."

Chord gives me a lopsided smile and moves all the way into the room. There's nothing materially different about him today—he wears a t-shirt and jeans, his hair is neat but a little longer now than it was at the start of the summer, and his feet are bare inside the house—but he's exceptionally beautiful for some reason, and I swallow the lump in my throat.

He takes a step forward. "Are you okay?"

"Yeah. Yes. I'm great." I stand and slide my palms down the front of my jeans. "Were you looking for me?"

"Um, yeah." He crosses his arms, watching me like he knows something isn't right. "I'm starving, and I noticed you barely ate any breakfast this morning. Do you want to walk up to The Hill for lunch?"

I glance out the window at the view that's been mine for more than two months. The never-ending blue of the California sky. The vineyards. The gardens. The mountains. The ranch. A whole life. And I burst into tears.

Chord rushes around the desk and gathers me into his arms. "Hey. Don't cry. Whatever's wrong, we'll fix it." He smooths a palm over my hair and kisses my head. "Tell me what it is. Let me take care of it."

I cover my face and lean into his chest, the frustration and despair of the last few days crashing against me in a wave of overwhelm. I cry until my hands are wet and his shirt is soaked and when the tears stop and my breath evens out again, Chord moves his hand up and down my back in long, soothing strokes.

"You have to say yes," he whispers.

I jerk back and crane my neck to look up at him. "What?"

"You have to say yes to the job in Milan."

"Chord, no. I—"

"Let's just talk about it, okay?"

I sniffle, and he takes my hand, leading me through the foyer to the living room, settling me onto the sofa, and tucking me in under a blanket. He holds up one finger, then leaves the room, and by the time he comes back with two steaming cups of tea, I've calmed a little, and he knows it.

"Better?" he asks as I accept my mug.

"Yes." I inhale the steamy aroma of peppermint curling from my cup and let out an exhausted breath. "Thank you."

"Good."

He seats himself next to me, then indicates I should swing my legs up over his lap. Soon, we're snuggled in together, Chord's large, heavy hand on my thigh, both waiting for the other to speak first. This time, it's not me.

"I've been thinking about this thing with Charlie," Chord says, surprising me. "With the ranch and the wine and the money. I saved her when she didn't ask to be saved, and when she finds out the truth, it's going to hurt both of us."

Empathy swells in my chest. "You did it for all the right reasons, and when you explain that to her, she'll understand. She has to."

His mouth tips up at the corner, like he appreciates my faith but doesn't share it. "Maybe." He squeezes my thigh. "But the reason I've been thinking about it is because I've gone and done the same thing for you, haven't I?"

Emotion catches in my chest because he's right, but it would hurt too much to say it. "Chord—"

He clears his throat. "Just be honest, Wallflower. Nothing you say could be wrong, and I'm not going to get upset or angry as long as we're telling each other the truth." He smiles encouragingly. "Do you want to go to Europe?"

A single tear tracks down my cheek. "Yes. No. I don't know."

"Okay." He nods to himself. "That's okay. So... Let's talk about it. Let's figure it out. Together."

It takes courage to say the things in my head, but I've kept my hopes and fears locked away for so many years that, on some level, I know that if I never let them out, I'll also never have the things I want.

"I love you," I whisper, "but I've spent the last ten years loving another person—my dad—more than I love myself, and it didn't bring me happiness."

Chord's brows draw down, and his mouth is flat, but he nods and circles his palm over my leg. "I know. You've sacrificed a lot to be the person your father needs."

"And I could keep doing it. I could stay here and negotiat
a part-time position with the Fury so I can keep covering m
dad's therapy bills and still have time to run a studio."

"No." Chord scowls. "You're better than that job. I don'
want you to have to do that anymore."

I smile sadly. "Staying is the selfless thing to do. Th
responsible thing. The safe thing. Probably even the righ
thing. But..." I close my eyes and dig deep for strength. "But i
I stay here instead of taking the chance to live a life I've alway
dreamed about..." I shrug and scrub another tear from m
cheek. "What will happen then?"

Chord stares at his hand where it rests on my leg. "I neve
want to be the reason you look back on your life with regret."

I snatch up his hand and press his fingertips to my lips
"I could never regret you. That's not it at all. But Chord... I
I stay, I'll always wonder if any success I have is mine. If I'm
here in California, designing in a studio you bought for me
starting a career I never had to work for, how can I be sure tha
I earned it? Deserve it? Am worthy of it?"

He sniffs and sets his tea on the coffee table. "Can yo
help me understand what Milan and Leonardo Bellucci wil
give you that I can't?"

My heart breaks, but I'm not going to lie to him now
"Three years of working for a world-class designer will teacl
me things. And while I'm there, anything I design won't hav
my name on it, so if people love what I do, it'll be because it'
good—not because I'm on your arm on red carpets or being

photographed with you in private moments. I need to prove to myself that I've earned this, and I'm not getting it just because I'm your girlfriend."

Chord hunches forward and drops his head into his hands, fingers clutching his hair. My heart gallops hard and fast enough to hurt, and I wish I could take back everything I just said.

"Chord, I'm sorry. I don't mean..."

He doesn't look up. "I hear what you're saying, Violet, and I understand. I wish I didn't, but fuck, I do. But if you could just see yourself the way I do. You're extraordinary. You're smart and driven and talented, and these people who want your designs love you for you. They might not know it yet, but they will, and you don't have to do it alone. Let me be there for you, Violet. Let me give you the life you want. Not because you didn't earn it or don't deserve it, but because I want to. Because I can. Because I love you."

"I can't," I whisper, letting the tears fall. "I'm so sorry."

His head moves in what I think is a nod, and when I set a hand on his back, his muscles are hard as stone under my palm.

"You don't have anything to be sorry for," he says, staring at the floor, "and fuck if this doesn't make me love you more. I'll take care of your dad. I'll set him up with a proper job here at Silver Leaf. Full benefits. And if he doesn't want to live permanently on the ranch, I'll get him his own place in Aster Springs. If he needs new doctors, I'll take care of that, too. You don't have to worry about him while you're gone."

My ribs pull so tight I can barely breathe. "You don't have to do that."

"Yeah, I do." He stares at his open palms. "If you're going to do this, you can't be worried about what's going on back here. This opportunity needs to be all about you. It's time to be selfish. You've earned it."

Panic hits me as I try to work out what he's saying, but I don't get a chance to ask before he lurches to his feet, hand worrying the back of his neck, not quite meeting my eyes. I set down my tea as he paces a few steps from the sofa, and when I reach out like I can draw him back, he glances at my hand and then drags his focus to my face.

I'm afraid the answer to my question might be written in his glassy blue eyes.

"I can do this for you, at least," he says. "I can give you the freedom to chase the life you deserve. Don't worry about a thing, Wallflower. I'll take care of everything."

"Chord! Wait!" I throw back the blanket and jump to my feet, but he's already out the front door. By the time I step out onto the porch, he's jogging in the direction of the main house, and all I can do is watch him go, my throat tight and my cheeks wet.

I've always known this about dreams: they require sacrifice. And I think I just lost the best thing to ever happen to me in exchange for a future I gave up on a long time ago.

THIRTY-EIGHT

Chord

9 DAYS TILL HOCKEY SEASON

THE RUN FROM MY PLACE should have worked the edge off my agitation, but when I thump on the door to Charlie's office at the rear of the Silver Leaf reception house, I'm overstuffed with emotion and ready to explode.

Violet's leaving, and I can't stop her. She chose Milan, and even though it makes me so damn proud of her, I've also never been so furious—with the world, with myself, with whoever thought it would be a good idea to throw Violet James in my path, give her enough time and power to dismantle all the walls that kept me safe, then tear her away while she's got a death grip on my heart.

Charlie calls, "Come in!" and I throw open the door with more force than necessary. My sister glances up from her computer and I pray for a fight. I could do with a little yelling.

Instead, she takes one look at me, closes her laptop with a slam
jumps to her feet, and rounds the desk.

"What's wrong? Is it Izzy?"

"What? No. It's— Everything's just—" I sift my finger
into my hair, then tug to send a sting through my scalp. "*Fuck*
What's wrong with me?"

It hurts to swallow, and my brain isn't firing right, so
I stare at my sister until she closes the distance and guides me
into one of the two chairs on this side of her desk.

"You want to tell me what's going on?" she asks.

"Violet's leaving." I roughly clear the pain in my voice
"She got a job with a design house in Milan, and I'm so damn
proud of her, but she's going. For three years. And I just bough
her a studio in San Francisco. I had it all set up, and she saw i
for the first time yesterday. It felt so fucking good to give he
something she wanted. To be able to take care of her. To show
her that I want a future with her. To make her happy. And i
didn't matter. She doesn't want it. She doesn't want my money
or the life I can give her. She wants to do it all on her own."

"Chord." Charlie sets a hand over mine. "Violet ha
worked hard for a long time to make something of herself
If she's been offered a job that she earned on her own, you
can't expect her to throw it away just because you can give he
the same for free."

"I know. I *know*. But I've worked hard too." I clench
my jaw and my nostrils flare with a sharp intake of breath
"I've sacrificed so much. I've got money and power and th

ability to make life easier for the people I love—and none of you want it. I could walk onto the street right now and hand everything to a stranger who'd be beside himself to take it, and yet the people I want to share it with refuse to accept it. Fuck, Charlotte. I don't need another car, another watch, another house, another business, another person in my bed. I just want to take care of my family and the woman I love, because what's the point of any of this if I can't do something as simple as that?"

Charlie's brows furrow. "Chord—"

"I have to tell you something."

The timing couldn't be worse to confess the biggest secret I've ever kept, but it's intentional. I'm looking for something—anything—to make the pain go away. The only emotion I know how to live with is anger, so I need Charlie to fire me up. I need something—anything—to trigger my old defenses because they're failing me now.

"All right," Charlie says slowly.

I snatch my hand out from under hers. "There is no catering client that buys enough wine for an army every month."

Her lips twitch like this is a joke she doesn't get yet. "What?"

"There is no Five Fools Holdings. It's me. I've been buying wine from you for the last ten years so that there would be enough money in the business to keep the ranch from going under."

SAMANTHA LEIGH

Charlie's sun-bronzed cheeks grow pale. "You're lying."

"I'm not. I've given Silver Leaf more than three million dollars without anybody knowing it. You expressly told me you didn't want any of my money, but I found a way to give it to you anyway."

She sits back in the chair, hands clasped in her lap, and is silent for a long time, staring into nothing. I grow impatient waiting for her to snap.

"Say it," I tell her. "I know you want to."

She turns her head and narrows her eyes, and finally I'm feeling chastised—and pissed about it.

"Say what?" she asks.

"Say I'm a selfish asshole. Tell me I've fucked up. Say you were right, and I was wrong, and I've screwed my family. Again."

Charlie's face is so still, I can't read a single emotion on it. She's composed. Cool. In control. Unlike me, who is completely falling apart.

"Are we the five fools?"

I give her a sharp look. "Huh?"

Her lips twitch again, but her gaze remains impassive and steady. "You, me, Finn, Dylan, Daisy. Five fools. Yes or no?"

I cross my arms over my chest and ignore the humor in my throat because she's right.

"Possibly."

"Interesting. Three million, you say?"

I've got no idea what's going on. "Give or take."

"Hm."

Charlie goes back to her side of the desk, sits and opens a drawer, then tosses a bound stack of paperwork at me. I flick it open and scan what looks like a contract, eyes snagging on the San Francisco Fury letterhead.

And Charlie's signature on the last page.

"What is this?" I ask.

Charlie holds out her hand to take it back, flicks through the contract, then returns it to me, opened to a particular page. There's information about Silver Leaf on there, a wine order, and the Fury home stadium. VIP suites. A lengthy list of terms and conditions.

I frown at the page, then at Charlie. "The Fury bought our wine?"

Is that... Did Charlie smile? I've been too caught up in my own shit that for the first time since I arrived, I notice something different about Charlie. She seems... Is she *happy*?

I look around at her workspace. It's carefully constructed chaos. A giant desk that belonged to our dad, the timber top carved with forty years of paperweights, whiskey glasses, and wine bottles. Charlie's chair is new—ergonomic, practical, hideous—while Dad's old armchair sits in the corner with one of Mom's blankets slung over the back. The canvas on the wall above it is something Mom painted for Dad's birthday the year he took an art class—an abstract of riotous color she called *Without Rain*.

Glass vases of wildflowers. A dirty plate that was probably

Charlie's lunch, and another underneath that was likely from breakfast. A coffee machine in the corner. The impression that Charlie rarely leaves this room.

And my sister, mouth twitching like she's got a secret of her own.

I toss the contract on a stack of paperwork. "Explain, Charlie."

"About a month ago, Violet gave me a lead on an opportunity with the Fury to supply wine for the home arena VIP suites."

My heart stops. "Violet?"

Charlie's blue eyes shine. "Yep. She got me a meeting with a guy on the administrative team, and I pitched. Put together an entire business plan. Public relations. Marketing. Contingencies. The works."

"*Violet* did this?" I don't know why I'm surprised—it's just like Violet to go out of her way to support the people who are important to me—but just when I thought it was impossible to love her even more, she gives me a reason to fall all over again.

"No. I mean, Violet gave me a business card, but *I* did this." Charlie stops fighting her grin, and her pretty smile transforms her face. "I got Silver Leaf on the books for a contract worth a lot more than three million, and it feels so damn good."

"I, um..." A mixed sense of pride and redundancy settles over me, and I pull on the back of my neck. "I'm proud of you, Charlie. That's... That's fucking impressive."

"Thank you. I'm proud of me too." Her smile falters and she drops her eyes, then raises them again with a chagrined smile. "And thank you for Five Fools Holdings. For supporting our family even when I pushed you away. If it wasn't for you, who knows where Silver Leaf would be right now? You did good thing. Not a selfish thing. Not a wrong thing. Was it stubborn? Yes. Sneaky? For sure. But am I mad? Not entirely. Part of me might even be grateful that you did it."

I release a heavy breath, and my shoulders sag. I've wanted this for so long without realizing just how badly I needed it. "For real?"

"I am. Thank you, big brother."

My throat grows tight. "You're welcome."

We awkwardly avoid eye contact for a moment, and study the row of photo frames on her desk to give me something else to look at. The first has a picture of Isobel beaming with the evidence of her first lost tooth. I turn the silver frame a little to get a better look at it.

"She's adorable," I say.

"She is," Charlie agrees.

I pick up the frame behind it, this one holding a picture of Mom and Dad when they were in their early thirties. Mom is pregnant with me, and they look so damn happy underneath the silver leaves of the old olive trees, the sunlight scattered through Mom's blonde hair in a halo that makes my eyes burn.

"I've got this same photograph in my wallet," I say.

"It's a good one." Charlie takes the frame when I offer i to her and studies Mom and Dad with a soft, sad kind of smile "Maybe the best we've got."

There's another picture of Izzy, this time with Dylan One of Finn in his military uniform. The next is Daisy on horse with her head thrown back mid-laugh. I pick up a fram holding an old photograph of our family. The seven of us ar in the living room of the main house, lined up in front of th blinking Christmas tree, the debris of our gifts lying thrown a our feet. Daisy looks about Izzy's age, which would make m thirteen, all puffed up and proud with a new hockey stick i one hand, my other arm thrown around Charlie next to me She'd be eleven here, tiny compared to my fast-growing frame her skinny arm tight around my waist and her pink-cheeke face beaming up at me.

"You used to like me," I comment, returning the frame t its position on the desk.

Charlie snorts, setting down the picture of Mom an Dad, but there's an odd curve on her mouth. "I was young."

"Yeah. It was a long time ago."

Charlie sighs and hands me the last frame in the line. It's picture of me. I'm about twenty-two in my Tampa Bay Titan gear, sweaty and laughing after a game we must have won.

I raise my eyebrows at Charlie, and she rolls her eye "I still like you. Are you happy now?"

I huff out a laugh that I don't feel. "Not really."

Charlie sighs. "Violet."

"Yeah. Violet." I clench my fists on my thighs, push against the hopelessness that surges inside me, and focus on doing what I came here to do. Making Violet's dreams come true. "I have a favor to ask."

"Okay. What is it?"

"I told Violet I'd take care of her dad while she's gone. Set him up with a proper job and complete benefits. A place to live. Good doctors."

"You think he'd be interested in staying on here?"

"I hope so."

"Me too. He does good work, and he's an asset to the business. I'll sort out the paperwork straightaway."

I should be relieved—I am—but the last obstacle between Violet and Europe was swept out of the way too easily, and now I can't think of a single way to make her stay.

My shoulders fall, and Charlie gives me an empathetic look. "What is it?"

"I have to let her go, don't I?"

"To Milan?"

I shake my head. "Not only Milan. I have to let her *go*. I don't want to limit a single opportunity that might come her way. Not when it comes to her career. Her confidence. The possibility that in the next three years, she'll catch the future she's been chasing so long. Fame. Fortune." I swallow painfully. "Love."

"Chord—"

I stand abruptly. "I can't be the selfish jerk I've always been. I don't want Violet to waste time worrying about her dad, and I don't want her to spend a single second missing what's in front of her because she's too busy thinking about what she left behind. I need to get out of the way and give Violet the chance to *be* something—whatever that is. And in three years, if we're meant to be..."

I drag an impossible breath in through my nose, muscles firing with adrenaline and frustration as my instincts scream to fight for what I want, not turn my back on it and walk away.

Charlie sighs. "If you love something, set it free?"

I scowl at nothing and try to find my cold, confident center. "Thanks for helping with Luke. Let me know if you need any help sorting it all out."

She moves around the desk with an expression of concern. "Chord—"

"I've got to go, but I'll check in with you later, okay?"

"Okay."

"And I really am proud of you, Charlotte. You did good and maybe later, when all this is... over... you can tell me all about it."

Charlie forces a cheery smile, but the sympathy in her eyes is too much. "I'd love that."

I nod and rush from the room before I give away more of myself than I have to spare. I hate feeling vulnerable. I can't stand the pity. And I don't want to accept, even for a second, that Violet isn't supposed to be mine. But what choice do I have? Charlie knows as well as I do that I have to let Violet go. It's the only way for her to move forward without looking back on her life and always wondering *what if*.

I push myself to my physical limits running back to the house, my footfalls kicking up dust along the dirt paths crossing the fields of Silver Leaf. If three years in Milan is what Violet wants, I'm going to make damn sure she does it right. And I'm not going to miss a moment of our time together now that all we have left is to say goodbye.

THIRTY-NINE

Violet

DAY 82 AT SILVER LEAF...

ONCE I DECIDE TO TAKE the job in Milan, everything happens unbelievably fast. It takes me hours to find the courage to hit "send" on my acceptance email, then just five days to finalize the paperwork, organize a place to stay, and pack up what's left of my life in my San Francisco apartment. The week passes by in a blur.

I rarely have a moment to myself—moments to breathe and take it all in. There's no time to talk myself out of my decision and few quiet moments to dwell on my fears. Chord keeps me so busy I suspect the whirlwind days of packing and planning followed by long nights of soul-shattering sex are intentional. He knows that if I stop moving, I'll start thinking. And if I start thinking, I'll talk myself into staying.

I'll choose him instead of me. And I can't do that.

Chord is quiet and determined with his eyes on the end goal, solid and certain that this is the right choice, and his strength gives me the resolve to keep going. He stands behind me at the desk in the home office, massaging my shoulders with his clever hands as I send my acceptance email. And he's here when I send my resignation letter to Courtney. That feels pretty darn good.

He drives me to San Francisco to help me pack the rest of my stuff. When I find my passport, he comments on the fact that I've had it for six years and it's still without a single stamp.

"I got it when I graduated college," I explain. "Just in case I received a job offer like this, but I never did."

His face grows still as he hands it back, turns to another drawer of my belongings, and stuffs them with renewed determination into the new luggage he bought for me. I keep packing too, ignoring the way thoughts of leaving him make me feel unsteady and unwell.

Five days pass, and every minute is more precious than the last. Each touch and look and word imprints on my DNA. Our nights together, with our skin sparking, our hands roaming, and our mouths exploring in the dark...

The nights are the best and worst of my life because I don't know if we'll ever have this again. Are these desperate moments the last we'll spend together? I'm too afraid of the answer to ask the question out loud.

The night before my flight, Chord surprises me with dinner at The Hill. He tells me to put on something that

makes me feel great, then knocks on my bedroom doo
wearing a pressed white shirt and tailored navy pants, hi
hair immaculately styled and a heavy new Rolex on his wrist
looking like he stepped off the cover of *GQ* magazine. H
grins like this is a date night like any other, but the energ
between us is heavy. It ticks with finality.

Chord holds my hand across the center console, and h
drives us around to Dylan's restaurant in his sports car. An
when he leads me to the private dining room, everyone'
waiting for us under a *bon voyage* banner—Charlie, Finn
Dylan, Izzy, Daisy, and Dad—and as I walk through the door
I'm greeted with a chorus of party poppers, tiny streamer
flying over my head, and shouts of congratulations soarin
with them through the air.

I'm warm with overwhelm and gratitude, and my eye
well up as I stammer out half a dozen barely audible *thank
yous*. Chord's arm tightens around my waist like he knows it'
the only thing keeping me upright, and as everyone takes a sea
at the exquisitely set candlelit dining table, Dad comes ove
and kisses the top of my head.

"I'm so proud of you, Blossom." He blinks back the tear
in his warm brown eyes. "You deserve this, and you're goin
to do so well."

"Thank you, Daddy," I reply around a sniffle.

Chord's fingers squeeze my hip, but he doesn't get it
This isn't about being the center of attention. I don't feel th
weight of the spotlight with him beside me. I'm burdened b

xpectations. By my father's pride, and Chord's faith, and his
amily's acceptance. By the secret that ever since I said yes to
his job, all I've wanted is to take it back.

And though I know it's only the fear talking, my brain's
aving trouble telling that to my heart.

I try to relax over dinner. The food, as always, is beyond
ompare. The wine flows, and I forget my troubles for a while
hen Charlie pulls me aside to explain the deal she made with
he San Francisco Fury.

She's wearing a pretty blue dress that hugs her curves
nd simple black pumps that show off her legs, and it's the
rst time I've seen her out of her Silver Leaf shirt. She looks
appy, and I remind myself that this is what it looks like when
woman realizes her dreams.

Three hours later, the dark sky is blanketed with stars and
hord pulls the car into his garage. This is the final step in our
st night before I fly to Milan and if he tells me this is it—that
's over between us—I won't be able to go. Maybe that's why
e haven't spoken a word since the restaurant.

He opens my door, takes my hand, and leads me inside.
Ie doesn't say a word, doesn't pause to turn on a light,
ecause the urgency has grown too great to waste time on
nything as insignificant as speech or illumination. His
ride is measured and single-minded as he leads me up the
airs and down the hallway, and when he opens the door to
is bedroom, I gasp.

"How did you...?"

Chord pulls me into the room. "I called in a favor with th
Silver Leaf staff. They set it up while we were out."

His bedroom is filled with candles. Dozens, mayb
hundreds, of votives and tapers and pillars, each one simpl
and white with a tiny golden flame that burns strong an
steady in the still air. It's too warm for the fireplace, but a smal
blaze burns there anyway, and there's wine on the table besid
it. Chord doesn't acknowledge any of it. He pulls me into th
room and pushes my sundress off my shoulders, quicky bu
gently dragging the sleeves down my body until the fabri
gathers around my waist. Then he unclasps my bra, peeling i
off me with reverent silence, letting it drop to the floor witl
his eyes on my tight nipples, tweaking one then the other as hi
lips meet mine and his tongue slips into my mouth.

We're beyond conversation now. No words can expres
the love, the hurt, the pain, the hope of tonight. And so, whe
Chord moves his hot mouth to my throat, I twine my finger
in his hair and drop my head back, forgetting who I am an
what this is while Chord works his magic on my body.

His mouth is never far from my skin as his hands curv
around my waist, his fingers dipping into the bunched-u
cotton of my dress and sliding into the waist of my panties.

He drops to his knees and takes my clothes with him
dragging everything down my legs, then spreading my thigh
latching onto my ass, and yanking my pussy against his mouth

My first orgasm hits me fast, standing and riding Chord'
face as he kneels at my feet and sucks my clit. Echoes of m

climax still reverberate through me as Chord stands, sweeps my trembling legs out from under me, and lays me on the bed.

"Wait," I say as his fingers go to the buttons of his shirt.

He drops his hands and watches me with fevered, pained eyes as I climb to my knees and perform the task of undressing him. This might be the last time I explore his body, and I want to remember every inch of it. So, in the way he did for me, I relieve him of his clothes, following every brush of my fingers over his skin with the press of my lips. The swirl of my tongue.

I unbuckle his belt and push his pants down over his hips, letting them drop to his ankles as I drag down his underwear. His incredible cock springs out, and I dip my head to take the crown into my mouth.

Arousal and satisfaction throb wetly between my legs as Chord groans and drops his head back, his hands twisting into my hair and tugging the strands as he can barely control himself. I latch onto his hips and take him deeper, noting the powerful flex of his thighs as he resists the urge to thrust into my throat.

"Damn, Wallflower," he says between heavy breaths. "Fuck."

No sooner does the salty flavor of him hit my tongue than he roughly pulls away from my mouth, hands cradling my jaw as he arches over me for a deep, hungry kiss. I whimper as he guides me down onto the mattress, laying down beside me with his mouth still on mine, palming one breast as his dick digs into my thigh.

"I want to be inside you so fucking bad," he mumble between kisses across my jaw, my neck, my chest, my nipples My legs fall open as he works his way down my sternum around my navel, and down my hip bones. "But I don't wan this moment to end. I want it to last forever."

Me too, I scream inside my head. *I want this. I want you.*

But I don't say it. I just arch my back as Chord buries hi head between my thighs, clawing at the sheets as his tongu hits my core and his fingers glide across my clit.

Aching and throbbing after another climax, I've barel caught my breath when Chord stretches out beside me on th mattress, lifts me up to straddle him, and guides me onto hi towering cock.

I sink onto him with a gratified moan, my pussy quiverin with the need to come around something solid, and I rid him. I ride him hard and without thought, meeting his eye as he thrusts up to me, my hips bucking and my heart racin as we give each other all of ourselves. We keep nothing t ourselves. We leave nothing behind.

We come together hard and fast, and although w collapse in a sweaty, satisfied jumble of arms and legs, w don't sleep. We just start again. Slowly at first, with kisse and touches, until Chord is hard and I'm soaked with desire He enters me again. Over and over, until we're both spent and I curl against the warmth of his body, inside the curve o his arm.

I wait until I think he's asleep so he can't give me a

answer, but I know I can't leave tomorrow without asking him what will happen next.

"What was that?" I whisper into the darkness. "Was it goodbye? Are we breaking up?"

"Oh, Wallflower—"

I press myself tighter against his body. "Maybe we can try a long-distance relationship, or keep dating in secret? Nobody has to know. We can work this out, can't we?"

I hold my breath, scared of his answer and just as afraid of his silence. His voice is low and strained as he presses his lips to the top of my head.

"I've been selfish my entire life, and I refuse to make the same mistake now. I need to be better than that, which is why I'm not going to limit a single opportunity for you. Not your career. Not your confidence. Not the possibility that in the next three years, you'll find the future you've always dreamed about. I won't let my name, my money, or my baggage overshadow your achievements. This is your time, and you have to take it. No second thoughts. No looking back."

My heart breaks as his arms grow hard and possessive around me. "I love you, Violet James, so damn much, and that's why I'm letting you go."

My thoughts are all muddled, my emotions are a mess, and I don't know if he's right, but when has he ever steered me wrong? So, like I always do, I let Chord take the lead. I'll go to Milan, and I'll fulfill my dreams. It's the only thing for me to do.

Chord tilts up my chin and drops a soft, sweet kiss on my lips while my silent tears roll down my cheeks and land on his wrist.

"We were supposed to have more time," I whisper. "Summer ended too soon."

He lets out a long, heavy breath as his arms get tighter around me. "Summer might be over, Wallflower, but the life you've been dreaming about has only just begun."

Chord sleeps beside me, but I lie awake and watch the candles flicker and extinguish one by one until the bedroom is lit only by the moon and stars sparkling silver outside the enormous windows. I turn my head on the pillow, and through my tears I study Chord while he sleeps.

His arms, even at rest, display the hard lines of an athlete. His back is muscled and strong. His tight, bare ass peeks out from the tangle of sheets. His dark hair is almost black in the shadows, a mop of waves with a single lock tumbled over his forehead, and the moon glow glances off his high cheekbones, straight nose, and smooth bronzed skin.

The scar slashing his eyebrow is the only thing that could mar his beauty, but that one imperfection only makes the rest of him flawless by comparison. His dark lashes rest on his cheeks, and behind those closed lids are the cobalt blue eyes that once struck me still with fear and now give me life.

I know that if I look into them again, I'll never leave here. I'll never have the strength to walk away from him. And he'll never forgive himself if I don't.

So, I sneak away while Chord's still sleeping. I dress in silence and stand by my luggage on the porch while I order a car, then I swipe through to my contacts list and blink away tears as I block Chord's number. My hands shake as I tuck my phone away, and my empty stomach turns with regret. It's for the best, and it's what he wants. A clean break. A new beginning.

Headlights appear on the driveway, and I step out into the darkness. Then I go to the airport, and I get on the plane.

FORTY

❦

Chord

39 DAYS WITHOUT HER

THE MOUNTAINS ARE PURPLE, THE sky above them thousand shades of pink, and the air begins to cool as the su begins its fall over Silver Leaf. I cross my arms, lean my bac against the timber fence circling an open field near the renovate barn, and watch Daisy canter past on the young, athletic golde mare I bought her. She named the horse Chardonneigh, an behind her, Finn follows on a gray retired rodeo pickup w christened Stallion Blanc. He rides with the easy grace an competent circuits of someone who grew up around horses.

On the far side of the paddock, Dylan holds the reins o a gentle sorrel gelding, leading it in a slow walk with Isobe on its back. She named her horse Mabel, of course, even afte we explained that *Mabel* is a boy.

Daisy is never happier than when she's on the back of horse, and the way she squealed and unreservedly accepte

404

these three when they arrived earlier in the week should have been the balm I needed. Finally, someone I love accepted what I had to give them.

But it isn't enough. My family's joy is a tiny moth beating itself against the glass, trying to get to the warmth on the other side, not realizing the fire is a blaze of rage and grief that incinerates everything in its path.

Buying and preparing for Silver Leaf's newest additions was supposed to take my mind off Violet, but it didn't quite turn out that way.

The hockey season started less than a week after Violet left for Milan, so Luke did most of the grunt work—structural repairs to the barn and managing the delivery of feed, tack, grooming equipment, and all the other supplies.

It was a mixture of luck and abandonment that nobody noticed the stable's transformation, and I watched it all take shape via emails I read in planes, hotels, and my new San Francisco apartment—the cold, sterile penthouse that I hated at first sight, and not the warm, sunlit place I bought for me and my girl because it was her favorite.

With a determined scowl, I concentrate on the horses and what the next chapter will look like for Silver Leaf. With advertising and word of mouth, plus a little time for Daisy to reacquaint herself with the local terrain, the ranch can finally offer trail rides again. And when Daisy has time to hire a team to help with the horses, I'll buy her a dozen more.

Throw in Charlie's contract with the Fury, and we're

on track to reestablish this place as the best touris
destination in the region. The way it was when Mom an
Dad were still here.

That hopeful little moth starts beating its wings again
Something feels *right*. And it's still not enough.

I suck in a breath of country air, filling my chest until m
ribs ache, then let it rush out as I push off the fence, reach int
my back pocket, and pull out my phone.

I ignore the missed call from Coach Campbell, the ema
from the Fury media team, and the notifications on my tear
chat with Hayden, Jake, Breaker, West, and Theo, and I d
what I've done every morning since I woke up alone in m
bed five weeks, three days, and twenty-six minutes ago. I scro
through my contacts to Violet's number and glare at it whil
resisting the urge to call.

You let her go, I remind myself. And if she didn't answe
my first seventy-seven calls, she's not going to answer numbe
seventy-eight.

When the impulse passes, I open her social media page
instead. Scroll through her feed for updates.

She doesn't post every day, but there's a new picture nov
Violet's elegant hand holding a takeout coffee cup.

I swipe through the pictures of her life in Milan. Cafe
and boutiques and ancient architecture mixed in with sketche
and fabric swatches. Never a picture of her face, which make
me ache, but I open each image anyway just to torture mysel
with the comments.

haters_gonna_hate: Total social climber. You used Chord and dropped him when you got what you wanted. I'm glad you left the country. He's a fucking god who deserves better than you.

lives_for_fashion_99: STFU! Violet is talented. She'd never get an offer from Leonardo Bellucci if she couldn't do the job. Jealous much?

hockeyhotties: Hard agree. If Violet left Chord Davenport, she had a good reason. The guy's a jackass. Just ask his ex.

anon_31: I heard Chord dumped Violet because he found out she was using him for his money and connections. Just like his ex-girlfriend. Violet will be banging Spencer Cook next. LOL.

nhlnoos: I heard the Fury's going to dump Davenport because he's such a LOSER.

lives_for_fashion_99: @nhlnoos This is a FASHION page. Take your comments somewhere people care. (But even _I_ know that's total bullshit. The Fury is going to come back this season. Chord is HEARTBROKEN. Give the guy time to pull his head together.)

violet_james_fan: You're all terrible people! LEAVE VIOLET ALONE!

I read this shit to stay angry. It was supposed to stop when I let her go, but nothing has changed. I can't stop people from talking about Violet, and I can't protect her from any of it, so if she has to wade through the vitriol every goddamn day, I'm going to do the same.

When I check again in a few hours, the most hurtful comments will have been deleted, but I hate that Violet read these at all. Reads them and removes them every single day while she's alone in a foreign country.

Even though she chose to be there. Even though she left my bed without saying goodbye.

I clench my jaw and keep reading, tapping through to a notorious hockey page and seeking out the worst comments.

I've started to feed off the ridicule. Crave the rage. It's the only thing that feels real.

This season's going to shit—the Fury has lost five of its first seven games, Coach is on my ass, and team morale dips lower every week—but I can't dig my way out of this hole. The losses are depressing, my performance is sloppy, and I spend my nights afterward alone.

For the first time in my life, my career isn't enough.

I go to my contacts list again and stare at Violet's number. It's killing me how badly I want to tell her I miss her. I've got my first game against my old team this week; we fly to Calgary in three days, well and truly, the underdogs to play last year's champions on their home turf. Spencer Cook's waiting, and although I can't wait to slam him into the boards, Violet's absence will give everyone more reason to talk. To look at me for all the wrong reasons. Another thing for the press to throw around, and more ammunition for Cook's insane vendetta against me.

I want so badly for Violet to be beside me in Calgary. d give anything to know she's there. Her face in the crowd. 1y name on her back. And I've never experienced this kind f need before. I've spent my time in the spotlight alone, and 1st when Violet finds the courage to step into her own light 'ithout me by her side, I don't know how I'll do the same 'ithout her.

I want her to come home. I want her at this game against 'algary and every game afterward. I want to score goals and edicate them to the woman I love, and I want to go all the 'ay to the championship Cup for her. I want her to forget 3out Milan and work out of the studio in San Francisco. want to hear her scream my name every night and wake up 'ith her in bed every morning. I want her to make her dreams 3me true here with me, where she belongs.

I want. I want. I want.

It's all so fucking selfish, which is why she's ignoring my 1lls. I can be proud of her at the same time as I'm miserable. /hat I want doesn't matter.

"Hey, you." Charlie stops on the other side of the fence, imbs onto the bottom rail, and leans her elbows on the top. didn't know you were going to be here today."

I stash my phone and nod toward the horses. "Yeah. Four-1y break between games, so I thought I'd come by and see 3w the new tenants are settling in."

"No complaints so far," she replies.

"Good." I cross my arms and lean back on the fence,

more comfortable without making direct eye contac
"Did the woman from that events company call you?"

"She did. We had a good talk about how to use the win
in the warehouse for fundraising. I spoke to Finn, Dylan, an
Daisy about it too and they agree all proceeds should go t
local charities—not the ranch."

"I'd be surprised if they thought any different."

She hums. "Me too. Thanks for setting things up."

"Thanks for agreeing to take over the planning now tha
the season's started."

"No problem."

We watch our siblings and the horses in silence for a fev
minutes, my phone and Violet's number still on my minc
before Charlie clears her throat.

"Look. I wasn't going to stick my nose into this becaus
it's not my business, but given the stunt you pulled with th
wine, I figure I've earned the right to get involved."

I cut my eyes toward her, not liking where this is headec
"What?"

"What's going on with Violet?"

I straighten off the fence and turn to face my siste
My stomach rolls with a sick twist, and it takes work to no
sound desperate when I ask, "What do you mean?"

"I spoke to her yesterday, and she seemed a little off."

My heart lurches with panic and hope, plus a powerfu
hit of envy, but I try to stay composed. "You talked to Violet
When? Why?"

Charlie spares me a bewildered look. "She called to make sure things were progressing with the beverage supply contracts between Silver Leaf and the Fury arena, and to offer her help if I needed anything."

Fuck. That's so like her, and the reminder of her selflessness only makes me more pissed at myself. "What else did she say?"

"She *said* everything was going well and she was *enjoying* her time in Milan."

Her emphasis on certain words makes the hairs on my arms stand on end. "Why do you say it like that?"

"Because she *said* everything is fine, and I got the impression that it's not. She wasn't herself." Charlie lifts an incredulous eyebrow. "How do you not know this?"

I frown at her tone and my own frustration. "Because I haven't talked to her."

"Uh... why not?"

"Because Milan is something Violet has to do on her own. She doesn't need me getting in her way." *And she isn't answering my calls.*

Charlie grumbles under her breath—I catch the words "idiot men" and "stupid ideas"—as the sound of galloping hooves drums behind me, and I'm peripherally aware of Daisy pulling Chardonneigh to a stop beside us.

"Are we talking about Violet?" Daisy gracefully swings a leg over the saddle and dismounts from her horse. "Oh, that woman is miserable."

My heart thumps painfully hard, and all pretense of cool and collected deserts me. "What do you mean? How do you know?"

"I video-called her two days ago." Daisy strokes the nose of her mare and gazes into the liquid brown eyes like she isn't delivering the most momentous news I've ever been told. "She acts like it's all under control, but I've seen her happy, and Violet is *not* happy. She's quiet and mopey and... I don't know. Small. Beige."

"And you agree?" I demand of Charlie.

Charlie and Daisy exchange looks, and I ignore the inference that I'm losing my mind.

"I do," Charlie admits. "But you would know this for yourself if you'd just talk to her."

Daisy tries to shove me and only succeeds in pushing herself back a few paces. "You haven't talked to her?" she screeches. "No wonder she changed the subject whenever I said your name! The poor girl is in a mess over you! Why the hell haven't you spoken?"

At the sudden pressure in my chest, I throw my hands up and pace away before spinning back around. "Because she left my house in the middle of the night while I was still sleeping!" I shout. "She won't answer my calls or return my text messages. What the fuck am I supposed to do? She *chose* Milan. She *chose* to leave. And *I* had no choice but to let her go!"

Charlie shakes her head with disbelief, and Daisy echoes her with a dramatic groan.

"She's miserable," Charlie says slowly, gesticulating like a schoolteacher with an especially dense student. "You're miserable."

"And you're both idiots!" Daisy adds.

"No. This is the right thing." I run a hand through my hair, knowing that my desperation to believe my sisters is overriding what I know to be true. Violet chose her dreams over me. "This is what she wants and—"

"She wants *you*," Daisy disagrees, nodding her head at whatever wild hope or despair she reads in my eyes. "Yes, she wants to design, and she wants to be her own woman, but that doesn't change the fact that she also wants you. She wants it all."

And I want her to have it.

I pace again. Five paces away. Five paces back. Meanwhile, Finn canters over, studying me from the saddle with a confused expression. Dylan and Izzy aren't far behind, pulling up on my other side.

"What's his problem?" Finn asks Charlie and Daisy.

"Violet," they reply together.

Finn nods. "Tell me about it. It's going to be a long fucking season if he doesn't solve this shit soon." He transfers his attention to me. "It's the brotherly thing to watch your games, but it's no fun when you lose."

Izzy sighs dramatically and runs her gloved hand over Mabel's mane. "I miss Violet. She never even got to see me ride."

"We can send her a video," Dylan offers. "And you can call to tell her all about it."

My niece sighs again with a shake of her head. "It's no the same."

"It's really not," Daisy agrees, shooting a loaded loo my way.

"So, what do I do?" I demand.

"Call her!" they all shout.

"Jesus. Okay." I'm nervous and impatient as I fumbl my phone out of my pocket, then turn my back as I fin Violet's number and hit *call*.

My heart races in case this time she answers, but it goes t voicemail again. I spin back to my sisters. "She didn't answer.

"Try again," Charlie suggests.

I do, and when I get her message again, I look helplessl at my siblings. They swap uncertain looks, which fills me wit urgency.

"Just keep trying," Finn says with a worried frowr "She'll pick up eventually."

"No," I say.

"*Yes*," Daisy argues.

I shake my head to try and clear the confusion. "Nc Something's not right. She's blocked my number or something She's—fuck." With sudden insight, I figure out what she' done—and why. Violet has all my admiration and respec She's also the most exasperatingly selfless person I've ever me "She's making it impossible for me to go back on my word."

I do a quick calculation and work out that if I can get m hands on a private jet, it's possible to fly to Milan and bac before I have to be in Calgary. It's not enough to hear Violet speak. It's not enough to share awkward words when I could touch her. Kiss her. Love her. Admit I was wrong and figure this thing out.

I give my sisters a quick kiss on their cheeks. "Thanks for the advice. I'm going to Italy."

"Yes!" Daisy cries as I start to run back to my place. My car. My dreams. My wallflower.

FORTY-ONE

Violet

DAY 39 AT BELLUCCI HQ... ONLY 1066 TO GO

MY PHONE CHIRPS TO LET me know that the hour ha
finally hit six p.m., and I tap at it furiously while a dozen coo
sophisticated faces turn to me with annoyed disdain.

I shrink behind my desk—the one I've only had for thre
weeks and is already a mess of pencils and sketches, fabric
and sewing supplies, reports and research—then cast a quick
appraising look around at the Leonardo Bellucci fashio
office. Everyone's already dismissed the forgettable America
girl in the corner, which makes it an opportune time to escape

I throw my phone and sketchbook in my satchel, shru
into my baggy beige jacket, and slink around the room towar
the bank of elevators.

The space is brand new and frigid, with industri
minimalism and bad vibes. Lots of steel, glass, and concret
floors. And silence. No warmth or texture aside from one lon

all down the middle of the room covered in sketches and swatches and evidence of the team's collective creative genius. And everyone here *is* a genius. I was made aware of that on my very first day, along with the fact that I'm an influencer hire—a shameful label for someone who got lucky without necessarily needing any talent.

I was also told I'd have to prove myself before anyone took me seriously, and while I'm not afraid of hard work, I didn't imagine *proving myself* would include running out every other hour to fetch coffee and cigarettes and otherwise being ignored or talked about in a language I can't understand.

So much about this job feels familiar and not in a good way. There may be no Courtney Reynolds here and my contract might say I'm a junior designer, but in every way that counts, I'm not much more than a glorified intern—and invisible again.

I smack the elevator button and frown at the digital display, willing it to move faster. A quick glance over my shoulder confirms the whispering I can hear is coming from a knot of people debating something on the design boards, not judging me and my exit, but I still hunch my shoulders and hit the button three more times.

The anxious introvert in me is relieved nobody cares enough to notice me. The woman with her own studio standing empty on a beautiful street in San Francisco is devastated she's here at all.

When I'm finally free on the pavement outside Bellucci

headquarters, I retrieve my phone, dial Dad's number, and se
off toward my apartment.

The weather is mild, my temporary rental isn't far, an
I call Dad every day at this time in a new version of our ol
ritual.

"Hey, Blossom," Dad says. "How was your day?"

The sound of his voice loosens something in my ches
He sounds happy—genuinely happy, not some act he's puttin
on to ease my concerns—and it fills me with both solace an
loss. It's a horrible combination when I'm trying to fight wha
feels like an impending breakdown.

"It was great," I lie. "We had a big important meetin
this morning to discuss next year's collections, an
I'm working closely with a lead designer on his brid.
couture line."

All not-quite-lies that are believable enough to be tru
I took notes in that meeting, and I fetched that lead designe
his lunch.

"I'm so proud of you for taking this chance. For havin
the courage to do something scary and for putting yourse
first. You'll be running that place in no time."

I concentrate on the ground in front of me as I wal
among the end-of-day foot traffic. The sun has almost set an
I'm sure if I look up, the architecture and the color and the li
in this city would be inspiring, but I can't find it in me to li
my chin.

"Thanks, Dad."

"So, where are you going for dinner tonight? I've been reading all about the food in Milan. You must be spoiled for choices."

"Um, yeah. It's fantastic. So much to choose from."

I pause out front of the quiet little delicatessen near my apartment. When I finish talking to Dad, I'll go inside for more of the bread, olives, and prosciutto I've been living on since I got here. Nobody at Bellucci headquarters has offered to show me around or take me to dinner, and I'm too shy to suggest it myself. I'm also too anxious to go to a restaurant alone and attempt to order food in my non-existent Italian.

"But what about you? How are things at Silver Leaf?"

My stomach twists as I deliberately skirt the topic of Chord. I want to know how he is, but I don't want to ask. I want to talk only about him, but I'll fall apart if I have to say his name. I want to ask if he's happy, but it'll break my heart if he is.

I've been following the Fury's performance this season, so I know things aren't going well for him professionally, and it's a constant stone in my stomach. But I've had to limit my time on the internet to avoid commentary about our relationship.

I hate that people think I used Chord to get this job. I hate that others say I was never good enough for him in the first place. I hate that anyone thinks I didn't earn this opportunity, that I'm no better than Chord's ex-girlfriend, that he deserves better than me.

I hate that every night, I'm forced to sift through my own social media accounts and delete the vitriol. I hate that when I was doom-scrolling instead of sleeping late last week I discovered that the website Chord commissioned for my studio in San Francisco is still live on the internet.

When I used my login information, there were six requests for my custom couture in my inbox, and I sobbed into a tub of chocolate ice cream as I declined them all.

I hate sleeping alone every night and waking up by myself every morning. I hate that I can't find anywhere that sells Pretzel M&M's. I hate that maybe all of this means I made the wrong decision coming to Milan.

"Things are great," Dad replies, and I think fast to remember my question. "Business as usual for the most part, although Chord was here this morning to check in on the horses."

"That's—" I swallow the lump in my throat. "Oh, Dad. I have to go. There's a cute little *trattoria* here with a fantastic pasta menu, so I'm going to stop for dinner. I'll talk to you tomorrow, okay?"

"Of course. Go. Enjoy yourself. You've earned it."

I stuff down the heartache and homesickness as I stow my phone in my satchel and step inside the *la gastronomia*. In a few short minutes, I'm back on the street with a paper bag of solitude, sadness, and sauvignon blanc.

The place I'm living is only another block away, but when I get to the front door, I freeze on the doorstep, glaring at the key in my hand like it's the reason for my problems. Inside this building is the Violet James who lives alone in a foreign

untry with nothing but her stupid dreams to keep her warm.
nd I'm too sad right now to spend another night with only
er for company.

I'm so *mad* at myself for being in this situation.
veryone who knows me is so sure this is the right thing. The
eople I love are proud of me for being here. And it's only
een a month!

No matter how badly I want to go home, I'd look like an
iot if I threw it all in so quickly. But then... didn't I accept
is job just as fast? With no consideration for what was in my
eart and every action dictated by the things I was supposed to
ant? Or more importantly, used to want.

People walk past behind me, and maybe they glance over
nd wonder if something's wrong, but I ignore the noise and
e press of their eyes. I can't make myself walk inside this
uilding. I can't pretend that everything about this place
oesn't feel temporary and wrong.

It's hard to believe that by achieving something I wanted
r so long, I lost everything I gained at Silver Leaf. Confidence.
career. Friends. Family. Love. I moved halfway around the
orld to live out a fantasy, only to end up right back where
tarted. In a job I hate and an empty bed dreaming constantly
out a life on the other side of the world.

Someone passes behind me in a rush of air, bathing me
a fragrance I know so well. Whoever it is wears Chord's
logne, and the scent triggers a tidal wave of emotion.

Love. Need. Hope. Regret.

I sniffle as a memory of butterflies and sunlight take flight in my chest, and it's been so long since I felt that kind o warmth that I close my eyes and lean my forehead on the doo like I used to lean on Chord's steady, solid chest.

I focus on the sunlight. I focus on the butterflies. I focu on the promise of joy.

Milan was supposed to feel like *this*. I was supposed to ste off that plane and into the Bellucci offices, and every momen of my life was going to feel the way it did this summer. But it' not like that at all. My stomach is always in knots. Food taste bland and uninteresting. I have no interest in exploring th city, and my daily walks to and from work have blended int a hazy nothingness. I haven't listened to my music or opene my own sketchbook since I got here. I haven't thought abou Mom's wedding gown in weeks.

The butterflies and sunlight start to dwindle away, an I reach for them the only way I know how. I think abou Chord and Silver Leaf, and euphoria explodes in my veins.

A choked laugh surprises me through sudden tears as th answer to my problems floats on the back of this feeling.

I wanted so badly to do the right thing that I never gav myself permission to do the thing that felt right. And wha feels right is designing my own line. I want people to wear m name. I've missed the opportunity to do exactly that for th privilege of pouring coffee and taking notes for people wh don't see me, let alone respect me.

Why on Earth did I choose to be invisible again whe

'd only just started feeling comfortable in the spotlight? There are smarter and more rewarding ways to prove my talent than by sacrificing my confidence and happiness on the altar of the world's most prestigious fashion label.

And I'm not *really* back where I started... am I? There was at least one person in the Bellucci offices who thought I was good enough to hire, and if I'm good enough to design for Leonardo Bellucci, then I'm more than good enough to go it alone.

All the things I miss so fiercely are exactly where I left them back in California. And the only person I'm letting down by staying here is myself.

Hot, stubborn fire burns in my throat.

Chord wants me to be selfish? Fine. I'll be selfish. I'll do what I want and stop caring about what anyone else thinks. And what I want is to not be here anymore. I want to hear his voice and touch his skin and feel his mouth on mine. I want to curl myself into the cage of his arms and never be free again. I want to be tethered to Chord for the rest of my life and chase new dreams with him by my side. I want to go home.

I squeeze my eyelids closed as a single tear escapes.

I want to go home.

"Eyes up, Wallflower."

My pulse leaps with shock and hope, my breath comes short and fast, and I close my eyes tighter because the voice behind me cannot be real. But my heart knows it's him before I turn to see the proof, and I sob with relief against the wooden door, tears flowing as all the pain leeches out of me.

I sense him move closer, the scent of him enveloping m
before anything else, and then his warm, tender fingers fin
my chin, and he gently turns me to face him.

"Eyes up," he says again, slipping his hand around m
neck and cradling my head as he turns my face up to his. "An
keep them up."

I open my eyes, and there he is. Here. *Mine.*

Chord leans in, hovering over my mouth, blue ey
drinking me in as he traces every line of my face like he's bee
waiting for this moment the way I have. The warm caress c
his lips on mine is excruciatingly perfect, and the taste of h
tongue mingles with the salt of my tears. It's soft. Sweet. Sacred

I latch onto his shirt and hold on tight to prove he's not
hallucination. "What are you doing here?"

"I came to tell you I love you, Violet, and that I was wron
This *letting you go* thing isn't going to work." His thumb
caress my cheekbones as he sinks into my gaze. "I don't war
that to get in the way of all the opportunities and experience
you're supposed to have in this life, but I miss you, Wallflowe
I can't eat. I can't sleep. I can't think straight enough to get th
fucking puck in the net, and I can't win. Not in hockey. No
in life. Not at all. Not without you."

"Chord—"

"I don't care how we do it, but we'll find a way to mak
this work." His fingertips twist harder in my hair, and his glass
eyes burn into mine. "I'll take you home right now if that
what you want. I'll go back to California if this is somethir

you need to do alone, but I'm going to fly back and forth every chance I get so I can be with you. I'll get you a jet whenever you're homesick. I'll call every day just to hear your voice, and I'll dream about you every night until you're back in my bed."

He presses a kiss to my forehead, and I clutch his wrists as his lips move against my skin. "The only thing I won't do is let you go. I'm sorry if this makes me the selfish asshole everyone thinks I am, but I can't live without you. I don't know how."

"Chord, I—"

He cuts me off with another kiss, twisting us until my back is pinned against the door, his mouth so insistent I give up on talking and give myself over to him.

"Please," he whispers, nose in my hair and mouth at my ear. "Find a place for me in your dreams, and I won't rest until every one of them comes true."

"Chord." I twine my fingers in the edges of his hair, breathe him in, and release all my inhibitions with a trembling sigh. My thoughts slow, and my worries float away, and I finally surrender to what feels right. *This*. This feels right.

"I left California because I was too busy doing what I thought I *should* do instead of what I *wanted* to do. My life in Milan and the dream it represents—it doesn't fit anymore. It's too small, and I don't want it. I want something bigger and brighter and infinitely better. I want to create dresses with my name on them. I want to stand in the spotlight with you. I want to be there when you win the championship Cup and be the woman beside you every hour, every day, every year

after that. I want you to trust me and believe me when I te
you: *you* are my dream. You and me together, whatever th
future has in store. You make me happy, Chord, and I ju
want to be happy."

He smiles that bright boyish grin that lights up his coba
eyes and makes my body pulse with wild, needy heat. "D
you mean it?"

"I mean it." I tighten my grip on his hair to prove ho
serious I am. "Let me be the selfish one this time. Let me d
what I want. I want to get on that plane and go home with yo
now. Tonight. Forever. Please?"

Chord closes his eyes and exhales with a sigh, brush
a barely there kiss across my lips, then the tip of my nose, the
rests his forehead on mine with a crooked, satisfied smile.

"When will you learn, Wallflower? You never have to be
me for anything."

FORTY-TWO

Chord

7 DAYS AFTER MILAN

THE SLIPPERY TIPPLE IS AT capacity with a rowdy crowd that includes half of Aster Springs, my brothers and sisters, and my Fury teammates. Twenty-four hours after our win against Calgary and forty-eight hours until we're in San Francisco for our next game, it was my idea to bring the boys back to Aster Springs for a long overdue round of drinks and a slow dance with my girl.

For now, Violet snuggles contentedly under my arm, her earnest face lit up by her phone as she checks her appointment schedule.

Soon after we landed in San Francisco last week, Violet reached out to the people who inquired about her couture while she was stuck in Milan. She'll officially open her books and her studio next week—quietly and under the radar the way she wants it, even though I suggested a blowout launch party.

It's a fucking rush to watch her breathlessly an
beautifully build her brand-new business. If I didn't believ
it when she told me she was happy before, I've got too muc
evidence to doubt it now. My wallflower is in her element–
vibrant and confident. In breathtaking bloom.

"Everything okay?" I ask as she tucks her phone into he
new leather bag.

"Mm-hm. Just confirming my bride for Monda
morning."

"Your first client, Wallflower. I'm so proud of you."

"Thank you. I'm kinda proud of me too."

Her cheeks flush from what I suspect is part exhilaratio
at her new couture label and part the half-glass of Mona
white wine sangria in her system. Tendrils of her dark cur
have pulled free of her ponytail, and I twist one around m
finger as I lean in for a kiss. How can it be that only a week ag
I was on a plane to Italy, hoping that one day, three years fro
now, we might have a life made of moments like this one?

And here we are, back in California, Violet in my arm
where she wants to be. Where she belongs.

She eases away from my mouth with a satisfied smile, the
takes a sip of her sangria and lifts her eyes to the oversize
television mounted above the bar.

The screen flashes with a replay of the Fury's game again
Calgary last night, and because I know what's coming nex
I grin around the neck of my beer and tighten my hold o
Violet as she flinches at a violent hit she's already seen thr

times—once at the game and twice more tonight. We're on the third replay, and the drunk commentary from all corners of The Tipple just keeps getting better.

"Are you sure this is okay?" I ask Violet for the thousandth time. "Spending tonight here with the guys?"

She leans against me and burrows against my chest like it's possible to get closer than she already is. "It's perfect."

"Hm." I set down my beer and slide my hand under the table, coasting over Violet's bare knee and sliding my way up her thigh, running my finger underneath the hem of her shorts.

Goosebumps ripple over her warm skin, and she fights a little whimper as I murmur against her ear. "I think our first night back was perfect, don't you? Didn't you like the way I fucked you on the floor of our new apartment?"

Her eyes float closed before she remembers we're in a public place, and then they fly open as her cheeks flush with awareness—and, if I'm not mistaken—desire.

"Yes. That— That was perfect."

"And how about the way I made you come on my tongue in that hotel penthouse in Calgary? Do you remember? I hoisted you on the dining table and devoured you for dessert. That might be a close second."

She wilts against me with a near-silent moan. "Chord..."

"And that's nothing compared to what I plan to do to you when we're back at the ranch tonight. Making love in our bed, making you happy in the house I built for us before I even knew you existed."

Violet turns her head and leans in for a kiss. I slide m
tongue against hers, and when she allows the kiss to gro
deeper, my boys start stomping their feet and hollering lik
jackasses.

"Get a room!" Hayden hoots.

Violet pulls away with a shy giggle and a pretty blus
and I pull her in tighter as I shout at my team, "Shut up!" Bu
I smile when I say it because I've missed this kind of bante
with my guys, and besides, nothing in the world is going t
bring me down tonight.

Around the bar, a cry goes up at the replay as I score th
first goal of the game. On the ice, Jake and Hayden jump m
with congratulations before I coast around the glass, pausin
where Violet sits in the stands.

The camera pans in on her, and the thrill of seeing he
in my jersey at the game, blushing like fire but tolerating th
spotlight for me, only gets greater every time I watch it.

"There's my girl," I murmur, turning my nose into he
hair and inhaling the peachy scent.

Violet hums her agreement. "There's your girl."

Play starts again, colors flashing across the screen, an
I smirk with mixed humor as Spencer Cook checks me har
into the boards, but then The Tipple crowd boos loud enoug
to drown out the cheers of Calgary fans coming through th
television speakers.

"I hate that guy," Violet mutters, glowering with a rag
I didn't think she had in her as the camera documents m

once-over with our trainer. She's adorable, like a furious kitten, and I smile wider. "I can't wait for—"

She cuts off as someone skips the tape through the next few minutes, hitting play at the exact moment Jake takes out Cook hard enough to draw blood. Whoever has the remote control mutes the boos coming from the Calgary crowd, making The Tipple audience cheer even louder.

"You realize he's going to have an eyebrow scar a lot like yours after that," Violet muses. "I'm starting to wonder if that guy wants to *be* you."

I chuckle under my breath. "Good fucking luck to him."

At thirty seconds left in the first period, there's a fight for the puck behind our net. Shore slides in, takes control, and with a sharp shot, sends the puck gliding past the Calgary goalie's skate.

Hayden jumps to his feet, whooping as he throws finger guns to himself on the screen. "Fuck, yeah! And that's why they pay me the big bucks."

West yanks him back into his seat with a grunt. "Sit your drunk ass down before you embarrass yourself."

Hayden waggles his eyebrows at West, then tips his head toward the women watching him and whispering at the bar. "I'm done talking myself up anyway. I think it's already had the desired effect."

Hayden swaggers across the room as West shakes his head and takes a long draw of his beer. Only his second, I note, and the only one beside me on this side of sober.

"More sangria?" Poppy asks as stops at our table, a littl white apron around her waist and a full jug of Mona's liqui poison in her hand.

Daisy thrusts her empty tumbler in the air for a refi while Violet pushes her empty glass away. "I think I've ha enough," she declares. "But thank you."

"Smart," Poppy agrees before glancing around the table

Charlie shakes her head with a polite no, Finn's sti nursing his whiskey, and at the other end of the table, m teammates raise their beers to toast Poppy with rowd nonsensical rambling.

"Wings!" Theo slams a palm on the table. "We nee fucking wings!"

Poppy chuckles. "No problem. I'll hook you up."

"And laid." Breaker slumps in his chair with a moan, h half-empty beer bottle clutched against his enormous ches "I need to feel a woman's touch."

"Oh, Jesus," West mutters as Jake snickers behind his han

"Sorry, buddy. I can't help you there." Poppy hooks thumb toward Hayden, who looks like he's getting lucky ov at the bar. "Why don't you hit up your friend for some tips?

Breaker shakes his head with morose defeat and returr to his beer. Another cheer goes up around The Tipple at th Fury's third goal of the game. Mine again.

Poppy turns her attention to Dylan, who hunches ov his barely touched drink. My youngest brother is a litt quiet tonight, and Poppy flicks a puzzled look to Daisy, wh plies with a subtle shake of her head and a silently mouthed *'ll tell you later.*

I shoot Daisy a look to let her know she's going to tell e too.

"And how about you, Dylan?" Poppy asks with unusual re. "Another top-up?"

Dylan gives her a fast smile, then stands without looking rectly at anyone and shrugs into his jacket. "Thanks, but I've t to get back to Izzy."

Poppy takes a step back to let him pass. "Of course. Where she tonight?"

"Her mother's in town, and they're back at the ranch."

"Her mother?" Poppy's fingers flex around the handle of e sangria jug as her eyebrows lift with surprise. "I didn't alize she—"

"Yeah, so I've got to go. Thanks for the drinks. Food was od, too."

Poppy smiles with a small shrug. "Our pleasure."

Dylan waves a generic goodbye to the table, and it's teresting the way Poppy watches him walk away, staring d smoothing her apron before she gives herself a little ake and returns to the bar.

If I didn't know their history and how desperately Daisy d Poppy tried to shake Dylan from their tails as kids, I'd y she was disappointed to see him go.

As soon as Dylan disappears through the door, I turn to aisy with a pointed look. "What the hell was that all about?"

My baby sister purses her lips like she's debating how much to share, then throws up her hands with an exasperated sigh. "Dylan's in a weird mood because Annalise is here. We all know their parenting arrangement is a little unconventional, right? She never wanted custody of Izzy and she only visits when it suits her work schedule, but he was so damn infatuated with that woman when they met, and I'm not sure he ever got over it."

Finn's grunt sounds almost disapproving while Charlie hums her agreement.

"Annalise visits three, maybe four times a year," Charlie elaborates. "Stays in one of the cabins on the ranch and spends a few days or a week with Izzy. Dylan's a mess the entire time but he shuts me out when I ask him about it."

"Do you think he's in love with her?" Violet wonders.

"I don't know," Charlie admits. "Dylan's never suggested there's anything serious going on. She's got to be ten years older than him, a successful international lawyer working in diplomatic affairs. Always traveling and not interested in putting down roots. They've got nothing at all in common."

"Maybe not," Daisy agrees, "but she broke his heart."

"Fuck," I reply with a rough exhalation. "Really? I'll talk to him."

"You can try," Charlie says doubtfully.

"And I will," I insist. "Tomorrow. Right now, I'm going to take my wallflower out to the dance floor."

Violet's eyes light up, and I grin as I take her hand and lead

er to the darkest edge of the dance floor. The beat is too fast
or something slow, but I don't care. I twirl her out and then
join her against my chest, and we sway together in the almost-
shadows of the crowded bar.

I take off her glasses and hook them onto the neck of her
tee, and for a long while, I do nothing but get lost in her eyes.
The warm brown irises with flecks of gold that glitter in the
muted lights.

I coast the back of my hand down her cheek, and she leans
into it with a contented sigh. There are things I want to say to
her, and maybe a drunken dance floor isn't the most romantic
place to do it, but the words spill from my lips before I can
stop them.

"I almost can't believe how much my life changed in just
one summer," I tell her. "All because of you. Not so long ago,
nothing was more important to me than hockey. Nothing felt
more urgent than ending my career on top. I never thought
I could love anything the way I loved my career, and even
though I told myself I didn't care what people thought about
me, I've spent too long trying to prove my worth to assholes
who couldn't give a shit about who I was and what I wanted.
All I could think about was winning. All I wanted was to be
the best."

Her eyes are open and trusting as she stares up at me.
"And now?"

My throat feels thick as I press her closer, spinning us
around as I search for the right words. "Now, there's nothing

more important to me than you. Nothing has ever kept m
up at night like the thought I might never hold you again
Nothing ever twisted me into knots like the possibility of yo
falling in love with somebody else.

"The only thing that kept me going was believin
I'd finally done something that made me worthy of you. Yo
are capable and talented, and you deserve the world. I wan
you to have it all, and I thought loving you was letting you go.

"Chord." She rests her head on my chest and breathe
deeply. "I know we took a roundabout way to get here, bu
I've come to believe it had to happen like that. The lessons w
learned made it all worth it in the end. How else would I hav
learned to listen to my heart over all the noise in my head, c
that I have the power to choose what lights me up inside?

"Thank you for letting me figure this out for myself.
She runs the back of her fingers across my cheek, mirrorin
my own gesture of adoration. "And thank you for chasing m
halfway across the world to tell me you love me and to brin
me home."

I slide my hand around her nape and pull her mout
against mine, claiming her with a kiss. It's soft and lingering. It
demanding and possessive. It's more than a promise. It's a vov

And then I tilt her face up to mine, blinking against th
sting in my eyes. "I'll chase you anywhere and always, Viole
because it's the only way I know to catch a dream. And yo
my pretty wallflower, are my fucking dream come true."

EPILOGUE

Violet

SEVEN MONTHS LATER

RUN MY FINGERS OVER the delicate lace detail and fine beading of a simple but stunning ivory gown, and smile at the warm buzz of contentment I feel when I zip up the white *Violet James Bridal Couture* garment bag. The dress is from my new made-to-measure bridal line—an exclusive selection of silhouettes that I custom fit for a more affordable way to wear a Violet James gown—and the dresses are especially close to my heart. My bespoke couture does exceptionally well but it's hardly accessible for most people, and I decided early on that I didn't want to run my business like that.

Claire accepts her dress with beaming gratitude, her cheeks flushed with excitement and nerves, and I pray that the thrill of giving a bride the dress of her dreams never, ever gets old.

"I can't thank you enough, Violet," she says as we mov toward the front door of my San Francisco studio. "This dre blew all my expectations out of the water. It's perfect."

"You're so welcome."

Claire pauses to look around at the space, hesitating lik she's not quite ready to leave. "I can't believe I won't hav a reason to come back again. I was so nervous about findin a dress that would make me feel beautiful, but I loved ever one of our appointments. You've created a warm, sa space here. So bright and colorful and full of joy. I hope yo know that."

I scan the room, taking the time to really look at what I' built over the last seven months. Pristine ivory wedding gowr displayed on simple white mannequins. Rows of dresses in rainbow of colors for bridal parties and red carpets and gala and special occasions. Tuxedos and well-cut suits. Priva changing areas. Emerald-green velvet sofas around a coff table with printed catalogs for consultations. Candles and ru and soft music. Walls covered in photographs of celebriti and brides and everyday people wearing my designs. A clie schedule that's filled two years in advance.

Independence. Creativity. Satisfaction. Peace.

"It's easy for me to forget how far I've come," I reply wit a warm smile. "Thank you for reminding me to appreciate it

I give her a fast hug before opening the door, letting in a st of early summer air and the sounds of end-of-day foot traff on the busy street outside. "Now. Everything is ready to g for the weekend but promise me you'll reach out if you have any worries before the big day. And please send me pictures! That's my favorite part—seeing you and the dress the way it was intended to be worn."

Claire runs a hand over the bag like she's petting a cat, and she shakes her head in disbelief. "I'm getting *married* in a *Violet James gown*!"

I laugh as she slips through the door, then lock it behind her and rest my back against the wood with a sigh. It's been a long day in the studio, and as rewarding as it is to finally be creating my own lines, I've got something more to look forward to this evening.

Chord's been on a road trip all week, and he's due home for a single night before we fly out late tomorrow afternoon for his last game of the playoffs. The Cup decider. He's worked so hard to take the Fury to the top, and even though I'm a bundle of nerves for him, something tells me he's going to get what he wants. He's worked so hard for this. He deserves it. And he's determined to have it.

I'm already living my dream, but my man is *this close* to getting his too.

I lock up the studio and order a rideshare to take me to our apartment, then let myself in with a drop of disappointment that the place is still dark inside. I'd hoped Chord would be home and our night could start as soon as I walked through the door, but when I check the time, I remember he's not due in for another hour.

I slip off my shoes, throw my burnt-orange-colore
blazer over the coat rack near the door, and move through th
apartment, flicking on lights as I go.

I don't think I've smiled as much in my life as I have sinc
Chord and I moved into this place, and it's no surprise that I fin
myself grinning again now. I adore our little home. The dec
detailing. The timber floors. The fireplace and the bookshelve
The personal touches we've added together. The way Chord
scent lingers in the air even when he's away. The warmth.

As I move up the hallway, I brush my fingertips along th
frame of the bright, beautiful abstract artwork we bought o
our first date in Aster Springs, then enter our bedroom. It's m
favorite space—for obvious reasons—and I quickly wash m
hands in the ensuite bath before passing by the kitchen on m
way to my little studio nook in the living area. Nothing wi
make the next sixty minutes move faster than losing myself i
my music and sketchbook.

But before I reach my cozy armchair in the corner, I spc
a bright pink sticky note covered in Chord's familiar scraw
stuck to the front of the fridge and stop dead in my track
My pulse races as I rush forward again and snatch it up.

*Evening, Wallflower. Couple of things for your to-do li
tonight.*

1. Pack your bag for an overnighter.

2. Put on something warm and casual—and easy to remov

3. Be waiting downstairs at seven o'clock.

I look around, hoping to find Chord or at least evidence that he was recently here, but this note on the fridge and the possible tease of his cologne is all there is.

I read the note again, adrenaline and nostalgia heating my skin as I remember the notes he used to leave for me when I was his assistant at Silver Leaf. That was almost a year ago now, but with his scribbled instructions between my fingers again, my heart pounds with an old, intoxicating mix of anticipation and infatuation.

With just an hour until I need to be ready for whatever Chord has planned, I rush through a shower and throw some clothes in a bag, then hurry to the street with barely a minute to spare.

He's already waiting for me, leaning against the hood of his favorite cherry-red sports car, looking like a million bucks in his snug dark blue jeans, muscle-hugging white t-shirt, dark hair curling underneath a backward baseball cap. I release a happy sigh at the sight of his slightly amused face before throwing myself into his arms.

He slips a hand behind my head and tilts up my mouth to claim it with his own. Our kiss is long and hungry, tongues stroking, hands clutching, bodies pressing until there's only one way we could be closer to each other, and it would require removing all our clothes. I miss him so darn much when he's gone, and though I know this is the life of a hockey player, I'm secretly looking forward to this time next year when Chord will be ready to retire, and I don't have to share him anymore.

"I've missed you, Wallflower," he says, cradling my head and stroking my pink cheeks with his thumbs as he brushes the tip of my nose with a soft kiss. "So fucking much."

"I missed you too." I grip his wrists as he drops his forehead onto mine. "But you're here now."

He hums his agreement, then reluctantly removes his hands so he can pick up my bag and open the car door. "And I've got a surprise for you."

I slip into the seat and press my hands over the butterflies in my stomach. "You didn't have to do anything special. You're only here one night before your last game and—"

"And that's exactly why I want to do something special." He closes the door, throws my bag into the trunk, and rounds the car before sliding behind the wheel, taking my hand, and pulling out into the street. He presses my knuckles to his warm lips, then holds my hand on his thigh as he drives. "The next few days are going to be all about hockey, but tonight is all about us."

I've learned not to protest when Chord wants to spoil me. I don't need grand gestures to know I love him, but he's so cute when he gets an idea in his head, like a kid with a new toy, that I can't bring myself to fight it. And I get a kick out of watching him have his fun.

We cruise out of the city as the sun begins to fall, and though Chord refuses to tell me where we're going, it doesn't take long to figure out our destination. About an hour after we start the trip, just as the sun is sinking behind the horizon, we roll past the gates outside of Silver Leaf.

"We're spending tonight on the ranch?" I ask hopefully, twisting in my seat as the white timber gates slide out of view.

Chord casts me a wide grin. "Sort of."

"Sort of?" I watch the darkening scenery glide past my window as Chord ignores the private road to his house and keeps on driving. "What does that mean? Where are we going?"

His only response is a knowing little smile and his fingers growing tighter around my own. Soon he pulls the car onto a sealed driveway that wasn't there this time last year, and I frown as I try to get my bearings in the rapidly disappearing light.

We drive through a field that is wild and empty but for the road under our tires until suddenly, in the distance, something twinkles up ahead—lots of little lights wrapped around a frame, maybe?

I'm still not sure where we are when Chord finally pulls the car around the turning circle at the end of the drive and cuts the engine.

I peer out at what looks like an enormous concrete slab framed by poles slung with ropes of twinkle lights. The most romantic campsite with a linen fort-style tent and pillows and blankets and a firepit is set up in the middle of it all, and when I squint harder, I spy wine glasses and candles arranged on one side for a picnic.

"Chord!" I gasp. "It's beautiful but... Please tell me you didn't buy a road and build a concrete platform just for one night?"

"Not quite." He shakes his head with a happy smirk—lik
a kid with a secret, there's no other way to describe it—an
I force myself to be patient as he rounds the car, opens m
door, and leads me off the asphalt toward the campsite.

We step onto the enormous concrete circle, and th
setup is even prettier up close, with the low fire crackling an
throwing off an orange glow from the low steel drum and th
blankets beckoning us in the cooling air and falling night.

Before I can ask again what this is all about, Chord pul
me against him, my back on his chest, and loops his hard arn
around my middle, pressing a kiss against my hair before h
releases a heavy sigh of contentment. And suddenly, I don
care if or how or why he bought me a road and a slab c
concrete. I only care that he's here.

I sink against his warm, immovable frame and close m
eyes. I'm in the arms of the man I love in the middle of Silve
Leaf Ranch. My favorite places in the world.

"Are you hungry?" he murmurs close to my ear, his warr
breath sending goosebumps rippling along my arms.

"A little."

"Good. I had employees from Silver Leaf come by and s
all this up so it would be ready when we arrived."

He guides me to a cushion, covers me with a blanke
and retrieves a cooler hidden behind a stack of cushion
The amazing meal inside has Dylan's fingerprints all ov
it, and as the stars pop to life in the blackness above us, w
share dinner and Silver Leaf pinot noir the way we used to-

ithout ceremony, straight from the boxes, eating from each
ther's forks.

When it's done, Chord collects the empty containers and
ts them aside, then scoops me into the crook of his arm and
raws me down on the pillows, his other hand under his head,
gs crossed at the ankles. I snuggle against him, wrapping
yself in the warmth of his chest, the crackle of the fire, and
le smell of burning wood, and luxuriating in the feeling that
erything is right in my world.

Another sigh leaves Chord's lungs. "I don't feel right
hen I'm not with you."

I turn my nose into his shirt so I can inhale his familiar
agrance. Clean like powder. Fresh like mint. Earthy like cedar
ith base notes of man. Tall, delicious, devastating *man*.

"I feel the same. Something is missing when you're
ot here."

He hums and kisses my temple, then points to the sky.
rcturus," he says, drawing my attention to the brightest star.

"I know." I recall that night at the ranch so long ago when
hord showed me the stars for the first time. I think that was
e first time I saw the vulnerability hidden underneath his
rd, cold exterior. "I remember."

"Have you made a wish tonight?"

I burrow closer to him and close my eyes to create a
emory that will live with me forever. "I wish for a million
ore moments just like this one." A rumble sounds in his chest,
d I smile to myself. "How about you? Do you have a wish?"

Chord's throat bobs against my forehead, his ches
stills, and his arm curls protectively around me, but when h
doesn't speak, I open my eyes. And gasp.

"Violet," he says with an open jewelry box in his hanc
an enormous diamond glinting at me in the light of the fire.

I scramble upright, sitting back on my heels and coverin
my mouth as Chord shifts onto one knee before me.

"Violet," he repeats. "In a few days, I'm going to lead th
San Francisco Fury in the championship final, and we're goin
to take home the Cup. I'm going to achieve the one thin
I thought would make all my years of sacrifices and hard wor
worth it."

He pauses as his brow furrows, and I reach out to cup h
face. I love his confidence, and I have no doubt he'll accomplis
what he's set out to do, but something is obviously differer
tonight. "I know. And I'm so proud of you."

Chord blinks rapidly. "But, Wallflower—it doesn't fe
the way I imagined it would. It's taken me weeks to figure ou
why, but now I know. Nothing in my life feels enough unle
you're right there beside me. I can't picture a single momer
in my future that doesn't have you in it. And I don't mea
waiting at home while I'm on road trips, chasing a dream tha
I've already fulfilled five times over. If it was my plan to finis
my career where I started—on top—then I'm about to d
that. I don't need to do it again." Chord clears his throat an
blinks against the glassy sheen in his eyes. "What I need is t
live a new dream, and what I want is to make you my wife."

A choked sob escapes my throat, and Chord's mouth twitches with pleasure even as he blinks back tears, and his voice is gravelly and cracked as he continues. "Here's what I wish when I gaze up at your star—tonight and every night since I admitted to myself that I loved you almost a year ago. I wish I could wake up with you every morning forever and make love to you every night. I wish I could stand in front of our family and friends, and vow to love, honor, and protect you for as long as I have breath in me. I wish I could give you children and build us a life filled with laughter and tears and big, beautiful moments just like this. Hundreds of summer nights spent under the stars."

Chord glances around at the platform underneath us, the frame of lights all around. "And this... I thought this could be your new studio so we can make Silver Leaf a home for both of us. You can move your business here permanently or split your time between here and the San Francisco store—whatever feels right to you. I don't care how we do it, just as long as we're together. All the time. Every day. And every single night."

My heart races and my pulse rushes in my ears as Chord wets his lips and plucks the classic round-cut diamond from its cushioned case. When he holds it up between us with a questioning crease on his forehead, I offer him my shaky hand, and he holds it in his.

"Violet James," he murmurs as his warm blue gaze heats every inch of my body and the deepest reaches of my soul. "Wallflower. Will you marry me?"

"Yes." Tears slip down my cheeks as Chord slides th
platinum band onto my finger. "Yes, I will marry you."

He scoops me up into his arms and holds me tight befor
taking my mouth in a rough, insistent kiss and lowering m
onto the blankets. We make love, right there in the open unde
the stars. Exploring each other's bodies by the dying light o
the fire, our mouths and tongues and hands moving withou
rest for hours and hours. Falling asleep naked and twisted i
our blankets and around each other. Safe. Content. Loved.

With Chord's arms holding me, his breath on my neck
and his heart thrumming next to mine, I couldn't have wishe
for a more beautiful way to start the rest of our lives. It'
perfect and magical.

It's all my dreams come true.

BONUS SCENE

Violet

10 YEARS LATER

Chord and Violet's story doesn't end here!
Visit my website at samanthaleighbooks.com/books/
bonus-content or use the QR code to download
a bonus scene set ten years in the future...

ACKNOWLEDGMENTS

Thank you

Thank you for reading *Wallflower*! It makes me so happy tha
you took a chance on Chord and Violet and made room i
your heart for their love story. I hope that you found as muc
joy reading this book as I did in writing it.

Wallflower only made it onto the page with the help an
support of a small circle of wonderful people, and this is m
opportunity to thank them.

Shay Laurent—thank you for being the smartest, mo
enthusiastic, and endlessly generous critique partner and frien
a girl could ask for. I am so grateful we signed up for the san
writing course all those years ago! I don't know how I would d
this without your patient feedback and unfailing support, an
I appreciate you so darn much.

Stephanie Archer—you make author life a lot more fu
Thank you for your guidance and advice, the voice notes an
plotting help, the book recs, and the energy you've given th
book and these characters. I feel very lucky to call you a frien

Echo Grayce—thank you for taking a creative brief that as little more than "vibes please" and turning it into this ind-blowing masterpiece. Your talent, patience, and attention detail is unmatched, and working on this cover together is sily one of the highest points of my author journey so far.

Thank you to my editing team, Gina Salamon and randi Zelenka, for your clever insights, keen eyes, and kind ncouragement. I adore working with you both.

Truckloads of gratitude go to my beta readers: Tabitha, ss, Katie, Abbey, and Cal. This book wouldn't be what it is day without your brilliant contributions.

Thank you also to the people who have held my hand in g and small ways while I wrote this book: Hannah Cowan r answering my cover questions; Kels and Ada at Archetype r the beautiful branding and marketing support; Becca and iauna at The Author Agency for their promo expertise; id every book influencer and reader who reached out to tell e how excited they were to meet Chord and Violet. Your ithusiasm and support mean the world to me.

Thank you to my husband and children, who might not iderstand why I'm obsessed with this life but give me the ace and love to write because they know it makes me happy.

And last but never, ever least, thank you to my readers. ›u are the reason I write, and I couldn't do this without you. hank you for making my dreams come true.

xSam.

MORE STEAMY SMALL TOWN ROMANCE FROM SAMANTHA LEIGH..

Four dirty-talking sexy surfers find their
happily-ever-afters in Valentine Bay...

Josh & Emily

A Fake Relationship
Grumpy Sunshine Romance

Logan & Jess

An Enemies to Lovers
Best Friend's Ex Romance

Isaac & Birdie

A Girl-Next-Door
Spice Coach Romance

Will & Abbie

A Single Dad Forced
Proximity Romance

ABOUT THE AUTHOR

Samantha Leigh

Samantha Leigh is an Australian author of steamy
contemporary romance. When she's not playing matchmaker
in imaginary worlds, Sam is reading books with all the feels
and all the spice. In the tiny slices of time she has between
word wrangling, Sam likes to hit her yoga mat, go for walks in
the bush or on the beach, continue her search for the perfect
poke bowl, drown herself in coffee and hot cacao, and
binge-watch nineties television.

samanthaleighbooks.com

Made in the USA
Columbia, SC
17 November 2024

46732563R00276